NEB
THE GREAT

Copyright © 2013 A. K. Frailey. All rights reserved.

No part of this book may be used or reproduced by any means, graphic, electronic, or mechanical, including photocopying, recording, taping or by any information storage retrieval system without the written permission of the publisher.

A. K. Frailey Books
110 Possum Lane
Fillmore, IL 62032

Editor: Megan Guffey
Cover and Interior Design: Trese Gloriod
Cover Photos from Alaska: Michaela Houser
Map and Tree Illustrations: Trese Gloriod
Author Photo, Back Cover: Kateri Houser

ISBN: 978-0-9891035-3-4

*To him that shall overcome,
I will give to sit with me in my throne:
As I also have overcome,
And am set down with my Father in his throne.
He that shall overcome,
Shall possess these things,
And I will be his God
And he shall be my son.
Apoc.xxi.7*

*Our Father
Who art in Heaven, hallowed be thy name
Thy kingdom come, Thy will be done
On earth as it is in Heaven
Give us this day, our daily bread
And forgive us our trespasses
As we forgive those who trespass against us
And lead us not into temptation, but*
Deliver us from evil
Amen

NEB THE GREAT

SHADOWS OF THE PAST

A. K. FRAILEY

A. K. FRAILEY BOOKS
FILLMORE, ILLINOIS

TABLE OF CONTENTS

Map	iii	Chapter 15 Deceit and Treachery	87
Chapter 1 For Those Who Come After	1	Chapter 16 Hul's Defiance	103
Chapter 2 Neb's Awakening	6	Chapter 17 The People of Havilah	110
Chapter 3 Enosh and Kenan	11	Chapter 18 A New Leader Emerges	123
Chapter 4 Meshullemeth and the Dark Powers	16	Chapter 19 The Victory Shall Be Mine	135
Chapter 5 Hezeki's Choice	18	Chapter 20 Endurance	146
Chapter 6 Hopes and Sorrows	23	Chapter 21 A Time to Rebuild	156
Chapter 7 Eva	27	Chapter 22 Revelations	163
Chapter 8 Ashkenazi	32	Chapter 23 Eva and Leah	173
Chapter 9 The Oath	38	Chapter 24 Meshullemeth's End	182
Chapter 10 The People of Seth	47	Chapter 25 Accad's Return	188
Chapter 11 Arrangements	53	Chapter 26 Neb's Sons	201
Chapter 12 Eva's Observations	64	Chapter 27 Today's Joy Tomorrow's War	212
Chapter 13 A Father's Love	73	Chapter 28 Trader of Invention	220
Chapter 14 An Unwelcome Guest	80	Chapter 29 Leah's Sacrifice	231

Chapter 30 The Reason of War	245	Chapter 45 The Final Journey	355
Chapter 31 Hate on the Minds of Men	251	Chapter 46 Hagia	362
Chapter 32 If Only	255	Chapter 47 A New Day	371
Chapter 33 A Truce of Terror	261	Chapter 48 And it Begins Again	373
Chapter 34 Madai	276	Family Tree	388
Chapter 35 Serug	280		
Chapter 36 His Story Continues	284		
Chapter 37 Madai Reclaims What Was Lost	287		
Chapter 38 Travels	296		
Chapter 39 Eva and Ester	303		
Chapter 40 The Next Generation	314		
Chapter 41 And to Dust We Shall Return	319		
Chapter 42 Inner Exile	325		
Chapter 43 Torgama and Eymard	332		
Chapter 44 The Consecration	341		

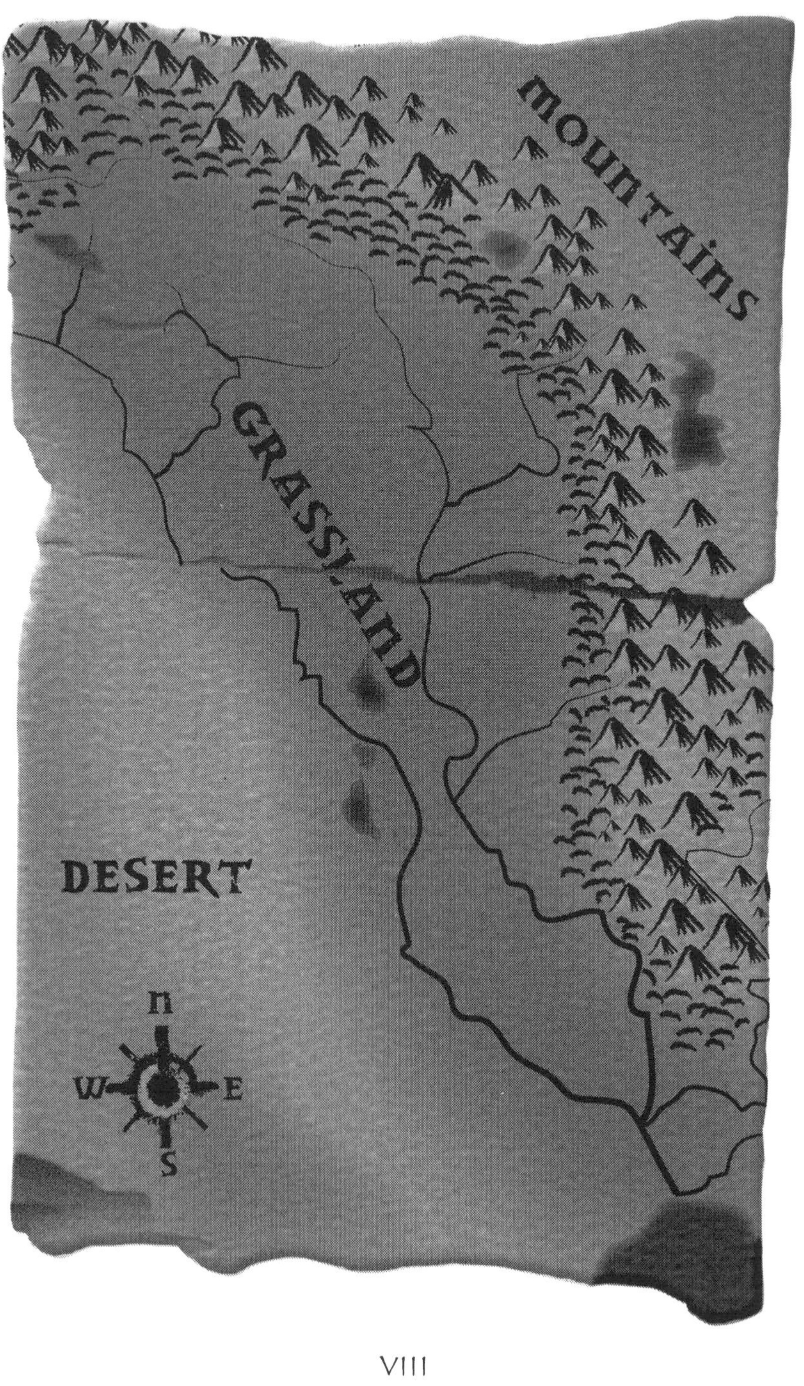

mountains
GRASSLAND
DESERT
n
W
E
S

CHAPTER 1

FOR THOSE WHO COME AFTER

Gizah looked at her husband, Ammee, and was reminded of her father, Aram. They were so alike—strong men who ruled the world around them—yet they were both rather bewildered by their own inner souls. Though the day was hot and bright, it did not carry the full force of high-summer heat. The sun, attempting to blaze down on them, cascaded through a soft, warm breeze that was stirring the branches of the few nearby trees. Insects were buzzing forcefully in their late summer activity, and the many various birds were chirping or crowing or cooing out their long and mournful end-of-the-season songs. Long stems of dark green grasses swayed in a mixed cacophony of undulating motion. Everything was drying out, readying for the harvest. Even as Gizah rejoiced in the healthy life all around her and the new life within her, she soberly understood that one man alone could not break down the old mass of the past season's experiences into a fertile soil for future generations. She watched her husband work and realized with sudden clarity that she completely understood Ammee's confusion, for she felt it too. She was often the one to temper his sometimes-irritated moods, yet at this moment she realized her limitations. She did not have the answers he was seeking—answers to questions she had not yet dared ask. At some point they would have to bravely face the past in order to build a future of hope.

Ammee and Gizah had been married for three years before they were finally granted their fervent though silent wish. Some had thought that Gizah's malformed hand and slight limp were signs that she would never bring forth life. Others whispered that it was because she was three years older than her husband that she was thus made barren, for it was unusual in the extreme for a wife to be older than the husband. But Gizah had come to know Ammee over many long seasons, and she had found him to be much more advanced than his natural count of years. Besides, she was like her mother in that she cared little for the opinions of gossips and talebearers. It would not be long now before she gave birth to her first baby, and her greatest concern was for the life growing inside of her. She and Ammee began to consider names and wonder if certain personalities from the past would reappear in their own offspring. This began a train of thought that led Ammee into some dark territory. Ishtar rarely spoke of his father, Neb, or his grandfather, Serug. This was quite unusual, for it was ever the clan's pastime to recite their lineage from long past into present day. The more Ammee considered his own ignorance, the more he felt bound to ask questions of the elders who might know about his father's youth, his grandfather, his great-grandfather, his great-great-grandfather and the long past. The bits and pieces of tales, poems, sagas and recitations he heard that directly related to his lineage were startling enough to make the most intrepid explorer reconsider. Here he was, exploring his own past and becoming more and more uncertain of his destination. One day while he was questioning an exceptionally garrulous elder, he was told that Aram and his own clan were related by blood from generations back. Though he had heard some rumor of this, it had never been fully explained to him.

One particularly dark and oppressively hot night, Ammee dreamed of his ancient relatives while haunting figures with weird faces floated around in the mist of his imagination, setting his heart aflame with wild grief and terror. He did not know what evil spirits he might have inherited, but he greatly feared that by marrying into his family, Gizah had put herself in some terrible danger. He now also feared for the very life of his new child. The frightful images that cavorted through his worried brain transported him into a nightmare of such proportions that he began to call out, thrashing about as if to escape the dark terrors. Gizah awoke, afraid that invaders were at their door. When she realized that her husband was just dreaming, she tried to awaken and comfort him, but the nightmare had such a grip on him that she could not release him from its terror. She was afraid of being hit by his flailing arms, so at last she stumbled out of bed and found a half-filled gourd and splashed the cold water in his face. In the sudden shock, Ammee's terror quickly turned to outrage until his wife made known to him what had happened. Ammee recognized Gizah's good sense and candor, so he quickly calmed down, but just as quickly the nightmare images came back to him even before his wide-awake eyes. Turning to his wife in his wet clothes, he tried to explain the horrors haunting him. She listened and wondered and grew afraid too. What was this past that threatened to invade their present world? Who were these figures from long ago that formed so much dark legend that few ventured to speak of it unless asked and then it was as if a torrent of terror were unleashed?

Gizah's father, Aram, had been a heroic man—someone who had lived valiantly and had become renowned as a model of men. She had loved him deeply while he was alive, and she loved him nonetheless when he died. She thought of him often, and she imagined that her mother, Namah, was finally at perfect peace in his company. When Ammee began to relate the strange tales of the past, telling her about their shared ancestry and the horror of one known as Neb the Great, she became uneasy. After listening to bits and pieces of various stories and legends, she put up her hand and intervened. She could hear no more without knowing it was the full truth. And there was only one person fit to reveal the fullness of their past to them.

"I think we need to do something more than gather scraps like wild dogs after a feast. There is one who knows the whole story about both of our peoples. We must go to him and ask for the truth."

Ammee shook his head. "I know who you are thinking of, but I cannot do it. My father does not relish his memories. His freedom from the past healed him of madness. I cannot ask him to go back and revisit that which once tried his soul so dearly. Besides, he is getting older now, and I wish more than anything to allow him peace in his final years. If we call forth those evil spirits now, who knows what vengeance they would wreck on him in his old age as they have been denied so much else?"

Gizah waited in silence a few moments as she pondered her husband's words. Then she took Ammee's hand and moved a little closer to him. "You forget that Aram, too, had a long memory, and I spent a great deal of time with him. It is true that I do not know all, but I do know some of the history. It is something we must face together so that we may overcome our past. I would not have our own son or daughter live in fear of a dark history that we were too afraid to face. Besides, I trust that Ishtar is quite strong enough to remember the past without reliving it. In fact, it might be a source of great comfort to see how things have really turned out and to know once and for all that our past does not have to be our future. A new day has dawned for this family. In his love for you, he crossed barren deserts and jumped through fire. I do not doubt his ability to pass through generations of memories so as to bring us and our new child hope and peace."

Ammee smiled. "I was a wise man when I chose you for my own." He lay back down while Gizah brought him a dry mat to lie upon and another gourd of water.

"Here," she said as she put the mat in place. "Now you will be comfortable through the night. And this," she put the gourd to his side, "is to keep bad dreams at bay!" After she settled herself next to her husband and finally heard his accustomed deep breathing, she lay awake staring into the darkness and knowing full well that in this world there was never a day without a night and never true hope without passing beyond despair.

The next day was still hot, but there were signs of a change in the weather. Clouds were building in the west, and the intermittent breeze was growing stronger. Gizah and Ammee visited with Ishtar in his dwelling, which was butted up against their own. As the recent years had passed, Ishtar remained as faithful to his chosen principles as any man possibly could. Physically he had slowed down, but his mind was still sharp and clear. He had rejoiced in his heart over the marriage of his son with Aram's daughter, and in a very tangible way it brought his old friend back to him. He could hardly wait for their first blessing. When he saw them approaching with sober faces, he smiled indulgently. But when Ammee stammered some incoherent sentences together about having strange and troubling dreams, Ishtar's heart fell. In some part of his mind, he knew that this day must come, but he had dreaded it as a little child fears the first night away from his mother. Yet he knew it was his duty as a father to spare his son the uncertainties of an unknown past. What future can a man have who does not know his own history? It is like taking a long trek through the wilderness—if one does not know where he has come from, it is hard to set one's direction so as to arrive at the desired destination.

As Ishtar was mulling over deep thoughts, Gizah broke in with a simple request. "Could you start by telling us about your great-grandfather, Neb the Great, as he was once known? You could tell about him as if telling a story, weaving in everything you have learned from all you have known and from your own insight. Let his story guide you, and as the day progresses, we will stop and do other things until it is time to story-tell again and then you can weave our histories together. Surely it is a saga well worth telling." Gizah folded her legs under her and sat at Ishtar's feet. Though she had never been beautiful, Ishtar saw in her face and form an attraction that went well beyond the physical into another much more powerful realm. Ishtar wondered if some chosen souls were simply not tied to the earth as others were and they lived in two worlds. He remembered Pele, and he smiled and nodded his head in agreement.

Gizah made herself comfortable beside her husband. Ammee looked up into the bright white–blue sky, wondering a brief moment at the billowing clouds that looked so wondrous as they passed silently overhead. He had a thought that perhaps he should be helping to do some work or another, and then he sighed. There was always work to be done, but the learning of one's past was a treasure no soil could produce. His job now was to listen, to learn and to remember well for the sake of those who would come after.

CHAPTER 2
NEB'S AWAKENING

Neb knew that he was destined for greatness. He was the first son of a first son who was also a first son, and when he was born, his mother declared that he would rule far and wide and that great would be his name. Meshullemeth proceeded to raise her first son as a ruthless despot who would let nothing get in the way of his all-consuming desire to rule everything within his grasp. As a baby, every whim had been seen to with alacrity. Servants were at his constant beck and call. His mother preened him and dressed him in the very best material available. She wanted him to be a confident child who would know no fear and would rule as one accustomed to having great authority. He began by ruling his own family. He laughed at and ridiculed his own father, Hezeki, until the older, more gentle spirit rebelled in sudden fury. In a stormy scene, the father asserted his patriarchal authority and defied a whim of his first son. The boy had been incensed by a servant's lack of respect, and he wanted the servant killed. His father knew the worth of this servant who, though young, was honest and strong. He was never one to kill without serious provocation, and his son's tantrum greatly offended the father's sense of both justice and simple good sense. The servant was allowed to go free while the son was reprimanded with strong, biting words. This first encounter with serious defiance further hardened the heart of the spoiled child. At the time, Neb was but a little boy of less than ten seasons, but he watched and waited, perceiving in his preternatural mind that an opportunity would arise when he would overthrow his father's authority and even his mother's manipulation. As he had grown in height, strength and age, her praise had grown almost hysterical as she tried desperately to control what she had wrought. In time, she secretly began to fear what she had nurtured. When she wished him to do her some service or alter his already determined plan, her son would simply stare at her and his eyes would bore into her soul like a menacing sickness seeping under the skin. Meshullemeth had two other sons and a daughter who had all grown under the shadow of the firstborn. They found that their worth was measured not by their own person but by their usefulness to their oldest brother.

It was a bright day in the southern hill lands with no hint of a breeze when Neb went out to seek game for his family. There were hunters in the clan who could do the job as well as he, but he enjoyed the hunt and liked to be the one to come home with a kill. Though his father had begun to look upon him with suspicion and doubt, he knew that no clan member would challenge the worth of a good hunter. He had heard that there was a bear of enormous size roaming the hills to the far south, and he decided that this would be a noteworthy prize to bring home to his people. He was not afraid as he searched the hillsides for tracks and other signs of the bear. His eyes noted the trunks of trees, scanning for claw marks or any remains of scats or bits of victims scattered among the ferns and saplings. When he came upon some promising marks, he moved more cautiously though quickly through the undergrowth. In time, he heard a sound that alerted his ears to the bear's presence some distance away. He stood and scanned the forest all around, and there in the distance he saw the brown humping form of a great bear. She was moving slowly, and there was a shadow to her left that followed her every move. Neb smiled. She would make a great prize. And her cub would only increase his status in the clan, as mother bears with cubs were very hard to kill. Few attempted such a feat.

Keeping his scent downwind, he stealthily shadowed them for some time, and then he came upon the mother from the right side. He readied his spear and moved in to attack. In his mind, he could hear his own father's voice warning him away from such a dangerous undertaking, but his sneer gave vent to his disgust with those who counseled precaution in the face of great danger. Neb lusted for danger as a warrior lusted for blood in battle. He watched as the mother took note of this sudden threat. She moved out in front of her young and lifted her paw in a gesture of defiance. She would not be taken without a fight. Neb's heart exalted at the sight of her concern. He wanted her to fight with all her strength, and he wanted to kill her knowing that he had defeated the strongest animal in the hills. He approached steadily with his spear upraised, and as his arm was readied, he carefully took aim and threw with all his force. In a strange contempt of all his certain authority, the spear did not make its mark. It fell short. In all his years of certain kills and demanding rights, he had never been so defied. No human or animal had ever so certainly refused his force of will. He had willed his spear into the heart of the beast before him, and yet it had landed softly, ignobly in the ferns. He stood as one transfixed by his own failure. There was no mortal present to tally his loss or record his shame, but the mother bear was not one to take lightly the sudden threatening gesture. She moved quickly with lighting force. She was pure instinct incarnate. Her thrusting shoulders throbbed to her desire to put an end to the life of her opponent. She would be upon Neb in a matter of moments, and Neb had no time to prepare another throw. His knife would be poor protection against the mass of muscle moving his way. Neb turned swiftly and began to run. In that race for his life, Neb realized for the first time what defeat felt like. It left a bitter taste. He had resented his father's interference in his whimsical demands, and now he realized that nature itself could thwart his will. His mortal frame was yet too weak to stand upon the mountain of destiny. He needed to be stronger. But where in this world of weak men and unintelligent animals was he to find the force that would enthrone him in perfect strength?

The bear gave up the chase after a time, but Neb was bruised and scratched on the outside and wounded in a way that would never heal on the inside. He refused the comforting ministrations of his mother when she saw his injuries as he refused to face his own limitations as a man. He would endure the suffering of physical pain as he suffered the search for a power that would never fail him. His father saw him and marveled at the boy's audacity after he heard the tale. He marveled still more at the defiant stare the boy offered in return for his consolation.

"You might have been killed, Son. A mother bear is a force of nature not to be reckoned with alone."

"I will challenge her again, and then I will kill her and her cub. She will fear me in the end."

"And who will undertake to support you in such a challenge? It will not be me nor any of my warriors. We have more sense. There are many animals good for food that may be had at half the risk."

Neb merely stared at his father. "It is not her flesh I wish to consume, but rather her life."

Hezeki shook his head at this senseless statement. He no longer knew his son. This was a youth who had neither wisdom nor true intelligence. He had only a will that could not be defied. He shuddered in sudden foreboding. Here was flesh of his flesh and blood of his blood, but he felt no kinship. In a helpless gesture, he threw up his hands in defeat. This was the mother's doing. He would let her see to her son. He would do what he could with affairs that were more promising. His life was nearing an end, he had no desire to struggle with a youth whose heart knew neither love nor respect. His other sons, Enosh and Kenan, were more manageable. He would see to their formation. His daughter, Eva, was too young yet to worry about. He shook his head once more as he left the room without looking back to his son. The boy did not even notice his departure.

Meshullemeth watched the exchange of father and son, and she narrowed her eyes in cunning. She realized that her son had outgrown her authority and that the father was helpless in the face of his defiant will. But this defeat of the bear was an ill omen. She worried that her son would be reckless in his fury to oppose the beast that had bested him. She realized better than he that the boy needed a source of strength that was beyond herself and her husband. She recognized her need to feed her son, as well as her son's need to become the strongest force in their world. Meshullemeth closed her eyes in concentration. There was an old man she knew who spoke of a God who controlled the whole world. He knew the stories of creation and destruction, how the animals came to be named and how they were to be sacrificed. He spoke to this God and called Him by name, and she knew he had powers of knowledge that no other man had. She would seek him out to discover how to appease this thirst of her son. As a mother, she could do no less. Yet as she watched her son take his rest and as his eyes began to droop in exhaustion, she blinked at the memory of his babyhood when he had been so innocent and so completely hers. Putting her hand upon his head, she could feel the same soft skin and smell his still sweet scent. Suddenly his eyes opened, and they were the eyes of a child searching for comfort. Just as suddenly they were the eyes of a man searching her heart. He peered at her, almost smiled and then closed his eyes in slumber.

Turning softly away and stepping out of the dwelling, Meshullemeth pondered once again what she had wrought in the youth she had carried as a baby under her heart. For now, though she could not help but nurture his ambition, she sensed a growing danger, not only to him, but to herself and her whole family as well. Yet as a man in bloodlust rushes into battle, so she felt she could not turn back. She wanted to make him powerful and become powerful through him, but doubt was a constant companion even as she did what she felt she must. Perhaps the man of God who knew so much about the unseen world would be able to direct her. If not, there were of course many other gods to choose from.

Neb stirred briefly in his sleep. The bear was before him, large and menacing, moving in great leaps directly at him. He turned to run, but then he stopped himself. He would face this bear. He held his ground. The bear stood before him and towered over him. Neb was overwhelmed with fear. He waited for the strike, but it did not come. The great hulking beast growled out human speech.

"Honor me, and I will spare you."

In response, Neb thrust forcefully at the beast. This time, his spear struck true.

CHAPTER 3
ENOSH AND KENAN

(Seven years later)

Enosh watched his younger brother Kenan with deep interest. The younger boy had been practicing using a large spear for some time now, and though Kenan was still a youth, he had come to master it with respectable skill. He was a large young man, possibly growing bigger than either of his elder brothers, yet he was not clumsy as most youths were at his age. Kenan's towering height gave him advantages, for most supposed him older then he was. Even his own mother often seemed to forget he was just a mere boy. Only his father treated him with the patience and understanding he deserved. Enosh was surprised at the determined care the boy took of his aim and stance and the power behind each throw. Clearly in his preoccupation with staying out of Neb's shadow, he had missed something of the developing potential of his younger brother. But where his elder brother caused him so much grief and searing pain, Kenan's success brought a sense of joy to his heart. The boy had never demanded much attention. As a matter of fact, Kenan had been virtually ignored for months at a time. If Enosh had not remembered his presence, then he would have been forgotten entirely. Meshullemeth seemed only to have the interests of Neb at heart, and Hezeki was preoccupied with the needs of each day.

Life was hard in the southern hills of late. The last few years had seen little rain, and the animals were scarce. There were threats of foreign clans in the area, and illness was a never-ending plague. Recently, Enosh began to feel that he was man enough to help his father in the cares of the clan, and so he had offered to take over the training of his younger brother. It was time now for the youth to become a proficient hunter and a brave warrior in their time of need. Yes, Kenan would prove to be an asset to the clan. Yet even as he recognized this truth, Enosh wondered what kind of a clan they were transforming into. His father was becoming an old man, and Neb was positioned to take over leadership when the time came. But Neb was an extraordinarily difficult man to understand. He was quiet and secretive. He went off by himself for weeks at a time and told no one of his whereabouts. He would offer no information about what he was doing or thinking or planning. He had grown into an adult—but not as everyone had expected. He had neither the height nor the muscular strength of either of his younger brothers. His frame was naturally thin, but he moved like a cat with stealth and agility. No one felt comfortable in his presence except those who wished to rule with him. Meshullemeth was a constant companion, though he would tell her to depart from him at a whim. Hezeki had little to do with him, while Neb merely tolerated his father's existence as an unfortunate reality of life. Hezeki had accepted the fact that he would have to resign the care of the clan into Neb's hands as a matter of tradition, although his hope was that the two younger brothers would hold him in check as they were becoming valued members of the clan in their own right and would one day, perhaps, become viable challengers should Neb overstep his authority or forget decency altogether.

A mild breeze blew, and a few white clouds nudged across the sky, changing and reshaping themselves so slowly that unless you stood and watched very carefully, you would perceive no change at all. Enosh smiled now as Kenan threw for the last time and made his best distance yet. The boy certainly had determination and skill.

"Good for you, Kenan! You are becoming quite a good thrower. Soon you will be able to outmatch any man in the clan."

There was a blush of pride on the youth's face as he smiled in gratitude at his older brother. There was little Kenan would not do for Enosh.

"I have a good teacher." He laughed at his own joke, knowing full well that Enosh had been the only one besides his father to give him any instruction. He ran, collected his spear and came up beside his brother. "Father has talked about a contest and inviting the many clans all around. Do you think I would be allowed to participate?"

"I do not see why not. After all, there is no man in our clan who could best you without serious effort, and few put forth the thought and time you do in improving themselves. Perhaps you will have a real part in showing the skill of this clan. Men will say that the youths of our clan can throw as well as a strong man, and that will impress many."

"I am not so much interested in impressing the men of other clans. If I could please the men of our own clan, then that would be enough for me." He seemed to sober as a shadow crossed over his mind. "Though there is one I know I can never please. My very existence seems to irritate him."

Enosh wrinkled his face in a gesture of distaste. "Do not let him worry you. He has . . ." His words were interrupted.

"No, little brother, do not let others disturb you." Neb had appeared as if out of nowhere. Neither had been aware that he was even in the area. They looked each other in the eye briefly before dutifully turning their full attention to their elder brother. Neb appeared not to notice their discomfort. He motioned for his little brother to take up the spear he held resting against his leg. The youth did so. Neb brought forth his own spear, which he inevitably carried with him wherever he traveled. He was never one to be unprepared for any sort of situation. Motioning again with his hand, he lined his brother up so that they were standing straight together, and he pointed silently to a distant target. There was an overhanging tree limb some distance away. Kenan knew without a doubt that he could never throw so far, but he could not think of any way of protesting the assigned target. Enosh frowned when he saw the limb in the impossible distance, but after a quick survey, his eyes made out a different, much more accessible target not too terribly far off. He looked his little brother in the eye for a brief moment and made a curt, almost imperceptible motion with his hand. Kenan made the connection and suppressed a smile. The two warriors stood parallel, and after a moment, Neb nodded for Enosh to motion for their throw. The middle son put up his hand and then with a quick thrust dropped his hand, and the two brothers made their throws at precisely the same moment. Neb's spear grazed the assigned tree limb and then fell harmlessly to the ground. Kenan's spear lodged dead center in a tree's knot hole, which was closer, but still a respectable distance away. Neb's eyes narrowed at this variance of his assignment. He could plainly see the suppressed smiles of his two brothers. He squared his shoulders and slowly but deliberately walked the distance to retrieve his spear. Kenan ran and collected his spear as well. The three brothers met, and it was Enosh who laughed as he put out his hand to Neb.

"Your throw was certainly the farthest, and your aim was very good, but it has always seemed more reasonable to me to aim for something that you could actually hit—especially if you are in a contest of skill."

Neb stared at Enosh, ignoring Kenan for the moment.

"You like to make sport where you will, but you will not always be able to pick your own targets. A time will come when the impossible must be made possible for your own survival. Do not forget, I am the eldest son, and when I set a target, it will be worth your life to hit it."

Kenan rested his spear butt on the ground, but his knuckles were white with anxiety mixed with fury. He looked to Enosh who only smiled lightly in return to Neb's taunt.

"You may be the elder son, but you may not be the leader—at least not of all the people. There are those who will not follow you. Do not speak of what a life is worth, for you do not know the true price as you care for no man." Enosh then stepped forward, and, putting his hand on Kenan's shoulder, they walked sedately away.

Neb's eyes narrowed in anger and vexation. This was an insult he would not soon forget, but he had no weapon yet in his grasp with which to properly return the barb. But in time, he would make his brother pay—both of his brothers—for he knew that they hated him and stood together against him. That was their choice. He would not risk his position for those who were weak with jealousy. But he realized his time was at hand. He must take possession of the clan soon, or there would be open rebellion. He knew Enosh was popular with many of the young warriors, and he might be able to sway them to follow him in a fight for leadership. This would be a waste of manpower, and at this point, he wanted every spear on his side. He had plans, and in order to carry them out, he needed many men. Watching his brothers' backs as they retreated back into the village, he smiled as an idea came to him. Dealing with his brother was much like his encounter with his first bear. The mammoth beast had frightened him the first time, but that was because he had not been properly prepared. He had gone back after that bear months later and tracked her. When he found her, he killed her, though he was never able to find the cub. But in his vengeance, he took the animal carcass and burned it so that its spirit would never be able to return to the earth. He had exiled it forever into the spirit world where it would never know the power of tooth or claw again.

He would do the same with his brothers. He would kill them and exile their spirits into the world beyond where they would have no power over him. But still he needed more men to accomplish his task. Where would he find more men? And when would his father die? Those were the burning questions in his mind. He refused to look like he was following his brothers back into the camp, so he turned and began running into the dense woodlands. Suddenly, he heard a yell. It was his father's servant. He was being called for. Neb turned again and began to return home. His father's power to call him home still held sway for the moment—but only for the moment. Soon he would find a way to call his father's spirit out of the clan altogether.

CHAPTER 4
MESHULLEMETH AND THE DARK POWERS

Meshullemeth watched as the old woman chanted incantations into the black night. The old man she had recently befriended again so as to learn the secrets of the spirit world had been of little use to her. The one God he spoke of could not be controlled, and He was Almighty in will. This had displeased her greatly. She needed a god a little more pliable and willing to grant wishes. It had taken her a great deal of time to track down this particular old woman and bring her into their own clan who, though of no great intelligence, did have some experience with the forces of the other world.

The fire flickered little sparks into the air. Suddenly the old woman's lilting chant stopped, and a familiar yet horrible voice came forth from the old hag's mouth. No longer was she a common old woman but a wraith of the spirit enchanted. The tone was demanding, and Meshullemeth became slightly afraid. She did not understand these powers of the dark night, but she knew that if her son was to rise to greatness, he had to be fed from a source that was stronger than anything she had to offer. The old woman had spoken of powers that were beyond imagining and could be had only if the seeker was brave and certain of his will. Meshullemeth nodded vigorously even as she felt her skin tighten at the sound of this dreadful voice. It had demanded that her son come forth. Reaching out, she pointed to Neb who was standing just outside the reach of the undulating, flickering firelight. The crone's voice called out to Neb, and he took one small step forward so that he was only half in shadow. He answered as if he were merely conversing with another clan member, though his voice was slightly more stilted and constrained. After several moments, the old woman collapsed and Neb retreated into the dark shadows once again.

Meshullemeth was not completely certain what transaction had just taken place. She only knew that she had arranged for the two greatest forces of willpower in her human experience to meet and come to some understanding. As she stood looking into the fading embers, she wondered why it was that she had understood none of their conversation. She realized with a start that only her son would know what had happened because the old woman never seemed to remember what had occurred when she came out of these spells. Now that it was over, Meshullemeth felt as if she had been relieved of a great burden. Neb would now be assisted by something greater than herself. She knew that her son would never have become what he was without her aid, and she knew that he was aware of that fact. However, she also knew that as she was getting older and she wished to rest more and enjoy the security of being cared for. She did not want to arrange matters for her son forever. Yet, as she watched the old woman sleep off her recent incantation while the embers burned slowly into black coals, she felt that old, familiar sensation of fear running down her spine. Her son could be so unpredictable, and it was clear that neither her husband nor her other children trusted or liked him. Still, that did not matter so much. As long as they obeyed Neb, then the clan would be safe under the firm rule of a certain master. Her jaw was set in clear determination. Now it was her time to enjoy the fruit of her labor. Her son would care for her as she had always cared for him. At least she hoped he would. She looked over at Neb one last time before the darkness took him, and she saw that he had retreated into himself. She shivered as the night air enwrapped her in its tight embrace.

CHAPTER 5
HEZEKI'S CHOICE

Hezeki could not sleep. It was deep in the middle of the night, and the room was covered in utter darkness. He knew that he would not truly relax again until it was time for him to take his final rest. He had to acknowledge the fact that his eldest son was his worst enemy, and he felt grieved beyond words at the thought of him. Yet he realized with a sense of certain shame that Neb's tyrannical selfishness was partly his own fault. He had allowed things to develop in this horrifying pattern as if he had no eyes to see with. His wife's tolerance for her firstborn's misdeeds was a sure sign that Neb would grow up to be a terror, but Hezeki acknowledged honestly that he had done little to reprimand either the child or the wife. The few times he had tried to interfere, he had to suffer through such looks of recrimination and accusations of cruelty that he felt it was not worth his self-respect to indulge in such emotional scenes. He seriously wondered if Meshullemeth was not just a little insane. He had known of those born with misshapen bodies and broken minds, but he had never encountered such a woman who would judge every situation as an opportunity for battle. She saw danger everywhere and felt misused constantly. Only in her eldest son did she latch onto a dream of perfect security. She imagined that Neb would someday grow powerful enough to offer her a life of ease and comfort where the woes of life and the hardship of duty would cease to trouble her. Hezeki had allowed her to imagine that Neb was in fact some great force of nature, and all the while he went about the business of actually keeping his clan safe and fed. He arranged for warriors to always be ready for sudden attack. He sent hunters out on a regular basis, and when they came home with little game, he forced everyone to share the burden of hunger equally. He encouraged spies to keep alert to the changes in the territory around them, and he made sure that the women who went to gather were well guarded. In truth, he was a very good clan leader, and his people knew this, though they were not a demonstrative people. Only his wife and son seemed to suspect him of being a lesser man who toiled at useless duties each day.

Still, even knowing that they thought little of his faithfulness and alertness to the needs of the clan, Hezeki had a hard time comprehending the deeper antagonism that his own son seemed to feel toward him. He had noticed of late that Neb neither looked nor spoke to him anymore. It was as if the youth had completely severed all ties with his father but had failed to tell him. The day before, Hezeki had stopped his morning activities to see to his younger son, Kenan, and found that Neb had thrown the boy to the ground. Neb had belligerently stood over the youth, claiming that Kenan had been insolent to him and demanding an apology, but the father knew the younger boy better. Kenan was never insolent. Hezeki approached closer, and upon seeing a red smear on the young boy's upper lip, his blood grew hot. He looked at Neb and demanded to know what had caused this incident, but Neb simply continued to stand over his younger brother waiting for an apology. Kenan attempted to get to his feet, but Neb pushed him down with his foot. Hezeki flushed with fury, strode over to his eldest son and pushed him with a great shove to release his youngest son. Neb had anticipated his father's move. He grabbed his father's tunic, and with incredible power, he flung his father to the side. Hezeki landed hard on the sun-baked earth and was completely stunned and dumbfounded. A son that had laid his hands against his own father was a curse beyond words. Kenan had yelled out at the sudden attack on his father, and Enosh, with several other men, came to the scene. There was silence and horror at the spectacle, though not a word was said out loud. Everyone feared to acknowledge what had happened, so no one dared to speak. Hezeki had forced himself back on to his feet, and Neb slowly released Kenan from the ground.

"You will learn to show me more respect, little boy, before many days pass. I will not have you challenge my authority again or refuse to offer an apology when it is expected. This clan has not many days left before the greater world demands an account of its men. When that time comes, a real leader must come fourth. Only those found worthy in my sight will be allowed to join me as I go into battle with the approaching enemy."

Hezeki stared at his son as if he were seeing an apparition from another world. Then, seeing his two other sons standing together as Enosh had gone to the aide of Kenan, he swore an oath. Standing his ground, he spoke loudly and clearly.

"By the gods above and those below, Neb, you will learn this lesson! Respect is earned through years of faithful service. It is not grasped at as a spoiled child grabs at a honeycomb. You, my disrespectful son, have no service to offer this clan. You are a usurper, an unnatural heir, a . . ."

Neb had raised the flat of his hand and began to talk loudly over the sound of his father's voice.

"A horror awaits you, but you stand here and act as if you have nothing better to do than stare at each other! Prepare your weapons! Send those you choose into the caves, and then stand guard day and night, for the enemy approaches! I have seen him, and he is fierce. He will kill you if you are not well prepared." In a mighty flourish of his arms, Neb turned and swept his way toward his tent. Hezeki and his other sons and clansmen were left standing in confused amazement. After a few moments, several whispered comments were passed back and forth, and men began to move off. There was general fear and concern on every face. Enosh first looked to his father and then to his little brother.

"He is mad! I think he has become dangerous. What will you do with him, Father?"

Shaking his head, Hezeki stood straight and tall. "I am not sure there is much we can do. He is well past being dangerous. As far as he is concerned, I am a dead man. He is attempting to take over leadership of the clan. Through threats of terror, he is trying to instill confusion and doubt in the men. Now we are no longer one clan but simply a gathering of frightened men. Everyone will want to go different directions. Strike the leader, and the clan will scatter." He paused, stoked his chin and rubbed his back where he had fallen. "I am not sure, but it may be safest for me to break away and move onto different lands for a time.

Your mother will stay with Neb, I am sure, but you two must decide for yourselves where you will serve. As a matter of fact, all the men must now choose. Neb was right; a terror has come upon us, but it was of our own making."

Enosh and Kenan led their father back to his tent. They offered him their spears and told him they would follow him wherever he went. Later after much talk and planning, the two boys went back to their own dwelling and gathered together their things. In the dark of night, Enosh left for a few minutes and then came back carrying his younger sister, Eva, who was fast asleep.

"She will be safer with us. I do not know what Neb is thinking exactly, but I do know I will not trust him with anyone that is innocent and defenseless."

Kenan looked more worried than ever. "But how many men will follow us do you think?"

Enosh rubbed his chin very much like his father was often seen doing. "Maybe half the clan if we are lucky. Many men do not like Neb, but they do see his strength and Father is no longer young. These new prophesies of doom and danger will cause many to side with him who might otherwise have followed us. It was a clever move on Neb's part to suggest we might be attacked."

"So, you do not think there will be an attack? It was just a story?"

"I do not know what Neb is talking about, but if there is an attack, I can only think he has something to do with it."

Kenan's eyes grew round with sudden shock. "He would not want his own clan decimated!"

Enosh slammed his hand against the doorpost of their dwelling. "Neb must rule, even if he destroys everyone around him to do it."

Kenan shook his head in dismay while the two went back to packing. Eva slept on in blissful ignorance.

Hezeki tossed and turned in his bed in silent anguish. The night was black, though a sliver of the moon and a myriad of twinkling stars shone brightly through the window space. Though he recognized the evil of his son and the madness of his wife, still he grieved as if they had died. In truth, he was facing the loss forever of that which he had once treasured. In his neglect, he had allowed evil to conquer, and he wondered if he would ever know peace again.

CHAPTER 6

HOPES AND SORROWS

Hezeki had a brother named Ashkenazi who was once mighty in the world of men, but he had chosen a life set apart. He did not like to live within the confines of a clan; he wished only to be left to his own devices. His mind was his whole world, and all of creation was his companion. He lived in a cave in the hills and drew pictures on the walls. He had no wife and no close friendships, though at times there were some who came to visit him in the hopes that he would pass some of his silent strength on to them. Even though he usually said little and often was gruff in manner, a few still traveled to see him and would always come away from him changed in some manner. His influence was subtle yet deep. He carried within himself such a certainty of quiet beauty and an enduring love for all of creation that his silent contentment was contagious. Still, he did not want too many visitors—or worse yet, long-term companions—for he feared the loss of his solitude. The world of men had a way of confusing his mind and dividing his heart.

Enosh, remembering the stories of his uncle's wisdom and strength, decided they should go to Ashkenazi and ask for his assistance against the tyranny of Neb, but when he spoke of the matter to his father, Hezeki tried to dissuade the boy.

"No one has seen Ashkenazi for many long years, and he may be little more than a wild man among the wild animals by this time. He may no longer even be alive for all I know. It is an uncertain task you set for us, and we need all our skill and clear thinking to make our escape. Besides, if I remember Ashkenazi correctly, he will not be pleased with our visit much less with our need for assistance. He is a man who wishes to be set apart from the troubles of men; that is why he hid himself away. Our father was not a gentle man, and it is best to leave it at that.

Ashkenazi learned early, as you have done, that blood relatives do not always make good relations."

Enosh's voice took on the urgency of one seeking a solution to an impossible problem. "All the more reason he should understand our need and be willing to assist us. He is but one man, but I have heard stories of those who have traveled to his cave and returned with tales of his prodigious strength and keen intelligence. He is a man who could do much to assist us in finding a new home and keeping Neb from hounding our heels, not to mention keeping the enemy he threatens us with at bay. Would your brother refuse to help us?"

Hezeki shook his head in a doubtful manner. "He just might. He is that kind of man. He would say it is for our own good that we should fight our own battles, though he would watch our progress from a distance. He might come to our assistance if we were being slaughtered, but what good could he do then?" Hezeki shook his head again. "I do not know." Taking a deep breath, Hezeki paused in thought. "I will tell you what we should do. There is a clan that lives about half a moon's march from here. They are in a valley between two foothills to the northwest. There is a pine forest there, and the men make good shelters from wood. They are more sedentary, though they do move on occasion. I traveled once into their territory, and they were very kind to me. Ashkenazi knows of them too. As a matter of fact, he used to live not too many days away from them, though he often changed his lodging. He prefers caves but will make use of any natural protection when it suits his fancy. I do not think we should go in search of him, nor so much as head his direction. We would do well to meet up with this clan that I speak of, for they were a gentle people and willing to offer assistance to those in need. If we could meet up with them, then we would not even need to ask for help. Just being in their territory would cause Neb to pause, for surely they have scouts, and he might think we have gone to make an alliance. He would not likely follow us beyond the steps into their hills. Then we would be safe in obscurity, and we could move on to any land we chose. The world is great, and we can undoubtedly make a new home in land as good as if not better than the one we leave."

Enosh was pleased with this plan, and in due time he shared the idea with Kenan. The two kept careful watch over their younger sister and prepared her for the long journey. She was a little frightened by all the confusion and hurried activity. She wanted to see her mother, and when Meshullemeth was brought to their tent, they carefully explained that they were leaving with their father and taking Eva with them. Meshullemeth was thunderstruck. This was completely contrary to all her wishes and plans.

"What kind of treachery is this that you would sneak away like thieves in the night? And you think you will take my daughter? Have you no shame? To separate a child from her mother is a crime against nature. She needs me, and I have plans for her. She will be of marriageable age in a few years."

Enosh almost shook with sudden rage. "Shame? You speak of such a word when you have encouraged Neb to become the spoiled tyrant he is? Do you not blush at your handiwork, Mother? You have chosen one child over three, and you are surprised that the three do not wish to live in servitude? How can you be so blind? He will not be good to you, Mother. He does not have it in him to love you. He may seem to care at moments for those who are of use to him, but he will wish you away when you can serve him no longer. Do not grow old mother! With such a son, you may find yourself alone in the cold."

Meshullemeth's face drained of all former color. Her own fury leaked away in the certain knowledge that what she had done was irrevocable now. In her primal desire for control, she made a choice that was to haunt her for the rest of her days. She recognized the truth of her second son's words, and for a brief moment, she clearly wrestled with her choice. She could admit her wrong; her planning and scheming had been based solely on pride and ambition. She could attempt some amends by assisting those she had left to pay the price of her favoritism, or she could refuse to see the truth before her. She chose blindness. And from that moment on, if she had wanted to understand her other children, she would be unable to do so. The bright glaring light of protecting Neb at all costs blackened out all other concerns.

She consoled herself with the thought that she was, in fact, an outstanding mother to at least one son and that he could find no fault with her. She closed her eyes for a moment, and a sudden dizziness passed away. When she opened them again, she looked at Enosh as if she had never seen him before.

"As your father denies his firstborn, so I shall deny my second born. I no longer recognize you. You are not flesh of my flesh or bone of my bone. I hate you now, and wish you gone from my sight forever!" She flung her arms out in a dramatic gesture and swirled her cloak around in a circle as she left the room, her voice carrying the warning in the wind. "Neb will destroy you if he catches you!"

Enosh watched his mother depart with sick grief. Despite her choices, he could not help caring for her. To be rejected by one's own mother is the deepest of human sufferings. He knew that in their small exchange she had made a definite and final choice and that he and Kenan had both been rejected. Eva was simply forgotten in the tumult of the eruption of her plans, but he knew she would remember before very long and would wish that Eva remain even as she wished her two sons out of her sight. But it was pride and ambition that ruled his mother's heart. Eva was not a daughter to be loved but rather a daughter to be used according to a set plan. Enosh shook his head in sorrow. This bode ill for future generations, for always it was the parents and grandparents who paved the way for the younger generation. Now they would not only have to forge their own way in this world but also find their way into the Land Beyond without the compassionate interest of loving family. They were now a family forever divided. A worse fate was not to be imagined. But as he considered the future, he knew that life under the rule of Neb would be unendurable as well. In this life as well as in the next, Neb would see them only as a means to his own personal glorification. In the Land Beyond, Neb would rule or fight those that refused him, as well as he did here. His life would be a continuous battle for supremacy. If he did not deserve his fate so completely, Enosh could take it in his heart to pity both his mother and his brother, for they would never know peace.

CHAPTER 7

EVA

Eva was a hearty child who, though young, was strong and able to fend for herself in many things. She was a small and slender girl with dark violet eyes and light brown hair, which lent her an aura of individuality that was quite unique in her environment. She was brave even to the point of being bold, and her heart was as faithful as the sun's continual return to the sky each day. Though she knew her mother's obsession for Neb was costing her much, still she had lived with her mother long enough to grieve the apparent loss of her love. Enosh could have turned her sorrow into anger if he had told her of her mother's plans for her, but he did not have the heart to do so. The less the child knew of her mother's plans, the better. She trudged along silently behind her elder brothers while some of her father's faithful men strode silently behind her. Her father, Hezeki, was in the lead. They had left in the night some days ago when there were few eyes to reproach them. Winter was coming on, and the wind had increased. Large white flakes began to drift out of the sky as she kept her eyes downcast. The tears she had shed earlier, she had brushed away in anger. She did not wish to grieve so much nor feel so deeply, yet she could not help it. She felt a terrible weight press on her chest as she took each step away from the land of her birth. She knew that her father had been forced to break away before Neb grasped leadership for himself, and it was a simple truth that they had made the only choice possible under the circumstances. Still, she could not deny a sense of guilt that they were leaving their family and people behind. Yet even as she acknowledged this guilt, in the next minute she was filled with fury that Neb had made this journey necessary. Why could he not wait until his father had died naturally before ascending to the role of leadership? What was the advantage of rushing the course of time? She brushed her futile tears away again. She trudged along resolutely and had to hurry her steps every now and again so as not to fall behind. She was not as tall or as robust as her brothers, but she had a strength that was all her own. In the recent turn of the seasons, she had learned to accomplish many tasks. She was handy at helping to tan a hide, and she could gather fruits and grains quite well, for she was observant and quick-witted. She had just begun to learn how to fashion clay into useful vessels, and she could do innumerable small tasks that helped in the running of any household. Wherever she went, she would be of assistance to those around her, but her most valuable asset at this moment was her ability to hold her tongue and keep her own counsel. She did not ask many questions or demand long explanations. Her trust in her brother Enosh was complete. She knew what kind of a man he was, and she also recognized the decency of her father, though she could see very well that at times he had been weak. She knew that this journey was both imperative and well considered. Her only wish was that it had not been so necessary.

After many days of walking northward and taking rests in the thick winter forests that they crossed through, they came into a new land that was less wooded and eventually became open grassland. In the distance, they could see the outline of a forest unlike any Eva had ever known before. The trees were darker and taller, and they covered high hills and led up into great mountains. The green covered mountains with white caps were beautiful, and they struck awe into her heart. In a sudden moment of bright hope, she felt her heart leap. Something about this vast expanse and the huge mountainous ranges that she had never seen before—as the trees had always been in her way—seemed to speak of something so great and wondrously powerful that her heart was filled with a strange joy. To her own utter amazement, she was filled with sudden gratitude that they had been forced to move to unknown lands and that she had been able to witness this wonder. The sky had opened up onto a vista unlike anything she had ever imagined. There were grasslands and tree lands and hills and fantastic mountains. She wished only to stand and stare and memorize the light pinks and purples of the sky as the sun blinked behind the mountains. The weather was colder as they ranged northward, and though she had seen snow before a few times, it did not appear every year. Most years they saw no snow at all. But now as she looked, she could plainly see accumulated snow fall upon the hills, and the sky was white with it, though there were muted evening colors seeping through the grey clouds. The few trees that grew upon the edges of the grasslands were bare of leaves, and their black branches stood still and foreboding in the evening light. There was something strangely beautiful in the contrast of the angular black branches and the softly falling white flakes. The white on black entranced her as she stood and simply stared, drinking in the beauty with her whole being. Then Enosh called to her, and she awoke from her awestruck state.

"Eva, keep up. Are you alright?"

"Yes, I am fine." She let her eyes fall to the earth as her brother walked back to her in a tired, shuffling manner.

"Come on then. Let's finish our traveling for the night. We will lay our blankets under that copse of trees over there, and there will be enough shelter from the wind to keep us through the night. You can help look for some branches, and we will make a fire to warm ourselves before we go to sleep. The wind is cold but not so fierce that we will freeze in the night. Take your pack off your back, and wrap yourself in your blanket now if you are cold."

Eva shook her head gently. She was not cold. Her clothing was well made, and she wore layers. Besides, the very thrill of seeing this magnificent view had warmed her blood. "I am alright. I can walk a little faster if you wish."

Enosh nodded solemnly, worried that his little sister was trying to cover her grief with excessive bravery. But as she seemed to be perfectly cheerful, he merely turned around again and ran up ahead, stepping once more into his father's footsteps. Kenan had watched their short encounter with a little concern brewing in his heart, so he fell back in order to walk beside his little sister.

"Are you sure you are alright? It is colder here, and it must feel strange to be so far from home."

Eva smiled at this. "Are you not far from home as well?"

Kenan's shoulders squared as he thought of his obvious superiority to his little sister. "I have been allowed to go on several hunting trips. I know what it is to travel a long distance and sleep out in the weather for many days, but this is a new adventure for you. Are you sure you are not worried?"

At this honest question, Eva did not smile. She let her eyes drop to the lightly snow-covered earth as she considered her answer. Their footprints were enough to melt the whiteness into a mere oozing wet, and she knew that if she looked behind her, their trail would appear a shabby, muddy mess in sad contrast to the wonder all around. She sighed deeply. "No, not really. I was sad at leaving home, and I am sorry that Mother is angry, but Neb is really the one to blame. I do not feel any grief for him. Perhaps Mother will come and join us someday after she realizes what Neb is really like."

Kenan pursed his lips doubtfully. "I wish that could happen, but the truth is that Mother has made her choice for good or for ill. I am not really angry with her either, but I fear she will not know any happiness as long as Neb rules the clan." He was silent a while as they marched along, the night taking over the day. Suddenly he looked over at her and spoke in a low, knowing tone. "From what I hear, it was well we got you away from Mother and Neb. If they had had their way you would be. . ."

"Kenan, I need to speak with you. Catch up with me, son!" It was his father calling to him. Hezeki could hear enough of their conversation to know when to intervene. He had a strong desire to keep Eva from worrying much about her future, and though he knew his son meant well, he realized that this was neither the time nor the place for any more revelations or evil portents. Kenan simply offered a comforting nod and smile to his sister as he ran to catch up with his father. Hezeki put his arm around his son in a confiding manner as they continued their march toward the grove of trees. Eva watched them and then looked at Enosh who was looking back as if questioning still whether or not she was well. She gestured briefly so as to allay his fears, and trudged on in silence. She tried to see the magnificent mountainous view of earlier, but it had grown too dark to see well. As they neared their resting place, she turned her head and caught a quick glimpse at the men following behind her. It seemed a small group to be making a fresh start in the world, but it was all they had at the present. Her brother's words echoed in her mind. What was her mother planning? What would Neb have done with her if she had stayed? She felt a shiver run down her spine as she hurried on through the darkening night. The mountains were lost to the looming trees and the spreading blackness. Suddenly her soul became as tired as her body. For all her short life she had lived under her mother's neglectful watch, and now she was about to enter into a new world. She hoped that when the sun shone bright the next day she would regain her lost joy and gladness would replace her present foreboding. Just as they were ready to stop for the night, she lifted her eyes up to the sky and saw that all the clouds had moved off. She could see the uncountable stars twinkling down in a vast array of mysterious whiteness. Though her heart did not leap this time, she did feel a swell of confident peace. Surely if the incredible beauty of the land in the daylight could be replaced by the startling beauty of the sky at night, then there was a reason to hope, for clouds only hid the sky, and trees only blocked one's view. Beauty existed beyond her momentary sight, and that was a comforting thought.

CHAPTER 8
ASHKENAZI

Ashkenazi was not a man to be trifled with. His temper was legendary. Yet as angry as he could be one minute, so he could change abruptly and become gentle and calm the next. Those who knew him even for a brief time were put in awe of his eruptions and equally of his sudden control of those passing storms. He was a fairly large man, though he appeared bigger than his mere body size simply because he stood very straight and always kept his feet widely placed on the ground. He was not one to leap or prance about, though he could run quite fast. As a youth, he would race with the creatures of the wild for fun. He once actually caught up with a young deer and was able to place his arms around her as if in a friendly hug. At the time, the doe squirmed away, but in due time and with great patience, he did manage to befriend more than one deer and teach it to feed out of his hand. On several occasions as a child, he had tried to race a squirrel to the top of a tree. He inevitably lost these ridiculous challenges, but he did manage to learn some handy skills. At the same time, his respect for the small creatures of the world increased. Now as a grown man with rich black hair and an auburn beard, he looked not unlike the wild world around him. For all his wild ways and unpredictable temper, however, he liked to keep clean and neat. He was rather an oddity with all his strange peculiarities in manners as well as in taste. His deep-set eyes were quick to notice the small changes in the world around him, and he enjoyed his peaceful sanctuary in the cave where he had made his present home. He liked to draw, and he had learned to use many various plants, berries and ground rocks to make rich colors for his paintings on the cave walls. He enjoyed depicting the wild things of the woods and hills as they ran free and innocent of evil, though he knew as well as any man that a hungry bear or lion would kill him without hesitation. Yet he also knew that the wild things did not bear the guilt of men in their murder. They killed to eat or to protect themselves and their young, but there was no evil malice in them. One would be just as dead, however, from their innocent hunger or fury. Still, though he was wise and prudent in the wild, he held no rancor in his heart against the animals for their bloody deeds. They were only creatures of the wild, and that was the best and the worst one could say about them.

His attitude toward men was more complicated. He felt a mixture of love and disgust toward humankind. On the one hand, he had been dearly loved by his mother and had loved her just as deeply in return, and he had known a few good friends in his youth. His father and his brothers, except for one, were a different story. His father was a mean and cruel man who thought little of others. His father's needs came first in everything. His brothers were much like him, except for the one named Hezeki, and he had not seen this favored brother for a very long time. After leaving their father's clan, the two had gone off in different directions. Ashkenazi had vowed to live where no man could find him and to be a solitary figure for the rest of his life. Hezeki had tried to dissuade him from this harsh choice, but Ashkenazi was young and stubborn. It was the terrible suffering of the innocent that decided him to leave the company of men. Hezeki did almost the opposite; he decided to form a clan where everyone could do as they pleased and where few rules and even fewer punishments would be imposed. Ashkenazi considered it a generous vision but one not based on a deep understanding of human nature.

Ashkenazi's peace was complete in the world he had made for himself in his little cave in the quiet, wooded hills. There was a clan not too far away, and at times he would go to them and visit, assisting as best he could with his little knowledge of herbs and healing potions, and from them he could get whatever he might need. The women in the clan treated him with generous benevolence, and they loved to bring their children to him. He seemed to have a special talent for attracting the children, and if someone was sick, he usually knew some nutritional plant or herb that would help remedy the illness. The men treated him with respect, and they allowed him to range freely throughout their village. When they migrated, he often was able to track them down. He also had several other clans he would occasionally visit and share a few meals, exchange news and get his clothing pieces repaired or replaced, and he would look in on those who needed a little help. Once he had set the leg bone of a man who had been terribly injured from a serious fall. When the man was eventually able to walk again, the news spread far and wide, and Ashkenazi was accorded a special status as a miracle healer from everyone who heard of his good deed.

He had been alone in his cave, painting a new scene on a prominent part of the back wall, when a youth from the nearest clan of the People of Seth rushed in nearly exhausted from his effort to get to Ashkenazi in time.

"Ashkenazi! There is trouble coming! It is said that there has been a disturbance in the Southern Hills. A clan has split, and the remnant is heading this way. I was sent to warn you. They may have heard of you and could be coming to seek your assistance. We know how you value your freedom and peace. . . ."

Ashkenazi held up his hand in understanding. "You did a kindness in coming all this way to warn me, and I much appreciate it, but it is you I fear for most. I am just an old man, and there is little anyone can want from me but perhaps a few herbs. From you, however, they might covet your strong arms and your stout heart to help them in their next battle, so I suggest you hurry home and stay well out of sight."

The youth looked alarmed at these words, and he turned to flee once again back into the wooded hills. Suddenly, though, he stopped himself and turned back to ask a question.

"How do you know the men coming are prepared for battle?"

Ashkenazi shook his head slowly. "It is what men do. Either they battle to conquer, or they battle to keep from being conquered. Now go on. I will be fine." He waved him away, and the youth sped up the incline like a deer with a wolf at its back.

It was not until the next day when Hezeki and his sons and daughter made their way into the hills that they found signs of a village close by. There were telltale smudges of smoke in the bright blue sky, and they had crossed over several well-used paths. On a sudden hunch, Hezeki changed his earlier plans and suggested that they try following a dimpled course through a heavily wooded pass. It was there that they came upon Ashkenazi's cave. Ashkenazi was outside, sitting on the ground and forming a clay vessel with his hands. His fingers were covered with wet, sticky clay, and the mound before his fingers was little more than a solid lump that looked like it could never be formed into anything useful or beautiful. For several moments before he spoke or moved, Hezeki stopped and stood staring at the man who looked so familiar and yet had changed dramatically with the passing of years. Ashkenazi had realized the approach of strangers before they saw him, but he had stayed in his place, sitting and dipping his hand into a murky water gourd, shaping the clay as if he had neither awareness nor understanding of their approach. Finally, Hezeki broke the silence. His husky voice betrayed a hint of his true emotion.

"My brother! I did not think you would be so easy to find. It has been long years since we greeted each other. I hope that the lapse of time has not done me a disservice, for many have been the days when I longed to look upon you and know that you were well."

Ashkenazi's head rose at the sound of the voice from his remembered youth, and he looked his brother full in the face. They simply stared at each other for several moments before Ashkenazi broke his silence with gentle speech.

"I, too, have often thought of you. Knowing you full well, I figured one day we would meet again." He smiled. "But I am glad of it. I am only sorry that it had to be under conditions so much like those when we parted. Who do you run from now? It cannot be our father, for he is long dead. So is it your wife or son?"

Hezeki's head bowed low as his eyes searched the dust for a better explanation than the one he knew to be true. He looked up and met his brother's penetrating stare. "Both, but how did you know?"

Ashkenazi waved the question aside. "Never mind. News travels faster than weary travelers."

Hezeki tried to sound hearty as he changed the topic. "Here are my two faithful sons and my daughter to become acquainted with their too-wise uncle."

Ashkenazi washed his fingers in the water gourd and then stood up and gestured for them all to come forward. Hezeki's men had stopped in the background, and only now did the whole assembly step forward into Ashkenazi's full view. Enosh and Kenan came closer to their uncle, and they bowed their heads and knelt in respect. Ashkenazi looked at the two youths, and he smiled upon them.

"They are younger than we were when we made our migration away from the Great Clan, but not by much. Do you remember how eager I was?" He looked over at Hezeki, and his smile bore a twinge of grief around the eyes. "Let me guess who the eager one is between you two." He looked them both over as he gestured for them to rise and stand before him. They did as he asked, and he looked deeply into their eyes. With a renewed smile, he put his hands upon the shoulders of each and laughed abruptly. "By the sun above, I see a matchless eagerness in both of your faces. You are brothers in mind, as well as in deed. That is well, for times are never easy in this world, and they are most dangerous when carving out your own place among men—especially men of ambition."

Enosh looked startled at his uncle's clear insight, but Kenan nodded in vigorous agreement as he spoke quickly. "It is the truth, though we do not deserve our fate. If it had been our wills, we would have lived among our own clansmen for the rest of our lives. We wish no inconvenience to you or to any other man, but an ill wind has forced us out into the world. We are now determined to find a land that will accept us and allow us to live in peace and prosperity."

Ashkenazi nodded solemnly while his hands fell to his sides as he looked away toward his cave home. He took a deep breath and sighed deeply before responding. "That is a noble endeavor—one I have spent my life trying to accomplish—but one must be willing to sacrifice much prosperity in order to live in peace. Believe me, I speak from long experience." He paused a moment and then seemed to make up his mind about something. He gestured abruptly. "Come into my dwelling, and let us become better acquainted and hear the stories of your past lives and your future dreams. You can rest in my humble abode and stay with me awhile. Your men can find trees and shelter enough to make a living near us for the time being. Tell them to do as they please, but if they hunt, ask them to go some distance north or south rather than disturb the sanctuary I have developed here for all living things. Besides," he whispered as an aside to Kenan, "I have my reputation to maintain. Having a large gathering at dinner might be hard to explain."

Hezeki spoke to his men awhile and told them to make a temporary camp a little further up in the hills. They could send a messenger daily and do some hunting and exploring while he and Ashkenazi shared stories and made plans. The group of men agreed willingly and headed off into the high hills with a stout-hearted leader named Thubal to guide them. Hezeki watched them go with a twinge in his heart. He knew their faithfulness had cost them much, and he was sorry for their loss and grief even though it was a free choice they had made in following him. Some would retrieve family later when they had made a new home, while others would probably never see their family again. A man could be broken into pieces in so many ways. His only hope was that with care and hard work his own life could be put back together again. Finally, Hezeki turned and followed his sons and daughter into the wide-mouthed cave.

CHAPTER 9
THE OATH

The chilly weather little affected Neb's behavior, for he detested the use of heavy clothing. He was constantly aware of how he might look to others, and the impression he wanted to give to the world was of a man who was beyond the flux and change of the land's dictates. Besides, Neb had much pondering to do after learning of his father's abdication. There was no question who would be leader of the clan now, but there were decisions that needed to be made about how his people would continue to live. Up until this point, they were a fairly prosperous clan in that they had food enough and their families had always been healthy.

Recent sickness, however, had thinned the community to a small degree. Still, they had plenty of children. But to his mind, children were only noisy, too often unwashed burdens unless they could be raised up to do the work of strong members and bring wealth to the clan as a whole and to him in particular. But it seemed to him that too many members of the clan had little thought beyond the needs of the present day. They spent an inordinate amount of time caring for those who would eventually succumb to sickness, weakness or some malformation. He had a visible dislike for old people, especially the toothless ones who drooled and stared vacantly ahead without useful occupation. No one, it seemed to him, considered the clan's long-term development or prosperity. He shook his head as if in admonition of an invisible crowd.

Some years ago, he had journeyed with his father across the woodlands into the high mountains. There they had met a traveling band that told marvelous stories about a great city over the mountains where there were houses of stone and monuments to gods and grand temples for their leaders. Those who ruled the people ate sumptuous food and had soft, colorful blankets spread everywhere—on the walls, under the feet and over large, plush beds. They offered rich and luxurious worship to their various gods such as few had ever imagined before. Neb's black eyes had narrowed in deep visions and extraordinary plans. How could he develop such a world for himself? Of course it had taken long years and generations of workers to build such a city as was described to him, but still he imagined that those who were granted the authority to rule such a great city in their lifetime would also rule it after their death. He was told that those men mighty in knowledge could capture death itself. He gloried in such a marvelous idea. Neb knew of no other man alive who so deserved the right to rule such a future as himself.

As he considered his plans, he realized that the most important thing he must do now was change how his clan viewed him. He was no longer simply the son of a weak leader. He had to raise the next generation to worship him as a god, and thus he must become a god in truth and take on all the attributes of a mighty being. Though he mused on the subject for some length of time, he was not certain how to bring his infallibility about. Finally, he decided he would go to meet with one of the old men of the traveling band, which had journeyed to the distant city over the mountains. His name was Uz, and his renown was great. He knew much about the dark spirits like the ones the sorceress, Cozbi, had brought forth from the Land Beyond for everyone said that he, too, had special powers. Neb had no desire to return to the old woman, for she was sick now with a never-ending illness that both disgusted him and satisfied his personal sense of justice. She had been merely a tool that had opened her soul to the dark spirits, but in her cunning and secretive mind, she had hoped to control both Meshullemeth and her son. When the spirits had opened Neb's mind to her visions, he had become aware of her deceit and saw her plans lay wide open. He knew she was not a trusted servant but rather someone who would forever desire to channel his will in order to satisfy her personal needs. Cozbi reminded him of his mother, and this he could not stand. The old crone's ambition was insupportable to him, and he felt a secret joy that she had become loathsome in her illness. Even his mother would have nothing to do with her now. The old woman's only hope was to die in peace and relieve them all of her presence, but even this she could not accomplish as she desired. No one wanted her—not the world of air and sky nor the world of darkness under the earth. Neb shook his head at the picture of her in his mind. Perhaps it would be best to put her outside of their clan, for indeed she could only bring her own curse upon them.

After returning from a long trek through the winter woodlands, he walked quietly over to Hul, one of the most trusted men of the clan, and gave him curt instructions before simply walking away. Hul had once been Hezeki's right-hand man, but he had felt that he had a greater duty to stay behind with the home clan when Hezeki left. His hair was as grey as the winter clouds, and he was old enough to be Neb's father. He listened in silence to Neb's request, but his face betrayed his surprise. Only after Neb had begun to walk away did Hul quickly follow and ask him to repeat his instructions. Neb looked momentarily irritated and repeated his harsh command.

"I told you to take the old sorceress and set her in the woods tonight when it is dark. Give word that no one is to give her shelter or assistance this night. By the morning, I am sure she will no longer be a threat to us."

Hul was incredulous. "Is she a threat now?"

"She carries a disease in her body and a terrible dark power in her mind. Haven't you ever watched her when she goes into her trance? She becomes the dread voices of those that would rule our people with horror and oppression. Cozbi must be sent out or killed directly. I had thought I was being merciful in simply putting her outside, but if you think it would be best to kill her outright, then you have my permission to do so."

Hul shook his somber, perplexed head in distaste. "I have never killed except in battle, and I do not think I could start with a defenseless old woman." Neb appeared to consider Hul's words with careful attention.

"It cannot be difficult. Come, first I will teach you the necessity, and then I will show you how easily it can be done. Bring four men that are trustworthy and strong to my dwelling this night when the moon is rising. I suggest Riphath, Torgama, Kittam and Puti. They are hunters who have faced the mighty forces of nature in the bear as well as the lion. After what I show you tonight, you will have no more questions and little to fear."

Hul slowly nodded his head in half-hearted agreement. Later that night after Neb had arranged for the sorceress to enter her trance inside his tent despite her continuous whining that she was too sick and too tired to do him any favors, Neb brought forth his men to witness not only her skills at calling up the spirits, but also her powers of reading their thoughts. Hul had at first backed away in horror at this demonstration, but Neb made sure that he saw everything. Puti, a lean, disheveled young man, was not disturbed in the least, as he had witnessed these events more than once since his boyhood. Torgama and Kittam, both strong, handsome warriors, were struck by the stench and loathsomeness of the old woman so much that when the choice was made to put her outside their clan or kill her outright, there was hesitation only from Hul who repeated somewhat shakily that she was still a defenseless old woman. Then something happened to Hul's sight, and he began to cry out that he could not see. He threw out his arms in an attempt to gain his bearing, and the other men backed away nervously. Neb shook his head as if in melancholy foreboding.

"See? It is as I foretold. She will bring evil to us all."

In her trance-like state, Cozbi made no sound to awaken the rest of the village as her life was ended. Hul was sickened by the act, but he stood by silently as Torgama assisted Kittam in the dreadful deed. Her body was then buried in a shallow pit outside the village in the silence of the black night. In the morning, Neb awoke refreshed and pleased with himself. He was to meet with Uz today, and he had the beginning of a plan in his mind that would bring all his clan under his dominion as certainly as his five brave warriors already were.

Uz was a small, shrunken old man with a full head of unnaturally dark hair who cared little for the thoughts of other men. What concerned him most was that his granddaughter and great-granddaughters would deliver him delicious food at regular intervals and forever see to his every comfort. He enjoyed lounging on a soft couch made of pillows in front of his dwelling so that any who sought him might find him accessible and he might see and comment on the entire passing world. He knew his time on the earth should soon be nearing an end, yet he had cheated death so many times before that he felt quite invincible. He had hunted wild game as a youth in a most reckless manner, yet he had always managed to come away unscathed. This was not always true, however, for his companions, but the hunting accidents had never been his fault. It was no concern of his if other men were unlucky. He had been graciously favored by the gods.

Once, when he was still youthful and full of much vigor, he had actually traveled with a company of men all the way across the woodlands, over the many hills up into the mountains and through the great pass into a great dry land—a place the likes of which he had never seen before and would never see again. It was called *The City of Prosperity* by those who lived there. His traveling companions had been foresighted enough to bring certain items from the woodlands that might interest those they happened to meet. Though their items were not considered unique, they were noted by a passing entourage of nobility, and it was he, Uz, who was chosen to come to the Palace of the King to tell the stories of his people. The magnificent structure was still being built, as much of the city had been under long years of construction. However, what he saw was so beyond his experience and imagination that though in generations to come the city would double in size, its earliest stages still filled him with indescribable awe and wonder.

The people of the palace were so clean, and the walls, ceiling and floors were so solid that it was too much for Uz to accept that these men who questioned him about the lands and people of his clan were in fact mere mortals. They wore clothing that rivaled that of a beautifully arrayed bird or the greatest beasts of the wild. But everything was made to endure through years untold: their homes, their clothing, even their own bodies. He learned of their houses of the dead, and he heard about those servants who would accompany the immortal soul to their new home with all the riches of their present life to accompany them. At first his youthful mind had been a little disturbed at the notion of killing useful slaves to travel to the Land Beyond as companions and faithful servants, but upon seeing the glory of their present riches, he came to doubt no more. A slave was a mere nothing in comparison to the destiny of those who could arrange such realities as he saw. No, the only souls that really mattered were those who had the skill to become full of power. He saw all this, and it remained clear and vivid in his mind during the entire return journey to his homeland and through all the many years that had passed since then.

On a certain day while he was still in The City of Prosperity, he had had the good luck to save the life of an old man who was full of the knowledge of secret temple matters by killing a serpent that had been poised for attack and had been in the position to kill. In gratitude, the strangely clad and bronze-skinned elder had put his gnarled hands on Uz's forehead and right shoulder and had spoken words completely foreign to the youth. Later he had been told that he was now ensured of a long life with invincibility while on the hunt. And so it had proven true. Even while traveling the long road home and for all the years that lapsed up until now, no matter how daring or reckless he had become, he was never once seriously injured. He was an old man now, but he had lost little of his relish for the hunt. He could no longer go on a long trek to track and kill his prey, but in his own mind he relived his youth and retold the stories of his journeys to any willing listener. Neb was such a listener, and in time Uz saw a resemblance between himself and the youthful clan leader who had come to see him time and time again. Though he could not call upon the powers of the Lands Beyond, he spoke as if he saw them every day. Neb believed his duplicity because the old man had proof of his power in his ancient years and the stories of his protection while on the hunt.

But it was on this last occasion when Neb had come to see him and hear again of The City of Prosperity and the powers that offered long life and invincibility, and after he had seen to the demise of the loathsome sorceress, that he felt it was his turn to receive the same gift that had been bestowed upon the old man.

Neb had bowed low to the ancient, wizened man and spoke a few soft words of respect. Uz merely laughed at him and demanded to know what he had come for besides the gift of hearing the wonders of his life once more. Neb's eyes narrowed in quiet concentration.

"I believe the time has come for your gift to be passed onto the rightful inheritor so that my clan might become as great as those you knew long ago in The City of Prosperity ."

"Ha! There can be no rival to the great city! I should know. I have been there. I have seen its wonders with my own eyes. Besides, my long life was a gift given to me for a good deed, and no one gave me leave to pass it on to another." He looked up with concern. "What might happen to me if I gave it away?"

Neb smiled with the barest hint of cunning behind his eyes. "You would be twice blessed, Old Man. What happened to the old man who gave you the gift? Was he not strong and powerful? How do you think he grew so strong? He exercised his power by using it. Like the sinews of the arm or the muscles of the cat, they grow weak if they are not used. Think of how strong and invincible you would have been if you had been willing to pass your gift on long ago."

Uz considered this idea some moments before a sly smile slithered across his face. "It could be so, as you say. Perhaps I should try, for after all, I am wearing out doing nothing but remembering." He paused in thought another moment. "But I am not sure of the words. I can remember all else, but the exact words escape me."

Neb took the old man's hands and placed them on his forehead. "It does not matter. Those who bestow the gifts will understand your intent and my need."

Suddenly Uz looked a little uneasy. "But there is one thing. I do remember that I was asked a question. It seemed a little matter to me at the time—just words really— so I assented. I had been warned that my certain conviction was needed if anything truly wonderful was to happen, so I listened carefully and I agreed. It was an oath really."

Neb looked down at his benefactor a little startled. "What did you agree to, Old Man?"

"I was asked as I ask you now, 'Will you worship me?'"

"Worship you, Old Man?"

"No, I need no man's adulation. But those were the words, and I agreed. Do you agree? You must be certain."

Neb looked over the old man's head to a small fire that was burning in an open space in the center of the village, and he stared intensely into the burning embers. He nodded his head slowly.

"You must say the words."

"I will worship you."

The old man sighed deeply as if he were suddenly quite tired. "That is right. You meant what you said, I could tell." He wiped his hand over his sweating brow. "You may go now. I have nothing more to tell you. My memories seem old today, and I wish to be left alone for a time. You can come back tomorrow, and we will talk. I will put my hand on your head and try to remember the words of blessing. You can wait a day. Come back tomorrow, and I will grant you my favor then. I must rest now."

Neb merely nodded. He knew that he needed no false blessing, for the commitment was enough. He let the old man's hands drop from his fingers, and he walked in a straight line through the center of the village. A few heads rose as he passed, and a woman let out a muffled cry of warning, but every voice was stilled as Neb unflinchingly walked across the embers of the burning fire and continued undisturbed on his way as if he were being led by an unseen hand.

Uz fell backward onto the soft pillows that supported his aging frame. His life's energy was draining quickly from his body. Using the last of his strength, he gasped, "Where is he? Where did he go?" His great-granddaughter reached out for his flailing hands and tried hard to understand his words as they were spat out in fury. "He took my blessing! He took my blessing, and now it has become my curse!"

The young girl looked up and saw only the straight and perfect form of Neb as he walked slowly away, untouched by the flames or the old man's plight. When she looked back down at her great-grandfather, she knew that all his life force had ebbed away. She shivered involuntarily as she gently closed the old man's eyes.

CHAPTER 10
THE PEOPLE OF SETH

Not very far from the home of Ashkenazi dwelled the People of Seth. Theirs was a simple village, built in a circular formation with huts of wood and stone hewn from rocks embedded in sloping hillsides. Mighty, ancient trees and green foliage dressed the perimeter while a central meeting place had lain bare from years of constant use. Dappled sunlight and softened winds made the people feel safe and protected even as they enchanted nearly every visitor who happened to stray near. Many generations ago there had been a great and holy man named Seth who ruled his people very wisely. Blessings fell upon the clan like drops of rain in a summer storm. As the tribe grew and developed, they came to look upon themselves as the True People from a long line of faithful. They lived lives of ritual where a portion of each harvest was offered in burnt sacrifice to the Creator of all things. Traditions had grown around every season and special occasion, and they had learned to celebrate the joys of life as well as mourn thoroughly the sorrows that accompanied every man on his earthly journey. Their leader was always the eldest male of the family of Seth, and he was always named Seth in honor of his heritage. As time had passed and the clan grew in number, strength and stability, they developed a variety of skills to enrich their daily lives, though they were still a very simple people and content to remain so until the end of their days. The leader at the time of Hezeki's visit was a young man whose father had recently died a peaceful and natural death. He inherited his role as leader in hopeful expectation that the wisdom that he required to rule well would be bestowed upon him as it was needed. Seth was as yet a little uncertain of his abilities in that he was still rather young, and though he had been raised to the position of leader, he never felt particularly comfortable giving advice or judging cases of any kind. He often wondered if there had been some mistake in his being born the eldest male of such a prominent family. He would much rather be the youngest son of a less noble line and have unimportant matters to occupy his distracted mind.

His best friends were a couple of brothers not much older than himself who were quite out of the ordinary in just about every way imaginable. Though they were close in age, they had some marked differences. The elder one, Accad by name, was very tall, heavy and dark with deep-set brown eyes. The younger brother, Jubal, was medium height, strong as a bear and had very light hair with piercing green eyes. Accad was one to try almost anything just to see what would happen and was a man full of deep complex thoughts, while Jubal wielded words like sharp blades and could discern a lie faster than the average man. The two were constantly in each other's company, and they enjoyed Seth's presence in all they did, though Seth was more cautious in both his words and actions than either of his friends. Still, whenever the duties of the clan allowed him the freedom, he would go hunting or exploring with his companions, and they would find themselves in the most ridiculous situations because Accad had thought it would be interesting to see what would happen if they tried a new direction or fashioned a new slingshot or entered an unexplored cave or climbed the highest tree. Jubal, on the other hand, had the magnificent ability of extricating himself from trouble before it actually entrapped him in its mesh. In fact, he enjoyed a good joke as long as it was on someone else, and pranks were a favorite pastime. Once Jubal had left an article of his clothing, well shredded, hanging from a tree, and then he disappeared for hours. When Accad and Seth rushed home to gather a search party, there sat Jubal, enjoying the warmth of a bright fire and eating stew as calmly as ever. His smile accompanied by his twinkling eyes was the only thing that kept his brother from pummeling him for his remorseless sense of humor. On various occasions, Accad would attempt to teach his younger brother a much-needed lesson in humility, but Jubal was a match in every wrestling competition or contest of throwing skills. While Seth watched and listened to their banter, his heart would unwind from its tormented constrictions of duty, and his burdens became somewhat lighter.

Shortly after their arrival on one particularly sparkling bright day, Ashkenazi brought Hezeki and his newfound family to meet Seth's clan. They had discussed matters thoroughly among themselves, and they had come to the conclusion that the People of Seth were the best authorities anywhere to help them discern where would be the best place for them to found a new home village. When Ashkenazi informed Seth of Hezeki's need, Seth agreed to meet with them. He knew Ashkenazi's excellent reputation, and to be of assistance to his elder brother, Hezeki, was an unexpected privilege. He was introduced to Enosh, Kenan and Eva in turn, and he was very pleased to welcome them to his humble, quiet village. He was struck by the quiet beauty of Eva, but he dared not ask why it was that such a young child should be separated from her mother. Surely there was something very strange at work that would cause such a sundering of family members who were naturally intended to be close companions this side of the grave. After they had all settled in his simple hut, he asked Ashkenazi to explain what he could do for them in their immediate need.

Ashkenazi merely looked tolerantly at the youthful leader and spread his hands out wide as if in offering.

"I think it would be best if they spoke for themselves."

Hezeki nodded his agreement and sat a little straighter as he began.

"First, I wish to thank you, Seth, for your generosity in allowing us to come to you in our time of need. We are not fleeing from an enemy as you might suppose. Our people have not been attacked, though we have heard of a rumor of some raiding clans in the area. However, our clan was safe and strong when we left, and, as the leader, I was very successful in bringing prosperity to my people. But my success with my clan at large was not so within my own family. It is an old story, though one you may not be familiar with as it involves treachery and deceit from within the family." He paused and took a deep breath as if he needed all his strength to explain any further. "It was my wife who raised my firstborn to believe that he was to inherit the role of leadership upon my death. As sometimes happens, we did not agree in many matters, and my son grew to disdain my opinion and presence. He also disregarded the rights of his younger brothers. He is a man who sees only his own needs and cannot share power. We were forced to leave our clan and seek refuge in the larger world in order to be free of his tyranny. We do not come to beg or ask anything other than your insight and wisdom. We need to find a new home, and we hope you might have an idea as to where we should travel in order to find a land safe from evil where we could, with time and hard work, make prosperous. We are too few to fight for land, and we would rather occupy some place in secret at least for a while." Hezeki seemed to have run out of words. He simply stopped talking and waited for someone else to pick up the thread of the conversation.

Seth blinked thoughtfully several times, running his fingers across his chin. He then nodded his head in an understanding manner, though much of what Hezeki had said truly baffled him. How could Hezeki's eldest son, who was to inherit leadership, take what was his before his time? Why here was a breach of decency beyond words to speak! He also could not understand how a wife would raise up a son when that was clearly the role of the father. Everything that Hezeki said about his own clan confused and disturbed Seth. His first inclination was to get these people to move on as far away from his own people as fast as decently possible. But as he pondered the situation in silence, he turned and saw the silent form of Eva as she sedately watched him. It appeared as if she could see into his mind, knowing full well his sudden distrust and dislike. Yet he was not repelled by her, and she was not angered by him. She simply accepted his reaction and was willing to wait and see what would happen next.

Seth took a deep breath and began speaking, though he was not yet sure what he would say. "I am a man of few words, Hezeki, and I am new to this role of leadership as my father passed on only a few months ago. But I will say that I will give your problem some thought. I do not clearly understand your reasons for leaving your clan. Because you are the leader, I do not understand why you did not simply assert your authority and demand obedience from your son. Frankly, if a son in this clan acted as yours did, he would have been dismissed into exile. To leave the leadership of your people in this son's hands does not seem like wisdom to me, and I fear you may not have seen the last of him. My father had a saying that those who do not stop evil when it approaches are doomed to be followed by it." Seth paused as he made motions to stand up. "But be that as it may, your decision has been made, and now you seek a new homeland. I can think of no good options for you at this time. There are other clans in the area, and I cannot speak for their willingness to accept new neighbors. I do not know of any good land open for the taking, for in truth there is always someone willing to challenge newcomers. But I will think on the matter and let you know in a day or so. In the meantime, you may feel free to mingle with my people and find shelter within our huts." At this, Seth stood and went outside his dwelling and called some women to his side. He spoke quickly and gestured, and they looked over at Hezeki and his sons who had followed him out into the sunshine. The women smiled and nodded their heads, and Seth turned once more to his guests.

"I have arranged a dinner in your honor. Ashkenazi is a man who has done much good in his many years living near us, and we are always looking for ways to repay his kindness. Please do us the honor of staying and eating with us; share stories and laughter with us this night."

Hezeki's shoulders relaxed in gratitude, and he looked at his two sons and smiled. Enosh nodded in pleased surprise, for he, too, had sensed Seth's wariness after the telling of their tale, but now he was so relieved that he spoke up in youthful ardor.

"Thank you for your kindness. Our hope is to form a clan much like yours where kindness is the rule and strangers are welcome."

Seth's eyes smiled in return, as his voice took on a more patriarchal tone than usual.

"I only do as my father would have done. He was my friend, my leader and my guide in all things. I honored him in life with my loyalty and obedience. I honor him in death the same way."

Enosh and Kenan looked at each other with sidelong glances, and they nodded their understanding. Hezeki only blinked in sudden grief. If only he had been such a father to such a son. But then he looked over to the two boys at his side and sighed in hopeful gratitude.

Ashkenazi looked around at all the waiting, sober faces of the villagers, and his voice seemed to boom as he called out, "So where are all the children? I must hear their tales of mighty adventures and learn what they have been doing since I was here last. And if there are any sick, call them forth now, for I plan on leaving early tomorrow to head back to my cave. Otherwise all the animals will wonder where I have gone, and they might come here to look for me."

There was a general outburst of laughter, for always it was thus with Ashkenazi. He inevitably insisted on returning to his home in the wild as soon as possible, and always the wild world would welcome him. But tonight would they all would feast and tell lively tales, and tomorrow morning they would bring those with various troubles to him so that he would do what he could. He would question and tease the children and women alike, and they would all enjoy his games and be truly sorry when he left. Ashkenazi knew that the strangers he had brought before them, though kin, carried too much grief in their hearts to be easy guests to manage. Yet for the night they would put aside all shadows of sorrow, and they would eat, drink, and be merry.

Eva watched them all begin to mingle as she stepped outside her family circle into the lengthening shadows. As she watched the hope-filled preparations, she shook her head in quiet wonder. She had sensed Seth's confusion and wariness but also his open generosity. He was definitely not like Neb who reacted to everything with arrogant determination. She considered the two new leaders in sober speculation. Which one would prove the most enduring?

CHAPTER 11
ARRANGEMENTS

As dark gray clouds saturated the skyline, Neb walked along the edge of a small river that meandered to the south of his village. The breeze had picked up slightly, and there was a cool edge to it as the light fabrics of his clothes rippled in reaction to the invisible wind. The sun was hidden and all colors were muted by the lack of direct light, but this mattered little to Neb as he stared unseeing into the racing current of the stream. He sat still, as motionless as a rock dug deep into the muddy depth, while the current moved on unthinking, uncaring, unaware, above all that lived or simply sat there beneath the living water. Two worlds coexisting—the one defined and shaped by the other—yet as separate as two worlds could ever be.

Neb had realized very quickly that being the leader of a clan held little meaning if you had no one to hold within your power. He had been pleased at first with his father's decision to leave the clan. As for his treacherous brothers, he could do very well without them. He was neither threatened by their absence nor in need of their assistance. In fact, he would much rather lead his men as a lone presence. But as time passed, he became aware of the fact that there was a grave difference between absence and death. If his father and brothers had died, he would be completely free of them, but the fact that they still lived—even though they were living far from them—meant their presence still existed in the minds of his men. For a reason he could not completely understand, his father's mere existence began to make him uneasy and disturbed. He did not fear his brothers' return, for he believed they were too cowardly to raise a revolt against him. He did, however, believe that these men he ruled now would forever remember that Hezeki and his brothers lived, and if there was ever any serious disagreement or danger, they might choose to follow the path his father had taken. This was a real threat, for he knew that men do not always need a reason to stray from their leader—they simply need an excuse. Men are fickle, and they often think that a new road or a new purpose will set old problems right. Neb shook his head as his own thoughts scaled the heights and descents of human behavior. He knew too well that the answer to nearly every problem lay in facing the very difficulty one wished to run away from and that the best solution was often the most uncomfortable and difficult one.

His problem now was no different than most other difficulties. It was always a matter of who was in control. He had to keep his men loyal to him, and he knew that the best way to do that was to eliminate any avenue of escape. The people must see him as the strongest leader anywhere, and they must not have any secret hopes of joining up with someone from the past. They must also fear being without his protective influence. There were many dangers in the world, and he had to make sure his men were aware of all of them. He wanted them to be completely convinced that he, above all men, could protect and enrich them. The first step in this plan was to secretly go after Hezeki and his brothers himself. He would hunt them down and kill them without ever appearing to do so. When he returned, he would send his warriors out on raids to make his men the most feared clan in all the land. As they would be feared, so they would be hated, and others would want to make war on them. As long as they stayed together as a unified clan, they would remain strong and undefeated. As long as they let him manage the affairs of leadership, they would be safe. They would also become rich. In his people's fear and greed, he would find his strength. He knew his plan was a risky one, but he was a man who loved a challenge. Great power was worth great risk.

Neb called together two of his men, Hul and Puti. They were quick and obedient men who believed that Neb had the power of strong leadership. They both feared and respected him, though Hul had begun to harbor secret concerns that he shared with no one. Since the death of the old woman, he had wondered whom Neb might choose next to put away, and in a deep corner of his mind, he feared his old age or some simple mistake would be his undoing. Yet by all accounts, he knew he was considered a loyal and well-trained servant. Neb called on him for almost everything he needed, and he was flattered by Neb's trust and dependence. Puti, on the other hand, was a hardened man who had seen much treachery in his days. His father had been a despotic parent, while his mother had been little more than a slave. He had started his young son out doing hard work when he was just a little child, believing it best to expose his boy to the harsh realities of life very early. When his mother would object, his father would admonish her with curses and insist that he would bear no weaklings in his family. So Puti knew the unforgiving trials of life only too well, but he knew nothing of dreams, hopes, aspirations or perfections; those had never been a part of his world.

Ned explained to Hul and Puti that he needed to impart some urgent information to his father and brothers so they needed to track them and find them. Hul felt a little uneasy with this assignment, but he said nothing to display his inner turmoil. As much as he respected Neb, he had a strong respect for Hezeki. If Neb had not been the next in line for the position of leadership, he would certainly have followed Hezeki. As it was, he could only see the logic of obeying the leadership of the younger and stronger next generation. Neb could manage any threat that would come their way, while Hezeki at times seemed to feel too much and hesitate too often to make the hard decisions that a good leader must make. Still, ever since Hezeki had left their village, Hul regretted his absence more and more deeply. He was glad that the younger brothers had gone too; there was only trouble fermenting between them and Neb. He had watched Enosh and Kenan on enough occasions to admire their spirit and charity toward each other, but he knew that eventually there would be a fight for control over the clan among the sons of Hezeki, and he was glad the younger two were well away from Neb, for Neb would never accept defeat.

Neb saw the flicker of unease on Hul's face as he explained his plans, but his own expression remained impassive. "I want to leave early tomorrow, and I want you two men to accompany me. I am putting Torgama and Kittam in charge while I am away, and I will also be bringing Riphath with us to cook and manage the things that I need personally. He will be my assistant, while the two of you will be my men of arms to do all the hunting, tracking and scouting. I believe I know the area into which my father and brothers were heading, and I may well know exactly where they are going. However, it will be a long journey, and there are many dangers along the way, so be well prepared and follow my directions exactly." Neb indicated that they were free to go now.

Hul had looked around aimlessly with a suppressed sigh and then simply nodded his acceptance and turned without asking any questions. Puti nodded his head also in acceptance, but his eyes followed Hul as he marched out of earshot. He stayed behind a moment with Neb while they both watched the slump-shouldered figure of Hul retreat toward his own dwelling. Puti's voice was slightly raspy as he uttered his personal observation.

"There is a man who does not rejoice in his duty as he used to."

Neb's head went up and down in a slow motion as if he were considering some secret thought. "I have noticed."

Puti's eyes slid to the side of his head as he peered indirectly at his leader. "Some men long for days past while others yearn for the future."

Neb turned and faced his companion. Puti remained still, unimpressive and unimpressed. He was a man who cared little for appearance. He was often a bit disheveled, and others wrinkled their noses behind his back when he passed, though his reddish hair was something of a novelty in the clan. Many treated him with deference on this account alone. He had light eyes, a quick wit and a sharp tongue, but he had the sense to keep his thoughts to himself most of the time. As Neb looked at him, their two pairs of eyes met. Puti neither squirmed nor looked away as he continued in his soft voice to speak his mind.

"I face each day as it comes. Regrets and dreams are for other men." He offered a slight bow in deference to Neb and then turned to go his own way.

Neb nodded his acceptance of this rather obvious statement, and then he, too, turned away to his next task. He walked the short distance across the dusty compound to the other side of the village where Torgama and Kittam were often seen together. Here were two men reared for battle whose whole purpose in existence lay in their ability to take whatever they could get from whomever they could subdue or outsmart. They were strong, well-built warriors who looked like they had been breaking rocks or heads from their infancy. When Neb gave his instructions to the two men, they merely gave each other sidelong glances and smiled in a respectably grim fashion. They were well aware that Neb was not one to travel a long way just to impart some forgotten piece of information to his estranged family, but it was not their place to question him. They needed only to obey and gain the respect and dependence of the one who held the greatest position of power in all the nearby land. Through him they were gaining much, and they would act as devoted servants as long as it suited their interests to do so. They listened intently while not appearing to do so, and then they sauntered away in the fullness of their new positions. Neb then finalized his business of the day by going to meet with Riphath. He once again explained the purpose of his planned journey. Riphath was a small, neat little man who was known for his efficiency in getting work done. He had watched the situation between Hezeki and Neb with intense interest, and he foretold to his wife that Neb would end up in sole leadership of the clan very soon. He even predicted Hezeki's departure, but he forbade his wife to ever tell a soul of his ideas. He was well aware that though Neb respected his ability to get things done well and quickly, he was not so enamored of him or any man that he would fear doing some nameless harm to exact revenge on incompetence or insult or both. Riphath bowed servilely.

"Yes, Neb, I will be ready to leave in the early morning. I could even be ready by this evening if you like."

Neb waved his hand in benign generosity. "There will be no need of that. The four of us traveling at good speed will easily be able to catch up with my father. I believe I know where he was heading. Do you have any knowledge of the hill lands to the north of here? I have heard my father speak of a brother who lived in that region."

"I do not know much about the lands far from here, though I have gone on many hunting expeditions in my day. But I do believe that Hul has traveled more than anyone in the clan, and he used to spend much time alone with your father. He may know something about your father's relatives and where they live."

Neb stroked his chin thoughtfully. "I am taking Hul with us, so he will be able to assist me in this matter. But while we travel, I want you to keep your eyes open and alert and pay close attention to those things that others do not usually notice."

Riphath nodded his understanding under hooded eyes, and after a few more curt instructions, the two parted. Neb walked back to his wood and thatch hut and began to make preparations. After a short time, Meshullemeth arrived full of her own importance. Her manner was agitated, and while Neb had no aversion to speaking with her, he realized that she might try and dissuade him from leaving, which irritated him.

"Yes, what do you wish to see me for, Mother?"

"Do I need a reason to visit with my son?"

Neb reached over and put his favorite obsidian knife next to his bag. He stood up and turned to face his mother. "Yes, actually, I do believe that you should have a good reason for visiting with your son, for I am no longer simply your offspring but rather the leader of this entire clan. I have much to do and think about this night."

Meshullemeth ignored her son's attempt at supremacy over her and smiled cunningly. "Why, are you planning something important? Perhaps I can be of assistance to you."

Neb's black eyes peered at her through the dwindling light. "Yes, that may be true. Perhaps you can be of great assistance to me." He paused as if considering his words carefully. "What do you know about my uncle Ashkenazi? I have heard that he is greatly renowned in the larger world and is known for his healing powers."

Meshullemeth waved her son's thoughts away with an impertinent flick of her finger. "I do not know how you would know any such thing as we have never seen the man. All I know of him is what your father told me, and that was long ago. He did not like to speak of his family much."

Neb's face was flushed as he took a step nearer. "And what did he tell you?"

Meshullemeth squinted in the failing light as she peered at her son. "What does it matter now? He is no concern of ours. He lives far away in the hills, and your father has not seen him for ages. It might be, however, that your father went to be with him now." Suddenly her face went rigid. "Surely you do not care about your father and brothers anymore? Why would it matter if they went to find a long-lost relative? He can be no threat to us."

Neb turned and continued to pack small items in his light skin bag. After a few moments of silence, he turned and faced his mother again. "I did not say that I was threatened or that I had any concern for the man. I am merely curious. Now tell me, where in the hills does he live?"

Meshullemeth tilted her head as if she were considering her answer. "I do not know, but I could guess. I have heard many things about that area, though it is far from here. It is said that a clan of long history lives in the area and that there is a man of good fortune who travels those lands. I have sometimes wondered if he was your father's brother that they spoke of, but when I mentioned it to Hezeki, he merely shook his head as if to say he would not speak of the matter." Her eyes grew large as she threw back her head with one finger up in pronouncement. "But I have the power of intuition, and I can guess much. Now, tell me before I reveal any more, why do you wish to know anything about that faraway land and your father's brother?"

Neb continued to move to and fro about the small room, speaking indifferently. "I wish to know because I may have a reason someday to contact my father and brothers, and it will be useful to know where they have settled. I plan on doing some traveling during the next few weeks, and if my ventures lead me in that direction, I may want to stop and meet my uncle and speak of family matters."

Neb's mother pursed her lips as if she seriously questioned the validity of the words she had just heard, but she would not openly challenge them. "It may be best to look for the clan I mentioned first rather than search for your uncle or your father.

After all, a whole settled clan is much easier to find than a few travelers or a solitary man."

Neb stood still a moment. "Do you know anything about this clan of the far hills?"

Meshullemeth smiled. "Yes, I believe I do. I know their name if that would be of any use to you, but I have a request to make before I give you that information."

Neb's chin went up just a small degree as he fastened his eyes on his mother's face. "What is it you want?"

Meshullemeth began to walk idly around the small room, touching small objects as she passed. "I believe that if you plan on traveling away from the clan for more than a few days then someone should be appointed to lead in your absence. Of course, as your mother, I am the most knowledgeable and reliable person to take care of everything while you are gone. So, before you go, let your men know that they are to answer to me. I will meet with them each morning and we will . . ."

Neb's hand came down with a curt gesture that cut off his mother's words in mid-sentence. His words were sharp and decisive. "I have already made arrangements for my absence. Torgama and Kittam will rule together in my place until I return."

Meshullemeth's turned to face her son, and her eyes blazed in sudden fury. "Torgama? Torgama and his imbecilic friend, Kittam? You must be joking! Those two are not fit to lead a hunting party. They are boorish men with little imagination. They are rough and hard spoken. They have no manners and less skill with . . ."

Again Neb's hand came down. "I do not care for your evaluations of my men! I know exactly what I am doing. I do not want men who are my equal to rule in my stead. When I come back, I want my people to rejoice in my return. Warriors do not need to be soft spoken or gentle in their manners. They need to keep everyone together and safe until I come back. Warriors are not nice men, Mother!"

"But I am your mother. I am more suited to rule!"

Neb looked at her hard and spoke his words with deliberate emphasis. "You are a woman. I will not have a woman rule my clan."

Meshullemeth's fury broke loose suddenly. "Why not? I was a woman when I bore you. I was a woman when I raised you. I was a woman when I gave you every opportunity to learn how to be a great leader. I made you what you are today."

Neb turned away, and his voice told her that she was dismissed. "You think too well of yourself, woman." In a swift gesture, Neb motioned that she could leave now.

Meshullemeth swept her large, well-developed form out the door. She stalked away from Neb's dwelling in a fit of rage. She would take some action on this matter. Her son was not going to dismiss her and leave two stupid oafs in charge while he was gone. She was the mother of the leader. With Torgama and Kittam, she had no sway whatsoever, and she wanted nothing to do with either of them. They disgusted her. But as she paused for a moment to collect her thoughts, she realized that there was a man in the clan who did respect her and was always willing to assist her. She decided that if anyone could help salvage this situation, it would be Hul. She went to see him right away.

Hul was just a bit younger than her, but he had long, grey strands of hair hanging from near his temples, and his gate had become slower in recent years. Meshullemeth knew that her son relied on him almost as much as her husband had and that he was an honest man. When she sought him out, he came out of his dwelling to speak with her. When he saw how agitated she was, he took her on a little stroll to the outskirts of their village.

Hul spoke softly and with genuine deference to Meshullemeth. "I am sorry to make you walk so far, but it is a fair evening, and I thought that whatever you had to say might be said better in the fresh air."

Meshullemeth read his mind easier than he thought, and she gestured her understanding. "Yes, the evening is beautiful—especially for those who are about to embark on a journey. Tell me Hul, do you know about this journey my son plans on taking in the morning?"

Hul seemed taken aback. "Why, I thought you would be the first to know of it. Neb just told me about it this afternoon. I have made all my arrangements so that I can assist Neb on his way."

He paused and looked at Meshullemeth a moment. "What is it you want to know?"

"Then you are going on this journey also?"

"Yes, Neb has asked me to." Hul stopped walking and put his hand out to her. "Is there a problem?"

Meshullemeth smiled and shook her head. "No, not at all. It just occurs to me that my son is still quite young, and he will need the assistance of an older and wiser man. I am quite relieved that you will be attending to him . . . But I do have a request to make."

Hul looked slightly baffled. "Anything."

"I would like you to report back to me privately everything that happens while you are away. I want to know where you go, whom you meet with and what events take place from first to last. Can you do this for me, Hul? You were a favorite of my husband's, and I know I can trust you with this little matter between us." She looked at him significantly.

Hul swallowed a couple of times and looked distinctly uncomfortable, but he knew that he was a man of his word and that Meshullemeth was Neb's mother. Somehow things had gotten into an awful tangle, and he desired nothing more than to be out of it all. He sincerely wished he had taken himself and his whole family with Hezeki to whatever end they would find, for Hezeki was not a man of deception or grasping for power. Here he was caught between two great forces each wanting what perhaps they had no right to take. Hezeki, on the other hand, had been a simple and clear-sighted man, except when it came to his eldest son. There Hezeki had failed, and they would all pay the price for this one weakness. Hul sighed despite himself. He raised his eyes from the ground and his silent inner musings. He looked the woman in front of him in the eye. "I will do as you ask, Meshullemeth. But I ask that you keep this conversation a matter just between the two of us."

Meshullemeth blinked her brown eyes in all innocence. "Of course, just between the two of us." She patted her friend patronizingly on the arm and then turned and walked gracefully away with her head crowded with many thoughts and plans. Hul stared after her for some moments, and then as his shoulders slumped, he began to head back to his dwelling.

Under a nearby tree, Torgama waited for the two figures to recede into the distance before standing up. He had been resting away from the noise and business of the clan for a time, but when he heard Meshullemeth's voice, he had sat up and listened attentively. Now he stood and rubbed his neck, which was a little sore from his uncomfortable nap. There was a smile playing secretly upon his lips. His whisper could barely be heard above the noise of the stream that ran nearby. "Just between the three of us."

CHAPTER 12
EVA'S OBSERVATIONS

For a girl of so few years, Eva had extraordinary powers of observation. As her father and brothers made various plans for their futures, she walked solemnly around the quiet village of Seth's people and watched as they worked. She was impressed with their contentment and industry. Everyone seemed to be occupied, but no one was in a hurry. There was a general air of peace among these people that she had not seen among her own people. Seth had awoken on the morning following their initial visit and had gone about his business as if he had little concern for her family or their troubles. She had no way of knowing that in fact her father and her brothers were foremost in his mind as a growing darkness and a threat that he wanted very much to banish to the furthest reaches of the land. She was struck by his quiet, gentle manner, so she shadowed him as he went from place to place. When she followed him to visit a sick, old woman, she was perplexed. Though she could understand why the old woman might be important to those in her immediate family circle, she could not understand the reason for Seth's tender concern. She quietly padded up to a neighbor who had also watched Seth enter the old woman's dwelling. The neighbor was smiling as she shook out her rugs and beat her pillows in the bright sunshine.

Eva looked up to the woman as she approached and asked in a modest voice, "Is Seth's grandmother seriously ill?"

The woman looked amused and laughingly gestured to the next dwelling. "Oh, that is not Seth's grandmother. His father's parents died long ago, and his mother's parents passed on in the epidemic we had a few years back. Though we are all related in some measure, he has no special claim on her any more than any old woman in the clan."

Eva shook her head in some surprise. "Then why does he visit with her? Does she have some power over him?"

The neighbor's eyebrows rose up in exclamation at this. "What do you mean by that? Seth is a good man, and he cares for all who live in these dwellings. She is an old woman who will probably pass on to the other side soon, and he wants to make sure she is comfortable and happy in her last hours, at least as much as it is possible to ease the way of the departing."

Eva was genuinely confused by this. "But I do not understand. If she is about to die, what use can he have for her?"

The woman put down the pillow she was beating and sat on a low bench built into the outer wall of her dwelling. "How strange you are! Does your father not visit those of his clan who are about to die?"

"Perhaps if he had a reason to do so he would. Sometimes those who are approaching death need to explain how to divide up their things or settle old disputes, but he could do little more than solve a few simple problems. The dying have no need of counsel. They have no future and nothing to consider beyond the next moment. Our clan does not spend much time worrying the dying with thoughtless visits when all they can possibly want is peace and quiet to die without discord."

"I have never heard such a view before. My people do not think dying is such a simple matter. Do you not consider where the spirits of the dying go?"

"Where they go? They go into darkness and silence. Where else can they go?"

"Most extraordinary! Come child and sit with me a moment." The woman gestured for Eva to sit next to her on the bench, but Eva was reluctant to go to her. She was afraid of magic. She knew enough of her mother's activities with the old woman of dark powers to know that spells were real and could do great damage. She did realize that there were dark forces at work in the universe, but she could neither understand them nor explain them even to herself. She certainly never considered that those who died entered that world of spirits. Suddenly a new thought clarified itself in her mind, and as she stood there looking at this gentle woman of the people of Seth, she felt afraid. She was not certain, but somehow she imagined that what she might hear in the next few moments

65

could possibly change her life forever. She was intimidated by that possibility. "I am not tired. I am content to stand."

"Very well, do as you please. But just step a little closer, can you, so that I do not need to speak so loudly? This is a delicate conversation and not for everyone's ears."

Eva took a couple small steps forward and stopped. "Why? What do you fear?"

The woman looked around as if discerning whether her words could be overheard. "I do not fear what I am about to say, but I do fear those who would scoff and confuse matters because it pleases them to do so. Even in this quiet village, we have those who would rather dwell in darkness." She nodded her head significantly at a hut not many steps away. "You see, child, I believe that our world is ruled by a single God who is good and creates all things. Our people have believed this since the beginning of time. The first Seth was a follower of the one true God. He was a descendant of Noah, and this belief has been passed down for generations. But as often happens, there are those who turn away and follow after other things not so wholesome so as to win success in this world."

Eva nodded her head in understanding, though much of what had just been said bewildered her. She only knew that those around her could cause her pain and grief or bring peace and joy as their own mood directed them. If there was a one true God who created all things and was good, then whom did her mother follow? Certainly she had never seen her mother do anything except encourage the extravagances of Neb, and that was not exactly good.

"But what does that have to do with the old woman?" She gestured back toward the hut where Seth had entered and was now leaving.

"Well, when a person—like that old woman—dies, her soul goes to join God in His land. And Seth wishes to send his greeting with her so that when his turn comes, he and the God who greets all at death will not think him a stranger."

Eva remained silent a moment. Her mind was whirling with new thoughts, but she was struggling to disentangle them from past conceptions. If those who believe in this one God go to His land, then where did those who did not believe in Him go? Would He accept everyone no matter what they believed? And what had happened to her mother's old sorceress? She was friends with dark powers who offered happiness on earth and not in any lands beyond. What happened to her at death? "I am not sure I understand you. I do know of spirit powers, for we had an old woman in our clan who called for the unseen spirits to do the bidding of the living. I do not know, however, about the Land Beyond that you speak of. Surely there must be two different worlds."

The woman on the bench stood up in fright when she heard Eva speak of spirit powers, and she took several steps away from the child. "How do you know of such things? Yes, you are right that they are two very different worlds. Each time a soul dies, it joins the world of spirits. The dark powers are evil and are involved in all sorts of terror and corruption, but the spirits of God are good and bring forth new life. But I think we have talked enough for one day. For the rest, you must ask your father. Surely he knows of such things."

Eva shook her head. "We are not a people of your God. We are a clan running from a man who rules through earthly powers. If my father had known there were spirits of good who could fight Neb, perhaps he might have stayed at home."

The woman shook her head in sadness. "Somewhere along the way, your people have become lost. If you do not know the one God, you will never find a home."

Eva nodded her head in acceptance, though she did not really understand everything that the woman was saying. She had seen Seth leave. He had entered his dwelling and then left again through a different doorway. He walked somberly toward the edge of the woods that surrounded his village. She gestured her good-bye to the neighbor woman and began to silently follow the path Seth had taken. As she walked, she considered the new thoughts that were now racing through her mind. If there were a God who owned a land into which the dead may dwell away from the powers of darkness, then she wanted to know more about it, but she felt wary; there was too much at work in her world that she did not understand, and she was cautious by nature. Still, if Seth visited those about to leave this world for the Land Beyond, then perhaps he knew more about it than anyone. In any case, it would be wise to learn what kind of man he was away from the watching crowd.

Seth walked some distance into the tree-covered woods with his eyes sweeping the ground. He seemed lost in thought, and it was after Eva had walked further than she really wanted to that he finally sat down on a fallen tree trunk. His back was to her, and she crept up very cautiously, stepping so slowly and quietly that he was completely unaware of her presence. She came near to a tree not far from where he was sitting, and she stopped and listened attentively. She could hear a sound that sent chills down her spine. It was so unusual a sound that she did not know what to make of it at first. She peered around the trunk of the tree and realized that Seth was sobbing. He was crying as if his heart were broken. This amazed her more than anything had in all her young life. Before she realized what she was doing, she was stepping forward toward Seth. Suddenly a loud rustling sound stopped her in her tracks, and she retreated once again into safety behind the tree. She could see two young men bounding through the vines and saplings, running as if in a race toward the village. One of them spied Seth, and he shouted out a greeting.

"Hello Seth! You are just the one we were looking for. We have been out in the world learning many important things! Come let us—" Suddenly Jubal stopped talking as he came to a quick stop in front of his friend. "Why? What is going on?"

His brother, Accad, stepped more sedately up to Seth and spoke in a quieter voice. "A picture of misery, you oaf! Can't you see Seth is upset?"

"I can see as well as the next man, but my eyes only work at close distance, and I wasn't so close when I started talking."

"Thus my description fits you exactly!" Accad folded his arms in silent vexation.

Jubal came and sat down beside his friend, and, while keeping his hands to himself, he nudged him with his shoulder in a friendly manner. "So, what is it? Has someone dared to insult my leader and friend? If so, name the brute and I will . . ."

Accad shook his head slowly and then proceeded to walk over and knock his brother backward off the tree trunk. "Please, let me handle this. At least I will let him speak for himself, you—"

Jubal put up his hand in warning even as he lay prostrate upon the ground, "Uh, uh, remember, I am your brother."

Accad grimaced and rolled his eyes skyward, murmuring, "You see what I have to put up with?" as he sat down next to Seth. He turned to face him and asked in a calm, coaxing tone, "So, tell us, what is bothering you?"

A bright flush had crept up Seth's neck even as he rubbed his temples. "Oh, it is nothing, really. I am just being a fool."

Jubal had righted himself on the log on the other side of Seth and patted him on the back in a comforting manner. "That is alright; you fit right in!"

Accad's eyes were very big as he silently mouthed, "Shut up, you idiot." He turned back to Seth. "Now talk quickly before he starts up again."

Seth stood and looked up into the great green branches overhead, which contrasted with the blue sky as a gentle breeze stirred the leaves. "It is just that when I heard what Hezeki said about his son, Neb, and how they had been chased from their homes by his threats of impending danger, I realized how lucky I have been and yet how much I fear the evil that they bring into our midst. When I went to visit old grandmother Zillah today, I realized that she will be on the other side very soon. In a way, I wish I could go with her. I miss my own parents even now. I know I am the leader and I should not be having such doubts, but I do not feel equal to face the trouble that Hezeki's family must bring. I do not believe that his son Neb will be content to let them escape in peace. Men like him are threatened by everyone—even those who wish nothing more than to live apart. He will come looking for them, and when he finds that we have given them shelter, he may take his anger out on us."

Jubal stood up and faced his leader with quiet determination. "You are fretting for nothing! This Neb, son of Hezeki, doesn't even know where they have gone, and if he should follow them, they will be far from here by that time. Even if he should find out that we sheltered them, he can have no grievance with us. We have done nothing wrong."

Accad stood up also, and, shaking his head sadly, he looked at Seth. "I guess I haven't explained the harsh realities of life to my brother. Some men do not need a good reason to make war. Some men just like to make war when an excuse presents itself, for they enjoy the battle and the power it brings them. There is nothing quite as satisfying to some men as killing a whole lot of innocent people so as to impress the clan."

Accad looked at Seth. "Do you seriously think Neb is that kind of man? Hezeki certainly is not. We have known Ashkenazi for many long years, and he has always been our friend and support. Could his own flesh and blood be so evil?"

Seth was quiet a moment as he peered through the woods. His eyes swept the ground and the limbs of the trees as if he were searching for something. He had heard a sound, and though it could have been anything, it disturbed his heart. He put his hand up toward his face and made a signifying gesture while he spoke in his usual tone of voice. "I do not know this Neb, but I have reason to fear him. Did you not notice his little sister who was among us yesterday? She is but a child, and yet she had to be taken from her own mother for reasons of protection. Something is terribly wrong in a clan where the mother is a danger to her own children."

Jubal had been listening intently while circling around the trees in the near vicinity. He saw Eva just as she saw him. She stood up and stared straight at him. Her voice was clear and strong. "You do not know what evil you face if you think my mother is the source of our danger."

Jubal simply gestured with his hand for her to come closer, but she turned toward Seth and walked straight up to him. "I have never seen a man cry before this day. And I have been told things today about your people's beliefs that confuse me, but

I think that your people have something my people lack. You have a strength that we do not even know exists. But it is not something we can receive from you; it is something we must find for ourselves. In the meantime, I think you are right. Neb is dangerous, and he just might come looking for us. He is rarely ever content. Though we can do nothing to truly threaten him, he could easily imagine it so and would follow us to ease his mind. We must leave your village as soon as possible so that he does not find us here. Your people are safe, for I do not believe he wants to make war with everyone—at least not yet." She paused and frowned as she considered a new thought. "Even though I saw you crying, I believe you are stronger than Neb." She turned and began to walk back toward the village.

Accad and Jubal watched her step silently and carefully away through the tangled woods. They turned simultaneously toward Seth who was still watching her. Jubal's hands went up in exasperation. "I feel a bit confused. I thought Eva was a child, but I have never heard a child speak thus. And what do we have that her people lack except a leader who knows how to cry?"

Accad shook his head warningly. "I think she is right. There is trouble ahead. She fits in with her whole family. They must be from some extraordinary line. Think about Ashkenazi and how he lives alone in the wild, healing yet never completely healed. And his brother Hezeki; why there is a man of much grief! His son Neb must be a force to contend with, for word has gotten out even to neighboring clans that he is a danger and a threat. He has a mind for conquest they say. That was the news we were rushing in haste to tell you. Now this child comes and speaks like an old woman who has seen too much. She is our ally now for her own reasons, but I would not trust any of them."

Seth nodded and began to follow Eva's path back toward the village. He stopped suddenly and turned toward the brothers with a grave expression. "I fear our lives will change in the near future. What we have to offer Hezeki may be very different from what Hezeki has to offer us. I wish more than ever that I was not the one left in charge."

Accad and Jabal followed slowly in his wake. Accad spoke aside quietly to Jubal. "We just better hope that whatever we have is stronger than whatever they bring."

CHAPTER 13
A FATHER'S LOVE

Enosh, the second son of Hezeki, ground a dead and brittle leaf through his dry fingers. All was quiet around him, and the crunching of the leaf turned into silence as he watched the separate particles fall to the earth. He knew without a doubt that time was running out. He could not explain where the certainty came from, but he knew that Neb had decided to follow them. He went to see his father who was resting in one of the tents they were using as a temporary shelter while they decided in which direction to move. They had camped just northwest of Seth's village, and though everything was peaceful and quiet, they were in fact not far from the daily bustle of the small village. Enosh stepped inside the tent and looked at his father's sleeping form. His heart was wrenched with unspoken grief. No matter where they went and no matter how hard they tried to escape, there would come a day when Neb would have to be faced and defeated. But in his heart, he knew that Hezeki would never be the man to defeat Neb. He simply could not. He may dislike what Neb had grown into, and he may hate his ambition, but he would still refuse to fight in open battle against his firstborn son. He was a good man in many ways, but he could not fight fiercely. He hunted safely, and he worked steadily, but he did not have the warrior's blood flowing through his veins. A deep sigh escaped Enosh's lips before he realized it. Hezeki stirred. His sleep had been light and troubled.

Hezeki looked up and over. He saw his son standing as a black shadow against a bright background. He was momentarily frightened.

"Yes? Has something happened?"

Enosh took a step forward, and the contrast diminished so his father could now more clearly see who was approaching. "No, Father, nothing has happened. Not yet anyway." He paused, unsure exactly how to say what he very much needed to say.

"Father, I think it might be time for us to move on now. We have learned all we can here. I have been told that there is a great river far to the east across expansive grasslands, and I think we ought to try and settle somewhere out there. I do not know much about the land or the people yet, but we will learn much as we travel, and it will be good to move on from here, don't you think?"

Hezeki nodded his head slowly. He could see his son's impatience, and he could see clearly the logic in moving on, but for a reason he could not explain, even to himself, he felt he needed to stop running. Somewhere deep in the core of his being, he knew that he had to face something that he had been running from for a very long time. He felt old now—so old that he was not sure how much time he really had left. In taking his true sons into a new land, he had done that which was most urgent. He had given them a head start. They must move on and forge a new home in a new land, but he knew that he would not be allowed a new life. He had tried to imagine himself in the future, but there came to him only visions of nothingness. He had no impulse, no spark, no creative wit to encourage him to start again. Slowly he sat up and motioned for his son to come and sit beside him.

"Enosh, I know this will be hard for you to accept, but you must lead your brother and sister and our loyal men into the new lands yourself. I know you want to go to the Great River, but I suggest you go south, deeper into the grasslands. Travel along the hills east a ways, and then suddenly go south. Leave no trail behind. Neb will think you have continued east, and he would not suspect that you would head south. He might eventually think you had gone into the hills and mountains to hide, but you will be free of him by then. You may well come into open, fertile lands with few inhabitants. Stay out of the mountains, for they can be treacherous. Do not travel too far east, for any land that speaks of great rivers and wondrous fertility will surly draw many people, and you do not wish to compete with others." When he paused, Enosh broke in with anxious questions.

"But I do not understand, Father. Why will you not lead us? Are you ill?"

"No, not ill, just old. I do not have many years left, and I think it is best that the men get used to you as the new leader. I was afraid to do this earlier because I worried that you were too young to carry such a burden, but after meeting Seth and learning of his wisdom and strength, even at so young an age, I am convinced that you are as much a man as he and can fulfill all that I ask of you."

"But where will you go?"

"I will follow my brother and either live with him or do as he does and live out my last years in peace." He looked at his son as if pleading for an exceptional boon. "Will you let me do this—go off alone and live untroubled by the affairs of men in my last days?"

Enosh was confused. He did want his father to have what he wished for—to live and die in peace was the goal of all men—but his heart smote him with fear and anguish. Was he strong enough to lead in his father's stead? Would the men follow his orders? And what about Neb? What if Neb came and found his father alone and unprotected? These questions stopped up his throat so that he was unable to respond for several moments. Then Hezeki spoke again.

"I see how difficult this is for you, but I can do nothing but make it necessary for you to do as I wish. I order you under obedience to me as your father and leader to take your brother and sister and our men and to go into the grasslands far from here. I demand that you explore the territory until you find a suitable land to settle for the course of one year. After that year is over and you have made the beginning of a village, you may come back and tell me about it, and I will consider joining you. But understand this: I will not see you before that year is up. Do you understand?"

Enosh nodded his head mutely. His father was not telling him everything. He could feel pain mounting behind his eyes. He simply stared one last time at his father and left his presence. After discussing the matter with Kenan and Eva, he knew that they must move on right away, for his own resolution was still uncertain and weak. He must make the break as fast as he could.

Then Enosh went to his father's men and told them that Hezeki had directed them to travel east and then south and that he would follow them later. The men accepted this decision without comment, and they prepared to move on early the next morning. Kenan and Eva went to see their father one last time.

When Hezeki, who was standing just outside his dwelling, saw Kenan and Eva approach, he gestured for them to come closer and he began in a conciliatory tone, "I am planning on joining my brother for a time. We have many years to catch up on. Do not worry about me. For an old man, I can take care of myself. Besides, if I need anything, the people of Seth are generous and will undoubtedly assist me. So you see, I will be safe and happy here."

Kenan just looked at his father with sad eyes. He did not know how to put his disappointment and grief into words. He was still young enough to wish for his father's presence. He was man enough to appreciate the danger of traveling out into the world without an experienced guide. Though his father had been weak at times, still he had been the leader of the clan for many long years, and he knew how to make decisions and command men. Would Enosh be so strong and wise? He felt like he was being abandoned anew, and it brought back all the misery of leaving his natural home, his mother, his friends and his relatives. Was he to never know the joy of being safe and secure ever again?

Eva looked at her father and then at her brother. She had observed Enosh's distracted look and the strain in his voice. Her eyes narrowed. Why was her father doing this? She knew that the men were under the impression that Hezeki would be following them in a few days. What would happen if he did not come? Would they follow Enosh's leadership even without her father to guide them? And was Enosh ready to rule alone? What was Hezeki thinking? Surely he was not ill or too old or infirm to travel. Was he afraid? Did he realize that Neb was coming? Did he think that he could save himself by hiding in obscurity? Eva felt her face flush in anger. She was being abandoned again. She stood her ground and stared at her father, vowing deep within her being that she would never do to another human being what was being done to her. She would grow big and strong—if not in stature, then in will—and she would be a protectress. She would take care of those who were left alone and uncared for. She would nurture and love and cherish the young, the innocent, the infirm and those not valued by a world that should have valued them.

Staring with cold, blue eyes, she looked upon her father for the last time. She was too angry to be sad. "I will say good-bye here, Father. We will leave early in the morning, and I would not wish to disturb your sleep."

Hezeki sensed her anger in her short, clipped words, and his heart squeezed in a tight grip. "Do not leave me with anger in your heart. I know you do not understand now, but you will understand later. I have been a weak man for too long. Now I must be strong. I must do what I refused to do when it would have been a much easier matter."

"And what is that, Father?" Her voice had softened just a bit.

"I must tame a wild beast." His eyes rolled over her as he reached out and stroked her hair. "Now, go along and get yourselves ready. The morning will come, and you must be off to your new home."

Eva blinked back the sudden tears that pressed against her eyes. Her vow would be even more dear to her now that she understood her father's love better. She turned to go, but just as she began to step away, Hezeki called to her and Kenan one last time.

"Remember, children, your true home is inside you. If your heart is disordered, so your life will be, for you cannot escape your own self."

Kenan and Eva nodded, and then they walked slowly away from their father.

It was in the middle of the night that Enosh was roughly shaken awake. Accad was standing over him, and, not being a very gentle sort, he was practically rolling the youth off his pallet trying to get him to awaken quickly. Enosh sat upright and put out his hands to stop the shoving.

"Alright, I am awake! What is it you want?"

"Seth sent me to warn you that a group of warriors has been seen traveling this way by scouts he had sent out. The leader fits the description of your brother. They do not look like they are coming for a social call. Your father has given word that you are to leave immediately. He says he has already given you your instructions."

Enosh nodded mutely as he sprang upright and used his foot to awaken his brother.

"Go awaken the men and get Eva ready. We will leave at once." He turned back to Accad. "Tell my father to hide with his brother in the caves. He will be safe there. The next time you see him, give him our farewells. Tell him," he paused with sudden emotion. "Tell him that I will do everything he asked and that I hold his words dear."

Accad nodded as he quickly exited. Enosh rubbed his hands together briskly to warm them against the chill of the night, and then he began to make quick preparations for their sudden departure.

It was late the next day when Neb saw the village of Seth. He stood for a moment in the shadow of the protecting trees, drinking in the view of a peaceful clan as they went about their daily duties. There were no hurried movements, though surely they must be aware of his approach. The sun was well past its zenith and was making straight for its nightly retreat. The air was warm and humid, though not hot, and the buzzing of insects hummed drowsily in his ear. He watched this clan in the silence of distance, and he judged them to be a weak, yielding people. He had found out all he wanted to know about the people of Seth as he traveled. He had caught one of the men of Seth when he had been out hunting, and he discovered both the location of his father and brothers in the village and also the cave of his uncle. Ashkenazi was so easy to find that it was almost a letdown. Neb felt no kinship with the big-hearted, gentle soul. In fact, he felt rather repulsed by his silent relative. When he had presented himself to his uncle, Ashkenazi had simply stared at him for a long time and said absolutely nothing in words but much with his eyes as they swept up and down Neb's cat-like form. Neb quickly grew angry, for Ashkenazi was neither welcoming nor courteous. When Neb asked him questions, Ashkenazi turned his back on him and acted as if he were not even there. This had been intolerable to a man so used to absolute obedience and deference. Finally turning to his unwelcome guest, Ashkenazi had dared to ask what Neb wanted with Hezeki. Neb replied that as the first son of Hezeki, he did not need to answer to anyone. Ashkenazi spat out his reply. "You are no son of Hezeki. Son of a demon is more likely, but not Hezeki!"

In cold fury, Neb gestured to his men and they understood all too well. There had not been much of a struggle, for Ashkenazi did not try very hard to defend himself. He seemed to think it was some sort of dishonor to fight a member of his own family. Neb had no such scruples. Though he realized even in his burning anger that it was not strictly necessary to kill the old man, he found that it was most logical to rid himself of a relative who would shadow his life with a claim of grievance. When a son comes looking for a father, he does not expect to be met with insolence and demanding questions. It only took one silent look from Neb directed at Puti to end the confrontation. Puti's throwing arm was quite strong. The spear was retrieved in little time as Ashkenazi took his last breath. Just as they were about to leave the cave, Neb looked up and noticed the painting on the walls. He felt a chill go down his spine. For a brief moment, he considered the idea of having his men smear the paintings with Ashkenazi's blood or at least throw mud upon them, but then he shook his head. He needed to go on and get to the village of Seth. He had a few more confrontations to face before the next day dawned. What did the dreams and fancies of a dead man matter to him? But after Neb had turned away, Puti, in a strange moment of self-direction, put his bloodied hand upon the wall as if to mark this deed as his own.

CHAPTER 14

An Unwelcome Guest

When Hezeki saw Seth early the next morning, he knew he had waited too long. Once again, his judgment had led him astray. Neb must have made up his mind to follow them shortly after they left, and he must be an uncommonly good tracker, for they had taken some pains to hide their trail. Hezeki sighed. This should not surprise him; yet in a way it did. Knowing Neb to be what he was—a spoiled and unruly child who had never learned to respect anything or love anyone—he knew that Neb would go to extreme lengths to have his way. Yet somehow in Hezeki's mind this was more than simple petulance unleashed— more than the injustice of an elder son wanting leadership before his appointed time. He sensed in the reaction of Seth and all his men that Neb's coming upon them was a danger that had a will of its own. He felt his skin prickle, and his shoulders slumped as he lifted his hand to his eyes, trying to keep the brightness of the new day from blinding him. His great fear was that Enosh had not had enough time to make a good escape. Now he knew what he had to do, but as in all things relating to his eldest son, he was not at all sure how he would accomplish his goal. If he could not tame Neb, could he at least delay him long enough to save his other sons? Ironically, it was Seth who seemed the more anxious of the two, perhaps because Hezeki's concern was buried deep under years of expected doom.

"Yes, Seth, I am quite certain that Enosh, Kenan, Eva and my men left very early this morning. I was told about their departure when the moon was still high, and I gave them instructions yesterday to go as far from here as possible. I told them to head north into the mountains. They can find shelter and plenty of hiding places among the rocks, hills and caves." He looked disarmingly at Seth. "You seem to be very worried today. I know

I have told you alarming things about my son, Neb, but surely he is only one man and your warriors are more than a match for him and few companions. It is quite possible that he just wants to know where we plan on settling and then he will go back where he came from." Hezeki stared ahead as if looking into a nameless future while the bright sun shone down unaware of the trials of men. A small breeze meandered through the village.

Seth looked at Hezeki out of the corner of his eye and nodded his head rather unconvinced, though he did not want to say so. He wanted to believe that his village was not in trouble, but he felt a doom threatening him and wished he knew how to prepare for an unknown threat like Neb. His men were trained in the art of battle, though they had seen very little of it for over a generation. They were a peaceful clan, and as they were small and not terribly prosperous, there had rarely ever been any attempt to raid or enslave them. They only maintained warriors because it had been a custom handed down from father to son and it was considered a point of honor to be able to fight well Still, as Seth considered the point, his men were good at fighting when it came to mock battles, but he had never seen them fight to the death. He was not really sure they had the bloodlust in their veins. The slight breeze had become stilled into a dead calm.

"I hope you will be able to convince your son that there is nothing of any interest for him here. I do not really enjoy a lot of commotion, and I fear your son may want to stay and trade or something and we might disappoint him. The sooner he decides to pass on, the better. But I am concerned that he may have some unwholesome desire to see his brothers. Do you not think it would be better to tell him a different direction than the one they actually took?"

Hezeki paused as if he had to think the matter over, but his musings were cut short by a runner coming up and panting out the message that Neb was less than a half a day's journey away. He was heading right toward them. Without any further conversation, Seth bowed his acceptance and turned toward his home to await the meeting. Hezeki stood alone for a moment as if frozen. He felt a cold sweat begin to break out on his forehead.

He tried to brush it away, but he knew it was useless. Neb would come and see him, and he would know instinctively that his father was afraid. He looked to the ground and felt very much like weeping, for he now wished that he had left with his brother and was safely hidden deep in a cave somewhere. He would not care about the physical hardships if only he could avoid this confrontation with his firstborn son, a son who was bright and strong and should have been his pride in old age. The doom of his guilt was upon him before his son ever came into view. He turned and strode across the village to his own dwelling and lay down, for he suddenly felt overwhelmed by exhaustion.

The air had become quite warm and still as Neb looked around at the cowering figures that were trying so hard to appear brave and warrior-like. He saw a few who, with training, might make useful servants, but the vast majority looked weak and unnerved. He felt disgust rising like gall up into his throat. He had merely walked into their midst, and they were afraid. He continued to stride through the center of the village. He saw his father standing with a youth at his side. At first he imagined it must be Enosh, but to his surprise it was a young man only slightly older than Enosh but not much taller and rather thin. He wore the ceremonial robes of one who holds the position of leader, and Neb felt a smile curl around his lips. Could this baby face be the leader? How had he assumed his role, he wondered. Neb stopped right in front of his father and stared at him for a long, cold moment. The uneasiness of the old man was palpable. Surely the youth at his side could sense it. Neb did not even greet his father. He merely turned silently and addressed himself to Seth.

"You are the leader of these people?"

"Yes, my name is Seth. You are . . ."

Before he could say any more, Neb waved his hand up in the air to stop him in a bored but commanding gesture. "I know all about you. I have learned much in my travels. I wonder, do you realize who it is that stands beside you?"

Seth looked a little confused and taken aback. "Yes, of course, here is your father and leader, Hezeki. Surely you . . ."

Again Neb raised his hand and began to speak over Seth. "I see you are not fully informed of the facts. Let us go someplace comfortable." He gestured to his men to fan out throughout the village. "My men will make themselves at home, so do not concern yourself with them. Where is your lodging?"

Seth's eyes had opened wide in surprise and irritation. Yet he was not sure how to refuse the incredibly arrogant demands of his sudden guest. He looked over and saw Accad and Jubal standing close by. They had seen all and were probably trying very hard to hear everything. He knew they would follow behind and would be near at hand in case there was trouble. So Seth merely gestured toward his home and began to lead the way. Neb followed, allowing his eyes to roam freely around at the lodgings and the inhabitants of this small village. Though it was insignificant, still he could see some useful elements. Like a vulture circling its prey, he seemed to be dissecting the place and making plans that no one else would approve. When they arrived at his house, Seth ushered Neb inside. Hezeki followed, though he had not been invited in by any direct manner. He felt that he perhaps was intruding; yet he knew that he, of all people, should be there to discuss matters with his son.

Neb sat down in the most comfortable location. He gestured for Seth and Hezeki to sit down also. Seth's set jaw and stiff movements reflected the incongruity of a guest telling him where to sit in his own house. Reluctantly he sat down on his own pallet and wondered if he should simply step back outside, for he was clearly losing control of the situation, and he had no desire to feed Neb's monstrous pride with his attention and servitude. But at the same time, he did not wish to spark a sudden confrontation. He was not ready yet. Why was he not ready? He wondered to himself why he had never considered the possibility that Neb would come and do this very thing? He realized that he had never imagined such arrogant rudeness because he had never seen or heard of it before. Here was a man who lived completely outside his neat world of tradition and convention. He played by no rules and was completely unpredictable. Seth ordered his mind to keep calm.

Neb began speaking in an authoritative tone completely unfamiliar to Hezeki. Never had his son assumed such an air of perfect control. What had happened to seal his confidence? "I have come into your midst, Seth, to warn you of a great danger. I have followed this man," he gestured toward his father with a dismissal of a few disdaining fingers, "because he is a traitor to his own clan and must pay the price that all traitors pay. He is not to be trusted. I know what he came here to do. He undoubtedly told you a story of how I am an evil, over-reaching son who forced him from his leadership role and how he has had to run for his life. I am sure that my brothers and the few weak-minded followers they brought with them were very convincing. But I am here to warn you of their treachery. They are not what they seem. They have come here to destroy you and your people."

Hezeki stood up. His face was flushed, and he wanted very much to strike his son, but his hand only trembled impotently at his side.

"How dare you accuse me of such crimes when it was you who treated your brothers with abhorrent disdain? You wanted to take . . ."

Neb also stood up, and he now faced his father. He pushed his face only a few inches from his father's face and spoke very, very slowly. "I wanted to take what? I treated my brother's how? I am the leader because you left your people unprotected. My people would have been completely unguarded if it had not been for me. When the attack came, as I foretold it would, we were prepared, and we defeated the enemy. I have come here to see that justice be done. You ran and hid as you always run and hide. I am surprised you are not cowering in some cave like your brother."

At the mention of Ashkenazi, Seth rose up and began to speak in a loud agitated tone.

"This is not the place for your accusations. If you have complaints against your father and you want to address them in this village, then you will have to abide by the traditions of this clan. I will hear both sides in the evening when the sun has set and tempers have cooled a bit. For the time being, I want you two to stay away from each other and . . ."

Neb turned and looked at Seth as if an insect had dared to land on his sleeve. "I have not asked for your assistance. I do not need your counsel. This matter is already judged, and I have decided the fit punishment. I will dispense my judgment as soon as I see my two brothers and have disposed of the disloyal members of my clan who followed my father into your midst."

Hezeki seemed to melt. He was horrified beyond words, yet he knew that Neb would be appeased with nothing less than his death and the death of the rest of his living family barring his wife. What part she still had to play in all of this was a black mystery. But he knew that every moment he could delay Neb, the better chance Enosh and the rest had for escape. His mind was whirling with what to say next.

Seth saw the situation as clearly as Hezeki and had come to the same conclusion, but he did not feel like melting in the least. His fury was as cold as ice, and, as with ice, the more it froze the greater it became. "I am the leader of this clan, and if you attempt any violence against me or against any man under my protection, then you will have to fight me and every man in this clan down to the last warrior. With the few warriors you brought, I do not think you are prepared for the battle I am willing to wage!"

Neb's eyes narrowed for a moment. For the first time, he felt a glimmer of respect for someone other than himself. Ashkenazi had not faced death so valiantly. He had simply been willing to die for some unknown reason that Neb could not imagine. When he had been told of his plans to find Hezeki, Ashkenazi simply would not say another word. He did not fight nor did he try to escape. It was puzzling to say the least. But that was no longer an issue. Now this Seth was becoming issue. Still, as Neb looked him up and down, he felt a desire to test him and see the proof of his words. This would be interesting. In the end, he would win, and Hezeki and his brothers would die at the time of his choosing, but there was no particular rush. He sat back down and gestured for Hezeki to leave the dwelling. Hezeki did not want to go, but Seth nodded his agreement. Neb sat back down and gestured for Seth to do the same.

"I see that I have a true man in my midst, and this pleases me very much. You have no idea how lonely my life is at times with so few who are strong-minded. I will speak with you, and we will come to an understanding. I do not see the need to destroy you or your people unless it is absolutely necessary. After all, I come with a just complaint, and you may well see my point after I have made myself clear." Neb stretched his arms and stifled a yawn. He looked about as if to ascertain what was immediately available for his use. "But right now I am hungry and a little wearied by all this nonsense. Please arrange for some meat and provisions to be brought to me, and we may speak of other things for a time. I will rest here, and tonight I will gather those whom I wish so that we can have full justice done before all. I assume Enosh and Kenan are hiding someplace. Please let them know that they can run but they cannot hide. It will be much better for them if they simply face me. After all, I may be in a mood for clemency. They are my brothers, after all." Neb smiled as if he had made a rather droll joke. "I will recline here until the food is prepared. You may go for now."

Seth was appalled at the situation as it spun out of his control, but he knew of no safe way to challenge the force that sat before him in the person of Neb. He stood and backed out, saying nothing, but upon his face he registered the insult done to himself as a leader and as a man. Behind his eyes, all the tears of yesterday had suddenly dried up; in his heart, all the sorrow was wiped away, and all was replaced with a furious rage. A vivid picture of his father and everything he had done to preserve and protect his people clarified itself in his mind, and with uncharacteristic determination, he chanted in a low whisper a single cold thought. "I will have my revenge for this."

CHAPTER 15
DECEIT AND TREACHERY

The village of Seth was arranged in an oval pattern around a central fire pit, which everyone gathered near for communal feasts. Seth's home was a simple, thatched wood hut with a central doorway much like that of all the other dwellings, though his was a bit larger as the central room needed to be more spacious to accommodate the many guests and council members who convened there when the weather was inclement. He also had the unusual benefit of two extra rooms in the back, which were private areas for the wife and children of the leader to work or rest at leisure while the men of the village discussed matters of significance. One of these rooms, designed by a Seth from long years gone by, had been arranged so that a small door was built into the back wall for the purpose of a secret escape if need or desire arose. Occasionally a leader would simply like to go out alone, and it was understood that when the back door was used, no one was to follow or ask questions. It was a convenient arrangement, highly satisfactory to the succeeding leaders of the clan. When the present Seth had taken his recent ramble into the woods, he had used this same door.

When Neb was left alone in this same dwelling, he explored the front room thoroughly and ascertained many new insights into the People of Seth. His eye was quick to notice two beautifully embroidered cloaks obviously intended for ceremonial occasions hanging upon ornate pegs on the right side wall. They were far richer and more detailed than the one Seth had worn to greet his guest. With a puzzled frown, Neb studied the pictures of sea and black sky with a multitude of various animals entering some sort of great structure as enormous raindrops pelted the world all about. Neb was mildly surprised that these backward people had it in them to produce such picturesque articles of clothing. He certainly did not have such cloaks of his own. This irritated him. In his mind, Neb could hardly imagine Seth being capable of filling such voluminous robes sufficiently. Puti entered silently through the front door and then stood ready and waiting with attention for any directions his master might see fit to give him, though his eyes did stray momentarily over the fine cloth that Neb still held between his fingers. Neb turned and let the cloth fall back into graceful folds against the wall as he gestured impatiently for Puti to come further into the room. Puti did as commanded, though his deliberate stare and slow movements only added to Neb's unaccountable annoyance. Neb waited until he was near enough, and then he began to speak in a whispered voice.

"Tell me what I want to know."

Puti hardly moved a muscle. He simply whispered back in his own particularly toneless voice. "Hezeki is in the dwelling directly behind this one, situated a little to the left. The people there must be weavers, for there are countless varieties of baskets about the place. He and Seth have been taking council together with several old men and a few warriors—if you can call any men in this village warriors." Puti's sneer was plainly visible.

Neb simply nodded his head in silence. After a thoughtful moment, he gestured for Puti to wait while he finished exploring the dwelling. He seemed to be looking for a window slot in which to look outside across to the dwelling Puti referred to. As he came upon the two back rooms, he entered each in turn. When he entered the left room, he immediately noticed the doorway. He almost chuckled to himself. He could too well imagine the purpose of that door. These people were not quite as obvious as he had thought them. Neb returned to where Puti still waited in observant silence in the front room. He paused a moment in deep thought, and then a light entered his eyes, and his annoyance vanished like a billow of mist before a hot wind.

"Go out and tell Riphath that I want him to help with tonight's meal. Explain that I want him to invite Seth's hunters to go with him to get some meat. Have him inform Seth of our desire to not be an unwelcome burden on his people. Tell Seth that I will rest here until the time of the feast and that no one is to disturb me. He should go and retrieve my brothers so they can attend the feast. Then after some time, go to the furthest end of the compound and take a burning ember from one of the fireplaces and catch one of the dwellings on fire. Make it look like a log was knocked out of place by accident. Then quickly join the hunters in a round-about path so it will look like you came from a different direction." He paused in thought once more before continuing. "Oh, and send Hul to me first."

Puti had the good sense not to ask any questions. He did not show any reactions to these commands. He simply nodded his understanding and then quickly went out the door. After he had measured out a few paces, Neb followed after him and called loudly from the doorway, "Good hunting!" As a series of eyes turned in surprise toward Neb, Puti merely acknowledged the surprising comment and turned away again. The sun was nearing the horizon, and the day was waning as the shadows of the mountains grew longer and all the colors of the day began to fade.

Neb strode to the back room and watched through a crack in the door until Seth and several men left the dwelling. He waited and watched a little longer. Finally, Hezeki came to the doorway with a few last men, and they also left the dwelling while Hezeki stood watching in silence for a few moments. Then he turned and went back into the inner room. Hul called out Neb's name from the front room, and Neb retreated away from the back door. He met Hul with clear, determined eyes. Hul seemed a little uncertain and embarrassed as if he had been caught doing something wrong. Neb did not need to hear about Hul's doubts; he could see them plainly on his face. "I have a job for you, Hul. I want you to go and inform Hezeki that he is to leave this village tonight to join his brother so he should make all necessary preparations. Then, after you finish, I want you to catch up with the hunting party I sent out earlier with Puti and Riphath. Do you understand?"

Hul seemed to unstiffen just a bit as the tiniest trace of a relieved smile played around his lips. "Of course, this is good news. I am sure Hezeki will be relieved. I mean, I am sure he will be happy to comply with your wishes."

Neb only stared at Hul, dismissing him with a curt gesture of the hand. After Hul had left, Neb retreated to the back door and watched the assigned conversation. When Hezeki turned back into the dwelling again and Hul marched off to find the hunters in his methodically correct manner, Neb returned to the front doorway to watch for the expected sign. The sun was getting very low in the sky now, and it would not be long before dusk arrived in full armor. When Neb heard shouts and yells coming from the southern part of the village, he quickly slipped on one of the ceremonial robes, and in the twilight as everyone's attention was focused in another direction, he dashed the few paces into the weaver's dwelling. Hezeki had been aroused by the urgent sounds outside and was just about to go and investigate when his eldest son barred his way.

"Do not worry, Old Man; this is just a little matter of no real consequence." He pushed his father farther into the darkness of the dwelling. Hezeki stared hard at his son and tried to push past him, but Neb stood like an unmovable wall. Hezeki knew this was his last chance to stand tall before his over-reaching son. Was there ever a chance of taming such a beast?

"So, have you come to say farewell before I join my brother?" His words were spat out in bitterness.

Neb only offered a secret superior smile. "Yes, I guess you could say that."

Hezeki shook his head. "Why come here pretending filial concern now when you have never shown any before? You do not care for me. We have nothing to say to each other. Leave me, and I will set out at once to meet Ashkenazi."

"No, I have nothing to say to you, but you do have one last duty to perform for me."

Hezeki looked momentarily amazed. "What could you possibly want now? You have everything!" Then with a low, bitter chuckle, he nodded his head. "Or do you have a request from your mother? She is never done with her advice or her ambition, is she? Beware your mistress son; women can lead a man into places he would rather not go."

Neb's eyes narrowed even as they grew colder than ice. "I

have no mistress, nor mother, nor father. I am a man alone in the world. I decide exactly how I will live. And I have decided that it is time for you to go beyond the reach of all living men. Die now, and rid me of your interference forever." He slipped his knife from under his clothing and pointed its deadly blade at his father. Hezeki blanched, though he stood boldly up to his son with his chest thrust out in an attitude of utter contempt.

"It is a curse beyond reparation to kill your own father!"

"Then it will be my greatest curse!" Neb thrust the knife at his father who parried the blow and tried to escape the room in a frantic dash to the door. He did not make it to the threshold. Neb's agility and bold determination quickly overpowered his father's ebbing strength. The brief struggle was soon over. After laying his father's body on Seth's bed in an attitude of slumber, Neb covered him with a blanket and then looked fugitively out the doorway. The dark night had quite covered the land, and all was fairly quiet, though there was still some commotion in the south. Only a few moments had passed since the fire had first been noticed, and though it was not serious, it had to be put out thoroughly to keep any further damage from being done. Neb retreated back into Seth's dwelling and disrobed quickly. There were now dark stains on the fine material, but Neb cared not. He decided to lie down to rest a few minutes before the hunters returned and the preparations for the feast began in earnest.

Jubal knew that the time for action had come upon them and that there was no solution but to drive the enemy away quickly before things got any worse. The only absolute solution was to kill Neb and do it before he suspected any serious opposition. Jubal knew he should consult with Seth, but he feared his friend's hesitancy. Was it not just the day before that Seth had gone into the woods to cry about such events as these? Surely he would not be master of himself to the point where he could do the necessary act without agonizing over it. Jubal thought of his older brother, Accad, and though he trusted his brother implicitly, he feared that as time was of the essence, even a short delay at this point and the eventual planning need to coordinate two men would be too long to wait. Neb would surely escape or do something terrible before they were ready. He suspected some treachery was planned for this night under the cover of a grand feast. So he crept up noiselessly under cover of dark toward Seth's dwelling. He knew full well that food had been brought and that Neb was undoubtedly tired from his long march through the woodlands. This would the optimum time to achieve his desired end.

He peered cautiously inside the dwelling, wondering if there was anyone with Neb or if by chance he happened to be alone. He figured that if anyone happened to question him, he could make up any excuse for seeing Seth as if he were unaware that Neb had taken over his dwelling. As it was, he saw no one, so he moved ever so slowly through the doorway. He looked around and saw before him a sight that almost unnerved him. It was uncanny the way that Neb was lying, staring up toward the ceiling of the dwelling, still as a stone as if in deep thought. He did not move or even seem to breathe, but his eyes plainly showed that he was awake and aware of Jubal's presence and intention. One hand clenched a spear, the other a short knife. Jubal crouched completely still, waiting to see what would happen next. He considered jumping on Neb instantly, but something held him back. The critical moment had been lost in his own surprise. Now he was the one on the defensive.

Neb spoke without seeming to speak. "I see Seth has friends."

Jubal stood erect and planted his feet firmly on the ground as if he had intended all along to have a serious conversation with this intruder into their peaceful village. "Many."

Neb sat up in a single, fluid action and looked Jubal in the eyes. "This is good. He will need many friends. Loyalty is not often found in the breast of a brave man. Either one is brave and independent of everyone, or one is loyal but afraid to act alone. You are both brave and loyal. I like this. You and I will be friends."

"I do not see how we can be anything but enemies as the very loyalty you so value must bar such an alliance. You have shown yourself to be brutal to your brothers and disloyal to your own father. How could a man like me become friends with a man like you?"

Neb allowed himself a small smile. "You have wit, too! Better and better." He stood up and walked over to Jubal and put his hand on his shoulder in an almost fatherly gesture. "For the moment, let us speak civilly at least. You may find that I am a different person from what you have imagined. I am sure that there have been many stories told about me. It is so with every man who must wield power. Surely you do not judge a man without hearing from his own lips the proof of his innocence? Or do all I have to do is go to the next village and spread lies and all will be on my side? Is this a battle of words merely? Does truth have no place in your society?"

Jubal shook his head warily. "You may speak for all the good it will do you. But remember this, honest words must be backed by honest action or they are phantoms at best and deceiving treachery at worst. I never trust a man who has once lied to me. Speak now if you dare."

Neb let out a soft chuckle. "I like you. I really do. My brothers are not half so clever. If they had been, things would have been different, believe me." Neb gestured for Jubal to sit down across from him as they both found rugs to rest upon. "Now, I will tell you my story, and you must judge for yourself the truth of it, if you dare, for judgment is a tricky thing. It requires some conviction, and conviction demands action—sometimes even loyalty." Jubal stared at Neb with a scowl embossed deeply across his forehead, but as Neb spoke, the crease lines diminished.

"I was raised mostly by my mother, for my father, though a caring man, did not have the strength or presence of mind to raise me as a leader of men should be raised. Had he been allowed to have his way, no one in my family would have been strong, for I would never have realized it was my duty to be strong and valiant for the sake of the clan, and my brothers would have never felt my shadow. They are stronger, in fact, for my exalted position, because they have had something to resist. If we had been raised as equals, we would have been equals in weakness. And," Neb paused and looked significantly at Jubal, "in times of trial, the weak die. My father and my brothers have decided that because I have grown stronger than they and I use my authority as needs must, they are in danger of my wrath. I do not fear them. I held them in no certain contempt, but because they have run from me in secrecy with all appearances of being in danger for their very lives, I must conclude that they have convinced themselves that I am a monster ready to devour them. It is quite apparent they have told everyone they met the same tale. Am I wrong in my assumption?" Neb could see the confusion in Jubal's eyes, and he allowed a soft smile to curl around his lips. "I see the truth of it in your face." Neb laid his hands out open at his side and thrust his head up with his neck exposed to the open air. "You can do to me now what you had planned to do earlier if you so desire."

Jubal only shook his head with his fingers running through his hair. "I do not know what I want to do now."

"As I thought; you are a more reasonable man than most. You are kinder than my own kin."

Jubal stood up. "There is much I do not understand in all this, but this I will say. I will not judge a man again unless I know the full story of why he comes into our midst. You have had that much influence on me, and I hope you are satisfied with that for I can make no other assurances."

"You are cautious. That is a very healthy attitude." Neb paused in thought. "I will tell you what I think we ought to do. Tonight, when the moon is at its zenith, bring forth my father, and we will discuss this matter in full. I want you to see that though he is weak and useless to me, unjust and even dangerous in his lies, I will spare him all discomfort. He can live out his remaining years with his brother, whom I hear lives not far from here. Let them keep each other company in their declining years. As for my brothers, I will let them go to live in peace wherever they may find it. I just want them to remain far from me so as not to taint the very air I breathe with stories of my ruthlessness. I am a fair man. I want to rule my clan in peace and justice. I had to follow them to make everyone understand that though I have good reason to kill them,

I may choose clemency. They are safe now, but they are not to return to cause rebellion and discontent among my men. I think I am perfectly justified in making that request."

Jubal nodded his head slowly several times. "Yes, I can see no fault with your summary. I will tell Seth that we will convene a meeting here tonight." Jubal stood and began to heave a relieving sigh as he retreated, but then he thought better of it and turned and walked away from the dwelling of Seth in brooding silence.

Neb turned back toward the inner room of the dwelling, and he poured himself a cup of amber liquid from a vessel tucked into a far corner. He tasted it and smiled. "Yes, we will convene a meeting tonight and see if we can call forth the tamed spirits of Hezeki and his brother Ashkenazi, for they can no longer wield the scepters of power or the weapons of war." Neb lifted his cup as if in a salute. "As neither leaders nor warriors will the world see the like of you two again. Depart from this present world, bodiless spirits, and lead me to rule as I see fit." He paused as he took one last sip, staring at the enveloping darkness that had consumed Jubal. "Man of Seth, you and I will meet again, and our conversation will be of a very different sort."

It was a dark night with the moon only glimmering faintly through gathering dark clouds when Seth, Jubal and Accad and many of the men of their clan met in the circle around a central fire near Seth's dwelling. The heightened moisture in the still air made it almost difficult to breath. Three wild boars were roasting over an enormous fire while women were milling about, bringing various items to a central location. Large clay vessels had been brought near, and strings of fish were being pulled free and piled onto a central platter. Jubal had tried on several occasions to tell his brother about his encounter with Seth, but each time he had found himself confused beyond words. He watched Seth with a concerned expression, for though he had believed that there might be some misunderstanding at work in the matter of Neb, still he felt no certain assurance that his leader was not in serious danger.

Seth turned to Jubal, and, sensing his anxiety, he tried to reassure him by giving him a simple task that would take him away from the scene for a bit.

"Jubal, I want you to go with another man of your own choosing and tell Ashkenazi that his presence here is required immediately. Do not let him put you off for any reason. Tell him that I waited until the last moment to make this known to him but that the life of his brother very well might depend upon his quick and courteous response to this request." Seth paused as he saw the slight hesitation in Jubal's eyes. "What is the matter? Your brother will be right here by my side, and nothing will happen while you are away."

Jubal nodded slowly several times and then looked his brother in the eye meaningfully. Accad nodded his understanding, and Jubal retreated into the darkness. Seth whispered just within Accad's hearing. "It is when he gets back that we will face our trial."

Seth began to walk around the perimeter of his village while the final preparations for the grand meal were being made. Neb had still not appeared. Seth had sent a man to tell Hezeki that the festival meal was nearly ready, but as Hezeki was exhausted with worry and appeared to be in deep repose, the messenger had let him sleep a little longer. Now after some time had passed, Seth and Accad passed near the hut where Hezeki lay. Jubal was due to be returning at any time with Ashkenazi, and the appointed time could be put off no longer. Seth put his hand softly on his friend's arm.

"I know that Hezeki does not wish to face his son again and he is undoubtedly worn out unto the point of sickness, but if Neb is true to his word, then he has nothing to fear. This will just be a confirmation of Neb's promise to allow his father and brothers to live in peace. I will go and tell Neb that it is time to join us in our communal meal, and you go awaken Hezeki, assuring him that we will stand with him and his brother no matter what Neb might say."

Accad nodded his acceptance of this simple task and sprang forward, stepping lightly into the weaver's dwelling. Seth walked a few paces around to the front of his own dwelling with a renewed irritation in his breast as he thought of the impertinence of a man pushing him out of his own dwelling in so unceremonious a manner. The blush on his cheeks reflected his burning embarrassment that he had been so impotent to stop Neb in his bold advancement. He resolved within himself that after he was assured of Ashkenazi's and Hezeki's safety in the comfort of their own peaceful establishment, he would quickly tell Neb he was no longer welcome in their village and that he must leave before the moon rose again. Once he made this bold speech to himself, he stepped determinedly toward the entrance of his dwelling. Neb was standing on the threshold apparently waiting for him. As Neb looked down upon Seth from his elevated position, he smiled in a welcoming gesture. Seth was immediately perplexed, and his initial determination to be forceful was struck a heavy blow in the face of Neb's exaggerated courtesy.

"I am glad to see you, Seth, son of Seth. Your dwelling is a most charming home, and I am grateful for your generosity in allowing me to use it this day. I am sure that you wish to sleep in your own bed tonight, so I have directed my men to make ready to leave as soon as this feast is over. I know it may not be customary for your people to travel at night, but I have been trained to travel at all hours, and I often find that night travel is exhilarating in a special way. Besides, once this business is over, I have no more reason to stay, do I?"

Seth could neither step up to be level with Neb nor would he step backward, though he felt an unaccountable desire to do so. He simply stared at Neb a speechless moment while Neb put out his hand and rested it gently on Seth's shoulder, speaking just above a whisper. "You have pleased me very much, and I will account your people to be among my friends." He took his hand off Seth's shoulder and strode past him toward the open fire where now only one hog was roasting, the other two being carved upon separate boards.

Seth watched him, stunned by words that he had never expected to hear and that he really did not want to hear, though he could not deny the fact that he could feel a slow relief begin to seep through his body. As he turned and began to walk back toward the assembled group, he heard a loud yell of someone calling out his name. There was a sudden commotion as Jubal came rushing up to him with another man in his wake. They were clearly agitated, and Seth put up his hand in warning. He did not want to make any unnecessary trouble just when it looked like things might work out peacefully after all. Jubal burst past him and ran over to where Neb was standing.

"You treacherous liar! You did it! No one else could have! No one from this clan would have harmed a hair upon his revered head. How could you? After all you said about being misunderstood. You devil from hell!" Jubal sprang at Neb, and if Puti had not been standing between them, it almost looked as if Neb might have been injured. Neb, however, had put up his hands in a strange posture, and few would have realized the quick, reflexive strength in his hands and his previous experience with deadly foes or foreseen the peril Jubal had put himself into by attacking Neb bodily. Seth came running up and began to pull at Jubal's clothing, attempting to drag him away from Neb before he did any real harm. Neb, realizing that he was in fact in no immediate danger, relaxed and stared at Jubal as if he had lost his wits. Seth continued to pull him away.

"What has gotten into you? I sent you to do a simple task, and you return acting like a madman!"

Jubal spun around and grabbed ahold of Seth's arm. "Ashkenazi is dead! He has been killed. His body lies in his cave. And that man," he pointed at Neb, "is the one who did it!"

Seth looked truly bewildered. "Ashkenazi is dead? Are you certain?"

Jubal flung his arms up in exasperation, nearly exploding with agitation. "I was not alone! Ask the men who came with me. I brought two friends, and they saw what I saw and know the truth of my words. Ask them if you do not believe me!"

Seth looked to the two men who had run up with Jubal, and they echoed Jubal's story and began offering proof in detail.

"He had been speared. His body was quite stiff. It can only have been . . ."

There was another babble of confusion as Accad came rushing forward. He strode with determined steps toward Seth, circling around Neb as if he did not want to be contaminated by the very air surrounding his person.

"Seth, I am very sorry to report to you the murder of Hezeki in the weaver's dwelling. He was alone and had been killed some little time ago. The body was still a little warm but growing cold quickly." He turned toward Neb and Puti. "I think we all know who did this deed."

Neb stepped forward into the firelight, and as he did, the flickering flames danced around his features causing him to appear something not altogether human.

"Once again I am judged not by what is known but by what is feared. I had hoped you people were advanced enough to discern truth from lie, but I see that it is time for me to retreat from this place. The whole purpose of my coming here has been destroyed by another's will." Neb gestured for his men to draw closer, but Jubal sprang at him once again.

"You lie too well, like you lied to me earlier today. You told me that you would let your father live out his last years in peace with his brother, and all along you knew they were dead!"

Neb shook his head. "How could I? I have been inside Seth's dwelling the whole of the day. My men were out hunting with your own warriors. And you and I spent quite some time in serious discussion." He looked at Seth appraisingly. "I had thought this man of yours was worthy of trust, but now I can see in your eyes that he did not share our conversation with you. No loyal servant would keep secrets from his master, especially in such an important matter as the one we hold between us. Do you not know he came to kill me this afternoon?"

An angry guttural sound burst from Jubal while Seth put his hand to his head as if to forestall any further disturbing revelations. Neb only shook his head in a disappointed manner, emphasizing his words carefully. "My father and my uncle have been killed while in your care and under the protection of your warriors. I think it is I who should be grieved and angry."

Accad spat out his words. "You did not care for them! Why pretend to suffer any loss?"

Neb merely nodded in agreement and looked at Seth with a penetrating stare. "And what have you lost? What do their deaths mean to you anyway? I have been informed of my brothers' departure early this morning, so I cannot see any reason for your consternation. Two men have died, and you have no idea how they were killed. One thing is certain; you cannot blame me or my men. We are leaving soon, so your village can return to its normal routine even as the moon descends this night. But first we shall accept the repast you so kindly arranged." Neb looked around and gestured rather eloquently. "Death happens. I would not let it disturb you much." Then Neb walked slowly over to a table with a wooden platter piled high with carved meat and joints of roasted pig, and he took a handful and began to chew thoughtfully. He gestured for his men to eat their fill, and then swinging his arms wide, he gestured for everyone to step forward and partake.

In stupefied silence, Seth took a step but then stopped in mid-motion.

"I will not eat a mouthful until I know the truth of who killed Ashkenazi and Hezeki. Though you are their kin, I have more friendship and feeling than you, for I am too grieved and disheartened to make merry at this time."

Neb had his back to Seth, and he continued to eat in an unconcerned fashion. "As you wish, but I find that nourishment helps me accomplish my ends." He gestured again to Seth to come and eat something, but Accad and his brother flanked Seth in their immovable determination not to accept peace at such a price. Though his mind was still numbed by the reality of what had happened, Seth knew that he should order Neb and his men out of his village immediately. However, a strange sort of propriety stood in his way. He simply could not prove what he knew to be the truth. Somehow Neb had killed or had arranged the murder of his uncle and father, for there was simply no other reasonable possibility; but under the cloud of confusion and uncertainty and Neb's extraordinary ability to lie boldly and with conviction, he was getting away with a heinous crime. His wrath by this time was nearly exhausted under the tumult of so many conflicting emotions. He looked around at his men and the women standing in the background with their children, and he took one more step toward Neb.

"You must leave our village now. There will be no feasting this night, for though you may not feel the weight of it, a terrible thing has been done. The evil mind that did this evil thing will contaminate us all in the end. Though I cannot prove your guilt, I am certain of it in my heart. My men should kill you and your men this night, but I have no bloodlust in me—only anger and grief. Go now before you kindle . . ."

Neb held a large chunk of meat in his hand, and he waved it in an amused manner. "Kindle? Kindle what? Your wrath?" Neb laughed out loud and looked at his men who also continued to eat though their eyes shifted uneasily around at the men of the clan who were standing a little closer with stiffened backs. "No, do not attack me, please. If you want to find the cause of all your grief, I suggest you speak to your man there at your own elbow. He was ready enough with a knife a few hours ago. If he were willing to strike at me to rid his clan of uncertain danger, would he not in vengeful rage kill my father and uncle to make me look like a guilty man? Doesn't he love you so much that he would do anything for you? Could you put such a question beyond the realm of possibility?" Neb turned back toward his men. "It is lucky for me that all my men were busy preparing for this feast in a fruitful hunt, or I might have doubted them. But as it is clear they were busily engaged in providing this exquisite meal, I do not have to rely on my heart to find the truth. I know it in the reason of cold facts." Packing some food into a satchel that hung from his shoulder, Neb gestured for his men to begin to leave the village. They had already packed their satchels to the bursting point and were quite ready to comply with Neb's unspoken hint. As he brushed some crumbs from his hands in an almost dainty manner, Neb turned once more toward Seth.

"You really should eat. It is very good." He smiled disarmingly. "Now how could a man who just committed two murders eat with such innocent relish?" He put his hand on Seth's shoulder in a confidential manner. "If you are going to rule your mind by your heart, I suggest you watch that one there." He nodded significantly toward Jubal. "He is not what he seems to be." Taking a few steps away from Seth, he turned once more and spoke so everyone could hear his voice. "Bury them with all honor as is your custom, so that when I come back, I might see where they lie and do their remains some homage. But do not grieve long, as they died as they lived—in obscurity and doubt. Farewell for now." Neb turned and walked into the black night as the living moon crested and began its decent toward the earth.

    Seth stood as one amazed by a strong wind that has just blown away his home. He felt a dark dread seep through his bones. Even though Neb was going away, he knew that he could never look at the world the same again. Evil had touched him too personally to be denied. He would retrieve the body of Ashkenazi from his cave, and he would help carry the lifeless form of Hezeki from his home. The two would be buried with the honor and love that they deserved. Yet no matter what care he took or what traditional forms he preserved, there was an omission and emptiness that he could not fill, for it was ever the duty of a firstborn son to bury with reverence the body of his elders—as much as it was the duty of a mother to nurture the life of her child. The murder of two innocent men was only the culmination of a series of crimes that had begun in the distant past.

CHAPTER 16
HUL'S DEFIANCE

Hul jogged along slightly behind his leader, and though his arms and legs performed their accustomed duties, his mind was far from the land he trod over. His eyes saw nothing of the sloping green hills that they were descending in all their natural beauty. He cared nothing for the sight of majestic trees, blue skies or even the very men who ran so near to him. His mind was still back at the village of Seth and the vision he took in when he looked upon the inhabitants' faces as they departed from their village. It was a sight he hoped never to see again. They hated him with clear and purposeful hate. Even more, they hated him with a justified hate. He knew that if strangers had come into his village followed by pursuing warriors and murder had been the final outcome, he would have come to the same conclusion as they had. It was only his certitude that Neb could not have committed the terrible deed that allowed him to jog along at his side at all. Yet there was a nagging concern, which caused him momentary blindness, that Neb might have had something to do with the twin dreadful deeds. He had gone over and over the past two days' events in his mind. Yes, Neb had ordered the murder of Ashkenazi for no justifiable reason, but at the time Hul had been forced to assume that his leader had some secret knowledge of the man that compelled him to take such drastic action. As he had never seen the man before and only knew of his determined refusal to obey Neb's reasonable request for information, it could well have been the act of a leader who wished to preserve his people's safety. But even as he mulled this idea over in his head, a sick dread continued to grow in his middle. While he had wandered around the village of Seth paying attention to every conversation he could as Neb had ordered him to, he heard a few snatches of conversations about Ashkenazi. Hul realized that the man had been loved, for he had been very kind and good. If that was truly the case, then Neb had done a terrible thing. But

103

how could he judge the truth of the matter? How could he be following the direction of a man who committed a blatant act of ruthless aggression toward an innocent person? Hul looked up and around, and he saw that Neb was still jogging slightly ahead of him, apparently deep in his own thoughts. The sun had risen even as they had marched and jogged further and further away from the Village of Seth. It was a cooler morning as the clouds hung low, and it felt very much like it might rain at any time.

It was the mystery of who had killed Hezeki that most tormented Hul's thoughts. Surely Neb would never commit such an outrageous act. He was a first son, and he of all people should be most determined to know the truth about the murder, but yet here they were quite literally running away from the scene of the crime. This did not make any sense. A sudden flash of insight blinded Hul, and he stumbled. He reached out before he fell and caught himself, but the thought that had come unbidden into the intimacy of his mind had knocked the breath out of him as if he had fallen upon hard rocks. Somehow Neb had killed his father, just like he had killed the old sorceress and just like he had killed Ashkenazi. Hul suddenly knew that he would kill again, for once a man has killed his own flesh and blood, he would likely have no inhibitions about killing anyone. Hul squeezed his eyes shut tight to block out the truth that was forcing its way into his brain. Yes, what Seth had said was true; he as leader should have killed Neb and all his followers before they left the village. If Neb had done this terrible evil, then they were also guilty for supporting such a leader. Their guilt may be less, but it was still a great doom. Hul had stopped in his tracks, and Riphath, who was following just behind, stopped short as well. He made an angry guttural retort in surprise, and Neb and Puti also stopped. Puti appeared cool because he was lean and in good health. This long jog, though even-paced, had been a stretch in Riphath's endurance however. Though Riphath was irritated by his own exhaustion and Hul's lack of warning, he was glad to stop and take long slow breaths once again. Neb was as calm and collected as Puti, and in surveying his men, he realized that Hul's short gasps for air, his white pallor and his wide searching eyes were proof of something more than mere physical exhaustion.

"You need a rest Hul, and it will do none of us any harm. We are well away now and can take our pace slowly. Let us sit and take a little food."

Each man found a place to sit and took out their bags. While they ate in complete silence and drank the last of their water, Hul sat eating very little but drinking a great deal, for he had begun to sweat in a most unnatural fashion. When Riphath felt a bit refreshed, he went to look for a fresh stream. He took each man's water skin along with him to refill. Puti decided to go explore a little, which left Hul quite alone in the presence of his leader. Neb looked over at him in an appraising manner and, after breaking a twig in half, he finally spoke out loud.

"Hul, tell me your doubts, for it is clear that you are disturbed by something."

Hul nodded in acceptance of the obvious fate that awaited him, which he knew he could not avoid. He would have to declare his disloyal thoughts, and Neb would have to act. Still, even in his forlorn state of misery, there was a tiny glimmer of hope that what he knew to be true was just a mistake. Perhaps a stranger had come to the village and had killed Hezeki for a reason of his own. Perhaps Neb had been correct in ascertaining that Jubal had killed Hezeki to make Neb look guilty. Perhaps . . . no. Hul knew. Neb had lied, for he had said that Jubal might have killed Ashkenazi when in fact he had done the deed—if not with his own hands, then certainly by his own authority. Hul could no longer deny the irrationality of his own crazy thinking. The truth was quite obvious. He sat slump-shouldered, and without raising his head, he spoke the words that he knew would seal his own doom.

"You killed your father, didn't you?"

Neb smiled and shook his head in wonder. "You still don't see the truth, do you, Hul? How could I be responsible for killing my father when my father had ceased to exist the moment he left his own people? I killed no man; I merely did away with a phantom, a ghost, a figment of men's desires. What defines a man, Hul? Is it his position in his society as a leader, a warrior, a cook, a weaver, a spy? By a man's wit he aids his people and supports his society. When he has children, they are raised with this same implicit understanding. If a child were unhealthy and unable to serve in any useful manner, that child would be nothing, worse than nothing, a mere drain on the humanity from which he sprang forth. No man could justify the continued expense of such a thing. I merely faced the truth of Hezeki's death before you did, and I ended the apparent contradiction. Do not think that you have been betrayed by the death of an old man. Realize once and for all that no murder took place, because no man was killed; he was mere flesh and blood, and really flesh and blood are of little account unless they are useful to our own ends."

Hul listened with care. Every word Neb spoke was a hammer blow to his heart. Every sinew and bone in his body cringed as the ideas filtered down into his soul, yet he knew that the minute he declared his allegiance to a different truth he would become as useless as Hezeki and thus just as dead. He remained in motionless thought for several moments, and then his words came out slowly.

"Your mother would probably agree with you, and there are many who think as you do, but the People of Seth do not live by your vision. They only saw men whom they knew, and they saw useful purpose to their existence in their own sphere. If your definition of purposeful existence is true for you, must it always be true for another? If a sick child was valued by her mother who found great solace in caring for her child, would that account for nothing? And," Hul finally raised his head just a bit, "what if there is some unknown person who values what we do not, whose judgment holds sway?"

For a moment Neb sat completely still. This was an entirely new train of thought to him. He had been raised to think only of his own purpose and agenda. As a leader in training and a leader in fact, his opinion always held sway in everything, but suddenly there was a large crack in his reasoning that threatened to burst through and demolish the very base of his majesty. He reached over to a slim stem, which had blossomed into a fragile little purple flower, and he picked it at the base and smelled its light fragrance before he threw it back to the ground.

"Hul, you surprise me. There is an order to the universe we inhabit, and certain things are ordained to be in certain degree and fashion. Imagine the animals that sustain us with their bodies. Do we ask permission to take their flesh? We do what we must because we must, or we would die. Preservation is the highest law, and that must be obeyed first. I am a leader, and I preserve my community. Thus, I must be obeyed. Seth is the leader of his community, and thus he must be obeyed by his own people. But when it comes to the two of us, I am of a higher order because I insist on it. I have more intelligence, more wit and wisdom, and I am more skilled and determined than anyone else. I will rule everyone I come in contact with because it is so ordered that this be so."

Hul felt the ache of tears behind his eyes as he struggled to decide how much of a man he would now be. He wanted so much to return to his own wife and family, yet he knew that if he did it could only be under the condition of agreeing to Neb's reasoning. In his heart, he saw the truth too clearly. Neb was blinded by his own ambition and desire to have what he wanted above all things. His own selfish desires ruled his very mind, and thus he would not see the balanced maturity of mercy, generosity, patience and acceptance that had been the law of Hezeki's life. Hul almost laughed to himself even in his misery, for if Neb had seen the value in such qualities, he would never have supplanted his father in the first place. Neb had murdered innocent men and justified his actions with the reasons of a selfish man. That was all there was to it.

"I would very much like to go home, Neb. I am missing my family."

Neb nodded as if he understood but was grieved that he could hardly comply with this wish. "We still have a mission to complete. I have not yet found my brothers."

"Nonetheless, I think I will serve you better at home."

"You will serve me best when you serve me first."

Hul looked up at this, and the two pairs of eyes met. Riphath had returned, and seeing the silent engagement, he said nothing. He merely handed each man back his water skin. Puti came within view, accepted his skin and stood waiting for further directions.

Neb rose and pointed to the south. "My father wanted me to believe that my brothers had gone north, but all evidence proves that they went south. There are few groups of men traveling with a single girl, and the signs are obvious. I suspect that they will continue south until they meet up with another friendly clan and then they will attempt to settle somewhere near there. They probably believe that we will give up the search in a short time, but once I am after my quarry, I will not rest until I achieve my aims. Enosh and Kenan can run, but they cannot hide forever. This time there will be no discussion. We will destroy them quickly and return home before the change of the season. It is time now to resume our hunt. We must be swift, so keep up with me." He gave one last look at Hul and spoke slowly. "I need you for now, but unless you grow strong under my hand, you will undoubtedly grow into a very noxious weed that must be cleared away in order for the strong to succeed."

Hul stood up. He dropped his weapons very unceremoniously to the ground. He unslung his water skin, which had been so mechanically tied to his waist, and let it fall beside the weapons of war. "I am already lost to you."

For the first time since childhood, real rage filled Neb's eyes. He stood up and thrashed his arms in the air. "Not until *I* say so! Not until *I* decide!" Neb took his spear and waved it at Hul. "You shall serve me with loyalty or without. I could kill you for this act of treachery!" After pacing a few steps away, he came back and stopped right in front of Hul. His words were slow and as cold as ice. "You are my servant, and I am your master. You will come now and do exactly as I say."

Hul simply stood motionless. He made no rebuttal or attempt to protect himself. In his rage, Neb screamed out, "Will no one rid me of this impudence?" As soon as the words were out of his mouth, Puti raised his spear and threw. Hul fell where he stood. For a moment, all three men stood motionless. Then with a wave of furious dismissal, Neb turned and walked away. Puti yanked the spear away and then followed Neb and Riphath away from the bitter scene. In his rage, Neb struck at every passing limb and hanging branch. Neb had not intended for Puti to act, but it was a moot point now. He was furious at his own success. His very wish was obeyed instantly by his loyal men, but somehow that was no comfort. In his vicious attacks upon the living things around him, he did not feel any relief, but in his mind, he consoled himself by imagining the final meeting between himself and his brothers. His victory would not be muddied by defiance and surprise.

CHAPTER 17

THE PEOPLE OF HAVILAH

The People of Havilah loved war games of all kinds. In each man's breast beat the drums of war. Their blood lusted for the excitement of serious competition. It was not for mere sport that they practiced and played their games. They inherited a code of honor that demanded that they protect the weak and demolish the arrogant whenever the chance arose. They were a tall, handsome race with mixed hues of light to dark copper skin with auburn haired children born to dark haired mothers. In the recent generation, the elders had established a code of behavior that they had marked in stone in a language so simple that anyone with an honest mind could understand its purpose and intent. The first rule was that respect was to be shown and adoration offered solely to the God of gods who was depicted as a single circle radiating outward. The second rule was that honor must be maintained in all things, and this was depicted with the figures of two men with two parallel lines drawn from one to the other. The men were equal in all respects, and it was apparent that they were to act justly in all things, meting out kindness with kindness and rightful retribution for all injury. The third rule was to maintain arms of war in case of need, and this was rather graphically expressed by the slaying of a dangerous beast that was half-man and half-animal. The fourth and final rule was that protection and assistance was to be offered to the weak and needy. This time the stone carver outdid himself in the expressions of tender concern for a mother and child by a group of elder men.

The leader of the People of Havilah was an elder named Uzal who had lived many long years upon the earth but was still hardy and vigorous, as he stood tall and majestic above his children and grandchildren. He had snow-white hair, and he had let it grow long as was his people's custom. He had been a mighty warrior in his time and was even now considered one of the best fighters in the village. He wore a long, loose tunic of animal's skin, though most of the women wore cloth of woven fibers. He liked to keep his garb rough and unornamented. He allowed the women some measure of ornamentation in their dress, but he did not encourage such novelties. His mind focused mostly on practical issues, hence there were few artisans in his clan. He like to compete with the younger men in the contests before the games, but he chose his battles carefully, and most often he had a silent desire to check an upstart's pride by inflicting some minor humiliation so that no one would ever think of entering even a mock battle unprepared. More often than not, it was hardly a matter of mere physical strength but of who had the quicker wit and the greater determination not to give in. On more than one occasion, Uzal had corrected a younger man's arrogance with a strategy that countered his every move and forced him to tire while Uzal outmaneuvered his thrusts by simply doing the unexpected. Uzal was known for his daring new moves, and rare was the youth who was willing to try a completely new move in front of an audience. It was lucky for everyone that Uzal did not have a vicious bone in his body, for often these competitions became very heated, and no man ever came away unscathed.

 The season was unusually cool, and the rain had been falling heavily for several days when Uzal decided that as the harvest was well over and the men had more free time, he would plan some extra games for his men. Everyone was in good spirits for though they all had worked to the point of exhaustion during the growing season and through the harvest and though the weather was far from pleasant now, it was well known and expected that the time of the games was coming upon them. There had been various lively discussions about who would enter which contest and how each family would be best represented by its ablest members. Each year there were entrance contests to see which of the young men would be allowed to participate, and those who failed to win first or second place in at least one entrance contest were forced to wait on the sidelines and watch the games in impatience for one more year to pass in order to try again. Their determination to practice longer and work harder thus achieving greater glory in the future was their only consolation.

There were several young men who had failed the previous year who were very determined to succeed this year, but the most determined of all was a youth by the name of Kryce. He had seen seventeen seasons of games pass, though the first few had been in his mother's arms, and he was determined that not another would pass while he stood on the sidelines. The year previous he had prepared himself as well as any youth could with long runs through the bramble woodlands and across the great grassy fields with nary a rest for his growing bones and developing muscles. He spent long days practicing his aim by throwing rocks great distances and attempting to hit a far target. He would gradually increase the weight of the rocks and stones he threw until he could throw even the largest rocks both far and accurately. He had practiced with various spears and had made himself the best knife he had ever owned from a blade that he had traded from a stranger who had come through their village the winter before. Everyone in his family was very excited about his first contest, especially his mother who had encouraged her auburn-haired son to try again every time he grew discouraged. Even his eldest sister, Tamar, who was married with two small children of her own, had offered to make him better-fitting clothes so that he would be more aptly appareled on the first day of the opening games. But two months before the entrance contests were to begin, his mother had fallen seriously ill and died very quickly. He had been very close to his mother, and though his father, brothers and sisters had all encouraged him to try his best despite their great loss, he had lost his spark and had performed badly by all standards. In this past year, he had grown much, and the ache of losing her had lessened just enough to allow him to concentrate on trying to win the competition for this new season. When Uzal had announced that they would have extra games this year, Kryce had rejoiced in his heart more than he had over anything in the past. It had come to him in a conversation with his Uncle Job that though his mother would be sad at his many losses, her spirit might be gladdened if he competed again and won. Though he knew his mother was lost to him in this present world, he somehow was cheered by this thought and grew determined to do what he could by preparing himself most perfectly.

His uncle was a wonderful trainer, and he also knew a great deal about the making of good, solid blades. As a matter of fact, the blade that was given to Kryce had caused Job much frustration. No matter how he tried, he had not been able to make so perfect and strong a weapon, and he knew much about metals—more than any clan member near or far. Though he was not a great fighter, he was of invaluable assistance to Kryce as he prepared for this year's competition.

This particular generation was most unusual because although they were quite ordinary looking, it seemed that fate had bestowed on each of them a unique and extraordinary nature. Some suspected it was the large spirit of Uzal that bequeathed some of his greatness onto his children, while others insisted it had been the mother, Judith, who had endowed them all with a charmed good will and inner strength. But despite their various conjectures, everyone unanimously concluded that they were the most unusual family anyone had ever known or were likely to know for generations to come. Why they were so attractive was simply a mystery—a mystery that had to be accepted to be understood.

Tamar was the eldest child, and she was of medium height with dirt-colored brown hair and nut-brown eyes. She was strong and able to take good care of her own household, while also managing the affairs of her father after her mother died. When one looked at her from a distance and did not know her, one might come to the unfortunate conclusion that she was rather ugly, for in fact her face was quite long and her jaw was a bit too square for the beauty of a woman. Her every motion was so confident and capable that one could almost consider her actions rather manly. But as one drew nearer and if one had the patience to wait and watch, eventually there would be an interruption to her household chores and then, when she engaged in conversation, nursed her baby or simply smiled, one would see the beauty underneath that was the bedrock of all her vital strength.

Dodan was the second child of Uzal, and though he was well-fed and grew proportionally, he never grew to a man's normal height. As a boy, he had always been very likable and had a quick wit that he learned to use to his advantage. As he grew older, he became more and more aware that his diminutive size did much to disable him in the war games, but after every effort had been tried to make himself grow bigger, he finally came to the dispiriting conclusion that he was never going to grow tall like his father and that, in fact, his own younger brother would grow larger than him in time, for he was fated to be unusually thin and small. It was not until he was a man in years, if not in height, that it was revealed how great a person he really was. An event occurred that could have cost their entire village much if Dodan had not had the wit and wisdom of a much greater man.

Many years ago, there had been a young girl in the clan by the name of Ophir. Her father died when she was young, and her mother married a foreigner from outside the clan and moved away. There had been much trepidation on the part of Ophir's grandparents, for they were uncertain about the man who was taking their daughter and granddaughter far from them. But it was the custom for the woman to break all ties with her old family and join with her husband's family, so this is what Ophir's mother did. No one ever expected to see or hear from her again, but to their amazement Ophir showed up one day several seasons later. She was older by more than count of time. She seemed to be somehow removed from the world as everyone else saw it. She spoke of a strange god and often spent long periods of time off alone by herself. In her forlorn and lonely state, Job found a gentle heart yearning to be protected and cared for. As was the custom of his people and by the direction of his own heart, he sought her out and reacquainted her with the ways of her own people. When she was asked about her mother and her new clan, she involuntarily shuttered and cried strangely as if some terrible memory drove her to senselessness. Job was the only clan member who was able to reach her mind, even during these times of inner torment, and he was soon seen as more than her protector and guardian. He told his brother that he wanted to marry her, but Uzal was set against the idea, and his opinion held sway. A great deal of time passed, and though Job was as patient and gentle as any man could ever be, there was no cure for the secret disease that afflicted Ophir's mind. She grew weaker and stranger with the passing of time, and though the clan was tolerant, her behavior became so crazy—she refused to wash and allowed herself to become filthy—that most found her disgusting. Her behavior toward others became more aggressive, and with young children she became positively dangerous. Finally after one particularly disturbing event where she appeared to have tried to push a little child into a fire, all the mothers of the clan and several fathers came to Uzal and demanded that she be banished or killed outright. Most favored her death as the only sure means of ridding themselves of her evil. Uzal was at a loss as to what to do, for though he quite agreed that the woman was both mad and dangerous, he also knew that his brother loved her like a wife and that he would go with her wherever she went if she was exiled and perhaps even fight to his own death to save her. It was at this time when Dodan was still little more than a youth that he displayed a wisdom and courage none had expected.

    Dodan had watched from a calm distance the grief of his uncle and the disturbance to the whole clan caused by this mad woman. Though he also felt repelled by her disgusting habits, he pondered what it was that had made her deranged in the first place. He asked permission from his father one day to take a journey and to try and find the clan Ophir's mother had joined. Uzal was disturbed by this proposal, but the request was made on a particularly troublesome day, and he felt forced into action despite his own inner conflict. He tried to persuade his young son to take a companion with him, but this Dodan would not do. Before his father could argue any further, he embarked on his journey. Through the clues he had gathered from various clansmen and from his Uncle Job, Dodan had a fairly certain idea about where these people lived. He found the remnants of the clan and was able to discover the secret horror that plagued Ophir's mind. After learning all there was to know, he returned to his people and quickly asked to see his father alone where no man could hear the conversation save the two alone.

Uzal motioned for his son to come away with him to a lonely spot among a few solitary trees near their village along the banks of a great sparkling stream while the sun shone down beautifully, enriching every leaf and blade with the intensity of vibrant life.

"I am very glad to see you well, my son. Many have been the moments when I deeply regretted allowing you to leave on such a mission. I know that we are a brave people long used to the dangers of battle, but I feared the enemy that might stalk you would be as mysterious and hard to counter as the secret malady that afflicts Ophir." He looked his son over with the searching eyes of a loving father who wanted to ascertain the full extent of injury if there be any injury at all.

"You need not look me over any more, Father. I am quite well, though my heart is sick with knowledge that I wish I could blot out of my memory. I understand all too well what it is that sickens the mind of Ophir, and I have pondered long the illness and its cure if one be possible." Uzal's eyebrows rose in anticipation while Dodan strode silently from one tree to another for several moments as if he had to decide how best to tell this story.

"I will tell the whole truth, for as the leader it is your right and duty to know, but I must plead that the fullness of this horror be kept within our own minds so that the knowledge of the depravity into which a man may sink may not be spread and on some future date do some untold mischief in the mind of the weak or disturbed." Uzal nodded his acceptance of this requirement, and he gestured for his son to sit on the great rock that was perched on the shore of the stream. Dodan simply shook his head as if he could not rest his agitated body while he had this story to tell.

"When Ophir's mother left with the stranger, your heart misgave you I am told. Right you were in your foreboding, for though the man himself was not terribly evil, he was a man of his clan. His people were not gentle or kind to women and children as we are, and she was not prepared for the hardships of the duties that would be imposed upon her. She grew sick, and her little daughter tried to shelter her mother from the punishments meted out to the weak and unproductive, but she was as helpless in her youth as was her mother in her innocence. The two suffered much, but it was the mother who first succumbed to the brutality of an overly harsh life. This in itself is nothing new or strange to your ears, but the seed of derangement occurred after her mother's death, for it is the custom of the clan's family to partake of some portion of the dead person's remains. This Ophir at first refused to do, but she was not allowed to follow her own will in the matter. To them, it was a ritual that drew them closer to the dead and to the powers of their god. To Ophir, however, who had been raised to revere the dead with a sacred claim on decency, this horrible act violated the very fiber of her understanding of what it is to be a human being.

"Thus it was that though after her mother's death she was allowed to leave the clan and return to us, she was never able to reclaim her mind as she had been before she knew of such horrors. The part she played, though against her own will, acted on her mind and she came to hate herself as much as she hated the clan that had done this thing to her." Dodan looked at his father with eyes filled with an ancient grief, "So, you see, she will never be well as long as she knows what she has done and cannot accept her part in it."

Uzal shook his head sorrowfully and dropped down on the great rock he had earlier asked his son to sit upon. Putting his hands through his pure white hair, he heaved a great sigh of weariness and asked with slow desolation, "How is it possible to remove the memory or the guilt when they are both true? In knowing this, she is more lost to us than ever."

Dodan sat down by his father and nodded his head in agreement, but then he put his hand upon his father's shoulder and spoke with a determined certainty. "Father, she was not a willing participant, and she was deceived because she really believed that the torment of her mother's death and her own pain at the loss would be lessened by this act. She accented to participate though only in a despairing and begrudging manner. Those who were actually there told me the whole story as if it had occurred only recently. Truly, they cannot forget anything, though I imagine they would like to forget much."

Uzal considered this new knowledge for several moments in complete silence. This was evil news indeed, for when a person has participated in so great a horror, they are contaminated by it, and she was twice cursed with past guilt and the prospect of further guilt through her deranged mind. The truth was that no one besides them knew the full story, and he could decide her fate without question, yet he felt uneasy with the picture of her execution in his mind. Harder still, he could see in his son's eyes the pity that demanded something more than strict justice.

Dodan nudged his father in a gentle manner. "But you, Father, are the voice for this clan, and only you have the authority to speak for others. Though she might not be able to hear your words of consolation, she might hear your words of truth and acceptance, for they would reach into the place she is most wounded. You alone can save her from the doom that awaits her."

Uzal looked up into the vastness of the bright blue sky and sighed deeply. It would only be a moment's act to kill her, and the clan would be free, though Job would grieve his loss for a time. Yet when such an act is done, there is no undoing it. Often there appear consequences to such things that one never thought of before. He realized rather starkly that he had two simple options to choose between. He could accept her with all her illness, allowing her to live out her miserable existence with what small comfort they could give, or he could rid his people of a repulsive menace. He turned and looked his son in the eye. "Though I am grieved by the truth you bring, I am also set free by it. Now I can act in honest response to that which was formerly a black mystery."

Dodan stood before his father and spoke with calm, deliberate patience. "If it were me, what would you do?"

Uzal's shoulders slumped at this, and once more he paused in deep thought. After a few moments, he stood straight, and with a clear decision finally made, he gestured for them to leave.

The two men stood, and though Dodan only came to the midst of his father's chest, the older man put his arm around his son with an air of walking with an equal. Uzal started forward only to stop in mid-motion and turn once more to his son who had stopped to pick up a particularly unusual stone.

"You said that you met with the remnant of the clan? What did you mean by that? What has happened to the rest of their people?"

Dodan shook his head as he blinked his eyes in apparent bewilderment. "I am not sure. All they told me is that everyone began to die, and there was no one to cure them. I was lucky that I went when I did, for they do not expect to survive as a people much longer. Strangely enough, they did not seem to be upset by their approaching extinction."

"Why not? Did they explain?"

Dodan shook his head. "I had already learned what I had come to find out. To be honest, I had no desire to learn more from them."

Uzal nodded his head in understanding. "You have grown wise, my son—very wise indeed. Now let us go and do what we can to save Ophir from her madness."

As the clan gathered that evening for the judgment of Uzal concerning the matter of Ophir, there was an expectation that she would be sentenced to a quick and immediate death. To most of the clan, she was a threat that needed to be cleared away. When Uzal made his pronouncement of clemency, there was a bitter response. One father spoke out boldly.

"How do you know she will not try to hurt another child or injure a clansman? She is mad, and by your decision we are forced to live in watchful distrust."

Uzal nodded his understanding, but he put his hand up to halt the surge of emotion that was beginning to run rampant throughout the village. "I know the full truth of her trial in the other clan, and I alone am the judge of her fate. I have decided that she shall not die by our hands, but I am going to release her into Job's care to be taken to a place outside our village where she can live out her life separate but at peace."

"Why not just kill her and be done with the matter?" There were many assenting voices to encourage this motion.

Uzal only raised his head and looked around at them in silence before speaking again.

"What if she were your child?"

There was silence for several moments. Then it was Dodan who stepped forward and spoke in a quiet, unhurried voice. "She is mad. We all know that. She will die in due time without our rushing the moment. As long as she can do no injury and commits no crime among us, then she ought to be free to live and die in what peace she can find." Though Dodan held no certain authority, still his bravery in seeking the truth and his good council were respected.

In the seasons to come after moving her to a remote location where there was little to disturb her, Ophir did improve a bit. She was never truly healthy, however, and one morning when Job went to look in on her, she was as cold as stone for her spirit had departed for a place of rest that she had never known in life. Though only Uzal and Dodan knew the whole of the truth behind her madness, everyone did believe that Dodan had done a mighty and courageous thing in searching for the source of her illness. Many had disagreed with the decision at first, but after her death, it was unanimous that they were glad they had not killed her, for she was less of a burden on their hearts than if they had done strict justice upon her. Many of the husbands told their wives during those days that they would rather fight a mighty host of attacking warriors than to challenge the madness that lay heavy on the heart of Ophir. Their wives inevitably agreed with their husbands on this.

The fourth child of Uzal was a beautiful young girl by the name of Leah, and she had the spirit and charm of both beauty and wit. She loved to run and play, and yet she was not too terribly adverse to work as long as she could make up stories as she toiled. She loved to invent imaginary clans with heroes and villains that came to life before the very eyes of her listeners. She was not very organized and was perpetually forgetting to do what was asked of her, but whenever there was a gathering, she always had an interested crowd that followed her wherever she went. Her laughter rang through the village like sparkling water over a parched land. When the games began, she attended with breathless interest, and her shouts for victory and encouragement to those who were falling behind made the games that much more exciting and enjoyable. Even when some particularly ugly altercation had taken place in which someone ended up seriously hurt, she was always near with her laughter, her vivacious interest and her infectious joy. There were men in the clan who, in the secret places of their minds, truly believed that to die even in mock battle would be no great grief if she were there to bid them farewell. Her mother's death only checked her spirits for a short time, for she invented a world of wonder where she insisted her mother now resided in with splendor and joy and that one day she would find this magical land herself and be rejoined with her mother. So for her, her mother's death was only a temporary thing that would lead to a greater happiness in the end. Many in the clan listened and came to believe as she did—except, of course, for Job and Dodan who knew that though she was a wonderful storyteller, she had, as yet, seen little of the trials of life, and it would be in the fire of real pain that her spirit would be tested. They knew that to live was to be tested at some time, and they watched her with both pleasure and concern. As brilliant as she shone now, they wondered how she would face the reality of grief.

    The youngest child, Sari, was the quietest and most reserved of the family. Her interest lay in plants and herbs, and she was wont to pick bunches of various wild grasses and herbs and test them for taste and food value. Her father had warned her on many occasions to be very careful about what she put into her mouth, for there were many dangers in the living world with which they were ignorant, but in her youth she was always quite assured of her success in learning something useful. When her mother died, she seemed to become even more determined than ever to prove her worth in the study of living plants, and her father watched her with a preoccupied attention and hoped that she would be sensible of danger. A few of the older village women discouraged her, for they too feared that she was too willing to try something that ought not to be tried. Their warnings went unheeded if not unheard.

It was this People of Havilah that lay some distance to the southeast of the People of Seth that would receive with friendly assistance the refugees: Enosh, Kenan and Eva and their few faithful men. It was also this people who would face the formidable assault of Neb and his warriors. When Neb learned of where his brothers had gone and among what worthy warriors they had settled, he had the wit to turn west and rejoin his own people for a time. He took a long while training his men for open war so as to overcome the People of Havilah. For the first time, he took it into his head to become a slave trader, for he realized that to conquer meant little unless you could take prizes home to reward those who had risked much. In slave trading, his people would become rich through plunder, trade and the service of those they used for menial labor. No longer would his people suffer the occasional want endured by migration and hard work. No, his greatness would be measured in the wealth and prosperity of his people. But first he had to overcome the People of Havilah, and this Neb was quite certain he could do. As for his brothers, he planned a swift revenge. He remembered Eva only as an afterthought. She would not necessarily be killed. He would find a use for her and perhaps gain more with her life than he would gain from his brothers' deaths.

CHAPTER 18
A NEW LEADER EMERGES

On a dark, gloomy afternoon Enosh, his brother, sister and their men arrived in the village of Havilah. Enosh stepped forward as leader and was brought quickly before Uzal and questioned thoroughly. He was told to settle his men nearby and wait to be summoned again, which took nearly three very rainy, blustery days to happen. When Uzal did meet with him again, he was told they could stay as long as they needed to so long as they followed the customs and traditions of the People of Havilah. Enosh was told about the contests, and to his understanding they were little more than mock battles for skill and amusement. When the ceremonial opening day dawned bright and sunny, Enosh was invited to compete against Uzal himself. Seeing the obvious age of his opponent, Enosh thought this might be an amusing opportunity to get even for having been kept waiting for three days. What he found was that he had to fight very hard just to stay on his feet. The games had been introduced to him as warrior training, and he had entered into the sport of it with all the enthusiasm of a young man in good health who wants to pit his strength and ability against the ablest of men. But what he found himself doing was trying to simply stay alive and not be pierced by a spear, clubbed by a cudgel or sliced by a blade of some strange making. Uzal made no tolerant excuses for weakness or foolishness.

When Uzal had heard about their trial and escape from their older, domineering brother, Neb, he had to refrain from expressing a certain level of disgust that they had run from such a challenger. Instead he spent some time among the loyal men who had come with Enosh asking questions and reading expressions in their eyes, and he came to the conviction that Enosh was in no way prepared for real leadership and that the few men who followed him came not from loyalty but rather from fear of Neb's revenge. Thus the opportunity for some real lessons in the art of manhood was presented to Enosh by Uzal as pure gift, but during the contest, the youth could hardly be expected to see that.

At the first moment of their contest, Uzal suddenly thrust his spear between Enosh's feet and knocked him to the ground before the young man could even get his bearings. He was surprised, but he figured that these games were more for fun than dangerous. He took his time getting back to his feet so as to better size up the old man who challenged him. Uzal had absolutely no patience with such an attitude. He swung his spear again and this time landed a stinging blow to the side of Enosh's head, knocking him back down. In searing pain, Enosh finally realized that he was really meant to fight seriously. He jumped to his feet, determined to show this old man what he could do. Uzal took out his blade and thrust quickly, cutting his opponent on the arm. It was not deep, but it bled freely. Enosh became enraged. Even Neb in all his cruel taunting had never attacked like this. Enosh gripped his own knife in his right hand while he began to twirl his spear with his left. He plunged forward with his head down at Uzal like a mad bull then stabbing and thrusting like an angry child. Uzal stood stone still for a moment and gave Enosh a clear target only to step aside at the last moment and let him plunge headfirst into the watching crowd. Uzal stood back and laughed at the absurdity of continuing this game. It was clear to everyone that in a few moments the white-haired old man could kill the young man without breaking a sweat. To Enosh's extreme embarrassment, he stood panting while Uzal chuckled deeply in his chest, laughing at him in a rather unfriendly manner.

"Enosh, you are dead! I could send one of my daughters to fight you, and she would win!" There was uproarious laughter at this while Enosh wiped the sweat from his brow and tried to shake the sting from his arm. His little brother Kenan had seen it all, though Eva was nowhere in sight. Still, as he tried to keep his burning face straight and proud, he could not help seeing the disappointment in the eyes of the few men who had followed

Hezeki and now him from their home to this point. After leaving Hezeki, their faithful warriors had hoped that Enosh would grow in leadership and strength, but he seemed instead to become more uncertain of himself. He had rejoiced a little obviously when they had found this settlement and learned of the warrior nature of these people. Enosh feared that the People of Seth were no match for Neb, but here was a clan that could meet a defiant warrior on his own terms. As much as Enosh had hoped for salvation from the People of Havilah, he soon realized that Uzal was not one to offer assistance except in extreme need. Uzal had told them that they should fight Neb for their own reasons and on their own terms but that if this Neb, eldest son of Hezeki, was to come and challenge him and his people in any way, they were surely prepared to oppose him. He then suggested that Enosh get his mind off his troubles by trying to win a place in one of the games. Enosh, thinking it would only be for fun and entertainment, readily agreed. Now as he stood before the crowd of bystanders—the source of their amusement—he regretted his acceptance of this challenge. Worse still, he regretted his unpreparedness to face such a formidable opponent as this unassuming old man.

"I regret that I have met you so unprepared. I did not realize the seriousness of this challenge."

Uzal looked him up and down with sneering disgust. "No man should ever be unprepared for a serious combat. It is the duty of a man to be prepared!" Uzal looked around, and he spied Kenan looking at him with eyes of hate. He smiled briefly as he swung his spear in the direction of Enosh's brother.

"I would like to challenge this one. He looks as if he is already engaged for a real battle."

Enosh looked over to Kenan who had kept his eyes fastened on the old man in an attitude of unmitigated fury. Enosh knew that his younger brother was no better prepared than himself, for he was the boy's own teacher, but when he tried to catch Kenan's eye to dissuade him from the challenge, the youth refused to see him. His unfaltering attention was fixed solely on the old man. Enosh shrugged his shoulder in defeat and stepped aside as Kenan took his own spear and knife and stepped forward into the ring of watchers.

    This time when Uzal attempted to knock Kenan off balance, the youth jumped at the right time, and the wood went swooshing under his feet. Even before he had regained his footing, Kenan swung a mighty blow at Uzal's head. Uzal was alert enough to the boy's determination to back away at the first sign of a swing, but as he tried to counter the move with a thrust, Kenan used his spear hand to block the move and thrust with his own knife. To everyone's surprise, the knife sliced Uzal's forearm. Uzal then moved forward, and with a blurry series of moves, he knocked Kenan down and finally used his spear to pin the boy's clothing to the ground, grazing his side at the same time. Then he jumped on Kenan's prone body and put an extremely sharp blade against his throat. There was complete silence as even the birds appeared to be waiting to see what would happen next. Kenan simply stared hard at Uzal, and with a last unexpected rush, he fingered his knife and attempted to thrust it into Uzal's body from underneath. Uzal nicked Kenan's neck quite purposefully as he twisted the knife from his hand and then rose while yanking the youth up to his feet and at the same time ripping his clothes and enlarging the gash upon his side. He forced the youth to stand across from him as he put his own hand upon the boy's shoulder.

    "You have fought well and regained the honor of your family, but you still have much to learn. If I was not so kind a man, you might have gotten hurt in this contest. As it is, you have a few nicks to remember this moment. Go now and tend to your men. If I were to assign a leader to your shabby little group, it would be you, not your brother, for a leader is not determined by age, but rather by valor and determination. Either your brother will win renown enough to regain his position, or you should take over leadership for the sake of those who still follow you." He turned and began to call on another man to come forward so he could test his ability against a weary old man. The crowd allowed Enosh and Kenan to leave freely, and they merged once again into a watching mass, expectantly surveying the next opponent to match his skill and wits against their leader.

Enosh walked away resolutely like a man who was stunned beyond all thought. Kenan walked quickly beside him, speaking in seething fury.

"He does not know what he is talking about. I am your younger brother in skill as well as in age, and everything I have learned I have learned from you and father. He does not speak for me or the other men!" Kenan stopped when his brother did, and they both looked to the men who had followed them from their home village through the Village of Seth to this point. Thubal was the leader of these men, and he did not look like he agreed with Kenan.

"We followed Hezeki because he is the leader of our clan while Neb was usurping him unjustly, but when he ordered us to follow you, it was in expectation that he would follow in a short time. We have made no determination as to what we will do if Hezeki does not come this way soon."

Enosh looked at Thubal with an expression of perplexity. "Then you will not stay with us? Will you go back to Neb?"

Kenan jumped at this and pushed himself right under Thubal's face. "You will not betray us if I have any breath left in my body. Enosh is a good leader, but he was not prepared for this fight. He thought it was all in fun, and Uzal took unfair advantage. If our father does not come soon, you know perfectly well that he has set Enosh as leader. That is what Hezeki wants and what Neb fears! Do not let your judgment be clouded by a few words from a man who knows no better."

Thubal pushed Kenan back with a sudden thrust. "Your brother had better become ready for anything from now on! None of us know what we shall face in the future, and if he is to lead anyone, he had better be able to stay alive!" At this, Thubal turned and stomped away toward the place where they had made a temporary shelter.

Kenan spat out an angry response and stepped forward intending to follow after Thubal, but Enosh put a restraining hand upon him and held him back. Kenan, in a sudden fury, thrust Enosh's hand off his shoulder. "I am loyal to you because I have set my heart on it, but you will have to fight for the loyalty of every other man who follows you."

Enosh stood solidly upon his feet and looked his brother in the eyes. The red stain had faded somewhat, though his shame was still acute. "What you say is true, and what Thubal said is true also. Even what Uzal said is true. I have learned a bitter lesson today. I think I am now beginning to see the success of Neb. It takes a certain arrogance of spirit to fight as hard as one must to succeed, and there are no fun contests. Neb believes he is the leader because he is the most ruthless and determined, and for that reason he could not let father live out his time in peace. Once he lost respect for his father, he could no longer follow him. He had to take over, you see. He is very much like our new friends; they see warrior strength as the very identity of leadership. Tradition and family ties have very little to do with the matter, I think." Enosh sighed deeply and then squared his shoulders. "I know now what I must do to lead our men and raise up a new community, but I am loath to do it, for it means I must become a bit more like Neb."

"You will never really be like him!"

"Let us hope not."

For several months Enosh prepared himself and Kenan in every way possible for victory in battle. They were offered the assistance of Kryce, second son of Uzal, who proved to be very knowledgeable and who won several positions of honor in the contests. He was even able to offer a challenge to the two youths when they fought together. Though he was only a little older, he was so far advanced in agility and sheer force of strength that there were moments when Enosh doubted his ability to ever compete in their games successfully. Neither Enosh nor Kenan participated in any of the games, but they watched with avid interest. They learned much—things that they doubted even Neb knew about—and their hearts rose for they saw the possibility that, given the opportunity to practice, they might become formidable opponents to Neb. But as time went on, they began to wonder if Neb were ever going to find them. Perhaps he had simply gone home. Perhaps something unexpected had happened to dissuade him from following after them. Perhaps they had hid their trail more successfully than they had dared to hope. There were so many possibilities, but every time they began to hope and expressed that hope out loud, Eva was sure to look at them with scorn as if they were younger than she and believed in the fanciful stories of children. She knew what she feared, and it was not make-believe. She knew that Neb was never one to give up on a quarry. She had heard all about his victory over the bear and had pondered it often.

Enosh had come back to their simple camp one day flush with all the signs of victory, and he grabbed his little sister by the waist and swung her in a great circle, shouting for all the world to hear.

"I beat Kryce today! I actually surprised him and outmaneuvered him, and he is the one going home with a sting to mend!" Eva looked at the beaming face of her brother, and she smiled for the first time in a long while.

"I am happy for you brother, though you know it will take more than a sting to stop Neb."

"Neb! Neb! The way you talk, one would think he was a kind of god who could not be beat. He is a man. He looks like a man, he bleeds like a man and he can be stopped like any other man. Kryce is a very good warrior—one of the best I might even say—and when I struck him today, I showed that I am stronger and better than I have ever been before. Can't you be glad about that? Can I never prove myself even to you?"

Before Eva could respond, there was the sound of pounding feet as Kenan came running up to the two of them. They were standing outside their dwelling, and the sun was bright overhead. Several of the men were away hunting, though a few were sitting around well within hearing range, and they looked up inquiringly at this sudden activity. Kenan practically collided with his brother in his haste to speak to him.

"Come quickly! Uzal is requesting your presence in his dwelling. Do you remember Hul? He served father faithfully and then treacherously decided to stay with Neb? He and Accad and his brother Jubal from the People of Seth have come, and they spent the morning speaking in private with Uzal. I just learned of this a few moments ago, and no one looks very happy. It is important news, I am sure. Hurry, let us go!" Turning to rush back the way he came, Kenan sped up a steep incline while Enosh nodded to one of the men, gesturing for him to come forward.

"Tell Thubal where we have gone and that I request he join us in the dwelling of Uzal. He has as much of a right to know what is going on as anyone else." With this he offered a curt nod to his sister who watched his back as he stepped determinedly up the incline after his brother.

Inside the dwelling of Uzal, the air was warm and stifling. There were quite a few men standing by, but clouds had swooped into the area, promising an impending rain. They all stood still and waited, though many wished to be out in the fresh air. Uzal simply nodded to Kenan when he came in, but when Enosh appeared, he gestured for Hul to step forward. Enosh quickly tried to cover his reaction. Hul was no longer the man he remembered. He could recognize the face and figure certainly, but the once robust man was now a shell of his former self. His skin hung in baggy looseness, and his eyes were merely black specks peering through grief into an unwelcome fate.

Speaking to Enosh, Uzal pointed to Hul and bid them both sit down.

"I believe you know each other so there are no introductions necessary. This man was brought into my presence by these two." Uzal motioned toward Accad and Jubal as they stood side-by-side looking to all the world like matched stone carvings. "I have been informed of serious tidings, and though it has taken long for word to reach here, I believe that we must not let any more time pass before we become equally informed of the threat that approaches. I will let Hul repeat his story for you so that you can judge for yourselves if my concern is valid." Uzal nodded once to Hul who sat up as straight as he was able. It seemed as if he had aged many years in the last few months, but no one said a word so as to better be acquainted with the news that much faster. Hul spoke slowly and with effort.

"Enosh, you must not blame me too severely for my confusion of loyalty toward Hezeki. If ever you are able to rejoin our people, please be merciful to my family, for they, like me, thought that it was best to follow the new leader of the clan rather than cling to one who was old and running away." Hul's eyes held such a note of reproachful grief that Enosh felt compelled to speak.

"You and your family have nothing to fear from me or mine."

Hul accepted this in quiet meekness and went on to tell the full story of what happened in the Village of Seth after they left, including how both Ashkenazi and Hezeki were murdered though there was no certain proof of who did the deed. Hul told how he learned of the truth and how when he could no longer follow Neb, he was speared and left for dead. He told the story of his long, torturous trek back to the Village of Seth, his ability to evade death's stalking grip and how the people there nursed him and provided for all his needs without even knowing what had happened to him. When the truth was known, Accad and Jubal went out scouting to learn where Neb had actually gone. They followed him through a long journey and discovered that he had returned to his original home. But then the story became even more painful, for it turned out that Neb had turned to marauding and enslaving other clans. He had attacked two clans in the area and had shown no mercy. Neb and his people now followed a god that they had abducted from one of the clans, and it was said that Neb now had powers no man should have. He was invincible, and every clan in the area was terrified of him. Some had even sent word that they would pay him tribute if he would promise not to attack. Neb had killed the messengers but kept the gifts that had been offered as bribes. He sent word back that he wanted more payments, but whether he attacked would depend on the quality of the gifts. Hul shuddered at the thought of what Neb had become.

"You have to understand. I did not see him for what he was until it was too late. My family still lives there, and I am unable to return. I can do nothing for them or anyone. My only hope rests with Meshullemeth and that she might oppose her son, but I am afraid she is not that kind of woman."

Enosh sucked in his breath and exhaled slowly. "No… she is not that kind of woman."

Kenan moved forward a bit, and, looking Hul in the eyes, he questioned him with a cold anger. "So, where is our brother now?"

This time it was Accad who answered. "He is heading here. He knows you have settled here, and he has heard enough of the People of Havilah to come well prepared. That is why he attacked the other villages first—to make his men battle-hardened. He comes to steal and destroy but most of all to kill all who remain alive from his own family. He cannot live with the possibility that one day you will challenge him."

Enosh almost shouted his next words. "Challenge him for what? Leadership of a clan that kills wantonly? I know the men who follow him most closely—Puti and Riphath and Torgama and his boorish friend Kittam—and they have no honor, no decency. They care for no one but themselves. The only reason they follow Neb is for their own gain. If Neb were to weaken, they would leave him too. I never want to reclaim the people of my birth again!"

"But they were not all evil." This time it was a young girl's voice that spoke. Eva had stolen into the dwelling while everyone had been intent on the details of the narrative Hul had been telling. She spoke now with tired certainty. "You know well the truth of this, Enosh. There were many in our clan who have helped a stranger or assisted those in need. They once had humor, and surely love still lives in their breasts. They were not beasts, though beasts they may have recently become under the evil influence of our all too evil brother."

Kenan almost spat out his words. "He was not alone in his evil. Remember well who trained him."

At this Uzal put up his hands and gestured for all to follow him outside. Once they were in the open air, Uzal called for his men. At the same time Thubal appeared, coming in from a hunt. He had a fat stag over his shoulders, and there was much excitement at this. Uzal called out, and everyone stopped in mid-motion.

"My people! War is upon us. A warrior clan comes to destroy us and take our women and children away as slaves. Prepare yourselves well. This will be no entertaining game, and there will be no second chances next year if you fail now. I want all of my men to set up guards and send out scouts. Gather all of our weapons; bring in tools from every place near and far. I want every blade at my service. We will meet this challenger, and we will teach him to bow before us as he wishes to make us bow. Go quickly to work now, and may every man be brave even to his death!"

Accad and Jubal stood off to the side with grave attention apparently awaiting their orders.

Uzal walked over to them and motioned for Hul to come along.

"This is not your fight. You have done well in warning us of the danger, but I suspect" he took a long appraising look at Hul, "that this man here has seen enough battle for his lifetime. He needs to find a place of rest before he dies. Take him to your home, and assure your leader that we will stop this menace here. Neb, eldest son of Hezeki, will surely go no further."

Accad and Jubal looked at each other and then back at Uzal. "We thank you for your kind words, but you see this is more our battle than yours. Neb came into our midst and did great evil. He lied and deceived us even as he murdered a friend of ours and an innocent man. We must regain our lost honor. Seth has promised to send men as soon as the time and place of battle is known. My brother and I will take Hul back to our village, but we will return here with men enough to destroy that which threatens us all."

Uzal rubbed his chin in an attitude of reflection, and then he spoke slowly and with great care.

"I am not averse to accepting the assistance of capable warriors, but I have heard about your clan, and they are not known for their fighting skills. Still, if you can find a few of your best men, you may send them. I would rather have a few well-trained warriors than a whole mass of incapable though well-intentioned fools. I hope you are not overly insulted by my words, but these are serious times, and I must not lead my people with kind words when there are evil men coming to steal their lives with sharp spears."

Accad nodded his acceptance and then spoke without rancor. "We will return soon with the best we have to offer."

Then the three men turned and strode off while the entire village watched in silence still amazed by the sudden and terrible news. Kenan and Enosh went to apprise Thubal of everything that had happened and to quickly get the stag dressed, for red meat was always welcomed by men about to do battle. As Uzal strode forward to direct his men, his daughter Tamar came and stood by Eva, gently putting her hand on her shoulder.

"Do not worry, Eva. These men know how to fight. You are perfectly safe in our care."

Eva simply stared ahead as she whispered, "If only you were fighting just men."

Tamar looked slightly taken aback. "Why, for goodness sake, who else are we fighting?"

"You shall see. There is something dark but invisible that creeps into a man's breast in war, and he becomes less of a man and more like a creature who does the will of an unseen power."

"Can no man fight with honor then?"

"Not for very long. When the passion takes him, reason flees and bloodlust rushes in."

Tamar bent down to look the young girl in the face. "Why, you are younger than my little sister Sari, and she has lived in a warrior clan all her life. How do you know such things when I am certain she does not?"

"I know Neb, and one evil man can teach a young girl a lot." With that Eva walked silently away. As Tamar watched her, a shiver ran down her own spine.

CHAPTER 19
THE VICTORY SHALL BE MINE

Neb exalted in his heart. He had come upon the People of Havilah far swifter than they had anticipated and from a direction they had never considered. Neb had recently learned that surprise and unremitting brutality were the ultimate keys to success. This he taught to his men, and the lessons were learned very well for they no longer even saw their acts of violence as particularly surprising or brutal. They simply had a duty to perform, and slaughter was rather easy, after all, especially if one did not think about who or what one was slaughtering. Yet despite the audacity and horrific daring of Neb and his men, Uzal's men were able to push Neb and his men back to the very edge of the woodlands surrounding their village. The fighting was fierce as the two nearly matched war parties battled back and forth, claiming advantage one moment and then just as quickly losing it. Still Neb's killing instincts had been sharpened to a keener edge than his opponents, and his men were slowly but surely felling men who would never rise to fight again. Despite their losses, Uzal and his men fought manfully to protect their own throughout the course of a long and bloody day. However, no one is immune to strange misfortune. Uzal, despite all his honorable intentions and skill, was capable of making a costly mistake. And Neb was quite capable of taking advantage of the smallest weakness.

Uzal's second daughter, Leah, had been kept indoors during the worst of the battle and was directed to assist those aiding the injured and watching over the children. After a bout of especially fierce fighting near their dwelling, she became frightened and had called out to her father to help them. Everyone inside had tried to stop her clamoring and had chided her for her foolish attempt to distract Uzal when he had far more serious matters to attend to. Yet she had become obstinate and had run outside the protection of their simple shelter to look for her father. In a short time, she found herself trapped between her falling kinsmen and the enemy. Uzal heard his young daughter's frightened call, and his heart responded to the danger she had put herself into. At the same time, Neb found himself in a small clearing with no one left to attack him. He saw Leah as she was being directed by Uzal to escape through some trees into a wooded grove. The smile on Neb's face was not one of a love-struck youth but of an opportunist who saw a magnificent chance to strangle the very heart of his enemy. It was the work of a moment to circle around where none could see and track the girl into the woodlands and surprise her. Leah was, at heart, a sunny child who had known little servile fear, so when Neb approached her, she was as saucy and abrupt with him as she had been with the men of her own clan. She had seen little of the battle, but she had heard much. Though her heart was confused with bitter grief, still she had never taught her tongue to obey her mind, so she spoke out belligerently when Neb blocked her path.

"What have you to do with me, oh terrorizing demon?"

"I have come to save you from a fate worse than death."

"You? Save me? Why would one so skilled in the art of death wish to offer salvation to an innocent enemy like me?"

"Are you innocent then? You hardly look the role. You are too fair and your tongue moves too freely to convince me that you could be anything but a companion to power."

Leah's face scowled with utter contempt. "A companion to—" There was a sudden rush of activity as a figure leaped down from a tree branch upon the back of Neb who for the first time in his life had been so consumed with a sudden interest that he failed to keep his eyes and ears completely alert. Leah shrieked as she watched her father ride the back of the man she had been briefly mesmerized by. She stumbled backward as the two struggled for supremacy. In that shriek, she cost the life of the man she loved most, for in response to her terror sprang the defensive love of her father, and as he attempted to turn to assist her, Neb grabbed his blade and slashed at Uzal's neck, which was still riding on his shoulder, and the knife went deep and did a great deal of harm. Uzal, realizing the blow was mortal, was thrown to the side, but he managed to right himself in time to attempt a thrust at Neb. The two struggled in back-and-forth combat for some moments, but as Uzal's mortal life seeped from his body, his opponent took strength from his obvious success. Still, Uzal was too well-trained a warrior to offer his life to the enemy cheaply, so in a daring and brilliant maneuver, he twirled around with surprising speed, swinging his knife and spear and amazing even Neb as he caught a blow to the side of the head and a long gash down his side. Still in his certainty of success, Neb only shook off the blow to his head and smiled at the gash. He let out a deep and guttural laugh. "You are a worthy opponent! I am impressed by the spirit of you and your men, and I would have you live on for years to come so that I may test my skill against you time and again."

Uzal lowered his head and shook it back and forth as an angry bull would do. "I would that you were dead and your body burned to ashes so as to free the earth of your vile nature. I vow to hunt you and your men until the last star falls to earth."

Neb stood breathing deeply, still with a mocking smile on his lips. "You are ambitious, but the stars will not be so kind as to hurry themselves for you. You are bleeding too freely from the neck, and I think I see the glaze of death before your eyes. If we cannot be combatants in an age-long war, let one of us die in battle now so as to satisfy the victor."

Uzal staggered a moment as his life's blood fell to the ground though he held up a hand to stanch the flow. He shook his blade at Neb. "I will fight you beyond this life into the next. You will know no rest, for where you go, I will also follow. Your every step shall be haunted, and eventually you, too, will meet a mortal blow that shall take you where you do not wish to go. I shall be waiting for you, and then I will have my vengeance upon you." Uzal fell to the ground, and Leah shrieked and ran to him as he fell. His eyes could no longer see her.

Leah cradled her father's head in her arms and spat out her words in a frenzy of distraught fury. "You are a murderer! You have killed the most noble of men!"

Ignoring her grief and anger, Neb grabbed Leah and dragged her away from the body of her father, turning only once to speak grimly to the body of his vanquished foe. "I do not recognize death, for I shall live forever. This I will do so you may see my victory more completely; I will take your daughter as my wife. She shall be mine so that if you haunt me, you will have to haunt her also and all our offspring too. Long will you wait for your vengeance!"

Leah only covered her face with her hands repeating the word, "No" over and over again.

The battle lasted long into the night, for neither side would retreat. Dodan discovered the body of his father soon after his death, and despite his best efforts, he could not keep the uncontrolled rage of the men from being spent in useless fury. He wanted them to rest and plan for the next day's battle, but Kryce screamed for vengeance in ranting fury while Enosh went with scouts to see if any preparations for a long siege were being made. Tamar had taken the other women and children to shelter them in her own home, and those who were not otherwise occupied were caring for the injured and preparing food for those who could and would eat. Sari hid in a corner, though Tamar ordered her to make preparations to ease the burden of those who suffered. The young girl was angry and frightened by the loss of her father and sister, but she complied with her older sister's demands with dutiful efficiency.

Eva, having learned much about healing herbs from Sari and remembering her vow to assist the helpless, tried to help as best as she was able. At one point, she took a dried herb and seeped it in boiling water, thus making a brew that she knew to be soothing for aches and pains. However, when she tried to give it to one of the woman who was quite exhausted and expecting a baby, Sari rushed over and knocked the bowl from the girl's hand.

"You can't give her that!"

"Why not? I thought it would be good for what ails her. She is in desperate need of soothing medicine. This day has been a trial on the strongest of us, but upon her it has been a day of horror. She lost her brother and her husband today."

"She will lose more than that if you give her the medicine you thought to."

"It is only a common soothing herb!"

"For most of us that is true, but for her it would end the life of the child that grows inside of her. You must be very careful and ask before you give anything I have not directed you too. Too late have some women learned the bitter truth of that soothing herb!"

Eva bowed her head in acceptance, and the black hollowed-out grief she had felt with the attack of Neb on this people only increased, as she was now uncertain of her own good use. A vow to be of assistance to the needy was not worth much if in blind ignorance she hurt them beyond repair. In only a brief moment she could have done a terrible wrong without ever intending to. Was there no end to the evil her clan inflicted on others? Ashkenazi had been brutally slain because her father had brought Neb in his wake. Now, though war-like, this clan was battling for sheer survival because Enosh had hoped to find allies in war. Allies they proved to be, but would they be able to beat back the forces of Neb? And what about her brothers? Were they capable of escaping the clutches of one who hunted them so relentlessly? Some had said that the Clan of Seth was going to come and assist, but that hope had proven fruitless. The worst had already happened with the death of Uzal. Eva walked out of the simple dwelling without saying a word, black despair being her only companion.

Neb was eating heartily as Leah lay in a stupor off to the side under a large spreading tree. He was smiling and laughing with his men as if they had just come home from a successful hunt. Riphath was tending to the meat roasting upon spits near the center of the camp, while two other men were pulling out supplies that they had pillaged from Uzal's village.

Torgama wiped his dirty hands across his tunic and laughed at the story Neb was telling about his encounter with Uzal and the dead leader's curse to haunt him into eternity. Khtam smiled knowingly as if he had seen hauntings enough and they only amused him. Puti came up and bowed before Neb in the ceremonial manner Neb had taught him and made his report.

"They are tending to the wounded and attempting to ascertain what our next move will be. They have scouts out. I believe one of them is the son of their leader. Everyone defers to him even though he is still young."

Neb smiled again. "Ah, here is my first opportunity to show what kind of a man I really am. Go and capture that son of the late father who is brother to my soon-to-be wife." Neb gestured for Kittam and Torgama to go and assist. "I want that boy alive and unhurt if possible, but if he must be injured, then do what must be done. I warn you, however, he is of no use to me dead or near death beyond healing." Neb smiled as if he had a delightful secret. "Believe me, you will prefer my method to your madness."

Torgama merely got to his feet and awaited Kittam and Puti to join him as they bowed and turned away. They disappeared into the outer darkness as Neb made himself comfortable. In a remarkably short period of time, the three men returned to camp with company. By that time the moon had risen and Puti came and found Neb resting. He offered a slight cough before he spoke. Neb returned to full wakefulness and looked at his men expectantly.

"We have brought you what you asked for and a little more. I hope you are pleased." Puti retreated a few paces as Kittam and Torgama came into full view leading two captives. Neb rose to his feet, and a smile broke across his face, illuminating the dark night.

"Ah, yes, you have done well. This is an unexpected treat. To have the son of my enemy and at the same time to be reunited with my own dear, lost sister." Neb turned to the young man who had obviously not come willingly.

"So, what is your name, son of so noble a leader?"

Kryce stood between the two men who were holding his arms behind him in no gentle a manner, and he stared with a look of such hatred that if his eyes could have killed, Neb would have burst into cinders. He said nothing until Kittam squeezed his arm a little harder. Then under panting protest, he spoke out biting words.

"My name, for what it is worth to you, is Kryce. I am the second son of the man you have so brutally slain for what purpose I have yet to understand."

Neb stepped a little nearer. "Oh, I will explain the matter to you so that when you go home you may explain it to all the others. I have no complaint against you or your men. On the contrary, I am much impressed with your people. You are so much better adversaries than the People of Seth, I must tell you. I could not bring myself to attack them openly, though they did deserve annihilation for opposing me and allowing my brothers to flee when they knew full well that I wished to speak with them. In that situation, I was content to suppress those who would hinder my leadership and then retreat home for a time of needed rest and composure. Now I have come here seeking my own flesh and blood, and again I am opposed. I killed your father against my own wish. It was not his death I sought. And I do not seek your death either, though if you oppose me I may be forced into unhappy action."

"You are a liar." It was the soft voice of Eva who spoke from the dark shadows. Neb turned his attention toward his little sister.

"Oh, yes, I almost forgot about you." He gestured for her to come a little closer, but she would not move. He put up his hands in a motion of futility. "It is of no matter. I have little use for you, but" he smiled grimly. "I do know someone who will be delighted with your return. Our own mother's heart was broken when you were spirited away. It will be my pleasure to reunite a mother with her long-lost daughter."

Eva shook her head. "Have you no acquaintance with truth at all?"

Neb smiled at this. "Whose truth do you prefer?"

Eva nodded toward Kryce. "What do you intend to do to him?"

Neb nodded in a decisive manner. "Watch and see. You will learn much about truth now."

Neb retreated into the shadows, and after a few moments, he led Leah into the light of the glowing fire. She put her eyes up against the brightness of the sudden light, but then she lifted her head and saw the face of her brother. An exclamation of surprise ushered from her lips as she attempted to run and embrace Kryce. Kittam and Torgama did not release their grip on their prisoner, and Neb held Leah near to his own side.

"I will tell you what you want to hear after a moment, but first I must have your word that you will stay right here with me. I will order my men to release your brother so that we can discuss matters as they now stand, and if all goes well, he will be released and the fighting will end. Do you agree to stand by my side during this discussion?"

Leah nodded her head silently as she looked furtively upon her brother. The minute Kryce's arms were freed and Neb had dropped his own restraining hand from Leah's shoulder, she rushed into her brother's arms and clung to him like a vine to a tree. Neb nodded his head with a knowing look on his face. "You are as predictable as you are beautiful." He motioned for Torgama and Puti to stand back a few feet. Kittam remained close to Kryce's side.

"I will say this for all to hear so that there will be no misunderstandings later about how things stand. I have chosen Leah as my wife. She will come home with me and so will Eva. Eva will be returned to her mother, and Leah will be my companion in all things. Now, before I can leave to begin my delightful new life, I must finish up the matter of my two brothers. I want them brought before me so that I might pass judgment upon them. A great deal of trouble has been caused by them, and I mean that this toil and hardship may end here."

Kryce spoke first, even as Leah spat in Neb's direction.

"My sister will never be your wife! She would rather die."

A slow smile spread across Neb's face. "Really? Leah," He walked toward the girl and put his hand to her face to look her in the eyes. He spoke slowly, emphasizing each word with clear meaning while he pulled out his blade. "Which would you rather: a quick death here and now or a long, useful life with me?"

Leah attempted to bury her face in her brother's shoulder.

In agitation, her brother spoke out almost hysterically. "I am her brother, and I speak for her. She would rather die than live with you and your people!"

Neb looked closely at the girl and shook his head slowly. "I think you are wrong. Besides, you have not heard all. I am going to make Leah my first and only wife. She shall rule with me. She will be in everything my equal unto death." He turned toward Kryce again. "So you see, I am offering an alliance between our people—a much better bargain than the one you got with my brothers and the People of Seth. By the way, where are your friends? I have not seen the brothers. Those most amusing twins, Accad and Jabal, where are they? And Seth? What became of him?"

Kryce looked momentarily deflated. "They have not come. You have killed them for all I know."

"Killed them? Why no, I haven't laid eyes on them in many moons." His eyes surveyed the larger surrounding, and he assessed the need to move things to a quick conclusion. "Though they did amuse me, this is hardly the time for such remembrances. I have things to attend to now." He paused in thought as he eyed Leah carefully. She had moved away ever so slightly from her brother's embrace and was now standing on her own two feet with eyes that were casting every which way. Neb went and stood beside her, letting his hand rest ever so gently on her back while speaking softly into her ear. From Kryce's perspective, it looked as if an offer were being made while he could barely make out his own name. She looked up at Neb, and she wiped the tears off her face with a look of deep concentration. She nodded to her brother with stark acceptance and waited passively for Neb to speak.

"I have offered Leah her first gift. I will give her your life and the freedom of your clan, and I will leave the field of battle tomorrow if it pleases her for me to do so. As my wife, her wish is my command."

Kryce shook his head violently and tried to edge nearer his sister who had taken a step toward Neb. "He is a liar! Do not trust him to keep honest hold of his words. He will betray you and all of us!"

For the first time, Leah's head snapped up in irritation. "How do you know? All you know about him you have heard from his brothers. What if they are the liars? What if . . ." She broke down crying with her hands over her face.

Eva spoke quickly. "Have you forgotten your own father then? He lies dead and awaits burial in the cold, hard ground."

Neb lifted his hand to strike his sister, but Kryce jumped forward to stop him, and Neb looked down just in time to see the horrified shock on Leah's face. He instantly regained himself and motioned for Kittam to lead Kryce away.

"I will make myself abundantly clear this time. Kryce may go free, but Leah is here to stay. I will meet my brothers sooner or later, depending on how long the People of Havilah wish this destruction to go on. Remember, it is not my choice, but rather it is yours. I would leave today if I were allowed to."

Kryce shook the hands of his captors off his shoulders and straightened himself up.

"You will leave this place as my father did, though there will be no honorable burial for you. I will offer your dead flesh to the woodland scavengers as meat for their young so that at last you may serve some good purpose."

Neb bowed in mock honor. "How kindly you speak." He looked to Leah who still stood alone and uncertain. Taking her hand, he turned and led her to the food laid out on leaf mats upon the ground. Kittam gave Kryce a mighty shove into the darkness.

"Off you go! You are no longer wanted. Go home and await us with the rising of the sun!"

Leah stood by her father's killer in silence as if she had no will of her own. Kryce gnashed his teeth as he ran through the brambles trying to find his way back to his own home. Various imposing threats and clever responses arose to his lips time and again, but the trees cared not, and even the sleeping animals resettled soon after he left, leaving little trace of his furious trail through their quiet home.

Eva was taken to a tree and bound so that she could sit and rest but could not run away. She was given food, but she would not eat. She merely sat and waited, pondering what this new turn in her fortune would bring. She would have been desperately sad but for the fact that her emotions were now frozen like the snow at the peak of a great imposing mountain. Was it possible that she had been taken from her home and brought to the People of Seth and then to the People of Havilah for no good purpose? As she pondered her present situation, she realized that she was no longer the person she had been. Now she did know something about medicinal herbs and also something about plants that can do a great deal of harm. As she laid her head against the tree and stared at the silent twinkling stars overhead, she wondered which of her new skills would prove the more useful: the knowledge to heal or the knowledge to kill. A look of serious wonder crossed her face as she debated her own strength and imagined Neb's look of incredibility when he finally faced an undefeatable enemy

CHAPTER 20
ENDURANCE

Throughout the night, the expected rains came, and it poured down in great pelting drops, soaking anyone who ventured out. The wounded had been retrieved from the fields and woods and brought inside their dwellings to be gently tended. Those beyond all healing and care were laid ceremoniously on hard beds carved from soft stone in the walls of a cave not far away, which was known as the Home of the Dead. The night had been bitter, and few slept except the sleep of utter exhaustion, though troubled dreams haunted them all even as the storm raged outside. In the morning, the mountainous dark clouds had moved off, and a soft, cool breeze flew between low white clouds and a muddied earth.

Tamar's grief was doubled in the dual loss of her father and her husband. Her time of grief-stricken mourning was intense, though, by necessity, brief. As she recovered her sensibilities and looked about, she realized that, though much of what she had loved most dearly was gone from the reach of her arms, she herself was not yet dead, and her children lived also. The warrior spirit of her people did not flow in her blood in vain. She recognized the need to reorganize the clan with a new leader immediately, and she considered her brother Dodan. She thought he was the most logical choice while they prepared themselves for the next battle. It was during a meeting of elders and warriors that Kryce found his way home after having fallen into a tormented sleep somewhere in the wooded hills. His mind and body had become so exhausted by the fierce battle with Neb's warriors and the even fiercer battle with Neb's will that he had found himself overcome with weakness and had slept into the late afternoon. When he finally stumbled, dirty, wet and completely disheveled, upon the assembled group and heard what was being suggested, he waved his sister away, and forcing himself to stand tall and defiant, he told the story of what Neb had done. Tamar had thought that Kryce had gone out to find their sister, Leah, and bring her safely home. When she learned the full truth of what had happened, she put her hand to her lips in a desperate attempt to calm the rising panic in her chest as it heaved in sudden shock and horror. Sari rose too, and her agitation was just as great, but she spoke not a word. Her comfort was in healing herbs, but she had no remedy to cure what ailed them now.

Kryce looked to Dodan, and their eyes locked in mutual understanding. Dodan stepped forward into the inner circle, and he spoke in his slow, measured tone. "Long have our people valued our sacred traditions, and in truth we will continue to follow the noble path set for us by those who have gone before us. We are a people of high honor, and though we have fought valiantly, we have lost much." Dodan's voice almost faltered a moment as he looked fixedly ahead. "I am my father's first son, and by right I should lead our men into the next battle. However, I know myself honestly, and a great warrior I am not. I was made for another purpose. I am Kryce's elder by nature, but he shall be my elder by choice. I shall serve him with loyalty and bravery. I submit that Kryce shall be the leader of the People of Havilah, and once we have our revenge, so we shall know prosperity once again." Dodan stepped back into the folds of the circle of men amid a loud silence. Then Tamar stepped slightly forward again, and she had her hands folded up under her arms and her head was bowed.

"I have attempted to remedy a great injury with the wrong cure. I agree with the wisdom of Dodan, though I do not believe that the size of a man measures the greatness of his spirit."

In anxious excitement Kryce stepped up even before his sister had stepped back.

"I have cursed Neb to his face and vowed to kill him for what he has done to my father, my sister and all our clan. We will end this contest between us before very long. I will lead my men in battle against him. Dodan will stay here and protect all who remain behind."

Then Enosh, who had been standing silent on the sidelines with Kenan and his men, stepped out front. He was clearly overwrought, for the horror of Uzal's death had touched him deeply. He was affronted by his brother's audacity in taking Leah away as a captive even as he chided himself for being so surprised by this new treachery. His desire to run away to a place of safety had been turned into a desire for revenge. He wanted nothing more in the world than to hunt his brother down the way he had been hunted and end Neb's reign of terror and madness.

"I know my brother, and he is aided by a power that cannot be easily overcome by the will of a warrior no matter how skilled. But I also know that he relies heavily on the skills of a few of his most trusted men and that they have no such protection. Ruthless brutality is their only aid, but as they give, so they shall receive. I suggest that instead of attacking Neb personally, my brother and I will go after Torgama, Kittam and Puti. They are a source of strength to Neb, and if we take them down, he will lose some of his confidence and protection."

Kryce thoughtfully nodded his head and gestured his acceptance of this plan, and they prepared to go into battle even before the next day dawned. That night was dark and restless. In the cool damp few animals stirred, though there were various cries of wild things as they smelt the aging field of battle. Kryce, with Enosh's help, was able to survey the camp of their enemy and determine which position would be best in order to attack most effectively. Enosh had sent Kenan to ascertain Torgama, Kittam and Puti's positions, and the youth had found them assembled together. Two were sleeping, and only Puti was standing awake and alert as a sentry, though he did not sense the silent youth who viewed him through the veil of a clouded black night. Kenan smiled to himself, for he knew what a victory it would be to take these three away from Neb's use. Kenan was about to back up and turn away to tell his brother what he had discovered when a sudden wrong move dislodged a twig, and it snapped quite loudly and caused an echoing sound to reverberate through the sheltering woods. Puti jumped and stared hard in the direction of where the sound had come. He gripped his weapons tightly and advanced. Kenan did not bother to think out a plan; he simply acted on instinct. He unsheathed his knife and ran straight at Puti, plunging the sharp blade deep into his opponent's middle as the two wrestled on the ground. Puti, though strong and not willing to die easily, was no match for a furious and determined opponent after he had been so fatally injured. Torgama and Kittam awoke to the struggle, as did many other men, and in the darkness—for the campfire had burned low—they confusedly attempted to see and understand what was happening. Kryce's men, sensing trouble, rushed in on all sides, and there were yells and shouts from every direction as the new battle commenced without ceremony. In the dark disorder, some of Neb's men even attacked each other. Like enraged bulls, madness reigned. Neb, who had taken to sleeping a little distance from the main camp, awoke as suddenly. Upon seeing the melee, he stood back a few moments, ascertaining what action would be best in order to take victory from sudden chaos. He had placed Leah near to him, and when she awoke to the noisy violence, she was too frightened to move. She sat up with her arms wrapped around herself, crying but making no attempt to run away. In truth, she was not sure in which direction to run, and she was frightened of what Neb would do if she were to get up. She watched him in silent terror as he moved away from her.

    Neb crept slowly closer to the fighting men until he saw the struggle between Kenan and Torgama and the body of Puti lying to the side near the burning embers of the fire. He wasted no time considering the loss of so valuable an ally. Kittam was engaged in hand-to-hand combat with Enosh, and Neb now realized that this was a perfect opportunity to finish what he had long desired to do. He silently moved from tree to tree until he was just behind Kenan, and then he launched himself onto his brother much like Uzal had jumped upon his back before. He knew it was a bold and dangerous move, but he also knew that his youngest brother could not hold his weight for more than a few moments, which was what happened. The two brothers crashed to the ground in a perfect swirling confusion. Torgama stood back a moment, and then, grasping his spear in fury, he threw with all his might at the form of Kenan as he lay just under Neb's body. But at just that moment Neb had decided to plunge his own knife into Kenan, and to do so he had risen from his position, thus putting his thigh over Kenan's lower chest. The force of Torgama's throw was enough to pierce Neb's thigh to the bone. He screamed like a wounded bear, and with a mighty stoke, he stabbed his brother in one vicious act as Kenan struggled to get away. Torgama, realizing in amazed shock what had happened, threw Kenan aside and wrenched the spear from his master's body. He grabbed Neb around the waist and with incredible strength ran carrying Neb into the covering darkness of the wooded hills that surrounded them. Enosh heard the scream and, he as well as Kittam stopped their own combat for a moment to witness the events. In their shock, their own personal battle was forgotten. Enosh ran to the side of his brother while Kittam began to run into the woodlands, following the footsteps of Torgama. In a sudden reversal, he strode back to the now nearly fainting form of Leah whom he grabbed and unceremoniously carried off into the woods. She attempted to call out, but her own faint voice could not overcome the sounds of continued battle. Enosh had not even realized she was so near.

In a short matter of time, it became apparent to Neb's warriors that their leader was gone from them for a reason they could not fathom. The fact that he had been seriously injured never entered their minds, for they imagined him unassailable. They pulled back from the area and began a retreat that they had never experienced before. Kryce's warriors followed them, and Dodan, hearing that Neb was wounded and the enemy was fleeing, joined in the pursuit. Though they actually only killed a few of the fleeing enemy, in their imprecations and threats they did everything they could to dishearten those who had come to conquer and were now retreating in humiliation.

When the new day dawned, the clouds had vanished, and a blue sky ruled the heavens; so too, the coolness began to burn away, and the air turned hot once again. Enosh and his men returned to the village of Havilah while Kryce helped to gather the bodies of the newly slain. Sari did all in her power to assist those not wounded unto death. Kenan, though seriously wounded with a deep gash in his side and a hard blow to the head, had not passed on to the other side, and Sari, as healer, was doing everything in her power to save him. Those she could not save, she succored with the aide of her assistants, and they were allowed to die in peace and goodwill, honored for their brave deeds and great service. The bodies of the conquered and hated enemies were taken outside the village and buried in a massive unmarked grave.

As Sari came around to try to soothe the burning pain in Kenan's side, he saw her furrowed brow and sad face. Despite his own pain, he knew her wound was perhaps even deeper than his. He attempted a little humor.

"A little cut like this is nothing. I've heard of men who returned from battle carrying parts to be added back on later."

Sari grimaced. "I have enough healing to do without having to do the impossible as well."

"You are a good healer. Perhaps you don't know your own powers."

Sari shook her head in bewilderment. The strong drink she had given him would only numb the worst of the pain. She could not imagine trying to talk with such a wound. "You are never going to recover if you don't lie still and rest."

Kenan stifled a groan as she began to peel off the old bandage. Suddenly he felt a wretched nausea strike. He tried to force himself into calmness, though the thought raced through his mind, as he saw the wound in the light of day, that he might die. He reached out to her. "I choose not to die. I have much yet to do. Do you understand?"

Sari wrapped a fresh wet cloth over the wound while bundling the blood-soaked bandages in her hands. She seemed not to notice his hand on her arm. She bent toward him and looked into his eyes. "I don't want you to die either, but such things are not for me to decide. I do what I can and I—"

In sudden impatience and fury at his own helplessness he hissed out his words. "Don't say that! Don't speak as if what you do and what I will are of little importance, as if the matter has already been settled by some council far from here. I live now because of your care, and I will continue to live because I must!"

Sari looked into his eyes, and with her free hand she patted his arm. Slowly she smiled at him, and a mischievous twinkle animated her eyes. "Well, if a strong will makes for a speedy recovery, you will be up by tomorrow!"

At this Kenan sighed and let himself fall back onto the soft skins covering his pallet. "Maybe not that fast, but soon, I will be strong again."

Sari nodded and let his hand fall softly to his side. She stood back up, and with a long backward glance, she went on with her work.

Tamar washed the bodies of the slain with her customary care before they were taken to the House of the Dead while Enosh watched from the side with weighty grief. He knew that now he and Kryce were bound by a joined desire for revenge, as both of their fathers had been killed by the same man who had also abducted both of their sisters. He was not sure what his position in this clan would be now that he had suffered the loss of so many of his men. His own brother was now seriously injured and unable to assist in anything. He did not have family or warriors enough to seed another clan, and he wondered where he would go now and how he would survive if he were sent away in retaliation for what Neb had done. Yet as the day wore on and Kryce said nothing to him, Enosh began to hope that he could stay. He made no attempt to communicate his fears and hopes to anyone.

Kryce had intended to follow after Neb a few days after the battle, but he found that too many of his men had been killed or seriously injured to make any profitable attempt. It would have been foolhardy to try to strike at Neb, even an injured Neb, with only a handful of healthy warriors. Also, he realized that he was exhausted by recent events and that he was in no condition to go on the war path far from home. His men needed to heal, and so did he. He watched Enosh move silently around the village, and he pushed down his mixed feelings of vengeful anger and sorrowing pity. He did feel sincerely sorry for Enosh, but his own weight of grief was so heavy to bear that part of him wanted to lash out in anger that Enosh had ever come into their midst. He knew they had suffered much the same losses and that in fact Enosh bore the heavier load in that he endured the guilt of knowing it was his own brother who had done these things. Yet it was a great struggle not to express his anger that if only Enosh had never come this way, his father would never have been murdered and his sister would not be lost to them.

Tamar watched over her children as carefully as ever, and even though she continued to grieve the loss of her husband, she realized that what her babes needed most she could not fully give them. No woman can be both mother and father. A complete family with both mother and father bred the most stable families, for each had much to add to the whole. She watched Enosh move throughout the village, helping as much as he could, silent yet not morose, and she pondered her options. Finally she approached Enosh as he sat resting under the shade of a large, spreading tree on a hot afternoon. She carried her little girl on her hip while her young son trailed slowly behind. In one hand swung a water skin.

"You must be tired, Enosh. I never usually see you resting."

Enosh looked up and smiled at the approaching figure. He took a deep breath as was his custom when he was about to face a trial. To him, speaking to a woman not of his own family was a bit of a challenge. "I do not really have an excuse, for I have not worked very hard today. It seems I have run out of usefulness around here."

Tamar's smile widened. "Oh, I doubt that. You just don't know whom to ask."

A puzzled expression crossed Enosh's face momentarily, and then a look of dawning light spread across his features. "Perhaps I have been blind."

Tamar held out the water skin and smiled again. "Perhaps you could use a suggestion?"

Enosh moved a little to the side and nodded ever so slightly to his side. Tamar took the suggestion and came around and put her baby girl in her lap while Put played at her knees. Enosh took a small sip and then very gently handed the bag back to Tamar. He sat quietly a moment, watching the two little ones with good-humored amusement. "What are their names?"

153

Tamar ruffled her son's hair. "This one is named Put after a father's father, and my baby is named Rachel after a mother's mother. My husband was fond of all things ancient. Tradition was sacred to him."

Enosh's smile vanished as he looked into the sky. "He was a brave warrior." His eyes slid to earth and then to Tamar, and he spoke while blinking his eyes rapidly. "In all truth, Tamar, I wish I had been the one killed and that he had lived. If I could make the trade, I would."

Tamar bit her lip as her eyes blurred in sudden pain. "We live through these things because we are not the fate makers. We are not God. If we tried to be, we would be consumed by our own madness. I think that is what has taken your brother, Neb. Our lives are like our bodies—not of our own making."

"But that is not completely true, for what we do matters. Surely it must! Otherwise why do anything? Why resist evil? Why care about anything?"

Tamar let a single tear drop as she smiled again. "You are right. What we do right now does matter. And what you have done to help my people has been very good. I thank you for your generosity."

Enosh shook his head in wonder. "Generosity? Was it generous of me to share my evil brother with you? Was it generous to bring rampaging warriors to your village?" He put his hands up to his head as if it pained him to think. "If I were you with your loss, I would hardly call me generous."

Tamar bent low to look into his fallen face. "You carry too great a weight for one man. You are responsible for your own offences, but not your brother's. Was it your wish that he come and act as he did? No. You did not wish to leave your home in the first place. We all suffer at the hands of those who want what is not theirs to have. You have not taken; you have given, and I do thank you for that." As Enosh raised his head, Tamar adjusted her baby in her lap. Then she called for Put who had begun to wander off. The little boy was obstinate, and he continued to toddle off toward the center of the village. Tamar began to get up, but Enosh put up his hand to stall her.

"No, let me. I can get him." Enosh started to move toward the little boy when a stray dog ran past and jostled the child so that he fell down. Enosh swooped in and scooped the child into his arms and soothed his crying almost immediately. When he sat down with the little one in his lap, Put was playing with the hem of his garment and attempting to put his head under his shirt in a game of hide and seek.

Laughing, Enosh held the boy up to take a better look at him. "So you want to play, do you? Well, I have a fine idea. Why don't we go and collect some wood for the fire, and we can then help your mother with the dinner. How about that?" Put nodded his head agreeably with his face was hidden inside Enosh's tunic.

Tamar laughed and clapped her hands at her little child. "I think we can do better that. I will get the dinner ready, and afterward we will visit Kenan. Perhaps you can make him laugh."

Enosh smiled, "Look who is being generous now." Tamar blushed, and the two rose together.

CHAPTER 21
A TIME TO REBUILD

Tamar thought deeply about her future, but whenever she tried to mention her ideas to Enosh, he seemed to hesitate and become wary. It was as if he could say nothing about his own future, and therefore he could do nothing to add to hers. Clouds of frustration rose up and choked her until she was almost distraught, for she felt a deep need to settle her future for the sake of her children, especially considering the fact that there could be future battles that would leave other women without husbands and there were only so many strong, capable men in the world. While they worked together one hot afternoon, Sari sensed her elder sister's anxiety and mentioned her observation.

"You seem out of sorts of late. What is disturbing you? I thought that you would be very happy now, as Enosh and you have become such good friends." She smiled as she pounded the course grain in her bowl.

Tamar sighed deeply as she cracked the shell of another nut, pushing her baby's fingers out of the basket. "I am happy we have become friends, but I would like to . . ." She hesitated and seemed to lose her words.

Sari smiled. "It is not like you to grow so embarrassed and hesitant. If you would like to marry him, tell him, and if he is willing then ask permission of Kryce."

Tamar's face soured instantly. "You think I wouldn't like to do that very thing? It would be so easy and direct, but there are things you do not understand. Mother did not live long enough to tell you of the delicacies involved in such matters. I will not have a husband who thinks he was trapped into marrying me. He must think of it himself and ask me." Tamar pulled Rachel's hands out of the nut basket again and sat her in the grass.

Sari laughed out loud. "I think Enosh would love to be trapped by you. As a matter of fact, I think that he feels so guilty about his brother that he is incapable of having the audacity to ask you."

"How do you know such things?"

"I have spent a lot of time with Kenan. The two are brothers after all."

Tamar turned to face her sister more directly as she bent in to look her in the eyes. "What are you saying? Have you become friends with Kenan?"

"Oh, I say nothing for now. After all, I am a healer and that keeps me quite busy enough, but there are times when I consider the future and wonder what will happen to Kenan and Enosh. After all, they have no real home now, and they do not have enough men to begin another clan. Who knows, but I may take pity on Kenan and save him from a dreadful fate."

Tamar had gone back to pounding her nuts. "And what fate would that be?"

"Marrying you if Enosh should fail."

Tamar's eyes grew large and round with sudden rage, and then she looked over at her sister and heard the girl's merry laughter rise up into the boughs of the trees overhead. Her fury was washed away in her humility, and she had to smile. Sari nudged her sister with her foot.

"You never know. We may be double sisters before very long."

Tamar put all the cracked nuts into her basket and swung its long loop over her shoulder. She stood up then, brushing the broken shells from her long dress. In one graceful movement she swooped down and scooped Rachel onto her hip. "Not if I don't do something about it." She grimaced as she sighed, and then she wiped her moist brow, looking up into the bright sun. "Why do the women always have to be the brave ones?"

Sari watched her sister walk away with the basket slung low over one hip and the baby on the other. Enosh, leading Put by the hand, came up from the other side of the village. Put saw his mother and came running. Sari was not at all surprised when Tamar managed to find room for the little boy in her arms also.

It was not many days later that Tamar caught up with Kryce and Dodan as they were setting out together.

"Kryce, may I speak with you a moment?"

157

Kryce stopped and turned to face his sister as Dodan stood off a little to the side. "Certainly, what may I do for you?"

Tamar looked hesitant, and then she swallowed and finally began to speak quickly as if to recite a memorized piece. "It is just that I have been thinking about our future. We have suffered great loss, and without our father and sister and many warriors, we are not so mighty a clan as we used to be. And as you know, we have in our midst one who has equally suffered. As I lost my father, my husband and my sister, so he too has lost a great deal. We all have much to grieve, but also much to recover. Eva and Leah are unwilling captives to an evil man who may or may not die soon. In any case, their place is at home with those who love them. I need a husband for my children, and Enosh needs a clan and a home for his few men who have fought bravely and loyally in the defense of us all. I think I should take Enosh as husband, and after some time of recovery, we should plan our revenge and the return of our own."

Kryce stared hard at her sister a moment as if he had not understood a word she had just said. It was Dodan who stepped just a bit nearer and put his hand on his brother's shoulder. "May I speak with you a moment please?"

Kryce nodded mutely, and the two moved a few paces away. Dodan smiled at his brother all the while keeping his hand on his arm. "I understand what you are thinking, and I feel your anxiety. But you know that Enosh is not at all like his brother, and though one of our sisters is lost to that family already, this is another matter entirely. In fact, you may have to accept more than even this."

Kryce's brows were furrowed in strong irritation. "What do you mean by that?"

"Nothing as of yet, but everything that Tamar just said is true, and I tend to agree with her. Enosh needs us, and we need him. He has done no wrong. To the contrary, he has displayed great bravery and skill. He is a warrior in heart as well as in body. And Tamar does need a husband and a father for her two little ones." Dodan looked over Kryce's shoulder and observed Enosh some distance off holding little Rachel in his arms, swinging her ever so gently while Put attempted to climb up his leg. Kryce turned to see what his brother was looking at, and he winced ever so slightly.

"It appears that the matter is already settled." He walked over to where his sister stood waiting, and he nodded his head silently. "I give my approval. Enosh is a good man. You may tell him I said so. You may be married when the moon is full." He paused in thought a moment. "As for the other matter, that is best left to the men to decide. But do not worry; revenge will be ours, but all in good time." Having nothing more to say, Kryce nodded to Dodan who simply smiled in return and gestured for them to resume their business of the day.

Tamar bowed her head as her brother passed by, and then she turned to rejoin Enosh and her children. There was a great smile spread wide across her face.

Enosh was joined to the People of Havilah as Tarmar's husband, and the men who had followed Hezeki and then Enosh, when given the option of staying or leaving, decided to join also. Generally speaking, it was a smooth transition, for as far as the clan member's hearts were concerned, they were too grieved and worn to bother with minor complaints or particular irritations. There was much to do to repair homes and mend things broken by the fighting and replace lost items and food stores destroyed in the days of battle. As accustomed as the men were with the warrior spirit and as prepared as they were for battle, there were few who wanted to go into another battle soon. So the months passed, and another harvest season arrived. The rains came, the contests were set up again and the games were played. However, there was a lack of joy in the traditions, for they remembered those who had participated in those games and contests in the past. Kryce was still a young man, but as the seasons passed, he grew older than time could account for, and he became quieter and kept his own council. His anger abated, and he grew fonder of Enosh as he watched him care for his sister and their little children better than her late husband had ever thought to.

Occasionally the two would walk together and discuss matters of mutual importance. Being of similar age and temperament, they found solace in their mutual, though distinctly unique, charge to discover what had happened to Neb and to bring back their stolen loved ones.

It was during the dark days when the light came weakly through ever-hanging clouds and the weather was cooler that they decided to take a hunting trip into the hills together. They took only a couple of men with them, for neither of them enjoyed the company of a large group of men. It was on that trip that they met with another band of hunters who were from the clan of Seth, and the two groups met warily with the uncertainty of whether they were friend or foe. Jubal recognized his old friend and stepped out first to greet Enosh. Kryce gave a silent signal that they could stop and speak together for a time. Jubal ordered his men to continue their search for game while he spoke in council with Enosh and Kryce. Kryce in turn ordered his own men to continue their hunt in another direction but to return before the light failed entirely.

Enosh spoke first after they were settled. "You order your men with authority, Jubal, and not as an equal among peers. Has there been a change in your clan?"

Jubal let out a bitter laugh. "A change of fortune leads to a change of order. Ever since Neb came among us, evil has haunted the steps of our people. Word spread throughout the territory that we were an unprepared clan, easy to attack, and after Neb set the pattern of destruction and conquest, other clans began to raid and pillage. We were attacked twice in a matter of two moons, and then our people took ill with some mysterious sickness. Hul soon succumbed, as did many elderly and young children. My own brother, Accad, was stolen away, and I have yet to find him. Seth has been laid so low by his own struggles with both injury and illness that he has not been able to lead the men for some time now. He should be married with a little Seth to someday lead the clan, but too much evil has come upon us in too short a time that our traditions have not been enough to properly meet the challenges we face. Seth appointed me as temporary leader in his stead, and though I am reluctant in the role, I do as I must to assist our clansmen in our distress. One more attack and we might be scattered to the ends of the earth."

Enosh had kept his head bowed at this description of their tragedies, and he raised it only slowly when Jubal finished. Kryce spoke softly so as to not sound bitter.

"I wondered why you never returned to give us aid in our need. Neb did terrible harm to us also, though he was wounded seriously in the end, and the hope is that he went home to die. Little word has reached us of him for a long time." Jubal nodded at this and spoke softly, almost in a whisper, as if he did not want to share his news with the wide world.

"We had heard the rumor that he was dead, but then it later turned out that he had not died but was simply injured. The injury then apparently became inflamed and he was near death. Several times we have received reports that he would not survive the season and that he had appointed another to take his place, but later he was seen walking and talking in apparent good health. I have come to the conclusion that he is not a man at all but rather some spirit from the world beyond that is led by an evil god."

Enosh nodded his head in understanding. He looked away toward the distant mountaintops through the green boughs overhead. "You are not far wrong. A man cannot do such evil as he has done without first aligning himself with something very terrible. Naturally evil will destroy itself eventually, but much damage is done along the way." Shaking his head, he turned and looked at Jubal and then pointed to Kryce. "Kryce is now the leader of the people of Havilah, and I am his brother for I have married his sister Tamar whose husband was killed in battle. I inherited two small children, a little boy named Put and a baby girl named Rachel. After so many lost so much, it feels rather wrong to gain a bounty, but I am doing all I can to become a worthy member of so noble a clan. I am sure that Kryce would agree that we are your loyal friends also, and though you could not come to our aid, you can trust that we would come to yours if you had need."

Kryce nodded his head in silent agreement, but Jubal put up his hand in friendly warning. "Until I know better what it is that afflicts us, I would rather you not come to us and experience our horror. Too many young are dying quickly, and the old linger in suffering. I go out for meat and provisions and to hear the news from afar, but I want to spread our bitter fate no further."

Kryce stepped forward and put his hand upon Jubal's shoulder in friendly defiance. "We are brothers in suffering. Enosh's offer holds. If you need aid, send word and we will come no matter the dread, for a fate awaits each man, but I would rather face it doing right than live in cowering fear."

Jubal nodded while a brief smile flickered over his face. "Though I still mourn my lost brother, my heart is gladdened by your words, for if brothers of flesh are lost to us then we must forge our own brotherhood. I commit our clan to your service in return. Though we have many ill, most of the warriors remain in good health. They have learned well, however unwillingly, the skills of fighting men, and they know now how to defend what would be lost but for their valor. We are committed to ending Neb's reign of terror, but we await the right moment. If you learn of an opportunity, call for us and we will go with you. We have much innocent blood to avenge."

Kryce put out his hand, and the two men clasped their arms in response to their decided commitment. Jubal turned and began to lead his men who had returned with a few small game back into the flickering green wilderness. Kryce whistled for his own men and received a whistled response. Enosh looked Kryce full in the face, and the two understood one another's silent grief. While they began to follow after their men, their minds were full of the knowledge of the depth and width of human suffering and endurance.

CHAPTER 22
REVELATIONS

    Neb had never endured so much suffering in all his life. As he sat leaning against a great tree, he looked at the quiet stillness all around him, and he smiled for he knew that his strength was returning though he still needed to rest often. He had managed to convince everyone, even in the worst of his weakness and agony, that he was still strong in a mighty way. Therefore no one had seriously attempted to take over leadership of the clan. Torgama had become for all intents and purposes his very own slave. Though he attempted to act as if what he had done was not so serious and that it was not really his fault anyway, Torgama found himself being led down a road of unremitting guilt through Neb's twisted sense of justice. Neb had found to his silent amusement a very effective way of making Torgama aware of his guilt by insisting that the incident was really someone else's fault. He insisted that Torgama could never have pierced him through the thigh and that it had been some unseen assailant who had done the treacherous deed. At first, Torgama had actually attempted to correct Neb in his ridiculous notion, but Neb would have no other explanation. Thus Neb could freely express his hatred of the terrible deed while Torgama was stuck with the certain knowledge that he was the one who had done it but without the strength of spirit to face Neb's wrath. So they lived a sort of game where Neb cursed in horrific language the man who did him such an injury all the while Torgama became the best of servants. Torgama, in his own uncertainty and guilt, found himself drawn into a web of servitude, the bonds of which he could not break no matter how he tried. His life was now simply to do the will of his master in whatever menial task was required at the moment. Quite gone were the days when he and Kittam would smirk and laugh behind Neb's back or imitate his orders with a snide remark in the secrecy of their own silent amusement. Even Kittam was a changed man, for he found himself without his allies in the death of Puti and the isolation of Torgama's guilt. He knew the truth as he had seen the entire episode. In a strange irony, he almost wished for the honest witness of his enemy to clarify the matter, for he knew that Kryce too had seen the incident and that he would verify the truth with no uncertainty. But as Neb graphically described the kind of torturous death he wished upon the man who had injured him, none dared speak. As it were, Neb was healing and growing in strength, and his men were more devoted to him than ever in their very confusion and their admiration for Neb's refusal to be conquered even by the worst of pain.

Neb continued to watch the quiet activity of his people. Torgama, as usual, was in the background, ready to assist him at even the slightest gesture. The sky was blue, a comfortable breeze blew and majestic white clouds were serenely sailing across the sky. Leah crossed his path, and Neb's smile grew wider as he approved her growing body as well as her position of respect in the clan. Very soon now a son would be born to him, and he had already chosen a name. His first son would be named Madai after a long dead grandfather who had been known for his strength and endurance. Leah had accommodated herself to the reality of being his wife better than he had anticipated. She was quiet now and rarely offered a word in conversation, but she was attentive to his commands. He, in return, offered her the respect of a well-loved wife. He made sure that her every need was met and her every comfort attended to. She was fed well and given the most comfortable place to sleep and rest. Neb never made reference to her old clan, and she acted as if she had forgotten them as well. Her eyes were frequently downcast, but this Neb approved of as a sign of her increasing modesty and a deeper understanding of her role as the wife of the leader and the mother of the future ruler. He would raise a son who would carry on his success and help him rule even greater lands than they presently knew.

The bright white sun was finishing its decent from its pinnacle high above, adding rosy colors to the horizon ever so slowly. The warm breeze softened, and Neb leaned back to luxuriate in the quiet, refreshing air while all around him everyone finished their toil for the day. He closed his eyes and rested his mind a moment. Birds were singing their evening songs, and he could hear the hum of bees as they hurried home with their bounty of pollen from the flowers all about. Suddenly he heard a sound that instantly made mountainous scows rise across his forehead. He turned his head away. He would not hear. But the sound was repeated. In a gesture of futility, he opened his eyes and looked for Torgama to assist him, but Torgama was already responding to another's call. Neb's scowl deepened as it crawled across his face. Meshullemeth was speaking in her own gestured language; her words were shrill and sharp while her hands flailed like the aimless darts of a fish in the stream. He could just barely hear what she was saying, and he grew impatient to stop her ceaseless harangue.

"I want her moved into my place today. She will give birth to the most noble of babes, and no one else knows as much as I do in the matter. I do not want to wait until the last moment. Get her things now and make the transfer before the sun has set. Do you understand?"

Torgama was doing his utmost to appease the mother of his leader, but he knew that Neb had no desire to see Leah removed from his side. Yet he could not contradict this maddening woman, for she would simply pretend not to hear.

"I must speak to Neb on this matter before I do anything. He has not told me to make—"

"He does not speak for me. I know what is best for his wife. Do as I say!"

Neb stood, and though he hated to hobble before his men, he had to work his leg as much as possible. He balanced himself against the tree, and then using a staff on which he had engraved various animals and fierce faces, he set his own face in his accustomed look of stern acceptance and faced the horrific pain of walking on his mending leg. He moved slowly with deliberate care to force his muscles to stretch and strengthen. He ignored a slight trickle of sweat, which began to slide down his face even as he forced himself to look only at his mother in anticipation of her complaint and trouble.

"Mother, Leah stays with me. She is my wife, not yours. Torgama can do nothing that you request because he knows my wishes in this matter. When her time comes, I have chosen three very skilled women to assist her. I want none of your charms and spells to interfere."

Meshullemeth took a step backward as if she had been slapped. She even put her hand to her face as if to cover the mark of the blow.

"How can you speak to me like that, my son? Have I no influence over your judgment? Does nothing I say matter to you? Was it not me who ran to gather you into my arms the moment I learned of your injury? Did I not arrange for your every comfort and watch over the needs of your new wife?"

"You almost killed me in you incompetence, and you nearly frightened my wife to death. You are skilled at making noise and little else. Now go away and do something useful. Why don't you oversee the making of the evening meal? I will be taking a journey in a few days, and I will need to eat very well in preparation."

Meshullemeth seemed to deflate like a water skin when the water leaks out through a gaping hole. She stared quizzically at her son as if she did not recognize him.

"Lately I have begun to wonder what kind of a blow you received to the head in that last battle. You have none of the gracious temper I honored you with and little of the noble bearing of your poor father. You have become little more than a brute animal of the wilderness. While Torgama at least gives me kind speech, you offer insult and odious accusations. I can find no fault with your wife, but I fear a child of you now will be little more than—"

Neb pounded his staff upon the ground. "Watch your tongue, Mother, or you may see a side of me that you have yet to witness."

Meshullemeth shook her head at the wonder her son had become. "I can do nothing more for you then." She turned about on her heel, allowing her long, flowing garment to billow about her. She began to walk away, but in her own secret mind, she had conceived a plan to influence the forces around her as she had always influenced them. She had already befriended Leah, but she now planned to become indispensible to the girl. In turn, she would help to raise the next leader of the clan. *Neb will find himself supplanted as his own father had been.* She smiled at her own plot, for though she had formed Neb from her own body and had practically lived his every breath to make him a successful leader, he had thrown her aside like a useless rag. He would learn what she had bestowed on him, for as she had brought forth the dark powers to assist him, so those same powers could be set against him as they already had. She believed that it had been her dark prayers that had led to his being injured and returned into her care, but every time she tried to assist him, he rejected her and her dark prayers became more frantic and frequent.

    She returned now to her small hut and walked solemnly into her one back room where a small stone figure stood about the size of a wild dog on a flat clay pedestal. It was a squat figure with large ears and great oblong eyes, a fat little body and tiny thick legs squatting upon flat feet. She had decorated the figure with clothes that could fit a small child, and though they were nicely made, they only accented its hideous shape and very inanimate qualities. She bowed low before it and began to whisper her secret wishes and her ardent prayers. The silent stone figure stared ahead with a vacant expression, but she cared not for she believed her prayers were being heard nevertheless.

    Neb watched his mother stalk away into her own hut, and he let a low sigh escape between his teeth. She was becoming tiresome, and he knew what her evil mind intended. She would not survive this harsh world much longer, he predicted. His eyes roved over the village again, and this time they rested on his sister, Eva. She was small and thin, for she ate very little but remained active. She was forever experimenting with herbs and plants of all kinds. He watched her as she moved through the village with a bundle of fresh plants in her arms. He had allowed her a small hut of her own to make her brews, for she had proven several times in recent days her worth as a healer, though he would never actually imbibe anything that she had offered to him.

One time shortly after he had brought her home, she had made him a healing brew for his injury. Despite her apparent gentle concern, he only pretended to accept her ministration. Later he had given the drink to a bird. The bird died in a convulsive fit. He smiled at the memory. He was strangely proud of her daring. He still allowed her to continue in her work. He knew she had no plans to kill anyone else, and he was quite able to defend himself from her artless attempts to poison him. In fact, he considered her knowledge quite useful. There would come a day when he would be able to solve two problems at once using her skills. His eyes roved from his sister's hut to his mother's and then back up toward the great sky. The sun would set in a matter of time, and for some it would never rise again.

    Leah sat on the bank of a clear, flowing stream and watched the reflected clouds billow past in the small little side pools, which formed at odd spots. Occasionally she let her eyes follow the rushing flow down the center, but as it bubbled and twinkled in the failing sunlight, she felt her nausea and weakness increase. Only the silent, still pools seemed to help her feel any better. Though she tried to keep from remembering her past, she could not help herself at such quiet moments as this. She had relived her father's death uncountable times and heard her brother's defiant words over and over. Had she done the right thing? Should she have accepted death when it was offered? No, she put her hand to her belly, and though she could not say what child this would be, she knew that even if it were a boy it could not be as bad as Neb and thus deserved a chance to live. She was glad to be with child. It gave her a purpose in life that she had never known before. And most surprisingly of all, she realized that Neb was a different man with her. Though he was capable of great evil, he was not entirely evil. This knowledge had shocked her when she first realized it. And even as Meshullemeth tried desperately to gain some measure of control over her son, Leah realized that she in fact had complete control over her husband, for against his own will and understanding, he did really love her. What she would do with this knowledge she was not sure, but she knew that it was her only hope in a world with so little reason to hope.

Neb saw his wife sitting in her accustomed spot, and he stood a moment watching her. He felt the now familiar lurch in his stomach and his head became a little light, but he stood his ground. He was not sure what was the matter with him, but he knew that he would do anything for Leah no matter what she asked. He was astute enough to understand that this new dependence on her put him at risk, but he was unsure how to deal with his own feelings. He had overcome so many greater opponents, and he was sure that given time this threat would also abate. He began to hobble toward her. She looked up at him and smiled. Neb's stomach lurched again. He wondered if he were sick. Leah noticed his look of utter discomfort, and her clear eyes clouded in bewilderment.

"Is something wrong?"

Neb made a quick jerk of his head and attempted to smile back at her. "Not at all. I am quite well, actually. I just came to check on you."

Leah nodded her acceptance. "I am feeling better. The baby is moving, and I can tell he will be very strong."

Neb's false smile became very real as he gentled himself down onto the creek bank beside her. "He will be the strongest baby under the great sun." Neb winced at a sudden pain in his leg as he tried to adjust it. Leah pretended not to notice. Neb sat still, watching the shadows grow longer as the sky grew dimmer. He suddenly felt terribly afraid as if a hand had reached out and grabbed him by the throat. He was so startled by this sensation, even as he attempted to luxuriate in the quiet evening, that he shivered slightly.

Leah let her eyes trail toward Neb, and she instinctively understood his confused vulnerability. He was not a fearless leader any more. He was not a terrifying killer at the moment. He was not what he must be to survive in the world he was making. If she had ever imagined a perfect justice, it was this. He had planned to thwart her father's spirit when it came for revenge, but it was not possible. Perfect revenge had already been found in the undoing of his own self-image. Whether he liked it or not, he was no longer the man he had been. She felt the little motions of the man-child inside her body, and she knew that when this baby was born, Neb would lose himself even more. He was made strong only through complete selfishness, and to accomplish what he now wanted, he would have to sincerely care about an innocent life. She smiled to herself. Suddenly she heard Neb speaking.

"My mother has not been bothering you, has she?"

Leah turned to face him more directly. "Your mother? Bother me?" Leah blinked uncertainly a couple of times. "No, why would she? She has tried many times to be of assistance, but I have informed her that all the decisions are yours, not mine."

Neb nodded though he looked unconvinced. "I do not mean that she would be unkind. I mean rather that she would find some way to gain control over you. She wants to have the baby for herself."

At this Leah almost jumped inside her skin. "What do you mean have the baby for herself? This child is ours, flesh of our flesh."

Neb grunted. "Do not put anything past that conniving old woman. She wants to raise our son as her servant. She failed to mold me into the serving vessel she imagined, so now she wants to try with my son." Neb looked Leah directly in the eye. "Don't spend much time with her or let her feed you anything without my approval. She uses the dark powers to gain strength, and she would stop at nothing to use you to gain a new child."

Leah's nausea increased again, and she tried to stand up. She wanted nothing more than to get away from Neb and all his family. Was nothing safe? Would her child be used as a tool for the amusement of those seeking to gain more power? How much power did they need after all? They had her life bound completely. Was that not enough?

Neb saw her attempt to rise, and he grasped her hand to steady her. "I did not mean to upset you but rather to simply warn you. She is not what she seems."

Leah shook her head sadly. The words came out before she even had time to think. "Is anyone?"

Neb had begun to rise to help her up, but he paused and almost stumbled. "What is that?"

Leah brushed the question away. "Nothing, I said nothing."

Neb rose and put his hand out to her. She accepted his arm and rose up facing the failing light of the day. Neb began to lead her home when he stopped, turned and looked her in the face. "I want to know the truth. Do you believe I am not what I say I am?"

Leah felt immensely weary. "I can hardly answer your question. All I know is that you are neither as good as you claim nor as evil as you wish to be." Letting go of his gentle grasp, Leah slowly walked along ahead with one hand rubbing her aching back while the other rested on the jerking kicks of her son.

Neb watched his wife move away from him as if she were part of a dream from which he could not awake. After a moment, he heard his mother's commands ring through the air. Suddenly he felt as if his world were falling to pieces. The well managed self-control of earlier had been swept away. He shook his head as if to clear it of all troubling thoughts. Just then Torgama came walking up to him looking like an angry child.

"Neb, your mother wishes to have everyone eat right now, and she has sent me to tell you that if you do not come immediately, there will be nothing left for you later. Frankly, I do not think I can continue to serve her, for she acts as if I am little more than—"

"I know what she thinks and I would rid you of her troublesome nature immediately if it were a simple matter, but there are those in this clan who respect her and who are under her spell. Even with all my authority, I need a good reason to kill my own mother!"

Torgama shook his head in bafflement. "Why? You had no such—" He caught himself before he finished the sentence, and to cover his immense confusion, a sudden memory came to his recue. He remembered the conversation between Meshullemeth and Hul where she had asked him to keep an eye on them all and to reveal everything that happened in their travels to her in secret. Of course Hul had died before he ever returned home, but suddenly Torgama found himself telling Neb all about the incident with a few added details. This would give Neb exactly what he needed. Neb listened with care to Torgama's recital, and his face froze into an impenetrable mask. After hearing all there was to tell and a bit more, Neb dismissed Torgama and stood watching the clan gathering for their evening meal. They had a new tradition of communal meals in the evening for it facilitated a sense of unity, which was very useful. It was also a good opportunity for Neb to elaborate on any beliefs that he wanted to inculcate into the clan. He knew what he needed to do, and though he wanted to achieve his freedom from his mother, he found that it was a more difficult matter than with his father. Why, he could not fathom. The need was just as great. He began to walk forward toward the campfire, but his wife's words rang clearly through his mind.

CHAPTER 23
EVA AND LEAH

Eva tilted her head a little to the right as she concentrated on stirring her stew. One of the men had brought her a nice, fat rabbit that he had caught and offered to her in gratitude for what she had done to help his little son who had recently been ailing with terrible headaches. Eva pondered the strangeness of fortune, for she was not at all certain what she had done to help the child though there was ample proof the little boy was feeling much better, as she had seen him up and about and acting as frisky as a little goat. She tried to think of what exactly she had done so that if the situation ever came up again she would be able to repeat her success. To the best of her knowledge, she had simply made a strong brew from chamomile leaves and added a little honey for sweetening. Had it been the chamomile or the honey? Or both? She shook her head in frustration. How could such a little thing help a child feel better when he had been plagued with headaches ever since his mother had given birth to another boy a few weeks earlier? Eva straightened up and looked north to where the child lived with his family. Yes, there he was, playing and running outside his dwelling while his mother looked on. Though his mother had had a fairly simple delivery, she had been quite tired from her exertions. Eva had recommended rest for an extended time, and the father, in natural concern, had sent his other children to be cared for by an elder sister for a time. Now the mother was feeling better, though Eva had only offered her the usual poultices, salves and nourishing meals of red meat and soothing warm drinks. Eva watched the family for a few more moments, and the small crease that formed between her eyebrows whenever she was puzzled smoothed out. The little boy called loudly to his mother every few moments, begging her to watch him as he committed another act of surprising agility and daring in jumping over a pile of sticks. The mother smiled indulgently as she clapped her hands at his antics. Eva smiled to herself as she went back to watch her pot. Perhaps it had not been her ministrations to the boy that had cured him as much as her ministrations to the mother.

Suddenly Eva became aware of the fact that she was being watched, and though she knew she was safe, for even her mother had given up trying to control her, she felt always on the alert for some threat. She dipped her long, wooden-handled spoon into the pot and tasted it hesitatingly. After nodding approvingly, she turned and saw Leah standing behind her. She nodded slightly. The two hardly ever spoke, though they had much in common. Leah tried to speak, but no words seemed able to reach from her thoughts to the air. Eva reached over quickly and grabbed Leah's hand and led her to a bench that was built into the wall of her little thatched hut.

"Are you ill?"

Leah shook her head. "I do not know. I just keep having these pains, and I feel so tired and can't eat anything."

"How long has this been going on?"

"It started a few days ago, and it has been getting worse each day. At times it stops, but then it starts up again." Leah put her hands on Eva's arm, and her eyes grew wide and round. "Please don't let anything happen to my baby!"

Eva stared hard at Leah. "Do you really want this baby to live?"

Leah jerked away. A stifled sob broke from her, and she struggled to get to her feet. Eva became alarmed at what she had said to cause such a reaction.

"I am sorry. I was just wondering what you wanted. I mean, if I was carrying Neb's baby I would—"

A bitter strangled scream broke from deep inside Leah. "You would be its mother! And if you had a heart at all, you would love your baby with your very soul."

Eva was genuinely confused and concerned. She reached out and stroked Leah's arm compassionately. "I am sorry again. I did not mean to upset you. I am just trying to understand how I can help."

Leah straightened up and wiped her face with her hands. "You can help best if you forget about your hatred of Neb and think about the innocence of this baby."

Eva's eyebrows flashed up and then came down slowly as her pursed lips unfolded. "Yes, I guess I deserve that. Alright, in order to help you, I will forget who the father is and do all I can to save this baby."

Leah closed her eyes in a trembling spasm. "No, that is not enough. Neb will come along, and he will remind you quite forcefully of who the father is. He will never let any of us forget, but that does not mean he will have this child for himself alone. I am, and always will be, the mother of this babe. No matter what, he will carry me with him forever, and I am nothing like Neb."

Eva tilted her head again. She sat down next to Leah. It took her a few moments to put her thoughts into words, "You know, I hated you for choosing to live and becoming Neb's wife. I thought you were a coward, and worse even." She looked away up into the bright and distant blue sky as a single black bird flew in an arch far overhead. "But now I realize that you are braver than I am." She brought her eyes to earth again and looked at Leah with a passing glance. "Do you know I tried to poison him?"

Leah nodded. "Well, as a matter of fact, he told me one night that he thought you wanted to kill him. I was amazed."

"Why, I have every reason in the world to want him dead."

"No, I mean I was amazed he told me. After we were married and spent time together, he began to speak to me about things— things I don't think he ever told anyone else. It was as if he were a different man."

"Can a man be two people at once?"

Leah nodded her head. "Yes, I think that is more often the case than we realize."

Eva put out her hand to Leah again, and Leah took it in all simplicity. "So, what can I do for you?"

"I want to stay strong and well, and I want this baby to live. Can you help me?"

Eva stared across the village to the little boy who was now

sitting contentedly nestled under his mother's arm while she nursed her littlest son. "I do not know what powers I have, for they do not come from me. All I know is that I intend to do good and things generally work out well."

Leah let a small laugh escape her. "Well at least you won't try to kill me."

Eva shrugged good-naturedly. "I'm still not sure why my attempt failed. To be honest, a drink I gave him once shortly after he came back here should have killed him outright."

Leah smiled knowingly. "He never swallowed the brew. He gave it to a bird, which did die."

Eva swallowed. "So, he knew the whole truth? He has known all this time?" She sat totally still a moment in deep thought. "Why hasn't he killed me?"

"He told me that he was proud of your daring for it took an uncommonly strong spirit to attempt such a thing. It was then that he forbade your mother to have her way with you. He made her promise to leave you in peace, and he gave you this hut for your own. He respects you and he finds your skills useful."

Eva was more perplexed than she had ever been in her life. "How can such an evil man choose to be kind?"

"Evil is not the only force in existence, and there are untold battles inside each man. There is much more to this world than we can see with our eyes."

Eva stood up and walked inside her dwelling. She came back with a carved wooden bowl and a skin of some warm drink. "Well, you seem to be doing well enough to eat a little something, so we will start with that. It seems that hunger and thirst can make a woman begin labor early, so we must see to it that you are well fed and have plenty of good drink on hand. I will bring something by each day, and we will talk. If anything else happens that alarms you, just send someone to tell me and I will come to you."

"You won't be afraid of Neb?"

"He chose not to be afraid of me, so I suppose I can do the same."

Eva dipped out the rabbit stew and gave the bowl to Leah who sat and sipped her meal slowly. They had been quiet for some minutes and Leah had almost finished her meal when Meshullemeth came storming across the village, her voice raised in a screeching call.

"Leah! Leah, my darling, where are you?" She stopped dead in her tracks when she saw Leah sitting composedly on the bench at Eva's dwelling, eating from her bowl. A howl of protest came up from Meshullemeth's chest and echoed into the world at large.

"Don't eat that! Don't eat anything that little witch gives you! She is in league with the powers of darkness, don't you know? She will kill you and our baby! Get up, get up and come away with me. I will take care of you."

Meshullemeth had reached over and slapped the bowl from the girl's amazed hands, and then she attempted to grab her by the shoulders to drag her away from Eva's dwelling. Eva was so shocked and horrified that for a moment she did not move, but Leah felt a wave of nausea rise up in her from the very sound of Meshullemeth's voice that she knew she had best not stand or say anything though she tried to resist the older woman's advancement upon her. She squirmed and groaned to no avail, for Meshullemeth was quite determined to have her own way in this matter. Finally, seeing the situation become desperate, Eva was shaken out of her own stupor, and she raised her voice and called out for help. Many faces turned their way, but no one dared to interfere with Neb's mother. Eva realized that she had no choice but to get Neb and bring him to rescue his wife from his mother's hands before Leah was sent into early labor. Eva ran to Neb's dwelling, but he was not there. She continued running, panting and throwing dust up from her feet as she scampered down an incline toward a place she knew that Neb liked to go for peace and quiet. She was just about to jump over a large rock that was in her way when she heard a voice call out to her.

"Why are you running like a frightened rabbit? It is not like you, Eva."

Eva turned, and there was Neb standing against a great tree with his one bad leg lifted up on a rock as if he were stretching it into a straight position.

Eva noticed everything, and though several thoughts ran through her mind at the same time, she simply blurted out the situation at the village with Leah and her labor pains coming early and Meshullemeth forcefully attempting to bring the girl to her own dwelling.

"You must stop her, Neb, or you could lose both Leah and the baby."

Neb did not appear to hobble much as he scampered as fast as his legs would carry him back up the incline into the heart of the village. Meshullemeth had gotten Leah as far as the door of her dwelling, though Leah looked as if she could hardly walk another step. Eva rushed to her side and helped to hold her up, for she was near to collapsing. Neb's eyes glowed with red fire as he looked upon his mother.

He saw the urgency of the situation, and with surprising control and astuteness, he picked up Leah and carried her back to Eva's dwelling and laid her on Eva's bed. He yelled for one of his men to gather all the skins from his own dwelling and to bring them there. When that was accomplished, he set everything with tender concern as comfortable as possible for his wife. Eva stood back and watched his ministrations as one amazed. She could not have been more surprised if a tiger had suddenly begun to act like a mouse. She sensed not only Neb's love for his wife, but also his fear. He was obviously terrified that Leah might die and the child with her. When he stood, he took ahold of Eva's arm and led her to the doorway of her dwelling.

"You will do everything possible to save her and the life of the child."

Eva looked intently at Neb, and she did not even know why she said her next words except to torment him one last time. "And if I must choose between the two?"

Neb squeezed her arm painfully. "You will not choose. It is not for you to decide."

Eva nodded her head slowly. "I will do everything that is in my power and beyond, but I can make no promises. Unlike you, I do not control the forces I serve."

Neb looked once more at Leah who was lying down with her eyes shut though she moaned in discomfort every few moments. "I have to attend to something so that this never happens again, but I will be back. If she needs anything, send me word and I will see to it."

Eva merely nodded as she turned away to see to Leah's care. She did not even notice the dark, angry mark on her arm.

Neb knew that though she deserved instant death, it was not possible for him to do away with his mother as he had with his father, though he could not account for the difference. He had long ago chosen to forget all the tender remembrances of childhood. He had blacked out of his mind every kind thing his mother had ever said or done, yet he could not kill her outright. He was not sure how to solve this problem. As he strode along, quite certain that he would end this conflict today, he suddenly thought of an idea. He turned completely around and returned to Eva's dwelling. Leah was sitting up drinking something from a skin bag that Eva was holding gently for her. Neb motioned for his sister to come to him in the front of the room. She put the bag in Leah's exhausted hands and followed Neb to the doorway.

Neb looked her intently in the eye. "Give me the same potion you tried to kill me with when I first came back."

"Why?"

"I need to kill someone."

"Who?"

"It does not really matter to you. Just know that my wife will live longer if I do this."

"Mother. You want her out of your way." Eva shook her head slowly. "I know what you will say, that our mother is an evil woman and she deserves to die, and after all I tried to kill you so what is the difference between one murder and another."

Neb nodded as if he could not have stated the case any clearer. But Eva covered her face with her hands. "But that was before I met your wife! She had changed me—perhaps ruined me in a way."

Neb grew angry and thrust his hand into the air in an angry gesture. "She has no power over you. You are strong. You attempted what no other woman has ever attempted. Now give me what I want."

"No, I cannot. I can never try to kill anyone ever again."

"Why not? There are many who deserve to die!"

Eva looked at Neb, and as the sun's rays shot out from behind him, it seemed as if his silhouette were enmeshed in complete darkness. She burst into ironic laughter. "This is so strange a conversation. The man I wanted to kill, I can no longer kill because his wife convinced me of some measure of goodness buried way deep down in his insides. And here you stand trying to convince me to assist you in killing our own mother. Don't you see? The same reason I can't help to kill her is the same reason I can never try to kill you again."

Neb looked absolutely baffled. His anger was mounting. "What are you talking about?"

"I don't want to be like you, someone who fills the world with anger and hate. I want to be like Leah, the one who draws love from the deepest well imaginable. I will overcome the infection of your malice and be healed by your wife's love."

Neb strode into the inner part of her dwelling. "You are not helping me solve my immediate problem. I cannot allow Leah to suffer again."

"Then send mother away. Let her go with some companions to follow her sons. Perhaps they will help her. Perhaps she will—"

Neb retreated out of the dwelling for a few minutes, and he came back leading a young child by the arm. It was the boy Eva had cured of the headaches. Neb shook the child's arm lightly and looked at Eva with his piercing black eyes. "Either you give me the potion, or I will have this boy drink a bit of everything in this room until I find what I am looking for."

Leah moaned lightly again as she stirred distractedly in her soft bed. Eva's eyes widened in horror as she stepped toward Neb. "How can you be so evil?"

Neb shook his head. "I am no more evil than you are. I just do what I have to do. My wife and child are important to me."

Eva reached over to a high shelf and felt around until she was able to grasp a small, clay vile. She took it down and stepped toward Neb. "I am sure you felt the same when you killed our father and every time you slayed another man. I am sure you always had a good reason for your deed."

Neb snatched the small vile from her hand and pushed the boy out the door. "I do not need to justify my actions to you or anyone. I am Neb, the leader of this clan." He turned on his heel and walked through the doorway, attempting to stride purposefully toward the center of the village. His limp continued to hobble his every step. Eva turned back toward her patient and drew back toward the skin-covered pallet. She looked down at Leah who was sleeping calmly now.

"Only you could love the unlovable." With a deep sigh, Eva sat down and watched over her friend.

CHAPTER 24
MESHULLEMETH'S END

Meshullemeth felt very old all of a sudden. She sat down on her pallet and heaved an enormous sigh. The light in her dwelling was dim as it was so small and there was only one thin window high up near the ceiling to let in the light. There were a few broad beams of light that slanted through the window opening and exposed the dust in the air and the oppression in her heart. Often in the morning, she was amazed at how the new light made everything look clean and fresh, but now in this late afternoon dimness, she felt as well as saw the uncleanness of her world. She looked around her space and was depressed. Everything was untidy. She had forgotten to wash her morning bowl, and her blankets were strewn in the dust. Worst of all, she felt so terribly alone. She imagined Hezeki in her mind, and she wondered what had really happened to him. Neb refused to speak of their meeting at all. In fact, he would tell her nothing of his journeys. He kept all the details to himself. She had questioned Riphath, Torgama and Kittam about the events, but they would say nothing. Hul had never come back from the first journey, to her infinite regret, for he would have told her the truth even against his better judgment. But what had happened to him was also shrouded in dark mystery. Only the fate of Puti was revealed, for Neb had told how he had died valiantly in battle and made every man among them jealous of the great praise heaped upon a dead man. Meshullemeth sighed again. There were too many mysteries, and what she did know, she did not like. Suddenly she shivered. She had heard the sound of her husband's voice in her mind. Hezeki used to joke with her that she should have married a god, as only a god could make her happy. She had always smiled at his teasing, for deep down she secretly agreed with his premise. She had always felt cheated somehow. She had been an only child to survive the many grave illnesses of her time. All her siblings had succumbed to ailments one after another, and everyone said that she was marked for some special purpose. When she married Hezeki, she was simply being obedient to her parents' wishes, but she had wondered often in the silent moments of the night if a mistake had not been made. She should have been married to a much greater man. But as time wore on and after Neb was born, her vision cleared, and she began to see that her purpose was not to marry a great man but to form one— to raise up a god from mankind itself. She shook her head. Her earlier doubts rose again to her mind as Neb refused to be led by her. Had her whole life been a mistake? Had she misunderstood her purpose? A terrible insecurity gnawed at her insides. She knew in truth that ultimately her attempt to take Leah from Neb and raise his baby was just a desperate attempt to try to succeed where she had already failed.

A shadow eclipsed the little light in the room. She looked not at the doorway where a man stood but over to the little window. The slanting rays had passed. The dust was gone, and somehow inside of her soul so was all hope. Neb spoke, his voice even and calm.

"I have a present for you mother."

Meshullemeth's head hung down low as she looked at the shadows of her hands. She barely murmured her response. "A present for me? How unlike you."

Neb took a step into the room. "I insist that you take it."

Meshullemeth raised her head and tried to look her son in the eye. "I want to know one thing. What really happened to your father? I think of him often, you know. Despite everything, I was really fond of him. He had a good heart, even if it was weak." She ignored the snorted response of disbelief and derision.

Neb stepped closer to his mother and handed down the small vile to her. "It is a calming medicine. Mix it with whatever you like, and you will sleep well tonight."

His mother looked at his long, brown arm extended down to her. She saw the small vile, and she shivered involuntarily. She had heard the rumors. She knew that many people thought that

Hezeki was dead and Hul too. She supposed that was the truth after all.

"Did you kill him?"

Neb stopped, his hand frozen in extension, trying to get her to accept his gift.

"Kill who?"

"Your father." She waved the vile away as she shifted her weight so that she could get more comfortable. Her back and arm were aching terribly. "Don't try to deny it. I know that is what you wanted from the first." She shook her head. "It is strange. I raised you to be strong and brave beyond the lot of mortal men, and yet you were afraid of the weakest man we knew. Why was that? What did you fear? He would have given you leadership in time. Why did you have to snatch it early?"

Neb straightened up. His voice was cold. "You ask odd questions, considering you were my teacher. What I learned, I learned from you." He hobbled across the room and found her water skin hanging from a peg on the wall. He snatched it up and opened it. While she looked into the darkness, he poured the contents of the vile into the bag. He smelled it and wrinkled his nose. He put the bag near her bed. Meshullemeth nodded as if she understood everything he wanted. As he limped past her, she caught the end of his garment and stopped him in mid-motion. "And Hul? What happened to him?"

Neb shrugged. "He was a mistake. He died by accident." He started to go past, but her fingers clutched his garment even more tightly and almost tripped him. "And my other sons? What about them?"

Neb wrenched his tunic free and hobbled quickly away from her grasp. "Nothing! Nothing has happened to them. They are living with a clan to the southwest. They are probably very happy." His bitterness was palpable.

Meshullemeth heaved a deep sigh again as long grey strands of hair hung down over her face. Her despair was showing. "But you will not leave them be, will you?"

Neb shook his head as he stepped to the doorway. "You need to rest, Mother. Take that draught I brought you, and go to sleep.

Forget your worries and troubles for tonight."

Meshullemeth nodded slowly. She had the water skin in her hands. She murmured to herself. "I wonder if I will ever see him again."

Neb paused a moment in irritated distraction. "See who?"

"Your father."

"Perhaps someday." Neb walked outside the doorway. The sun had set, and the warmth of the day was fading. He began to walk slowly away. He heard a stifled choking sound behind him, and he kept on walking.

Meshullemeth wiped the tears draining down her face away in one angry, choking sob. She looked down at the water skin but she was not thirsty. She threw it to the side, and the contents began to leak out all over the bare ground. She felt terribly hot and extremely tired. She felt her chest pains start again. In instinctual response she clutched at her chest trying to stop the intense pressure from building, and she was on the verge of calling for help when she saw Hezeki's face right in front of her own. He stood there as he had stood in front of her so many times trying to reason with her, trying to calm her, trying to please her. She put out her arms to beckon him closer, but when the floating image came near, she became frightened and repulsed and just as hurriedly waved him away. She watched him vanish in an instant. Weakness swiftly enveloped her whole being. She needed to sleep, but she dared not. She did not want to dream only to wake to another day with Neb and his horrors, her horrors. What was the point of everything? Nothing she did ever worked. She had never really been able to fix things the way she wanted them. Neb may have grown powerful, but he cared nothing for her. In the corner of her eye, she saw the water skin again. In the darkness, it looked somewhat like a snake. Was it not very odd of Neb to bring her a soothing draught? He had never done such a thing before. Her eyes bore through the darkness, attempting to see the truth of the matter. A terrible crushing pain took her attention for a moment. She fell back on her pillows. Her head was hurting dreadfully, and she could not catch her breath. In her mind's eye, she could see the mound of earth that was the sorceress's final place of rest.

Long ago, Neb had taken matters into his own hands. He was not her child any more. Suddenly she knew what the draught was meant to do. She felt she was being choked as a strange darkness enveloped her that had nothing to do with the darkness of the room. She called out for Hezeki, but of course he was not there. She had chased him away through Neb. She felt very sorry for herself. Complete silence oppressed her. A sweat broke out on her skin, yet she felt nothing at all except overwhelming fear. She was leaving the room, but yet she had not stood up. She tried to reach out, but there was nothing to grasp onto. Even the empty water skin was beyond her reach now.

"Neb!" There was no response. She could hear laughter, a strange horrible laugher, at the irony of her death. Neb had not killed her as he intended, but she was lost nonetheless. Neb would think he had done the deed. He would live with yet another curse, but in truth she had cursed herself.

When Neb was told of his mother's death, he said nothing, though Leah gasped in surprise. Neb had been sitting by his wife's side the whole morning, and though they had said little, they both felt better in the morning light. Torgama held the water skin in his hand, and he seemed to want to say something more, but the words would not come. Finally Neb reached over and took the water skin from his grasp and tried to pour its contents on the ground, but there were only a few drops left in it. Neb looked slightly puzzled as he shook the empty skin thoroughly and then handed it back to Torgama.

"Burn that in the fire. I don't want anyone else coming down with whatever she had." He paused in thought. "Go and burn her whole dwelling down to the ground, and throw her little god into the fire as well."

"It is made of clay and stone."

"Then smash it to pieces, and bury whatever is left."

Torgama nodded. "I will see to it at once."

Neb turned back to his wife. "I must travel in a few days, but while I am gone, I want you to stay under Eva's care. She will watch over you, and my men will protect you from all harm."

Leah looked a little startled. "What harm could come to me here?"

Neb shrugged. "None that I know of, but it is always best to be prepared for the unknown."

Leah shook her head to object, but Neb put up his fingers to her lips to stop her protest. "Just do as I ask, and rest easy until I come back. I just want to check the boundaries so that no one will come upon us unprepared. The time is right for raiding, and I am not fool enough to think that no one would like to conquer me."

Leah nodded her head in quiet acceptance as Neb rose to his feet. She put out her hand to him. "I am sorry about your mother."

Neb simply nodded once and turned and left the room. Neb crossed the village to Eva's dwelling. She was quietly sitting on her bench outside in the sun. Neb stopped for a moment to speak to her.

"You will do all you can to help Leah and keep the baby safe."

Eva nodded silently, though when she raised her head, she looked Neb directly in the eyes. "I will be kinder to your wife than you were to our mother."

Neb shrugged unconcernedly. "She was never very kind to you."

"But she was our mother."

"What does that matter?"

Eva shook her head as she stood and turned to enter her dwelling. "You will know the answer to that when your son is born."

Neb looked after her a moment and then turned and walked away.

CHAPTER 25
ACCAD'S RETURN

(Ten years later)

Accad chopped the winding vines down from his path with quick, ruthless cuts. He wondered how thick this wilderness would get and whether he would ever manage to cross through the interminable foliage. His family had been traveling with him for days uncounted, and he was losing his patience. His wife was a strong, stout woman with a good heart and a strong back, and he adored his three children, but he was so angry at his own confusion that he could not help snapping at them to keep up better even as he slashed at the saplings in his way. Where in the world was he?

"Don't fall behind, Obal, or I'll lose you altogether!"

"I am doing the best I can. Why don't we take a rest? We are just getting more and more lost."

"We are not lost! I am just a little delayed."

"Delayed? You said that we would reach the grasslands in a few days. It has been long past a few days."

In a fury, Accad turned and slapped at the green leaves between them as he began to shout. "I know what I said, and I know—"

Suddenly there was a wailing sound as Accad's youngest responded to his angry tones by crying loudly. Accad threw up his hands in frustration. Obal comforted the child on her hip even as she tried to comfort the other two who had also began to sniffle in fear and bewilderment.

Accad muttered out in his frustration. "Oh, alright, we will stop, though I do not know what good it will do us. We will just be stuck out here in the dark."

Suddenly there was a loud rustling sound, and everyone in the family stood completely still. The vines and plants were parted, and three men and a large youth appeared almost out of nowhere.

Accad peered at the three men as they peered intently back at him and his family. Finally Accad decided he had better do something. He swung his spear up into the air and sliced the nearest vine with his knife in an attempt to show both his bravery and his skill. Abruptly, one of the men began to laugh. Enosh stepped forward into their little circle, and he put out his hand to Accad in a friendly gesture.

"Please don't kill me, oh mighty warrior!"

Accad's jaw dropped slightly as he kept his weapons ready and his arms spread in front of his wife and children. He turned his head to the side, peering intently. "Do I know you?"

Enosh dropped his own hands down to his sides. "Oh, how you crush me! I thought that when we came to your village bringing Neb in our wake that you would never forgive us, much less forget us. It is I, Enosh, along with my brother Kenan, and I have a son now. Do you not recognize us?"

Accad dropped his arms to his side almost in imitation of Enosh, and his words came out haltingly. "I am sorry. Yes, I can see you clearly now. It's just that it has been so long, and I have had many changes in my life." He stepped back and gestured to his wife and children. "This is my wife, Obal, and my children. We were just traveling."

Kenan stepped forward and nodded his salutation even as his words expressed his incredibility. "Through this trackless wilderness?" He paused in thought. "Where have you been all these years? We have visited the People of Seth on many occasions, and they speak of you as if you were dead."

Accad looked slightly ashen. "In a way I was." He looked around hopelessly. "Is there any way we can get out of this thicket and find a clearing in which to speak?"

Kryce stepped forward. "We are not far from a table land. We can climb up there, and I can show you the surrounding area so that you can get your bearings. Where are you heading?"

Accad looked at his wife, took a deep breath and smiled. "We are going home."

It was about noon when they all reached the tabletop and had a chance to rest and eat some of their provisions. Accad started the conversation by asking Enosh in a rather gruff begrudging tone, "So what ever happened to Neb?"

Enosh shook his head as he swallowed the last of his dried meat. "He lives back at his home village. He attacked the People of Havilah and killed Uzal and took his daughter as wife. He was injured and went home, and though he did make some raids, he never came our way again. He has a family now, I hear, and he keeps to himself. When he does go on a raid, he goes far from us. I think his wife keeps him distant."

Accad looked amazed. "Neb would never listen to a woman, no matter who that woman was."

Kryce spoke up. "He listens to this woman! She is my sister, and a more beautiful woman you will never meet."

Accad pursed his lips. "I doubt that not, but Neb is a man who cannot be tamed. After what he did to me . . ."

Accad trailed off mournfully, and Kenan spoke first the question others were wanting to ask. "What did he do to you?"

Obal squeezed her husband's hand. Accad sighed. "By his own hand? Not a thing. But by example, he sent others to attack my people. He brought hate into the world around us. We resisted every raid manfully, but eventually I was injured and taken as a slave. I was tied like an animal and marched far from home. Because I was uncooperative, I was traded uncountable times. In the end, I was sold to a small clan deep in the mountains, and it was there that I met Obal. She had been a slave also, but we were married and began to have children. We were as happy as it was possible to be under such circumstances. The people of that clan did not treat us badly. We were given a decent place to live, and we worked hard, but we were not brutally handled. But then last season we found out that the leader was considering trading our children to another clan. We made our escape quickly before anything could happen to divide us. But I was not able to get my bearings, so I wasn't sure where I should go. I just took my family away, and we moved as fast as we could from those mountains down into the hills and into this woodland. We soon got lost, however, and I have been looking for some way to return us to the People of Seth ever since." Accad looked away with his eyes downcast.

Enosh's eyebrows had risen in the telling of the story. "Your life has become an adventure."

Accad shook his head. "Not one any man would want to share." Every time he wanted to see someone clearly, he turned his head to the side. Finally, Kenan could not keep his curiosity at bay any longer.

"Why do you always turn your head to the side when you speak?"

Accad looked up into the sky as if considering his words. "It is the price one pays for making a master angry." He turned so they could see his full face more clearly. One eye had a deep scar running through it. "Like I said, it was not an adventure any man would wish to have."

It was Kenan who looked ashamed now, but Enosh stood up and shook out his limbs as if getting ready to do battle. "Alright. Are we ready to get through this thicket? Home is still several days away, and we have to get our food along the way."

Kryce nodded his head thoughtfully. He stood up and pointed to Accad decisively. "We will take them to the Village of Seth first, and then we will go home." He looked at Accad's young family and smiled. "And we will bring enough food to make a banquet. How often does a hero return home?"

Seth wandered alone along the gentle flowing river. His back was to the sun, so he could clearly admire the sparkling water and the reflecting pictures of waving grasses in silent, still pools trapped between great boulders. He felt a great deal of joy and contentment in his heart. It had taken him a long time to heal from his many injuries and illnesses, but he had grown strong again, and his life had changed for the better in more ways than he could count. He had married well, and his wife, Debora, had already born five children. Though only three had survived infancy, she had now given birth to another healthy son. This would make four sons, and he felt blessed beyond words. It had taken him a long time to find a wife, but the one he had finally chosen was worth all the pains he had taken to find her. He felt a slight blush rise in his cheeks when he thought of some of the other women he had nearly chosen. He felt the sensation once again that he had just barely missed being flattened by a huge rock. The memory of one woman in particular caused the hair to rise on his arms. She had been a beauty, but only in looks, for her moods swung up and down like a bird in summer flight. He had heard recent reports of her from the clan that she had finally married into. She argued bitterly with her poor husband from morning until night, and when she did finally give birth to a healthy baby, she neglected him to the point that others had to take over the care of the child. But then he thought of Debora, and he smiled. This time he had brought home a treasure. She was strong and had her own opinions, but she let him lead the clan as he saw fit, and she managed her own affairs with grace and wit. As a matter of fact, that was one of the things he most loved about her. She was always laughing. Debora had such joy tucked deep inside that from time to time it bubbled out and even the children laughed when they didn't know what they were laughing at. Seth took one last look at the mirrored image of the perfect sky in the calm, slow-moving river, and he turned and went back to his home.

He was just about to crest the slight hill that led into his village when he heard a shout. Jubal was running toward him with unusual speed. Seth put up his hand to stall the coming excitement. Of all days, he wanted to keep things calm for his wife's sake. She hated being left out of any fun or excitement, but she must rest for days yet to come. When Jubal came to a stop in front of him, the two looked at each other. Suddenly Seth's heart clenched tight. There was ill news, and he feared for his wife and their new baby.

"What is it? What has happened?"

"There are men coming from the west."

Seth took in a deep breath of air and let it out slowly. "And that alarms you?"

Jubal looked slightly taken aback. "We can never be off our guard."

Seth nodded his understanding. "How many men are there do you think?"

Jubal looked a little sheepish, even as he kept his face completely straight. "At least five and maybe more. It looks like there are some children and a woman."

Seth's eyebrows went up as he pursed his lips and looked grim. "This could be serious. You had better get the best warriors ready in position."

Jubal's shoulders went down a slight bit. He shifted his eyes toward Seth to see if he was smiling. "I did not say we were going into battle. I just wanted to prepare you for visitors. We have not always had the best of luck with our visitors."

Seth's mind shifted back to the woman he almost chose as wife and then to the curse of Neb, and his shoulders slumped just a slight bit. "Yes, that is true. It is always wise to be careful." He paused in thought a moment. "How far away are they?"

Jubal shifted his weight as he fingered the knife tucked inside his tunic. "Not far. They will be here before the noon meal."

Seth nodded decisively. "Then I will check on Debora now, and then I will come with you and wait for them. If they are harmless and only looking for a night's shelter, we will offer them what we can. If it looks like trouble follows them, then we will send them on their way as quickly as we decently can." Seth blinked as he remembered Hezeki's visit and all the horrible trouble that followed him and his sons. He would not repeat such a mistake twice. Now his men were better trained and much more battle-ready. If anyone like Neb ever came into their midst again, he would find no welcome here. Seth had learned through death and much destruction that kindness in the face of evil could become an evil in itself.

Jubal nodded in understanding. He had to brush away the image of his lost brother. It was beyond the stars in the heavens to track how often he had thought of Accad and their last battle together. It had been a warm night so long ago that they would no longer recognize the youths they had once been, when a raiding clan had come in the middle of the night and attacked without warning and without mercy. Many had been killed, and many had been taken away. When the dust settled on the bodies of the slain and Accad had not responded to his brother's call,

Jubal had gone out looking for him. He followed the trail of the victors, but they had split up, and heavy rains had come and muddied the tracks. Too many of his men were sick and needed care, so he had turned around and come home to face the empty place of his mind and heart where his brother had always been. So many years had passed now, but he could never forget his best friend and brother. He had never married, for he felt closed up inside as if he could never love another until he let go of the love he bore his own flesh and blood, and this he could never do. Many were the nights he dreamed of Accad and cried as he searched for his brother's eluding figure in a dark wilderness.

Seth returned after a short visit with his wife and child. The smile on his face bore testimony to Debora's irrepressible humor, for he looked very much as if he wanted to laugh out loud in memory of something she had said. This had not been an uncommon experience of late. Jubal tried not to be irritated, but he found he was—very. Finally in annoyance, he had to ask.

"What are you smiling about? You look as if you swallowed—"

Seth let out a small, choked laugh. He stopped walking and turned toward Jubal trying to keep a straight face. "While I was speaking with Debora, my little son, Chus, was jumping all around. After a time, my wife asked him what was the matter with him, and he said that he had decided to grow up to be a grasshopper. Debora looked at him very calmly and told him that it simply was not possible. He was a boy and must grow up to be a man, but he continued to jump around as much as ever, so I took him in hand to scold him, and I said, 'Don't you hear your mother? You aren't a grasshopper. You are a boy.' So the child just turned around as determined as ever and said, 'Well then, I guess I'll just be a boy-hopper.'" Seth tried to keep his face straight, but he was having a hard time of it.

Jubal pursed his lips together tightly. He nodded soberly as if he simply refused to admit that his leader was acting like an idiot. Clearly there were days when Jubal wondered if Seth were fit to lead. It seemed to him that excessive happiness could unman a man. He then turned to face the arriving visitors. He watched as the figures came into focus, and it became clear that Kryce led the way with Enosh and his son to his side and Kenan directly behind. There were a few other people with them, but that hardly mattered now. Jubal's face broke into a wide grin. He sincerely liked Kryce, for he saw in him a man who had faced both death and tragedy and overcome them with wisdom and strength. They were men of equal size and stature, but while Kryce was brawny and large, Jubal was quick-witted and able to out maneuver every opponent; to him, even the smallest skirmish was a matter of life and death.

Jubal stepped out in front of Seth with his arms extended.

"Welcome friends! It has been a long time since we last saw you. How have you and your families been fairing?"

Kryce quickened his pace, and the smile on his face was enormous. Even his eyes were smiling. Jubal's step faltered for just a brief moment as the alarming joy on his friend's face seemed out of proportion to the occasion. Surely it was good to see each other again, but this was a little more than too much gladness.

The two friends met and embraced in greeting. Then Seth stepped forward, and greetings were extended between all the friends for Enosh and Kenan had come forward also. There was much back slapping, and Jubal shouted out to Enosh's son, "How you have grown boy!" He turned and faced Enosh. "What are you feeding him? Whole hogs?" Put grinned sheepishly, even though he had heard such exclamations about his size often enough. Enosh laughed and acknowledged that it was just about the truth of the matter. Then Kryce put up his hand to make an announcement. Everyone became suddenly quiet.

"I have someone here that you will want to meet, Jubal." His smile was alarming again. He stepped back toward the one man who had stayed in the background. The woman and children seemed to be rooted to the ground. Kryce put his hand upon the stranger and led him forward. He walked right up to Jubal and put his arm on his shoulder also. "I return your brother to you." Accad turned, and his whole face became visible. The two men looked at each other for several long moments in complete silence. Finally Jubal extended his own arm in welcome. "Long have I dreamed of this day." They embraced, as long separated brothers should.

The festivities of that night were not to be compared to any in memory, for the joy of the whole clan was great. Accad could only import a little news about others who had been taken away, but none of it was good. It was accepted by those who most needed to know, and then the whole clan went on to celebrate this remarkable reunion, for in truth a brother had been lost and was now found. Seth took Accad around and introduced his wife and family to his own wife and family. Obal was very glad to meet a woman who was willing to welcome her with such warmth and understanding. Jubal walked along with his brother and watched his every move as if he might suddenly vanish into thin air. The two hardly had a chance to speak, so great was the clan's desire to see and hear all about Accad's adventures. Obal and her young children stayed with Debora and assisted her even while she was comforted by the kindness of these new people.

It was late when most of the clan had retired, but Seth, Enosh, Kenan, Jubal and Accad sat close to the dying fire and spoke in soft voices. Seth was sleepy beyond words, but he wanted to stay in the men's company a bit longer. It had been a good night, and his heart was greatly relieved by Accad's return, for he had realized the depth of Jubal's wound, which no medicine could heal. Still, as he watched his friend, he wondered if it were a little too late. Despite Accad's return, Jubal looked as grim as ever. Seth shook his head at such oppressive thoughts and decided to turn the conversation to a lighter topic.

"I am curious, Enosh, how you grew such a large son. I realize that he is not your flesh, but I have never seen such a youth grow to be so tall. Are there many men of such height and stature in the People of Havilah?"

Enosh rubbed his hands together near the fire, as an evening chill had descended. He smiled as he responded. "No, actually he is the wonder of the clan. And I am quite glad he is on our side and a well-behaved son, too, for I would hardly like to discipline him at this point. As a matter of fact, I tried him in a contest a few years ago when he should never have been able to try out, and he beat almost every man in the clan. He is not simply big; that boy is unnaturally strong. He amazes me."

Seth yawned even as he spoke. "It must be your wife then—she or her first husband—who gave him the advantage."

Enosh shook his head. "No, that is what is so surprising. My wife is tall for a woman, but she is smaller than me, and her first husband, the blood father of the child, was not much taller than she was, though it was said he was uncommonly strong. No," he rubbed his chin thoughtfully, "there is no explanation for the child other than God wants him to be big. He must have a battle to fight someday that will match his greatness."

Accad looked over sharply at Enosh. "I did not know your people believed in God."

Enosh shrugged. "The People of Neb do not, but I am no longer of the People of Neb. When I married Tamar and took her child as my own, I also took the God of the People of Havilah as my own."

Jubal seemed slightly irritated. "And what do the People of Havilah believe about their God?"

Enosh seemed a little uncomfortable, so Kryce spoke up. "We believe there is a one God who rules the world. Our stories tell of the Creator of all things. He is benevolent and good. He hates those who cause injustice and suffering. We are a people who have chosen to become like Him in all things."

Jubal snorted. Pent up anger began to seep through his well-controlled posture. "As if such a thing were possible! The People of Seth believe in the one God, too, and we know the stories going all the way back to the Great Flood and the salvation of mankind through Noah. We are direct descendants of his most noble son, Japheth, but we do not claim to become God ourselves."

Kryce sat up a little straighter. "The People of Havilah do not claim to become God, but we do strive to imitate His kindness through strength. He gives us life, and the creatures of the world, all living things, are for our use, so we must act as stewards worthy of His great trust. We must be strong so as to protect those who cannot protect themselves. It is what He wants from us. We live by our honor. You know this. Why are you acting surprised?"

Jubal stood up suddenly and kicked at an ember, which had fallen from the glowing mound. "I am not surprised by anything! I just don't know how you can know what He wants. Does the Almighty reach down and speak into your ear?" The bitterness in Jubal's voice was palpable. "It seems to me that many innocent men, women and children have suffered death and destruction no matter what one believes. God has only offered silence to the People of Seth."

Seth woke suddenly from his stupor and rose quickly. He tried to reach out to his friend, but he sensed the angry tension, and he put his hand down by his side. "I do not agree with you, Jubal. You are angry and not thinking clearly. God does speak to us, though not in words. He speaks in the very life he gives us. He speaks in the breaking of a new day. He speaks in the quiet of our thoughts. We have survived much for a purpose. Perhaps we do not see all, but we see enough to trust that God exists, and so we must accept that there is more to our existence than what we see now."

Jubal pointed angrily at his brother while nearly shouting at Seth. "And does God have a purpose in the years of suffering my brother endured? A purpose for the loss of his eye?"

This time it was Accad who stood up. His back was not quite as straight as his brother's, but he made the most of his height. "Is it not strange, brother, that you are the bitter one when I have suffered the greater loss? When I was far from home and traded like a goat, tied and beaten, even then I had hope. I believed that I would get home someday, even when I ceased to look for that day. After a time, after I married and had a child, I realized that my home was where my heart resided. When they threatened to take my children away, I would have offered my life to keep them safe with their mother, for that is where my heart lived. Now we are all here together, and my joy is only clouded by your anger. Who are you angry at? God? Why? For it was only by the hand of an unseen God that my family and I met up with Kryce. Or are you angry with me for returning? Have I somehow upset your expectations?"

Jubal groaned, and his hands came up in an almost pleading expression. "No, no, you are most welcome. I am happy for you, and I am very happy that you found joy in a good wife and good children. It is just that . . ." He rubbed his hand over his head in a fierce gesture of impatience.

Accad came and stood before his brother. "What is it? What still ails your heart?"

Tears filled Jubal's eyes even as he tried to blink them back. "I believed you dead for all these years. I have lived too long without hope. And though you are returned to me, there are those who will not return. What about them? What about the wives whose husbands will never come back to comfort them? What about the children born who will never know their fathers? What about all those still held in slavery? What about all those who still suffer and are not released and who die in suffering? What about them?"

There was complete silence for several moments as the embers burned down even more slowly. Suddenly a slightly higher voice broke through the silence. It was Seth's wife, Debora, and she was holding her baby son in her arms as she walked slowly toward them. Her words were soft and cool like a gentle rain.

"Suffering brought forth this babe into the world. Suffering brings the seed into flower. Suffering is not the end. You agonize for good reason, for the suffering of men is terrible to behold. But do not despair, for though one may die in suffering as some of my babes did, they live on in my heart, and I believe that the God who made them recovered their spirits and brought them to a home without suffering." Debora walked over and whispered something into her husband's ear. Seth nodded and took a deep breath.

"Your wife asks for you, Accad. Debora will show you the way." Accad nodded and began to follow Debora toward the dwelling. But then he turned again and returned to his brother. He put his hand upon his shoulder and turned his good eye to see him as best as he could in the moonlight.

"Allow yourself to heal, brother. Grief does not have to become a life-long companion."

Accad turned again and walked into the darkness while Seth followed closely beside his wife. Enosh took a deep breath and spread out a pallet on the ground beside Kenan. Put had gone to sleep long before. Kryce sat down with his arms locked around his knees, staring into the fire. He was thinking of his father and his sister. Jubal stood watching the slow fading embers a moment. He knew he should go home to his own dwelling and get some sleep, but he did not want to leave things as they were. He spoke out as if including everyone within hearing.

"I apologize if I was rude." He rubbed his arms together. "I am not sure what got into me."

Enosh looked at him a moment and then volunteered, "You have had to endure much. Perhaps a wife would do you some good."

Kenan spoke up quietly. "It does help, Jubal. Both Sari and I have helped each other to accept our losses and our grief. We have yet to have any children, but we still hope."

Jubal said nothing in response. He simply nodded in the dark. Finally Kryce spoke up. "In the night when the dark comes, many men question the will of God, but with a new day, so hope is renewed. Just remember this, it is when the dark covers the day that the stars appear and we see without an earthly light. It is then that God makes true faith possible."

Jubal swallowed and picked up a stick that was lying off to the side. He put it gently onto the fire, and a sudden bright flame burst upon their eyes. "Perhaps I have become my own darkness." He turned and began to walk away. Suddenly he stopped. "Goodnight. I will see you in the morning. And if you don't mind, I would like to visit the People of Havilah again. I will see my brother safely settled here, and then I will go with you."

Kryce smiled into the night. "We will be honored."

Jubal turned and walked home alone.

CHAPTER 26
NEB'S SONS

Neb watched his two young sons carefully. His first son, Madai, was a strong youth though he never seemed to use his body to his own advantage. As a matter of fact, Madai had a rather soft and delicate touch. Neb's sour expression and downturned mouth expressed his feelings clearly enough. Leah liked to keep Madai near her, and the boy responded by being very dutiful in complying with her every wish. Madai saw as well as felt his father's disdain, and he knew that he and his mother were joined together by some mystery he could not explain. Neb's hand tapped impatiently at his side. His second son, Serug, was a different personality altogether. Neb's scowl cleared as he watched Serug attempt to bully his elder brother. Stomping his foot, Serug yelled for Madai to get him his favorite food while Madai simply stood off to the side looking mildly dismayed. Leah tried to gently intervene, but Neb called over and told her to let the boys handle the situation themselves. Leah's face clouded, but she obeyed in compliance to her husband's wishes. She did not like it when the boys quarreled though it had become a common experience of late.

Neb motioned for Leah to step away as he watched the drama unfold. Serug's temper was mounting into a full-blown fury. The little boy kicked his older brother and cried in a screaming, wailing tone.

"I want honey bread. I'm hungry. Go get it. Give it to me!" The chant was repeated over and over in louder and more desperate tones. Madai knew perfectly well that his brother had just eaten a full meal and that his mother wanted to save the rest of the honey bread for later. Past experience had taught him that as soon as he gave his little brother what he wanted, he would just as likely throw whatever he had previously desired on the ground and demand something else in the space of a few breaths. Madai, as was his custom, tried to explain matters in a calm, patient manner.

"You don't need to eat right now, and the honey bread is for later when you will really be hungry, so stop crying and go play."

Serug had no interest whatsoever in what his brother was saying. He threw himself down on the ground and sprawled in the dirt, kicking and screaming in guttural speech. Leah wanted to go to her son, but she was somewhat afraid of him. She had been kicked by him before, and it had taken days for the deep bruise to heal. Madai simply looked at his mother and then at his father and shrugged his shoulders. He knew that there was nothing he could do to help his brother or his mother, and he ardently wished he could get away from the situation as quickly as possible. Neb shook his head as if he were disappointed and dismissed his eldest son with a curt wave of the hand. He told Leah to go home and get some honey bread and bring it to him. Leah turned and did as Neb requested. Neb walked up closer to his youngest son. He could see the wild beast in the boy, and though he knew that the child cared for no one, he knew that if Serug was to be any use to the clan then he must be tamed and disciplined. He looked toward where Madai was sauntering away, and his flesh crawled. He would trade that son away if he could. He looked at Leah, and though he still believed her to be quite beautiful, he was no longer enamored by her. Her relationship with Madai had done much to cool his ardor. After a few moments, Leah came back and Serug was just beginning to show signs of tiring. Neb took the soft, round honey bread and broke off a small piece in his hand. He looked at Leah.

"You need to make more of this."

Leah understood. She was being ordered to go and make more bread for a child who wouldn't even want what he had. She shook her head and was just about to speak but then quickly closed her mouth again. She had realized recently that whatever power she once had over her husband had faded away like the early morning midst. He no longer cared to hear what she thought. He did not like her influence on Madai. For a reason she could not discern, he would not trust his eldest son. This realization had been a shock and a terrible disappointment. Neb had watched Serug carefully, and he made sure that Leah did not have much opportunity to spend time with her second son. He kept taking the young child with him on various errands, and when by chance Serug was home, Neb made sure that Leah was too busy to spend much time with him. Neb tried to be very imaginative in his excuses, but Leah saw her husband's mind quite clearly. He wanted Serug for himself. He wanted Serug to become like him and not so much like her. She sighed even as she turned and obeyed her husband's command.

Neb looked down at Serug who had finally stopped kicking and yelling. Sweat was beading on his round, red face. Neb held up a small piece of the bread.

"Do you want this?" He took a small bite and made a pleased noise as he swallowed the food. Serug watched his father very carefully. The boy seemed to know that he had met an equal in battle, but he was not about to give up his control of the situation. Still lying in the dust, Serug motioned for his father to bend down and give him the bread. Neb smiled.

"No, you must get up and come to me."

Serug began to kick and scream again. Neb ate another piece of the bread. There was only one piece left. Serug scrambled to his feet and snatched the bread from Neb's hand and stuffed it in his mouth. Neb laughed. He opened his other hand and there was another larger piece of bread.

"Come and stand by me and ask for it."

Serug looked to the ground, contemplating a repeat of his maneuvers in the dust. Instead he tried to snatch it quickly from his father again, but Neb was too quick for him. He shook his head and drew back his hand. Serug grew infuriated. He tried to reach up and grab Neb's hand, and when he could not, he reached over and grabbed his arm and tried to bite him. Neb pushed the child away roughly and took the bread and dropped it on the ground. He ground it into the dust with his heel and looked at Serug intently. The child began to cry again, but Neb demanded that he stop with a quick motion of his hand. Serug had learned by now what that motion meant, and he stopped his noise abruptly. Neb held out his hand one last time. There was the smallest piece left between his fingers.

"Come here and ask for it." Serug stepped forward and put out his hand and asked for the bread quietly. Neb smiled and handed it to him.

Leah watched from the distance of her dwelling, and she contemplated the evil that would spring from a child who was raised entirely by Neb. Her heart ached. No matter what he might grow into, still he was her flesh and blood, and she would always love him. But she feared for Madai. Neb would always favor the son who was most like him and oppose anyone not obedient to his will. She stopped grinding the wheat, and a sudden awareness came over her. She would not be able to protect her sons much longer. She would no longer even be able to protect herself. She looked out across the dusty ground, and a sudden movement surprised her. Her skin prickled. She looked more carefully, stretching her neck through the window. It was a large, boldly striped snake slithering away into the woodlands. She took a deep breath and shook her head and began grinding again.

A few years later, Neb took both sons on a hunting expedition. Madai was a fine hunter though he often waited just a moment too late to make his throw. Still, he often managed to return to camp with some kind of game even if only a bird or rabbit. Serug had killed a few small game as well, but he spoke as if he could kill a great animal if he were only given the chance. Neb had seen bear tracks the day before, so he decided to let his two sons attempt to take the bear together. Serug was pleased with his father's proposal. He wanted very much to show his cunning and strength despite his small build. He was thin but sinewy like a cat. His green eyes even reflected in the night like a cat, at least his brother thought so. Madai was less thrilled with the challenge. He did not want to kill a bear, though it would bring home quite a bit of meat. Still, he had seen those huge animals at the river, and he marveled at their strength and beauty. He did not want to challenge one because he that knew a bear of any size could turn on him and tear him to pieces. Besides, he hated to destroy such a matriarch of the wilderness. He knew that neither his father nor his brother would understand his reasoning or his fear. He was a large youth now, and he wanted to be considered a man, but he knew that his manhood would be defined by those he did not wish to emulate. He felt foreign somehow, as if he never belonged to this clan at all. He often wondered in the secret place of his heart if he had really been Neb's son at all. He desperately wished he were not.

   The bear tromped along noisily through the brush. It was a massive creature. She had reigned supreme for many seasons and had successfully raised three healthy cubs. She was hungry now and in no mood to be challenged by anyone. When Serug saw her, his heart leapt with excitement. He knew that this would be a kill worth every effort and daring. As he looked sideways at his brother, his brows knit together in a deep frown not unlike his father's common expression. How he had wished Madai were not traveling along beside him so closely. The stream was near, and the she-bear would stop for a drink undoubtedly. Serug paused to think.

   Neb had left them when they had found her fresh tracks. He said that he would see them at home after they had made the kill, skinned her and packed the meat in fresh leaves to be carried home in woven baskets they could make quickly out of hanging vines. Neb had made light of the situation, knowing full well the inherent dangers of the mission he was giving them. He knew this would be a quest that would decide their fate in his eyes. Only one son could rule, and he had to decide soon which son would be trained to inherit all. He had no question of Serug's daring, but he had some doubt about his ability. He was too rash a youth, despite Neb's best attempts to curb his impatience. In the case of Madai, Neb seriously doubted the youth would even attempt to accomplish this task if it were not for his little brother. He had seen Serug goad Madai to the point of extreme irritation, though Madai had an exemplary ability to keep his emotions under control. Neb had come to admire his eldest son for this facet of his personality. For Neb, this was a trial that would tell him much about his two offspring. He had once considered exiling Madai to the care of his mother, but after a time he came to see qualities that surprised him, and he was more willing to train him than he had been previously. Now he wanted to see which of the boys would reign supreme.

Madai had simply stared at his father, trying very hard not to show any emotion. He knew that questions or any sign of uncertainty or fear infuriated Neb. Still, he could not fathom how they were going to accomplish this horrendous task. This she-bear had more than twice the strength of a full-grown man, and it could kill either of them with a single swipe of her massively powerful paw. And even if they did manage to kill her, how would they manage to skin her in a single, complete piece, as was the practice among those who knew how? He had seen it done on smaller creatures, but he had never tried to do it all by himself before. Skinning a large bear was well beyond his skill. And on top of that, the meat alone would weigh far more than the two of them put together. Madai let out his breath and shrugged almost imperceptibly. He was used to being asked to do difficult, even painful tasks, but he had never been asked to do the impossible before.

Serug was not afraid in the least. He saw nothing but possibilities for personal glory. His only concern was that Madai might get in his way and would either ruin their chances of getting the bear or, even worse, actually succeed and get some of the credit. Neither option appealed to Serug. He looked around and considered how best to manage the situation.

"Madai, we have a formidable task ahead of us. Why don't we get things ready before we attack?"

Madai nodded slowly even as he peered intently at his brother. What was Serug thinking? His brother liked to use large words but was not known for planning out his actions. He folded his arms in front of him. "What do you suggest we do?"

Serug attempted to look innocent and pleased all at the same time. His smile was ingratiating, and his voice was mildly high. "If we make the baskets first and then get a space ready for skinning, we will be all set when the deed is done."

Madai shook his head. "She is liable to run far from here before we even make the kill."

Serug shook his head violently. "No, not at all. She has her territory. She likes this place. You can see she has come here often before. She will simply turn to fight, and then we will kill her."

"You make it sound like a simple matter."

Serug rolled his eyes in impatience while his lips pursed in annoyance. His hands were on his hips. "How you worry! You are like a woman sometimes."

Madai shook his head in slow irritation. First Neb had left them to accomplish an impossible task, and now his younger brother was making terrible plans. Madai realized that he was in no mood to deal with his brother's ill behavior. He stroked his still-clean chin and decided that this might be a good time to teach his little brother a well-earned lesson. Madai simply stepped back with a bow and waved his hands palms up to gesture that Serug could do as he liked. Serug knew his brother was weak, but he was a little surprised Madai had given in so easily. He thought Madai must just be afraid. Still, Serug's smile was quite genuine.

"Alright, the first thing we should do is get the baskets together. You can go back into the woodlands and gather some vines. I will work here to make a clear space, and then you can circle around and make noises so that she runs this direction. You follow her, and we will make the kill together." Madai knew he should say nothing and let the little idiot get killed, but he could not in all conscience let him use this plan. It was simply too dangerous.

"What if the bear turns to pursue me? Will you come after her to help? Or what if I am not able to follow her fast enough? How will you take her down by yourself?"

Serug shook his head as if he had to explain his ideas to a slow child. "Listen to me again. I am going to be close at hand when you scare her. I will back up drawing her toward me, and when you have caught up, I will throw my spear right into her heart. Then you can come around and help me to finish her off. Do you see? It is a perfect plan."

Madai swallowed hard. He could not see how this plan would work, but at the same time, he could not see how he could honorably leave his little brother, knowing that the fool would undoubtedly attempt to take on the bear all by himself. If he refused to allow this to happen, Serug would tell Neb that he had directly disobeyed him and allowed a perfect opportunity to feed their clan for many days simply walk away. Madai thought of his mother and their many conversations together. She had taught him much about her own people and their belief in the one God and their noble aspirations to become like Him. Madai had always believed that his mother's wisdom even in her humble situation was more reasonable than his father's arrogant pride. Serug was proof of what trouble Neb's thinking would lead to.

"I think I will stay here, and you can go around to frighten the bear. Then when she comes this way, I will attempt to kill her and you can finish her off."

Serug's eyes grew round with anger. His plan was being ruined. He stomped his foot in irritation. "That is all wrong and won't work! I am a better thrower, and you will probably run away when she comes at you." His voice had risen to a shriek. He threw down his spear in fury. Madai held his breath a moment. He could hear an unusual sound moving through the brush toward them. His eyes grew wide, and his skin prickled in fright. His brother was still thrashing about and whining his commands when a large, furry figure broke through the brush. The she-bear was angry, and the noise had irritated her even further. She stood on her hind legs and let out a bellow.

Serug fell backward in sudden surprise. The bear was much bigger than he had realized. Madai gripped his spear, but the bear had come down on all fours and was tromping noisily toward Serug who had scampered to his feet, looking wildly about for his spear. Madai yelled to him to run, but the bear was almost on him, and Madai had to circle around to get to her front. He saw his little brother unsheathe his knife and hold it with both hands high into the air. Madai saw the boy's spear, and he quickly grabbed it up. Just as the bear was coming down onto Serug, Madai swung in and forced the spear under her so that her own weight would drive it into her chest. The spear snapped, but not before it cut into her enough to make her raise up. Madai stepped back and threw his spear with all his might. The spear caught her in the stomach. She was in pain and furious now. She clawed at Serug who had been knocked off his feet again. Her long claws scraped at his face and his arm and his side. The boys screamed. Madai grabbed his own knife. He jumped into the bear and stabbed at its neck over and over again. The animal tried to swing up and grab ahold of her tormentor, but as she swung, the spear dug even deeper into her insides. She fell and rolled. Madai was kicked and scraped by her thrashing leg, but he managed to limp over to her. His bloody hands could hardly hold his knife, but he was able to get in one more powerful thrust, and she finally lay still. The world was no longer clear. The trees seemed to sway sideways. Madai fell not far from where his younger brother lay.

When Madai awoke, he was lying in his own bed. His mother was sitting beside him with her hands clasped in tormented anguish. His head hurt dreadfully, as did his leg and side, but he was able to make himself sit up a little bit.

"Mother? What happened to Serug?"

"He will live. He is injured worse than you, and he will carry many scars for the rest of his life but, Neb says that they are wounds of glory."

Madai fell back onto his pallet. "Some glory." He shook his head and closed his eyes. "Did he tell you what happened?"

Leah closed her eyes. "He told me that he took down the bear all by himself."

Madai groaned. "He would lie, even about this?"

"Serug looks to emulate his father in all things." Quickly Leah patted her son's hands. "But you are alive, and that is what matters most to me." She looked her eldest son in the eye and took a deep breath. "This cannot happen again."

Madai shook his head. "As long as I am Neb's son, then this is my life. Just wait till he sends me out on a raid."

"That will never happen."

Madai looked up surprised. His eyes were filled with questions. Leah heard footsteps coming toward the room. She stood and put her finger to her lips and then kissed her son on the cheek. "I will let you rest now. You still have much healing to do."

Neb entered the room. He nodded silently to his wife and then looked down at his son.

"I thought I heard voices as I went past." He paused. "I am glad to see your eyes are clear and steady." He turned to his wife as if waiting for her to leave. She took the hint and passed through the doorway with a single backward glance.

Madai watched her leave and then turned his eyes toward his father. He said nothing. Neb sat down near his son. He cleared his throat. "I want you to tell me exactly what happened from the time I left you two." Madai nodded and told the sorry tale. Neb listened without comment. Madai's side was hurting dreadfully, and he was hungry, but he did not want to mention his suffering to his father. Still Neb seemed to sense his needs. He put his hand upon his son's and began speaking in a sincere tone. "I am glad you lived." He looked around and then stood up. "I will arrange for food to be brought and someone to care for your wounds."

Madai looked confused. "Mother is used to taking care of me."

Neb shook his head decisively. "I have learned what I needed to know. I have decided that you will be trained to rule the clan with me. We will expand our claim and make ourselves great throughout the land."

Madai was deeply disturbed. He hesitated, but he forced himself to speak. "I thought you favored Serug."

Neb shrugged as if the matter were beyond his control. "I cannot train someone who will not be disciplined. Besides, his injuries are quite severe. He may never be truly whole again."

Madai's eyes widened in horror. Grief welled up despite his anger at his brother's stupidity. He was the elder son, and he should have taken better care. He was truly sorry for his brother's loss. Yet at the same time, he felt a strange pride and gladness when he thought about his father choosing him over Serug. But then his eyes shifted to the doorway where his mother had just passed through. His stomach churned with hunger and pain. He felt light-headed. What would he do now? Which parent should he follow? Alone he must decide what his fate would be.

Neb turned to toward the doorway. "I will go now, but trust that you will be well cared for. I will take over your training completely. Once you are healed, we will go on our first raid. I have an old matter that must be attended to. I can see no more fitting companion than my son to settle matters with my brothers." He smiled grimly and then walked through the doorway.

Madai lay down on his pallet again and stared at the rafters above his head. This was not what he wanted. But he did not know how to turn the hand of his father. He tried to breathe deeply, but every motion was painful. He closed his eyes, and he felt a hand touch his. It was his mother again. She was looking intently into her son's eyes. "Do not worry. You will not go on any raids. You will not be trained to become like Neb." She looked down suddenly. "I was afraid to die before, but not now. For you, I will gladly lay down my life." She looked around and whispered softly. "We will steal out of here in a few days, at the first opportunity when you are well enough to travel with me. We will do the one thing that Neb does not expect." Leah patted her son's hand and kissed him silently. "I am stronger than Neb ever realized. In this I will have my way." She smiled and turned to walk away. "I will never be far from you. Hurry to heal and grow strong. Just do not let Neb know the truth." She slipped out of the room. Madai suddenly felt a quiet confidence seep into the hurt place of his heart. He wondered at his own feelings, but he closed his eyes and he rested as instructed. He was not alone, and the sensation comforted him. He fell into a deep, restful sleep.

CHAPTER 27
TODAY'S JOY TOMORROW'S WAR

Enosh smiled as he watched his sons play fight with their long, stripped sticks. Though his little son, Gomer, used every ounce of his childish strength to swing his staff through the air, his aim was wildly inaccurate, and he rarely struck a true blow. As the older brother, Put enjoyed allowing him to make his mark every now and again with much dramatic grimacing and grunting. Enosh's eyes twinkled at the display. Though Put was not flesh of his flesh and bone of his bone, still he felt the youth was his son in complete entirety. The baby boy he had inherited had grown into a strong able youth and now was a man under his guidance and tutelage. In his experience, there never had been a more receptive, good-natured young man put upon the earth. His next son, Gomer, was late in coming, and there were two sisters between them, but the two brothers were practically inseparable. While Put was tall and massive with thick black hair and rich brown eyes and quite a grown man, his little brother appeared to be simply a miniature little person. Gomer wanted so much to be big like his brother that he would try to eat mouthful for mouthful what Put ate, though he often nearly made himself sick in the attempt. As Enosh watched, they were in the midst of a serious battle. Each had a long, smooth stick in his hand, though Gomer's was quite a bit longer. Their quick, deft moves pleased Enosh.

He saw Put offer a quick thrust toward his little brother who managed to offer a surprisingly able defense by slashing Put in the thigh with his stick. Put, unwilling to let his little brother win so quickly, returned the thrust, but Gomer sensed the coming retribution and attempted to out-run his brother. Put quickly caught up with the little boy and swung him up in the air and then gently thrust him to the ground. Gomer then surprised them all by whacking his big brother over the head with his stick.

Put responded by using every bit of his dramatic skill as he fell slowly to the ground, uttering horrible groaning sounds. Gomer smiled broadly at his grand success ready to fling himself on his opponent when Put suddenly sat up, rose to his feet, and grabbed his little brother once again. Gomer squeaked, half believing his own imaginary game that he was about to be eaten by a giant, and howled for assistance.

A quick thrust by Put, an able defense by Gomer, and Gomer swings and slashes Put in the thigh. Put attempts to rally his strength as he thrusts at Gomer who manages to outrun his brother. Put catches his little brother and gently thrusts him to the ground. Gomer surprises them all by whacking his brother over the head with his staff. Put throws his hands up in despair, falls ever so slowly uttering groaning sounds while Gomer smiles broadly at his success. The little fellow flings himself forward to finish off his deadly opponent when suddenly Put sits up and surprises him, causing a little high-pitched shriek to sound off flying off across the grasslands. Put rises to his feet majestically, grabs his defiant opponent by the arms and swings him up into the air, sending more squeaks across the land. Gomer thrashes about wildly in mid-air, half believing that he is about to be eaten by a giant who looks remarkably like his brother, and he howls for assistance.

Enosh had been standing transfixed and watching the engagement with one hand on his hip while holding a long rope vine in the other. Kenan happened to walk by, and he, too, stopped to see the fight between the two brothers. Without any warning, he dropped his tools and rushed to Gomer's rescue, attempting to take him out of Put's mighty grasp. Put laughed at this new challenger. Kenan pulled Gomer out of Put's grasp and attempted to run off with him. Put followed in pursuit. As they rushed around the village center, Kenan grabbed up a stick while holding Gomer around the waist with one arm as he attempted to fight Put who now had two sticks. A fierce battle ensued between Put and Kenan with Gomer either slapping Kenan onto success or grabbing him heartily around the neck in fright and nearly choking him. Enosh laughed. When Gomer hurled an imaginary stone at him, Put reeled, fell and died dramatically though quite efficiently onto the grassy plain. Kenan slid Gomer to earth to pay his worthy opponent a final farewell. Gomer bounced over, all fear and apprehension gone, and he sat down right on Put's chest. The game was over, and he was the victor, of that there could be no doubt.

Enosh walked over to Put and gently laid his hand upon him. Gomer got off his triumphal throne to watch this impressive ritual. Always after these splendid battles, his father would awaken the fallen. Gomer liked this part almost as much as the entire battle. Put awoke and shook himself off. He smiled down at his brother who smiled back in glad relief. Put's face became serious once again.

"So what is your plan, Father?"

Enosh blinked as if awakening from a dream. "Yes, the plan. Well, I have been thinking of enlarging that small patch of peas by the house. I was thinking that perhaps it would be better to place the whole patch with everyone else's near the creek so that we can bring water to the plants better during the dry times. I have talked with Kryce, and he said that though few would want to give up their own family plots, it might be good for the clan to have an extra store of lentils in case of necessity. So we are now put in charge of making a large garden full of good things we can store up. We can ask for help as we need it."

Put looked pleased. "I will be glad to help, and I think I can find a few more volunteers." He looked down at his little brother and smiled.

And so it was that Put was established as the eldest son of Enosh, and when important tasks needed to be done, Enosh turned to his trustworthy son. Kryce saw this development and was pleased, for he felt that indeed he had gained much in the addition of Enosh to his family and clan. But when word came to him through travelers that Neb had begun to move out again with grown sons at his side and that he was moving toward their established village, Kryce wondered if Enosh would be interested in redressing old wounds. Though the People of Havilah had built a new life from the ashes of Neb's fury, still Kryce well remembered the murder of his noble father and the loss of his innocent sister. He wondered whether the first son of Hezeki, he who should most naturally claim revenge, had the heart to face war once more. Had Enosh been made perhaps a little too happy in his new home?

So Enosh lived on in the joy of his family while Kryce made plans for battle. Jubal and his men often came down to council with Kryce, and the two made up their minds to organize war parties to face the coming threat. This time they would not wait for Neb to advance upon them. They would go out and destroy the evil in their midst like attacking hornets. Kryce knew that Enosh had begun to live as if in a dream that had never known a nightmare. He also knew it was time for him to wake up. Dreams do not last, whereas approaching death was forever.

It was still early in the season, but Enosh was busy with his son in the newly prepared field. It had been a hard job turning soil to rid the earth of weeds that they both knew would reappear. However, they had to begin somewhere, and by sowing the seeds in a relatively cleared field, they hoped to give the new plants a good start. Enosh had stopped to rest and was sitting down upon a rock off to the edge of the field when he saw Kryce coming near. He stood and waved toward his son and the new field.

"See what industrious workers we have become? We shall have a field of wheat great enough to feed the whole village!" His face was bright with sweat from the heat of the day. His smile was genuine and broad as he faced his friend and chosen leader, but it soon faded as Kryce came closer and there was no matching look of joy or pleasure.

Kryce merely nodded absently toward their field and then turned to look his friend in the eye.

"I have come to tell you serious news. Word is out that Neb is preparing to raid again and that this time he will bring his grown sons when he heads this way."

Enosh looked as if someone had hit him across the face. The red blush was quickly replaced with a pale pallor. He had tried so hard to put Neb out of his mind. For so long he had wanted revenge and hate had burned deep in his heart, but in experiencing the love of Tamar and the healing peace of fatherhood, he had learned to forget old hate. From his sons he had found new meaning. A lump rose in his throat, for he feared that all he had ever known of joy was now about to be thrust away. He did not want to reenter the world that Neb created. It was a life he had rejected completely through much grief and bitter loss. He did not want to remember. He did not want to face Neb and all that he represented again. He attempted to speak, but words did not come readily.

Kryce saw his friend's discomfort, and he clenched his jaw. He had not expected Enosh to be happy at his news, but he had not even considered the idea that he would be afraid. Enosh looked terrified.

"I realize this is ill news, but I thought you would want to know." Kryce paused and waited in silence for Enosh to speak. No response was forth coming except a repeated shaking of the head, so he continued speaking. "After much consultation, Jubal, Seth and I have decided to form war parties and go out and surprise Neb and his sons. We will defeat them before they have a chance to attack us."

Shock was plain upon Enosh's face. He had maintained a good relationship with Seth and Jubal, and neither of them had forewarned him of this. It was true that Kryce had been acting rather secretive of late, and he had seen him with Jubal many times, but he had not thought much of the matter. Why this sudden need to take action?

Enosh's voice had steadied some, though his heart was still pounding. "I must admit I am surprised. I have heard nothing of this from Seth or Jubal."

Kryce shrugged his shoulders. "They did not want to worry you, though they do indeed know of the matter for we have discussed it much this season."

Enosh froze. Suddenly he stood up straight and his shoulders squared. His jaw came out from where it had been hiding, and he took a deep breath. When he spoke, his voice was low and barely controlled. "Worry me?" Enosh's eyes blazed. "Why was so intimate a matter discussed and decided without me? Am I not a member of this clan? And what about Kenan? When was he going to be told?"

Kryce heard the anger in his friend's voice, and he became defensive. "It seemed most appropriate for me to tell you and then for you to inform your brother."

Enosh shook his head in deliberate rejection. "Most appropriate? Were you afraid of our loyalty? Did you question our manhood? Do you think we have forgotten Neb? How could you—"

Kryce raised his hand and spoke loudly and clearly. "For these past many years we have been good friends and relations. I am the leader of this clan if you may remember. I make the decisions, and now our clan, as well as the clan of Seth, is committed to facing Neb and destroying his power forever. Do not let your fears or misunderstandings bring a division between us. That will only give Neb the edge he needs. I am telling you now that we need your strength and courage to help us defeat your brother, for his power is like no other I have ever known upon this earth. If that is not trust and confidence, then I do not know the meaning of words."

Enosh let his eyes fall back to earth as he looked over the broad, clear horizon. He contemplated Kryce's words. Finally he raised his head and looked his wife's brother in the eyes. "I and my brother and my son will fight by your side, and we will end Neb's threat forever." He paused a moment in thought, looking far away beyond the grassy plain. "I wonder what ever happened to Eva?"

Kryce, too, stared out toward the limitless sky. "I share your wonder. Many have been the times I wished to gaze upon my sister Leah's face, yet I have only been tormented by her loss in the black of night, as well as in the searing light of mid-day. In my mind, she is forever sad, and our coming to destroy her sons will only add to her grief, but if they fight for Neb, they have grown evil, and it is either their destruction or ours."

Enosh sighed deeply. "How is it that Neb could never learn… to love?"

Kryce spat out his words. "He loves himself too much!" He then patted Enosh on the shoulder. "Call your son in from the field. We have much to do before we depart. I want to be off within three days. Seth and Jubal and their men will be joining us the day after tomorrow."

"What about Accad? Surely he has as much cause to fight as any man. Does he not want to go?"

"Oh, he begged to lead a party of men, but Seth refused him. He has already suffered much, and Seth wants someone he trusts at home to watch over those left behind." He paused in thought before he continued. "At least those are the reasons Seth gave Accad. But in his heart, I think he fears a one-eyed warrior. Mistakes are easy to make on the field of battle with two good eyes. Accad is not strong or well. His years of suffering weigh heavily upon him. I think Seth is wise in keeping him at home."

Enosh nodded soberly and then called his son to come home as the two men began to walk toward their village. The sun was now lower, and a reddish hue was coloring the sky. Birds were singing their last songs of the evening while a soft breeze blew in from the west. Put rushed up to his father. His face was flushed and happy.

"I heard some of what you said. Are we really going into battle?" His feet were moving in quick, light steps. Clearly he was eager to spread the news.

"Yes, Son, we will go to battle as soon as Seth and his men come."

Put's smile broadened. "And I may go too? I am old enough to fight. I am strong and able."

Enosh stopped walking a moment as he looked at his son. He swallowed hard, and the words seemed to stick in his throat. His face was oddly contorted. "Yes, Son, you will come. In truth, we need your help." He looked away a moment toward the once-burning sky, which had grown suddenly cold. "Go tell the news, but let your mother hear it from me."

"Yes, of course. I will be careful. I will go ahead now!" Put let his feet lead the way like wings on a bird. His excitement filled the silent air. Kryce had begun to move forward again, but Enosh kept still. Kryce stopped and walked back to his friend.

"What is the matter? Your son wants to fight the enemy. How could that displease you?"

Enosh shook his head. "He does not displease me." A small sigh escaped between his lips. "It just occurred to me that he will be fighting his own uncle and relations. He will be fighting men that were once my own clan."

Kryce looked dismayed at this sentimentality. "Who is your clan? Those you are born with or those you choose?" He strode off at a quick determined pace.

Enosh followed in his footsteps, his eyes sweeping the ground. Only the slanting rays of light upon his check could have heard him mutter, "Both."

CHAPTER 28

TRADER OF INVENTION

In those days, there were a few men who traveled freely, trading whatever it was that would give them good profit. Often these men would travel in small groups for safety and protection, but there were those who by their very impetuous and daring nature eschewed the companionship of fellow travelers and walked alone, venturing from one village and clan to the next, always seeking welcome and trading more than goods; stories and news of the clans near and far was treasure in and of itself.

One such man named Adam was completely ordinary in every visible way. He was bequeathed by his parents with light brown hair, dark brown eyes, dark tanned skin, a medium build and nothing extraordinary of manner or style. His voice was quiet and deep, and he spoke with few words, but when he did speak, those near him bent in to listen for he had an invisible air of authority. Though few could explain why they liked and trusted him, almost everyone did, though no one called him a friend. He was too distant and formal for ease, and he never stayed long in one place. Just as Kryce was preparing his men to face Neb and as Neb was working his way toward the People of Havilah, there strode into the middle, quite unaware of the impending danger, this innocent though not ignorant trader. Neither Kryce nor Neb would have cared to pass the time of one day with this man, for they both had far more serious matters on their minds than the trading of simple goods or the passing of village gossip. But had they realized the fullness of what Adam carried, they both would have stopped to take serious notice. In fact, they would have gone out to meet him so as to make him most welcome, and they would have plied him with sweet drink and every good thing there is to eat in order to get him to talk about what he had recently discovered on his travels.

For it had been in the not-so-distant past that Adam had met with some other traders for a short while, and as he had just come from a village rich in wine and had quite a ready stock with him, he was willing to share most liberally, which was not usually his custom. But on this occasion, he had acted the generous host and made donation after donation to their goodwill, and the acquaintances, after a time, grew quite generous in return. One in particular became almost fatherly as he gave advice to the younger man. He warned him of the dangers of traveling alone and tried to persuade him to travel with them, but to this invitation Adam said nothing. Then on a gushing whim of sentimental kindness, the old trader began to share their greatest secret. A new weapon of war had been invented out in the far distant lands, and it was something that could change the fortunes of war in these places of woods and grasslands. The old man took from his bag a curved piece of wood with a strong, thin string of sinew tied from end to end. Then he took also from his long bag another bag with thin sticks sharpened at one end. He fitted the stick up against the sinew to the wooden bow, and while standing though not steady, he managed to pull the stick quite a ways, stretching the sinew to great tautness so that when the stick was let loose it flew over a surprising distance. The young trader was astute enough even with wine in him to realize that he had just acquired a prize. He had seen, and though the other traders quickly encouraged their elder drunken companion to put away his prize, the young trader would not soon forget what had passed before his eyes.

    After a groggy morning and many hearty slaps on the back, the elder traders were on their way once again and the youth was left to himself to travel as he had always preferred to do, alone, and deep in thought. He thought much about the weapon he had seen, and after a time, he decided that he could improve on what had been created before. He hunted a young deer, and after eating his fill and taking the parts most useful, he found a slim sapling and carved a wooden bow better curved than the one he had seen with slightly less give. He found just the right thickness of sinew to his liking, and he made himself a new weapon. It worked, though not as well as he hoped and not nearly as well as his imagination told him it could work. It took many days of serious thought and much practice, but by the time he had wandered into Kryce's neighborhood, he had struck upon a good invention that would save one clan from extinction and propel another clan into great dominance.

But Neb saw him first. Neb had little patience for wandering traders, though he found that at times they could be of invaluable service by describing the clan movements in the area around a certain location. When this trader was seen from a distance, Torgama was out hunting with Kittam. They both stopped what they were doing and followed the trader with such excellent tracking skills that the young man did not even know he was being followed until they surprised him with a sudden attack.

"What is so noble a youth doing so far from home?" Kittam's voice was as dry as his sarcasm would allow.

Adam looked at his two interrogators with a silent, steady smile. He was not accustom to fear, and though he had heard about raiding parties in the area, he had felt as safe and comfortable as when he lived under his own father's roof.

"My name is Adam, and I am a trader of goods and news. If your leader is near, I would be happy to speak with him."

The easy confidence of the young man surprised both Kittam and Torgama who were rather used to people trembling in fear at the very sight of them.

"Well, Adam, Neb the Great is our leader, but he is not a man to trifle away his time in wasteful speech. He has a battle to plan, and he has little desire for what you carry."

Again there was that rather curious smile about Adam's eyes, which perplexed Neb's men. "You do not know what it is that I carry, so how do you know that Neb won't want it?"

Torgama looked at Kittam who furrowed his brows in concentration. Finally Kittam spoke with a mock bow. "Show us, boy-trader, what you have to offer, and we will decide its worth."

Adam stood with one foot resting comfortably on a large boulder that was sticking conveniently out of the earth near him.

His hands were clasped gently at his waist as he stood as tall as he could, looking generally amused.

"I have goods that are only for the bravest and the wisest. I can show them to no one else on pain of death." Adam's face became still and serious now.

Torgama laughed in an abrupt manner. "On pain of death? We can see that arranged neatly enough! Come show us what you have, and we will decide whether you should be allowed a visit with Neb or feel the pain of death yourself." His voice was cocky, but irritation burned through his eyes.

Adam simply shook his head as he threw his long bundle over his shoulder in one swift, easy motion. He always carried his goods in small groups and buried his most valuable work in secret locations. What he carried now would impress no one. Torgama ran ahead to stall his leaving.

"I thought we made it clear to you that you are to show us what you have."

Adam dropped his bag back to the ground and with one swift fluid motion he dumped the contents out for all to see. Kittam and Torgama stood and stared. Torgama walked over and shuffled through the simple goods with the great toe of his foot. Then he kicked at the things as if they were garbage to be broken and dumped into a pit.

"What is here that should be brought to the notice of a great man like Neb? Your insolence tests my patience. We should kill you now!"

Adam laughed outright, though the seriousness of his situation was very real to him. He knew that his fate lay in his words. "I did not say that what was most valuable was carried in my bag. I have stores of goods that you cannot even imagine but that Neb would be pleased to have. Now, unless you plan on telling Neb that you killed an innocent man who only wished to do him a good turn, you had better let me meet with your leader without so much ado." Torgama and Kittam both seemed to be lost in thought when Madai came upon them. He had been listening to the conversation for some moments, and he realized that this young trader was more of a man than his father's men were ever capable of becoming. He was made curious by what he had heard, and more certainly he wanted to know if this young man had anything he could use to escape from his father's grasp.

Though his mother had promised to get him away from Neb before they began this arduous journey west, that plan had been halted for she had been laid low by a sudden illness. Madai had survived this long campaign by appearing to obey his father's every command, but in truth he had done much secret damage. He had led men in the wrong direction, and he had helped to spoil the food. He had poisoned water with noxious weeds and put ants in the bedding of the hardiest of travelers. At first, Leah had suspected Neb of poisoning her, but Eva assured her that it was just a common malady that often happened at this dry time of the year. Eva had conspired with Madai before he left, and she had given him every possible aide in both advice and herb to make Neb's journey as difficult and unpleasant as possible. So far Neb had not realized the root cause of his difficulties, though Madai feared that Serug, in his sneaking watchful way, had begun to suspect. Madai tried to appease his little brother by doing special things for him and giving way to his temper before it flared, but that had little effect. Serug was never one to appreciate a kindness. When this trader appeared out of nowhere promising a mystery of something too good to believe, Madai was determined to know the secret before anyone else. He only wished his mother or sister were near enough to tell him how this was to be done.

Madai gave an imperious wave of the hand and let it be known that Torgama and Kittam's services were no longer required. He began to speak in a light, almost humorous tone, but all the while his eyes followed his father's men carefully as they slowly made their way out of the woodlands and toward the grassy plain where Neb had camped.

"So how is it that you find yourself so honored as to be accosted by the worthy warriors of so noble a leader as Neb the Great?"

Adam's smile had vanished the moment Kittam and Torgama went out of his sight. He looked to Madai, and his eyes searched and appraised the youth not much younger than himself. "Who are you?"

Madai bowed and gestured dramatically with open hands. "I am the firstborn son of a firstborn son of . . . Well, it goes on and on."

Suddenly Adam smiled again, and this time it was genuine. "I, too, am a firstborn son, though in my case the lineage is not so noble. My father was the son of a mad man."

Madai looked seriously interested. For a moment, all thought of Neb fled from his head.

"A mad man? Really? Is it true?"

Adam shook his head and sat down upon the boulder he had earlier perched his foot upon. "Oh, I do not think so, or if it be the case then most men of adventure are mad men. My grandfather simply liked to do things his own way. He was not afraid to try new things. He would eat things never eaten before. He could go places never gone before. He would say things never said before." Adam smiled. "He often got in trouble with my grandmother for that."

Madai came nearer and found a rock of his own to perch upon. He leaned upon it and breathed deeply. The heat of the day had cooled slightly, and there was a gentle breeze in the air. Then he gave a long and searching then finally appraising gaze at his new friend.

"I am not so sure you want to offer your wares to my father."

Adam looked up surprised. He had been rubbing a spot where he had just been bitten by a small insect. "Why not? I do have something worth his while to see."

Madai clenched his jaw and looked around fugitively. He wondered where Scrug was at this moment. "That is the problem. You may be offering it to the wrong man." He looked hard at Adam. "Do you even know who my father is?"

Adam shrugged. "I have heard of Neb the Great. It is said that he cannot be killed, though his men die like mortals. I know that he suffered great injury and conquered even while in pain. His sons are said . . . ."

Madai stared hard, and Adam's words failed him. Madai urged him on with a light gesture. "What about his sons?"

Adam was embarrassed. He could not fathom why he had become so talkative all of a sudden. "It is just that they are said to be as different as night and day. One is strong and brave while the other is . . ."

"The other is what?" This demand came from Serug, with his hands on his hips in his usual attitude right before throwing a fit. "Come, come, do not be afraid. Tell me about the other son!"

Adam looked to Madai who swallowed hard and made the slightest quick gesture with his hand near the ground where Serug could not see.

"It is said that the other son is brilliant with insight not given to ordinary mortals."

Madai sighed deeply while Adam kept his gaze fixed carefully on the little tyrant who was sauntering nearer with a slight swagger to his exaggerated step. Serug's earlier irritation had dissipated as fast as it had arisen. He only wanted to know now what they had been speaking of before he had come upon them.

Adam's masked smile covered his features again, and he nodded in understanding. "Of course! You want to report the news to your father, loyal son that you are." Adam stood up and stretched as if he were terribly weary. "I am so very tired. I have been traveling for a long stretch of days without meeting one friendly clan. Do you think your father would be kind enough to allow me a night's rest within your camp tonight? I will gladly share with him any of my goods, which," he looked over to the dusty relics of the goods that Torgama had kicked about, "I still have within my possession."

Serug did not even look to his elder brother for permission to speak. He was used to grabbing control of every situation and keeping it for as long as he could. "I am sure that if I speak with my father he will welcome you, though he may not have much time to spare in speaking with you. We are preparing for battle you know."

Adam's eyebrows rose at the significance of this news. "I did not know that you were in the midst of battle preparedness." He went and gathered his things, dusting them off as well as he could. "This is perhaps not a good time to stop for a visit. I am quite content to—"

"You will come with me and meet my father!" Serug turned on his heel and began to saunter away. He was not about to miss this opportunity to bring a prize, whatever its worth, to his father.

Madai went over to Adam and, bending down, he helped to gather the things that were not broken. Using his own tunic, he wiped them clean of dirt. He handed them back one by one and spoke not a word. At one point as the last article was lifted from the earth, Adam stood and, placing the object in his bag, he looked Madai in the eye.

"Who would you have me share my secret with?"

Madai looked back at Adam, and his face was in deadly earnest. "Anyone but Neb."

It was late in the evening after a heavy meal of roasted meat, flat bread and roasted nuts in wine sauce that they sat near the fire watching the flames dance in the blackness. Neb had not been around all evening, and many silent thoughts had canvassed the various possibilities of where he had gone and when he would return, when suddenly he was in their midst. He came and sat by his eldest son.

"I have news today, Madai, that might interest you."

The youth looked up and saw his father's profile against the flickering flames.

"It turns out that you have a choice to make."

Madai was baffled. This was not their usual sort of conversation. He felt something like a mouse in the paws of a cat. "Yes, Father?"

"Your mother is on the point of dying. She wants to see you, but we are very near to the greatest battle of our lives. You have a choice, as I said. You can either leave us to see your mother one last time, or you can stay by my side to fight and conquer our enemy."

There was a rather large crowd about the firelight that evening as a guest was something of a novelty, and many were anxious to hear news and tales. Now there was complete silence hanging heavy in the night air. Serug almost spoke up, but his father gestured quickly for his other son's silence. Madai knew it was his turn to speak, but he had no desire to say anything. His heart hurt like it had been stabbed in the dark. His head ached. Finally, he sat up straighter and spoke so slowly and quietly that several men leaned in to hear better.

"I will stay with you, Father, for it is not only my duty but my honor."

Though no one could be sure in the dim light, it seemed that Neb's smile spoke words of its own. His head nodded up and down. He whispered under his breath. "I knew you would."

This time Serug could not be silenced. "Why do you trust him, Father, when he means to do you no good? He is a liar and a thief. He has been playing mean sport with us. I saw him put something into one of the stews we ate last week when everyone got sick. He hates you, though he will not say the words."

Neb sat up straight and looked from one son to the other. Then suddenly his eyes fell on the stranger in his midst. He was not pleased that so much had been shown to a man unknown to him.

Neb gestured with his hand. "And who is this?"

Serug and Madai both began to speak at once. Neb held up his hand for silence. "I will allow the stranger to speak for himself.

Adam faced Neb with calm confidence. "I am Adam, the son of a trader and maker of things. I come from a clan far to the east near the mountains. We are a valley people, and many are the travelers who cross our lands. We live in a vast territory, and we move south each winter while in the summer we climb into the hills. It is a beautiful land, rich in gardens and alive with young animals. Our women are beautiful, and our children are strong and healthy. I am a man who likes to travel and share the goodness of the earth with many."

Neb nodded silently. He knew a well-rehearsed speech when he heard one. "And why does a man wish to leave such a perfect land and wonderful people?"

Adam offered one of his disarming smiles, though Neb appeared not to see it. "I simply like to travel and see new things. My father was much the same way, though my mother did not like it so much. Eventually my father turned to creating new things instead of . . ." Suddenly Adam seemed slightly confused. Neb raised his head. He looked intently at the youth through the dim light. He ordered that another log be added to the fire, and several men rose to obey.

"Have you much skill with invention?"

Adam nodded slowly. "I like to try my hand at new things, though I am no match for my father. He could make wonderful little figures from wood, and he made sharp blades strong and enduring."

Neb let his gaze fall back toward his sons. He stared hard at Madai who was looking intently into the flames. "So what have you to say about our new friend, Madai? Shall we keep him with us for a time?"

Madai felt a little startled as he looked over the flames at Adam, and though only silence passed between them, there was too much in their look for Neb's comfort. Serug smiled. He knew that Neb had seen something that had displeased him. Madai may be firstborn, but he would not long remain first son in all things. Neb rose and appeared to stretch in the complete ease of a man tired after a long hard day. "It is time I took my rest, and I suggest the rest of you do the same." He looked over at the young trader. "Adam, you will stay with us for a time. I have much I would like to learn about you and your people." Neb looked at the gathering, and he seemed to be ordering them all in their silence. Several of the young men stood even as the elder men rose also to turn in for the night. Serug appeared to be planted in place for the duration of eternity. Neb stopped and looked at him. Serug tried to ignore the look, but after a moment the heat of it bore into his skull, and he too rose to go.

"But why do they get to stay?" Serug was whining. "They are going to plot against you."

Neb shook his head once quickly, and Serug turned to go. His shoulders sagged even as he pounded his feet in pouting fury. Madai began to stand, but Neb spoke out clearly. "No, Son, you stay awhile and keep our friend here company. He can sleep near the fire. You have no hurry. Youth needs so little sleep."

Madai did not raise his head. He did not need to see his father's face to read the bitter irony. Neb was feeling old, and he counted on Madai to make him young again in war, but this was a dream fast slipping away. They both knew that Serug saw too much and spoke too truly.

Adam tapped a broken stick against the fallen log on which he sat. Several logs had been rolled near the fire for seats upon which to rest. Adam had chosen a particularly tall log earlier and then had taken a handy ax and chopped down one side just to the middle so that he could sit comfortably and rest his back. Madai had marveled at this ingenuity. Now as they sat in silence, they both pondered all they had heard this night. Both knew that not one word could be spoken aloud. It would take the ingenuity of them both to bring them out of the grasp of Neb the Great.

CHAPTER 29
LEAH'S SACRIFICE

Leah knew that her son was at a crossroads, and yet she felt as if she stood on the brink of a precipice every time she considered how best to help him. Neb had traveled several days to the west already and had inflicted minor indignities on the surrounding clans as he went. It seemed as if he wanted to send word ahead to the People of Havilah that he was coming without actually burdening himself with too many trophies as of yet. He was holding himself and his men back for the big battle.

At first she had simply stayed in bed and waited, hoping for word of her son. Her sudden illness had indeed laid her low, but even as her body healed, her mind raced on shadowing Madai's every move. She had runners go back and forth with news so that she could keep abreast of what was happening. She even learned that recently a trader had come among them who was a creative youth whom Neb had decided to adopt for his own personal use. At this news Leah had suddenly felt an unaccountable surge of new strength flow through her limbs. Somehow she knew that this portended some good for her son. At the first sight of dawn the next morning, she asked that Eva be sent for, and her friend quickly appeared, worried that some old symptom had reoccurred. When she saw Leah standing up near the window opening, she sighed deeply and, with a look of chiding chagrin, she entered the room.

"What is so important that you had to call for me so early? Why, the sun hasn't even shown its face."

Leah began pacing from wall to wall like a wild dog tethered before its execution. "I must go and find Madai and free him from Neb before it is too late."

Eva blanched and threw her hands up into the air. "Well, that is a wonderful idea! Why don't you free us all?" She shrugged her shoulders. "I wish I had when I had the chance."

Leah stopped her pacing and looked at her friend a long, searching moment, and then she walked over with her hands out, shaking ever so slightly. "I will free everyone I can. Mostly I will free myself."

Eva shook her head in an exaggerated manner that had always irritated Leah but now passed unnoticed. "You will be free of what may I ask? Are you going to run away? To your old home? Where Neb is heading at this very moment? So you can be slaughtered with the rest? Will that free you?"

Leah took ahold of her friend's hands, which were flailing in the air in a maddening attempt to express her frustration at Leah's conviction that she could ever be free of Neb. "I know what you think, but you are wrong. I tried to love Neb, and it did not work. Even when Neb loved me back, I was not free. I had too much guilt. I knew I had sacrificed my honor for my life, and I justified that choice by the life of my babe. Madai was all the justification I needed to stay alive. But if he is corrupted or killed too soon, my sacrifice will have all been in vain. He must live to undo some of the terrible wrong of his father."

Eva shook her head even more violently. "Why? He is not Neb's keeper. He does not bear responsibility for his father's deeds."

"Every son bears the sins of his father, for either he must accept or reject them. Madai wants to reject them, but he is afraid as his own grandfather, Hezeki, was afraid. He bears the weakness of fear, and he must be made strong."

"So where exactly will he get this mysterious strength? From you?" Eva pulled her hands away from Leah and stepped off to the side of the room. Her voice dropped almost to a whisper. "Don't you yet see where Neb gets his strength?"

Leah turned toward the opening of her dwelling. "I know better than you think. I have lived intimately with a man who has bound himself to darkness for the honor of great power. Yet I see him in his sleep. He does not rest easy. He is haunted, though he knows it not. He is not free from his own soul. Some part of his decent nature still exists and yearns to breathe free, but he will not let it. He could love, and he could be a new man, but he will not. He is overcome by his own chosen terrors. He is more tormented than his worst enemy."

Eva turned to look at the rising sun shining through the doorway at the profile of her friend. "If only that were true, I might be satisfied."

Leah turned around, and with a sudden vicious tone, she countered, "Satisfied? Satisfied with what? That evil has conquered a man?" She rushed toward her friend one last time. "Don't you see? We all lose every time one man becomes mad, every time one man gives up his soul. All of us—family, clansmen, all of us—become poorer and weaker by such loss!" She stepped out of the dwelling and began to walk toward the rising sun. "That is why I must go now and save my son. He is my only hope. Otherwise I have nothing left."

Eva ran several steps to catch up with Leah. "You are going now? You just got out of bed! You have been very ill. You need time, and there are things you could prepare." She had to run in order to keep step with Leah who was walking quickly. She tried to grasp Leah's hand, but she was brushed aside. Finally in desperation, Eva took a quick jump step and got in front of Leah "I could come with you! Just wait a day, and I will get everything ready for the two of us."

Leah shook her head as she walked around Eva in strong, determined steps. "I must go now."

"Why? Why now?"

"I have been summoned."

Eva stopped in her tracks and looked at her friend as if she had gone mad. "And who exactly has summoned you from your sick bed?"

Leah did not turn around as she continued her march. "I do not know. I only know I must go now."

Eva stamped her foot in the fury of her impotence. "Well, what about Serug?"

Though Eva could not see it, Leah's eyes swelled at the mention of that name. Her step faltered just a bit, but she continued to move determinedly forward. Her voice was too quiet to hear as she responded with a thick tight voice. "I have already lost him."

Eva stood watching her friend cross over the short grasslands until she ascended a small rise, and then she began her decent.

The sun had risen and was a glowing ball of white heat in the morning sky. Like a bird in flight, Leah became smaller and smaller as the hill took her from sight. Eva clenched her hands to her sides. She wanted so much to cry, but it had been long since she allowed herself that luxury. She wondered if she would ever be able to again. Then she thought of where Leah was going and what was probably going to happen to her, and she knew that the tears weren't far off.

Leah had set out in the brightness of the day when her summons was clear in her mind. She walked, not knowing exactly where she was going, for two days without food until she was faint with hunger and exhaustion. It was nightfall on the second day, and her conviction was blurring into the night sounds of animals that can smell fear and death. She had found a stream that meandered down from the rocky crags near the mountainside, and she sat and drank her fill. Her dress was dirty, though not terribly torn, for even while walking in her blind ambition she tried to take care of herself. She was not a hunter. Though she had found a few herbs, they did little to sustain her on her journey. On the first day, she had felt no hunger pains; rather she had felt invigorated and strong beyond anything she had ever felt before. But now, suddenly, she was weak, and a sensation of terror was working its way up from her stomach to her mind. She did not want to be afraid, and she could not give up her quest, but she wondered how she was ever going to accomplish the task she had set for herself. She began to think that perhaps she had gone a bit mad as Eva undoubtedly suspected. Had it been her illness that had brought this on? Was it a fever that made her think she could simply walk away from her village and find Neb's war party alone in the wild? She sat down on the grass and leaned her back against a great rock. It dawned on her that she had probably gone too far north or south and would miss Neb altogether. She closed her eyes and let the sound of the flowing water echo gently in her ears. She did not know how long she had been like this when suddenly she heard a sound that sent her heart beating and every muscle in her body frigid with fear. There was the thrashing sound of men's progress toward the same stream she was at. She was out in plain sight, except it was now late at night, and only a sliver of the moon shown. Perhaps it was only a wild animal that had come to slake its thirst. If that was the case, it was a large animal, which was almost as terrifying. She imagined the grunts and the sniffs it would make before it attacked. "Oh, someone, help me!" Leah pictured her mother and her father, but no more words would come. She could not plead with the dead to help the living. She curled up into a ball and squeezed her eyes shut. Whatever was to happen, she did not want to see it as it was happening.

"What is this?" It was a sneering voice that liked to belittle. Leah's eyes unclenched, though they did not open. She knew that voice. Torgama at his best. Torgama used his foot to kick not too gently at the curled up figure. He laughed. "I know who it is! The little mouse who likes to pile up mounds of weeds and roots."

Kittam's voice was soft and sibilant. "No, you are wrong. This one is too big. Eva is small, and her bones are like a bird's." He went over and grabbed Leah by the shoulder and pulled her upward so he could see her face. When Leah saw his face so close to her own, she spat at him.

"Get your hands off me! I am trying to find my husband. I have important news."

Kittam jumped backward as if a snake had bitten him, and Torgama laughed at his discomfort. "You shouldn't lay hands on Neb's woman. He might have something to say."

Kittam turned toward Torgama. "Shut up, you slave! Or I'll ask Neb how his leg is feeling today!"

Leah had stood up during this exchange, and she put up her hand in a commanding gesture, one she had never used before. Both Kittam and Torgama looked puzzled, but they stopped talking at once.

"I have told you that I have important news for Neb, something he will want to hear from me, and if you two value your lives, you will take me to him as fast as you can!" The two men exchanged wary looks and then pointed to the east across the small stream.

"He is less than a day's march from here to the east, if we go directly. That is not how Neb likes to travel, but you may do as you wish."

Leah wiped her hands on her dress and looked across the murky stream into the darkness ahead. "I have been resting, but I have not had anything to eat."

Torgama bowed in mock kindness. "Permit me to share my meager provisions." He grabbed up his bag, which he had flung on the ground when they first came upon her. He held out a dried piece of meat that neither smelled nor looked—even in the dim light—good enough to eat, but hunger was mistress of the moment, and Leah reached out and took the viand. Her hand accidentally brushed against Torgama's, and he moved his hand swiftly so as to prolong the touch. She jerked away as if stung, and Kittam choked back a laugh.

Leah swallowed and spoke in forced calm. "Once I am satisfied, we will go to meet my husband."

Both men smiled and nodded in silent agreement, though even in the dim light, Leah felt the predator presence in each of them. Of the two of them, it was Torgama she feared most. Though the heat of the day was quite gone and replaced with the shadowy coolness of a dark night, she felt a slight damp sweat on her forehead. How was it possible that she now looked for Neb, not so much to stop him from his evil, but to save her from this present danger? She tried to out-stare Torgama as she finished her disgusting meal, but exhaustion was seeping into every fiber of her being, and she knew it would take everything she had just to finish this journey much less battle the wayward wills of her husband's men. She closed her eyes and then stepped to the side to allow the men to lead the way. Torgama looked at Kittam who stepped in front, but Torgama chose to follow in Leah's wake. Should she fall behind or some wild animal attempt to attack, she was well surrounded. This did nothing to comfort her soul.

Neb was quietly deciding how best to approach the Men of Havilah when a runner came up to him panting with breathless speech. Neb assumed this was news from the scout he had sent out earlier to determine what kind of preparations were being made by Kryce. When he looked up, however, he saw not the man he expected but quite another—a camp guard.

"Kittam and Torgama have returned, and they are bringing your wife." Neb looked to the west and saw the guard's words come to life. He stood up, and a frown burrowed deeply into his aging features. His face had darkened of late, and when he was angry, his countenance looked much like a thundercloud. Most of his men knew to stay clear of him when that look appeared. As Leah came closer, he saw that she looked exhausted and very pale. Torgama and Kittam were walking on either side of her, and their faces were perfect masks of complete indifference, even as their steps marched out suppressed emotion.

For a sudden moment, Neb felt something. Alarm sprang forth from a pit very deep, and he wondered at it. What could possibly have happened to bring Leah out so far into camp on the eve of battle? He took a step nearer her. Her clothes were dirty, and her hair was matted with stray locks flying into her face. She looked very much like a wild animal caught after a fight to separate it from its young. She had the same haunted, hunted stare. Neb's eyes roved over his two warriors. Would they have attempted some disgrace upon his wife? He knew they would never dare to, but then also he knew they would have liked to. Undoubtedly Leah knew it too. Neb swallowed. For the briefest of moments he regretted that he had ever taken her from her home.

Neb stepped another pace forward and put out his hand. "Leah? Explain yourself."

Leah stopped in her tracks. This was not how she had imagined things would go. But then, she realized she had not really been thinking about how things would go. She had no plan. She did not even have a story to tell him. It would have been very convenient to faint or be suddenly overcome with a return of her illness, but though she was terribly tired and thirsty, she knew she could stand on her own two feet yet a while longer.

"Neb, I have come to warn you of danger." She had no idea what she was going to say next, but she knew those few precious words were enough to stop all conversation out in the open. Neb put up his hand, and indeed he seemed to stop the very birds of the air. His words were sharp and angry.

"Torgama, you and Kittam go and see to the sentries around the camp. Check every man to see that everyone is alert and watchful. I will speak with my wife a few moments, and then we will meet in counsel."

Torgama and Kittam said nothing but merely turned to obey. Neb stopped a moment, noticing the lack of the proper bow he had taught them whenever they entered or left his company. Why were they not offering him the small courtesies of respect that he demanded? He halted them as they turned away. "Torgama, Kittam? Have you forgotten something?"

They two men looked at each other, and there was a brief glance exchanged. They both bowed in union, but there was the slightest mockery to their motion that did not deceive Neb. For some reason he could not fathom, they were losing respect for him, and it was going to cost him much if he did not do something about it quickly. He turned to his wife and gestured for her to follow him into his tent. Leah stood stock still as if she could not be moved my human force.

"I want to see my sons first."

Neb looked at her and stared hard into her eyes. What was this, some new defiance? No matter, he would learn what was going on soon enough. He kept silent and turned slightly so as to gesture her to another tent right next to his own. Leah walked sedately ahead of her husband, and when she came to the opening of the tent, she called out softly.

"Maida? Serug? Are you within?"

Suddenly Serug's face peered through the opening. "Mother?" There was genuine surprise and gladness upon the face of her young son. Leah felt her heart clutch in anguish.

"Yes, it is me. I have come to see you and your brother. Is he inside?"

Serug's face pinched into a look of displeasure. "Madai? Why he is never here. He is always with that stupid trader, the son of an idiot."

Neb's voice rang out behind Leah. "That is enough. Your mother wishes to see you and know you are well. Come forth and tell her all the news. I will bring Madai." Neb turned and gestured for one of his men to attend him. He began speaking quietly to the side. Serug came out of the tent and stood in front of his mother. He had not grown or changed in any way that she could see, though it had been many days since she had seen him last. She tried to put her hand out to him, but Serug stepped back as if to disdain the touch of a woman.

"I am too old for your caresses now, Mother. You should not have come."

Leah looked slightly surprised and troubled. "Why do you say that?"

Serug offered a knowing smile. "Men are different when preparing for battle. We are not so nice. Father has been in a perfect rage lately. He snaps at everyone and questions everything. He is probably furious that you have come. He will send you home as soon as you have seen Madai and satisfied yourself. You have only done him harm. The men will be laughing behind his back that he cannot control his own wife. He does not need any more challenges to his authority."

Leah looked at her son without wavering and wondered how he managed to see so much and yet be so blind. She took a deep breath. "Tell me about this trader, the stupid one you spoke of."

"Oh, I did not say he was stupid, but rather that his father was stupid. The father likes to make things, and this pleases his boy no end. He is so proud of his father, though he can hardly fight to save his skin. I could kill him in a moment."

"Why would you want to do that?"

"I do not need a reason to kill. It is just knowing that I can do it that makes all the difference. I do not think he could kill me."

"Why not? You are young, and if he is a trader, he must be many years your elder."

"He does not have it in him."

"But you do?"

"If I wanted to."

"But he might not let you kill him so easily. He might fight back, and then where would you be?"

Serug looked wise and smug as he shook his head at his mother's simplicity. "No man can watch his back all the time, Mother."

Leah looked truly shocked. "Would you stab a man in the back, Serug?"

Serug looked slightly puzzled. "If I needed to." Serug had had enough of this conversation, and besides, Madai was now coming with his friend, Adam. Serug had no intention of being asked ridiculous questions in front of those two. "I will leave you to meet with Madai. I am sure my father needs me." He began to turn away. "You do know that we are set for battle tomorrow?"

Leah nodded her head. "Yes, I have been told."

Serug looked away to where Torgama and Kittam were now walking and conversing with various warriors. "You are lucky you weren't left with Torgama or Kittam."

"Why is that?"

Serug walked away as he flung back his last words. "Oh, they hate Neb. They would love to get at him."

Leah barely had time to catch her breath before Madai strode up to her and put out his hands to her in a gesture of welcome and love. Neb was standing near, but he said nothing.

"Mother, I am surprised to see you here." He looked to his side and brought Adam forward. "Here is a young man I would like you to meet. He is a trader from the east, and his father is an inventor."

Leah attempted to pull her eyes away from her son, but she had a hard time of it. She wanted to read in his face all that had happened to him and what had changed in his soul. Was he still her son? But upon her son's insistence, she looked into Adam's face, and she caught her breath. Here was a man who had nobility written upon every feature. Suddenly she knew why she had come and whom she could trust with her mission. She put her hand upon Adam's shoulder, and as she bent in to offer words of courtesy, she squeezed his shoulder and spoke so low that only the youth could hear the words.

"You must save my son."

Adam nodded his head as if he had accepted a quaint compliment. "I am happy to meet you as well. Your son has told me much about your people. I wish I could meet them." At this, there was a dread silence. Adam realized his mistake and bit his lip, but his eyes looked deeply into Leah's, and he offered one quick nod in understanding.

Leah leaned in again once more. "Soon!" She whispered this single word and then turned toward her husband. "I have seen them, and I am satisfied. I am very tired now, and I must rest before I speak any further." This speech was made loudly and with pronounced determination. There were many raised eyebrows. Neb was not surprised however. He knew that something was afoot, and he meant to get to the bottom of it. But he could wait a few hours. He made the one mistake he had counted on others always making—not taking the present threat too seriously. Neb gestured to his wife to rest with him in his own tent. She nodded her acceptance, and they both entered into the cool darkness of his temporary dwelling.

Serug had watched everything that passed with crude but accurate appraisal. His mother was here for a reason she would not tell, and it had something to do with Madai. Neb was angry, but he would not show it just yet. They had a battle to win, and Neb would not put it off. That would weaken him still further in the eyes of his men. No one knew what was causing the sudden threat to Neb's security, but threat there was, and every man both hoped and feared Neb's response. Serug did not like Adam, but he hardly understood why. It was enough that Adam made himself agreeable to everyone and was smarter than they knew. Serug did not like depths he could not fathom. But he figured that Neb was still the leader and man enough to see through a youth like Adam. For all his intelligence, if Neb could gain nothing from him, then the trader might find himself used as a shield at a convenient moment. It had happened before. And Serug pondered astutely that it would probably happen again.

Madai watched his mother disappear into his father's tent, and against his will, his heart ached. He had made his own emotions move to his mind's commands up to this point. He had thrust aside his mother's words, her thoughts, her moods, her gentle speech and the stories she had taught him of a life and world beyond that of Neb's ambition. But now all that came rushing back with all the feelings of a young boy who respects and loves his mother. Even when he had told Adam of her and the people she had sprang from, he had spoken as if mentioning a long ago past that no longer existed. Now he worried that for him, perhaps it didn't, but he wanted so much to live in her world and not his father's. He looked at Adam who had a very strange look in his eye. He looked to his side, staring at the figure of Serug who was watching them from a distance, and he whispered a single word. "What?"

Adam laughed as if Madai had made a great joke, and he slapped him on the back quite heartily. He spoke loudly one moment and then in a whispered undertone the next. "I like your jokes. You always know how to tell a good tale!" He moved Madai away from the center of the camp. "We are leaving right now. Don't call attention to yourself. Act like we are just going to the spring. I know what to do."

Madai swallowed hard and quickly covered his face with a mask of light amusement. "I just hope you know how to fight as well as laugh, or tomorrow the joke will be on you!"

Adam stopped in his track as if affronted. "Do you really want to see who is the better man? I will race you!"

Madai puffed out his chest in mockery. "I am the son of Neb the Great! Are you challenging me?"

"Do you accept?"

"I accept!" The two young men lined up shoulder-to-shoulder and then sped off without any further ado.

Serug watched from his perch on a rock off to the west and shrugged his shoulders at their games. "Stupid idiots! Wasting all their energy when there is a battle tomorrow! Well, it won't be my fault if they are too exhausted to defend themselves!" He stood and sauntered back to his own tent to rest. He knew his brother would be back before nightfall, for wasn't Madai afraid of the dark? In Serug's estimation, Madai was not a very brave person. Serug smiled. This time he would kill the enemy, be he man or beast, and everyone would be amazed. Neb would know which son he could depend upon most.

Madai and Adam ran on and on while most of their village smiled in complacency at their youth and vigor. Many older men wished they had such spirit and strength, though several also wondered, like Serug, if they would be fit to meet the enemy in the morning. But that was their problem, and life was very short on the eve of battle. There was certainly not enough time to worry about another man's wisdom. Madai ran as if the mother bear of his nightmares were at his heals once again. Sweat trickled down his face, and his legs became wobbly, but he would not stop. Adam ran calm and coolly without the fury of fear taking its toll. He practically sauntered at Madai's side until late in the day when the sun had moved far behind them. Then he motioned for them to take a rest. Both young men lay down in the grass and spread their arms and legs under the cooling sun. They had some shade as the sun was no longer directly on them, but they were hot nonetheless. It took a while for Madai to form his words.

"So where are we running to anyway?"

"Don't you know?"

Madai wanted to sit up and look at the man he had entrusted his life to, but he was still too tired. "Not really. I just heard what my mother said, and I saw that look in your eye, so when you began to run, I followed."

Adam sat up on one elbow and looked over at his friend as if he had just adopted a baby. "You are finally going to meet your uncles."

"The ones Neb is about to attack?"

"The very same."

"But we will be killed along with them! How will this help anyone? Surely my mother wanted me to run somewhere safe."

"Your uncles will be quite safe when they learn about what I carry."

Now Madai sat up and looked at his friend. Adam had nothing in his arms and wore nothing on his back. "What do you carry?"

Adam pointed to his chest. "It is something inside of me that will give strength to the weak and make the frightened brave."

Madai shook his head. He liked his friend, but he could not fathom what he was talking about. "All I know is that Neb will want to kill more than my uncles when night falls and we do not return." He stood up and looked back across the horizon from where they had come, and his voice was grave and sad. "And what will my father say to my mother?"

Adam rose also, and he began to jog toward the settling darkness. "Your mother loves you, and her heart will be most pleased by your escape. Do not waste her sacrifice."

Madai closed his mouth from all further comment and began to run with all due speed.

CHAPTER 30

THE REASON OF WAR

"You do not know my brother!" Kenan's face was contorted by sudden fury. "If you knew what he was like and what he wants, you would not be so complacent in the face of the danger that threatens us."

Sari slapped the wet rag she was holding down upon the sill of the window opening. She turned away from her husband and looked out into the wide expanse of open air, breathing deeply before she spoke, though her chest was heaving. At last she turned his way. "I was there when Neb attacked, and I remember washing the bodies of the dead. I remember well the long, wailing cry of the many women who lost husbands and brothers and sons. I lost my father and my sister in case you have forgotten. I know all too well what Neb is capable of, but . . ." She hesitated as if searching for just the right words. "I know that he is not the man he was. He couldn't be! So much time has passed. He is older, and he has had the influence of Leah for all these years. He has two sons now, and that will make a man take a look at how he wages his wars. He must be considering a successor by now, and perhaps Leah's sons will bring the clan—"

Kenan put his hands on his hips and stood staring at his wife as if she were mad. "You think his sons will be like Leah? Trust me, that is not possible. They will be like Neb, or he would have cast them out by now. He probably would have killed them at birth if he thought for a moment that they would not be true to his command." A flush had suffused Kenan's features, and he was obviously having trouble keeping himself calm enough to have a discussion. "You may be certain that I know all there is to know about not being acceptable to Neb. He has been trying to kill me and my brother for most of our lives. He killed our father! He is a killer, and his sons are killers too. The best thing we can do is go into his camp and kill Neb, all of his men and every child that sprang forth from that clan. Then and only then will we be truly safe. And if some day we have children, they will be safe too."

Sari looked back at her husband and shook her head slowly. "I understand what you are saying, and I know it makes sense to my mind, just not to my heart. Is there no other way? Could it not be that in your assault on Neb you are becoming too much like him?"

Kenan's voice was raised up a notch as he responded by stepping toward the doorway. "Neb *wants* to kill. He is an aggressor. I kill because I have to! My revenge is justified. His is all in his mind."

Sari watched as her husband stomped out the door into the broad daylight. There were clouds building in the west, and she hoped that a storm would come and wipe away the oppressive heat they had been experiencing of late. Her hands cupped her middle as she sighed deeply. Perhaps if they had known children of their own, Kenan would not be so eager for battle. As it was, he tasted the blood of revenge in his mouth more and more every day. She could see the change in him as he went from being a happy youth to an angry man. He was cheated of his home clan and denied the blessing of children. As his wife, she had tried to fill in the empty spaces, but she had seen him rejoice when the news came that Neb was approaching with his sons. Tears filled her eyes. If they had sons, then they would be going off to do battle, too, like Enosh's boy. Perhaps she should be glad she was childless. She closed her eyes and grimaced. Her grief was like a physical pain. She wanted to ease the suffering of her husband, but she could not even ease her own suffering. And now war was upon them, and he would go looking for death and glory. He wanted to kill men and their children. She grasped at the windowsill, her arms shaking. Why was she even brought into this world? Her herbs had done her no service in the most important matter of her life. She sat down upon her pallet and let her face rest upon her pillow. She felt terribly tired, so she closed her eyes. Where could she get a baby when her body could not conceive one? And why was she so stricken when so many others had more fertility than they knew what to do with? Silence filled the little room, and the heat suffused her face. She wanted answers to her questions, but there was no response to her inner search. She began to fall asleep. In her dream world, she could hear a baby crying, and she yearned to comfort it. She reached out her arms, but still it cried on and on in the distance. She stepped forward and saw that it was injured. It had a dreadful mark upon its face, and one arm was missing. She stood frozen still, frightened by what she saw, as the baby still cried out. She would not let it cry. She ran forward and scooped the baby up in her arms, and the tiny thing nestled against her bosom and was calmed. It laid its head down on her shoulder in security and trust. She hugged the baby close, and she was filled with a gladness she had never known. She thought her heart would burst. Sari slept on while a single tear slipped down her cheek.

Tamar watched her son prepare for battle, and she nodded at his repeated requests for various things. Yes, he could take that and use this, and she would make sure she had fresh provisions ready in time. Her heart was divided. She was proud beyond words of her son and his mighty strength, and she was sure that his help would be no small thing in the battles to come, but she loved him so much it hurt, and she did not want to see him suffer no matter how glorious the cause. Enosh slipped into the room, and, after looking at his son, he turned to his wife and spoke a single word. "Ready?"

Tamar looked at him and smiled. "No, are you?"

Enosh grimaced. "No, not really." He motioned for his wife to follow him outside, and they stepped into the blazing brightness of the day while mountains of clouds loomed on the horizon. The storm would arrive before the sun had set. He began to walk away from their dwelling toward a stream not far away. There were several women there doing various tasks, so he began to travel downstream until there was not a soul in sight. Tamar paced after him in silence until he found a welcoming spot and sat down against a tall tree that had its roots in the water. Tamar stepped into the cool running water and rested her worn feet. It was not often that she got a moment's rest during the course of the day. Enosh did not say a thing. He seemed to be watching the storm clouds gathering. Tamar looked up and saw them too, but her conversation was distant from the troubles at hand.

"It seems that my days are so busy that I have no to time to see the trees in the forest. I see only the outline, the great shapes, but never the details."

Enosh put out his hand to his wife and she stepped closer to him. "You see everything very well indeed. I wish I were as clever as you."

Tamar laughed out loud. "Oh, don't say that too loudly, or someone will come to set you straight. I am not clever or wise. I wish I were. Perhaps then my heart would not be so divided."

Closing his eyes, Enosh appeared not to have heard what his wife had said. But then he looked up again, for the clouds had almost covered the sun. "Perhaps it is not your heart that is divided, but rather our world." He shifted his weight and sat up straighter. Tamar was still standing but now nearer to him with one hand resting on the tree trunk. "It seems to me that we go into battle to reconcile an old injustice. Yet, nothing we do now can fix the past. Will Neb's death bring back my father or his brother? Will killing Leah's sons give her back her lost years of innocence?"

Tamar looked over at her husband and smiled. "Neb's death will free us from his threat forever. You need to look no further for the reason of this coming battle. We fight to keep the innocent safe from slavery and death."

Enosh looked away from her. "Yes, of course, I know that. And I want Neb to die. I just don't want to become like Neb to accomplish this mighty task. Kenan is looking to kill Neb's whole family."

"Not Leah, surely!"

"No, not her, but her sons. He cannot think that they are anything but Neb repeated twice. He wants revenge against the whole clan. He wants to see as many slain as possible. The bloodlust is upon him already."

Tamar nodded. "And upon Seth and Jubal as well. I have heard them speak in the quiet of the night with Kryce."

"Does this not trouble you?"

Tamar looked slightly surprised. "It is the way of men. There are hunters like Neb, and there are defenders like Kryce and Seth. Men will fight. It is what they do and how they live out their existence."

"What about me? I have no real wish to fight. I hate Neb with all my heart for what he has done, but still I do not look for the day of battle. What is wrong with me?"

"You are like your father and your uncle. You wish to repose in peace and build, not destroy."

"Am I not a man among men?"

"You are a man, but not *of* men." Tamar was watching the clouds now, too, but suddenly her eyes were wrenched another direction. She saw two young men running toward them. They looked exhausted, for their steps were beginning to stumble. One put up his hands in a gesture of defenselessness to tell them of their peaceful intent. She looked to her husband and touched his shoulder to draw his attention to the two figures.

Enosh stood up and stared. At first he felt merely surprised, but then a puzzled frown appeared across his forehead. "What does this mean?"

"I do not know." Tamar looked at one of the young men, and suddenly her face went grey. She knew that face. It was Leah come back to her, but yet not Leah herself. Her hand gripped her husband's arm and squeezed. He looked over at her and became alarmed at what he saw there. He looked back at the two approaching youths, and all he could see was two unarmed young men. Suddenly Tamar was running forward to greet them. Her arms were outstretched. Enosh was completely taken aback, so he followed his wife more sedately. When the four met, the young men stopped and the younger fell upon his knees trying to catch his breath. They were both of them handsome, and Enosh noted that one was older than the other. Tamar was searching the face of the younger man with an intense gaze. Enosh decided to step in before his wife did anything else embarrassing. This was so unlike her that he stepped in front of her and spoke to the young men without including her in the conversation at all.

"My name is Enosh of the People of Havilah. Who are you, and why have you come in such great haste?"

The younger of the two rose to his feet and stepped forward. "I am Madai, son of Neb the Great, and I come to save you from death."

CHAPTER 31

HATE ON THE MINDS OF MEN

Seth, Jubal, Kryce and Kenan looked upon Madai with cold, staring eyes. Adam had been told to stand back, for he was nothing more than a trader who had become mixed up in the mighty affairs of warriors. Their interest was in the son of Neb alone. Enosh had brought the youth forward with every intention of introducing him as a young man who wanted to help their people, but as soon as Kenan learned of the man's identity, he had Kryce, Seth and Jubal summoned. They had all gathered quickly, for on the eve of battle, everyone was ready for anything—anything other than the sudden appearance of the son of their enemy.

"We have Neb in our hands now!" Kenan was exultant. "Send a runner, Kryce, and tell Neb whom we have captured."

Kryce's eyes darted over to his friend's face. His own skepticism was obvious. "I doubt that Neb—"

"My father would not walk across the village to save my life if it meant a blow to his pride." Madai stood tall and defiant. "He hates me now as much as he ever hated you. I have refused him, and as you must realize, Neb cannot tolerate dissension. He will kill me himself if given the opportunity."

"So why have you come to us? Why do you aid his enemy?" Seth's voice was calm and low.

Madai searched the faces before him as if looking for someone. "I am my mother's son."

Jubal shook his head. "He has his father's blood flowing through his veins whether he accepts it or not. He cannot help being his father's son as well. We will never be able to trust him."

Madai's frustration was palpable. "Trust me or not, you will not defeat Neb on your own. His clan has grown in recent years. There are those who like the taste of victory, and men from all over flock to him for the spoils of war. His men trust him implicitly…though some he trusts which he should not." Madai looked to Kryce who was clearly the man in charge. "I want to end his threat so that I can live in peace. My mother is left behind in his care, and I want her freed at any cost."

Sarcasm was painted on Jubal's face. "And how do you propose to assist us? You are none too large, and I do not even see a weapon ready at your hand."

Madai looked over to Adam. "I do not have anything of value to offer other than my own two hands and a willing heart, but I have brought someone who can do more than offer his valiant will. He comes bearing gifts, though at the moment you cannot see them."

"Stop speaking in riddles and tell us what you have to offer!" Jubal was becoming impatient.

At that moment, Adam stepped forward. "I have the skills and knowledge to make new weapons that will give you strength like you have never known before." A look of disdain crossed over his face. "But at the moment, I am not sure I want to reveal my secrets to you."

Madai turned looking shocked and baffled. "I thought that was why we came here. You said it was the answer to all my problems. We would be free and could save my mother from—"

Adam shook his head in sorrowful denial. "I am sorry, but I do not see *nobility* etched on these men's faces. I had supposed that the enemies of Neb would be enemies of his hate but instead I see in their faces the same wrath he carries, only their anger has festered under the mantle of justice. What would I save your mother from? She would leave a husband who conquers to live with brothers and friends who conquer."

Seth stepped forward, his face blanched with suppressed rage. "How dare you make us Neb's equal?! We are nothing like him. My clan was set upon and my men enslaved for years of suffering untold. Ask Jubal here! His brother has only lately returned. Nor do the Men of Havilah battle for conquest but rather they have always lived in peace, protecting those who needed protection. And Enosh and Kenan, have suffered all their lives at Neb's unworthy hands. Do you not know that Neb killed his own father in cold blood? And yet you dare to compare us to him?"

Adam stared back at Seth whose blazing eyes bore into him with all the anger of a wronged man. "I must be sure. Once I let this knowledge out, it will change this part of the world forever. There will be no calling it back."

Kenan snorted. "You think too well of yourself!" He walked past the youth and brushed him as he went. "I do not think you could fight a child and win."

Adam stiffened, but he did not react. Madai looked from his friend to the others. "I do not know what to do. I came here wishing to assist the enemies of my father. I brought you the best gift possible, but in your arrogance and pride—and your stubborn anger, you can see nothing but the reason for your hate." He walked back towards Adam and gestured for him to come away with him. "We will leave here and find another place to stay." He spoke as he turned. "We do not desire your protection…or your friendship anymore."

Kryce stepped in Madai's path. "For whatever reason, you are here now, and we will decide your fate in our own time. As it is, we have to move on tomorrow. Our men are prepared for battle, and I will not disappoint them. Neb will meet justice, with or without, your help." He gestured for several men who were watching all the proceedings to step forward. They led Adam and Madai to a hut set slightly off to the side for the storage of surplus goods. Then after he had seen to their imprisonment and given directions to the men who would watch over them, Kryce walked sedately back toward Seth and Kenan and Jubal. The sky was covered in black clouds, and the light was fading fast. It would be an early night.

"We would all do well to get an early rest, for I want to start out well before the light of day tomorrow."

Jubal gestured toward the storage hut. "What will you do with them?"

Kryce shook his head. "I will keep them out of the way. I cannot trust them. They could be spies sent by Neb."

Seth shook his head. "Though he is a liar and a deceiver and I would not put it past him, yet I do not see treachery in those men's eyes. They truly believe they can help us defeat Neb."

Kenan looked over at the hut. "Be that as it may, we have our appointed task and it would be best if we accomplish it by our own selves." The three men nodded in union and then began to walk away with no other looks addressed to the silent hut guarded by three warriors.

Only Enosh watched from a distance. He knew he should have taken part in the discussion, but he could think of nothing to say to his brother's son. He only knew that he would go with Kenan and his friends into battle. For some reason, however, he was glad to know where the eldest son of Leah was being kept. He began to wander back toward his own tent, but as he passed Seth, he stopped a moment.

"Seth, stay a moment, I have a question for you."

Seth was obviously tired and irritated, having lost all of his natural joy. He looked at Enosh rather puzzled. He had noticed his silence in the proceedings. "What is it, Enosh?"

"It is just that I remember hearing the name of Adam before. Do you know what it means?"

Seth looked up at the blackening sky as great drops of rain began to fall upon his head. "I am not sure what it means, but there is a story about an Adam of old, the firstborn, who ate fruit from the tree of knowledge of good and evil…it is an ancient story." In no mood to give a history lesson, Seth began to walk away again to get out of the storm.

Enosh appeared determined to satisfy his curiosity. "So what ever happened to him?"

Seth moved away more quickly. "He was banished for believing a lie and bringing sin and death into the world."

Enosh stood still in the middle of the village as great rain drops began to splatter down over his head and with a bitter chuckle he spoke low under his breath. "I always wondered who started it."

CHAPTER 32
IF ONLY

Enosh sat alone in the dark for several hours, listening as the storm passed overhead. Tamar had finally fallen asleep, and Put was breathing deeply in expectation of the morrow's adventure. Childhood memories came back to him of his mother and father and his family as they had once been. If only Neb had chosen a different path and not forced his father to abdicate his role as leader before the rightful time. If only they had not tried to find his uncle and settle with the Clan of Seth. If only he had never met the People of Havilah. Yet he could not truly wish to change that. Though Uzal had been killed and Leah taken away, still *his* fortune had changed for the better. The People of Havilah were more like family than his own clan had ever been. He loved his wife more than his own life, and Put was a son any man might wish for. The antics of Gomer lightened his heart in ways no other person ever could. He deeply loved this clan and his new family. He sighed. Neb was coming very well prepared, and if all the reports were true, then the People of Havilah might cease to exist very soon. A lump rose in his throat, and he wondered at his unmanliness. He should be more like his younger brother, Kenan, thirsting for the blood of his enemy—no matter who that enemy might be. Or he should be more like Kryce who knew all the arts of warfare…or at very least like Seth who took command as needed and saw to the protection of his people. But he was none of these men, and he felt terribly alone as the darkness held him, awaiting the moment when he must face his fears. He stood up and walked to the doorway where a refreshingly cool breeze caressed his face. The storm had passed, leaving the foliage dripping slow drops upon the wet earth. What was he *really* afraid of? He asked himself this question brutally. Was it death? No, he had no fear of pain or dying. He had faced pain often enough to know that it was not his master. He did not want to leave his family to fend for themselves, but even that did not frighten him. He knew Tamar and Put were strong and capable and would see to every need. Was he afraid Neb would win? Yes, that was a terrible thought—to have his family enslaved by such a man and at his mercy. Enosh wondered if he would go mad. But even that was not the true horror that gripped at his gut. He could see the scenario clearly in his mind; Neb coming...killing and conquering... the People of Havilah putting up a bold and determined front but being pushed back and back again by this relentless madman. Enosh could feel his face growing red at the thought. He could see his wife being taken away by Neb as Leah had been taken. He could see his sons sold into slavery like dogs with ropes around their necks. He could feel the burning lash, the spears whizzing past his head as he tried to escape, his turning and finding Neb at his heels. There they would be, he and Neb, alone. He would look his tormentor in the eye, and the horror of it all would blind all reason. Enosh would grab Neb about the neck, and he would squeeze and squeeze and squeeze with all his might—with more strength than he ever knew he had, and he would be glad to do it, he would rejoice in his strength and ability to end the life of his tormentor. Neb would fight back and try to kill him in turn, and *he* would use all the powers of hell to conquer him. Enosh would feel between his fingers, in his mighty grip the sap of life seeping out of Neb and he would-

Enosh fell to the earth outside his doorway, sobbing beyond all comfort. He knew now what he truly feared. In the quiet of the night it was hard to keep his muffled sobs to himself, but he managed to do it, and when he had spilled every last tear he got back to his feet. Suddenly peace reentered his heart, and he realized what he must do. *He must stop Neb, but he must not want to destroy Neb.* He must leave Neb's final justice to someone better able to arrange it. He stepped swiftly back inside his dwelling and woke his son gently. Put was a sound sleeper, and it took several shakes to get him alert without awaking anyone else. Put was quick, however, and when he saw his father, he made not a sound as he slipped from the comfort of his bed. Enosh reached over and grabbed his provisions bag and hung it over his shoulder as the two left the quiet dwelling.

Enosh led his son in the direction of the storage shed, speaking in a low whisper.

"Son, I know how much you want to experience your first battle, but I have another task for you, and it may well make all the difference between our survival or our defeat." Put was quiet as he followed his father. When they arrived at the hut, Enosh gestured for his son to wait. Two of the guards were sleeping, but the third was wide-awake.

Enosh spoke softly but with authority. "I need to accomplish a task. Let me go in and speak to the son of Neb."

The guard was wary. "What is this about? Does Kryce approve?"

"Trust me. I know what I am doing." The guard looked a little dubious, but he nodded slightly, and Enosh was allowed to enter the small dwelling. Both Madai and Adam were sleeping. Enosh walked silently up to Madai and shook his shoulder.

"Wake up. I have something I need to ask."

Both Madai and Adam sat bolt up in sudden surprise. When they realized it was Enosh, they were uncertain but not uncooperative. They had never met Enosh formally, though they had noticed him standing off to the side. Madai rubbed the sleep forcefully from his eyes. "What is it you want? Has the time of battle come already?"

"Not yet, but it will be here soon enough—too soon really. Tell me, what is the secret Adam carries that will help us defeat Neb?"

Madai peered into the darkness, trying to see Enosh's face more clearly. "Why do you ask now? No one seemed very interested when I told them earlier."

"You were speaking to men on the eve of battle who have the bloodlust upon them. They are not interested in new ideas or a change of plans. They are interested in slaying their enemy."

Adam rubbed his face and shook his head at this exchange. "And what are you interested in, may I ask?"

Enosh breathed deeply and then exhaled. His voice was deep and almost choked as he spoke. "I am interested in remaining free. I do not want to become Neb in order to defeat him."

There was a moment of silence as Adam and Madai looked at one another. Suddenly Adam rose and walked over to Enosh. "In that case, I have a surprise for you." He stepped over to the corner of the room and pulled out a long, pliable stick and a bit of long twine. While he was doing this, Madai reached behind his pallet and pulled out several long sticks with slit shafts on one end and blunt ends on the other. Adam smiled in the darkness.

"We asked for these materials to amuse ourselves during the storm, and your men, seeing no harm in them, gave us what we asked for. We do not have the final weapon, of course, but if we can go outside, I will show you my idea and how these weapons work. I think you will see their usefulness."

Enosh nodded, though he was puzzled. He saw absolutely nothing useful in what Adam was holding—a bowed stick and a bit of string. He couldn't even make a boomerang or a slingshot from those materials. And those sticks, though strong enough to throw a short distance, could never be fashioned into spears or even knives. They would never hold a decent blade, and they were useless as spear throwers or darts. What could these two men be thinking? They walked out into the cool night air, which was still now. Enosh's son, Put, stepped forward to ask a question, but the intense silence and concentration of the men stopped him from uttering a sound. The guards came and stood around watching.

With great care, Adam took the string and fit it to the bowed wood. He tied it securely at one end and then pulled tight, bowing the thin wood even more. Then he took the long and thin straight stick with the shafted end, and he placed one end against the string. He pulled it back as far as it would go and then stopped and spoke in a whispered voice. "You have to imagine that I have secured a sharp small point to the end of this shaft." Then with a quick motion, he let the arrow fly through the air. It sailed high out of sight into the black sky and then fell to the ground several feet away. Madai ran over to retrieve the shaft. Adam spoke softly again. "These are but weak examples, as I was not given the best materials, but just imagine if I made this bow from strong wood and tied a good wiry sinew from end to end and attached a fine, sharp flint tip to the shaft. Then when I let loose, I aimed it at a beast or a man." There was complete silence as the images were securely placed into each man's mind. "I have practiced with various materials, and there were times I had an arrow tip fly deep into the trunk of a tree. With practice, I learned to take down a bird flying in the sky." He looked around at each man in turn. "I no longer have to stand near enough to touch my enemy. I can stand back at a safe distance and let my weapon fly into his heart."

Enosh shook his head in wonder. "With this weapon, we will outnumber Neb - no matter how many warriors he brings forth into battle. Each arrow is like a warrior flying from heaven to earth."

Put looked at his father. "What does this have to do with me, Father? Do you want me to learn this new skill?"

Enosh nodded vigorously. "Yes, and more. You have been to the Village of Seth many times. Take Madai and Adam up there. Show them what you have learned, and tell them to make as many of these weapons as they can and to come to us as soon as possible." Enosh looked intently at his son. "Do this, and you will be worth all the warriors standing upon the field of battle."

Put nodded his understanding and turned toward Madai and Adam. He stopped and turned slightly back to his father. "Are they my prisoners or . . ." his voice trailed off.

Enosh smiled and patted his son on the back. "They are giving us the gift of a lifetime. I would call them friends." He then turned to Adam and put out his hand in a gesture of friendship. "I do not have words to express my gratitude. You have saved us from a fate worse than death."

Adam stared right through the black night and nodded silently. "It was given to me freely, and I pass it along freely."

Then as the men began to move off, Madai stopped a moment. He turned and stepped back and spoke quietly to Enosh. "If you do meet my father, do not hate him…too much." He started to turn away but then spoke once more. "But if you find my mother, please, save her…if you can."

Enosh nodded mutely. He had no words to fill the aching silence. The guards stood to the side as Put led the way for Madai and Adam. They could see the reason for this departure, and they did not doubt Enosh's counsel. They would let him explain matters to Kryce in the morning, but they would not leave him alone in his judgment, for they had seen the wonder of the bowed wood and the flying shaft for themselves and imagined heroic possibilities. The art of war filled their heads for the rest of the night.

Enosh returned to his dwelling to rest until dawn. He lay down upon the pallet next to his wife and sighed deeply once again. He felt exhausted and yet refreshed. He closed his eyes. He wanted to sleep, but he knew that his dreams would take him to places that he did not want to go. So he simply lay in quiet repose, remembering, thinking, wondering, and even… daring to hope.

CHAPTER 33
A TRUCE OF TERROR

Neb was waiting for Torgama to attend him. He had learned of his son's departure from his camp with Adam, the son of the inventor, and he had been so completely stunned by this unexpected betrayal that he acted as if it had not really happened. He said nothing to Leah of the matter, though she learned of it through Serug who was determined that Madai be made an example of as a traitor. Neb did not respond to Serug's request to send men out looking for the two deserters, nor did he look his wife in the eye when she asked him what he was going to do. He did not even seem to hear Kittam when he gave his full report. He simply wanted Torgama to come and wait upon him for the night. He was going to sleep early in order to wake early, and if anyone had any news about the People of Havilah, he wanted to be the first to hear of it.

Neb retired into his dwelling as the clouds began to first show themselves. He slept through the pounding rain, and he awoke when the air had cooled into a soft breeze. He emerged outside to see Torgama standing in his accustomed place on the right side of the entrance. Neb walked past him a short way, breathing in deeply the fresh night air.

"Where is my wife?"

Torgama moved not a muscle. His eyes strayed only from left to right, scanning the empty blackness before him. "She sleeps not. She is over by the fire looking into the flames."

Neb walked to the fire and saw Leah still and slump-shouldered. He wondered if she had fallen asleep even as she sat there. He stepped softly up to her. She did not turn her head, but he could see her eyes were wide open.

"You should sleep. There will be much action tomorrow, and men will need tending. As you are here, you might see to their needs."

Leah shook her head. "I will do nothing."

Neb looked down upon his wife. He wanted so very much to hate her. He had good reason to hate her. If she had been different, then Madai would have been different. She did not admire him; she admired only Madai. She did not trust him; she trusted only Madai. She did not love him. Madai alone held her heart.

"I am still your husband."

"I care nothing for you or your men. I wish only for the life of my son, and this you cannot give me."

Neb walked around and stood between his wife and the red and white flames of the fire. Someone had put new wood upon the embers, and fresh life had been given to the old flame though it was the same fire her had ordered earlier. "I may save your son yet. It is still within my power."

Leah let her eyes roam over her husband's form as she shook her head in complete resignation. "Why? He has betrayed you finally and completely. He does not want to be like you." She let her eyes fall back to the flames. "He is what you could never hope to become; a man content within himself. You cannot not allow his challenge to become personal - for he would win." Her voice was heavy. "You know this is true."

Neb's voice was barely controlled. "I only know that my wife has conspired with my son to abandon me on the eve of battle. I know that I have been a good husband - much better than most. I have been a strong father who would have given his first son—"

Leah's temper flared to life. "You would have given him what? Your ambition? Your desire to rule at all costs? Is that what you call being a strong father? A man who teaches his son the art of war so he can conquer and rob and terrify everyone around him? Who loves his wife only when he feels like it and—" Leah stopped as a choking cry stopped up her throat.

Neb stepped away from his wife, his voice colder than the night air. "I am what I am. You had a choice. You could have chosen another fate. I make no apologies for my desire to rule. It is what I was made for. I unite men - I bring them strength and wealth."

"You teach men to hate."

Neb snorted. "You sound like Eva. Men have been hating other men since the dawn of creation."

"But not all men hate. Madai does not hate. He could rule with kindness . . ."

"You are a fool and do not know what you are talking about. I lived under the rule of a kind man, and it was like drowning in a swamp. No one ruled. Always there was dissent and unrest, for there was no progress, no strength, none had the determination to become great."

Leah stood up and began to walk away from the fire her face still warm from the flame. "You are only remembering how it was inside yourself when you were trapped between your mother's desires and your father's leadership. There is another path, though you cannot see it. One can be strong and yet remain kind." Leah stepped past her husband. "And you have a son capable of such a feat, but he will have to face one terrible truth in order to do it."

Neb said nothing. He stared at the fire and waited as his wife began to walk past him. Suddenly, he reached out and grabbed her arm. "He will not rule in my stead—not without killing me first."

Leah looked down at her arrested arm and spoke so softly that Neb could barely make out her words. "Yes, I know."

Kryce led his men across the grasslands with their weapons swinging haphazardly to their determined movements. Seth was walking at his right side, and Kenan was on his left. Enosh walked slightly behind with Jubal marching next to him. The advancing men were masked by the darkness before dawn, and they moved stealthily. They did not want to arouse suspicion of their proximity. Normally battles were not attempted right after a hard rain, for the ground became slick and difficult to navigate especially on hills or near creeks and streams. But Kryce was determined that nothing would stop his approach to Neb's camp. When Enosh told him of the new weapon he had seen and how he had freed Madai and Adam, he had merely shrugged in impatient irritation as if to say that there was nothing he could do about it now. He did not believe for one moment that the two young men would actually go to Accad, even with Put's direction and encouragement, and then return with anything useful. There would be no miracle to assist them in battle. Besides, Kryce had more important things to attend to than the wishful thinking of his friend. The fate of Neb's eldest, or anyone else for that matter, was not going to distract him from accomplishing this glorious mission. As far as he was concerned, Neb must be killed this day. Nothing short of that end would satisfy him or his men. They hurried their pace as the darkness began to lighten.

Neb had finally decided that his wife must be sent away for the safety of them all. She was no longer sane, and now that her favorite son, Madai was gone, he had nothing to hold over her. It occurred to him that perhaps it would be best to send her back to her family. Would it not be just? He rose from his place of contemplation just east of his camp. He had imagined himself on this first day of battle leading his men, marching determinedly across the grasslands toward the People of Havilah. He was well aware of the fact that they were waiting for him. He knew that they hated him. He also knew that his son was now in their ranks, probably giving them all sorts of insight and information as to how best to defend themselves. But his men were very well trained and he was a gifted leader. He knew that the People of Havilah had been accumulating wealth for many years and thus this victory would not be an empty one. His men were well aware of this fact too. No matter what he might say or do Madai had never been filled with enough bloodlust to kill wantonly as a good warrior must. The Men of Havilah were guided by a sense of justice that always stopped short of the mindless brutality needed to completely annihilate an enemy. Neb knew all of this, so he felt quite confident of his success…until the first light of the sun began to glow on the horizon.

Standing on his feet, with his men just behind him, waking to the new day, Neb the Great stood as one completely transfixed. There, in front of him and behind him, circling his camp as far as the eye could see, were the Men of Havilah. This was an impossibility! Havilah did not stand a chance against him. Yet there they stood, looking for all the world like the victors, though not a spear had yet been thrown. Suddenly a man stepped forward. He was large but not enormous, though his shadow was great. His body was silhouetted against the rising sun, and the rays seemed to come from behind and within him. This was not a good omen for Neb's men to see. They would think a god had come against them. Color rose in Neb's face. There was no god that could oppose him. He had bound them all to his will. He stared hard at the line of men, and then he sneered in silent relief. It was only Kryce, the son of Uzal, who he had captured and freed in a moment of clemency. These were no gods. These were only men, and among them, somewhere, were his little brothers whom he had sought through the long years, as well as the boy-leader named Seth, who always looked like he might cry. Suddenly Neb recognized his brother. Enosh's face was grim and determined. Neb grimaced in return. Was his little brother grown to a man then? He would enjoy killing him more than any other for it was his face that had haunted him more than even Uzal's imprecations. He had never actually seen or heard the spirit of Uzal rise against him, but he had often seen Enosh's face before his dreaming eyes. Today was the day to end that secret torment. Neb's searching gaze could not locate his son. Surely he was not a coward, though he had managed to find the one person besides his dead grandfather who would sympathize with him. But now there was only silence on the battlefield; the day of conflict had come at last. The sun was above the horizon. Neb turned to let out a rallying cry to his men, though they needed no cry of warning. They had seen just as well as Neb what awaited them with the dawn. They had all silently picked up their carefully prepared weapons, and they now formed a great circle behind Neb. He stood, turned and faced his men putting his back to the enemy as if he cared nothing for their presence. His men stood taller and prouder in his supreme confidence. He had planned for this moment a hundred times in his mind, but with the distraction of his son and wife, he had lost his momentum. Now was the moment of truth, however. He had planned to cry out, "Death or victory!" but suddenly he wondered at the wisdom of those words. There was a sound behind him. A shout had been called out to him. He did not want to hear it. He wanted to keep his men riveted upon him and his message, once he was sure what he wanted to say. But the shout came again. For the first time in his life, Neb, at a supreme moment, was undecided. His men saw the stalled expression. Neb knew they noticed, so he swung around in furious anger.

"What do the carrion of birds have to say to me?"

It was Kryce who had stepped forward. "Send Leah to us before we begin, and we may spare some lives."

Neb spat into the dirt at his feet. "Leah is no longer yours. She will never come to you! Prepare yourselves for death, for your final moment approaches, and the birds will feast upon your flesh….at least they will have what my men leave behind!" There was a mighty roar of brutal laughter from his men at this witticism. Neb had focused his men on him again. The light was rising, and Kryce was no longer in the glow of a new day. Neb smiled. He only had to bring the bloodlust to the surface, and all would be well. "It is time for my men to teach you a lesson for coming up against us unjustly. We will slaughter the weak and take many prizes this day." There was a chant beginning behind him, and Neb's smile widened. It was what he needed but had not supplied. His men were chanting louder and louder. "Neb, Neb, Neb, Neb!" They were beginning to move in gathering strength. He knew that now was the time to release them to their fate. "I command you - kill the enemy!" Neb stood still just a brief moment as his men rushed up all around him, and then in mass they began to rush forward.

Kryce raised his spear and waited a few moments for the first rush to come close enough. Then he threw his spear with all his might. All his men did the same, and then they gripped their short spears and knives as they rushed into the fray with all the weight of body and spirit. Kryce went blind with rage as he forced his way forward. He wanted Neb for his own, and then he wanted to rescue his sister. He could only imagine the hell she had lived through. He felt more incensed than ever, and the strength he used to move against the enemy was fierce indeed. At one point, he felt a tug at his arm and realized that one of Neb's men had been speared and was grabbing at him for balance before he fell. Kryce tried to shake off the grip, but the dying fool would not let go. Kryce turned and pummeled at the falling figure, but as he shifted his attention, he was hit on the head by a rock that had been thrown with good force. It stung mightily, and Kryce, in astonished appraisal, realized that he was going to fall. He wanted to find Neb and kill him, but with every effort he made, he found he was growing weaker. It was only then that he realized that the dying man had cut him in the thigh. He knew the danger that faced him. If he wanted to live, he must bind the wound quickly. He pulled at his own tunic, but it was too securely made to be used. Staunching the flow with one hand, he reached out with his other hand and grabbed at the tunic of the dead enemy. The garment tore easily. Kryce worked quickly even as darkness began to pass over his eyes. He looked around, but there was no one to help him. He was half lying on the top of another man near enough death to care nothing more for this battle. Clutching at his enemy, he tried to right himself, but weakness was master of his body though not of his will. He bound his wound as tightly as he could, and falling back, he just missed getting pierced through the middle by a well-aimed spear.

    Neb stood and stared to make sure the leader of the Men of Havilah was dead. Yes, Kryce, son of Uzal, had fallen, and there was blood enough to drown several men. Neb shook his head. This had been too easy. He fought and moved from place to place, yelling orders and slaying those unwary enough to have their backs to him. Once, he realized with chagrin that he had accidentally killed one of his own men. He shook his head roughly at the blunder. Still, they were winning and he had men enough to spare. He looked around and surveyed the scene, and he saw a sight that riveted his attention. Torgama was engaged in hand-to-hand combat with Enosh. This reminded him of the time when he had been pierced by Torgama's spear. Suddenly Neb felt a momentary hesitation. He considered whom he would like to kill first. He had never forgiven Torgama for all the agony he had endured, and this would be a prime opportunity to get even where no one would ever see. He aimed carefully, and then he threw his spear. Just at that instant, however, Kittam had stepped in the way, attempting to assist Torgama in his conquest. Torgama turned and saw his friend fall, and his eyes followed the direction the spear had come from. Neb was standing still in the posture of the thrower. In a flash of clear insight, Torgama knew the truth. He saw Neb's unforgiving cruelty clearly, and this dreadful vision brought bile to his mouth. He spat as he leaned down and grabbed the spear from his friend's body. Enosh was trying to edge away from the heat of this terrible combat, but Torgama was in the perfect position to do his worst. Enosh had been knocked to the ground by a heavy blow from the back, and though he had stood back up quickly, his weapon was not in his hand. Torgama looked to Neb to see if Neb was watching, and Neb's eyes flickered in angry jealousy. He wanted to land this blow. He stepped forward, swinging a heavy rock on a thong. He knocked down everyone near enough who did not see his movement. His right arm raised the swirling rock above his head while he gripped his knife in his left hand. He moved forward. Torgama backed away slowly. Enosh began to back away also, and then without warning, he bent low and rushed forward. Before he even got to Neb who tried to quickly brace himself for the blow, someone had flung himself on Neb's back. The rock was swung out into the open air to fall harmlessly to earth. There was a man's weight on top of Neb, and a voice from the long past was whispering darkly in his ear.

"Our father would want me to do this!" Kenan raised his hand to stab Neb in the neck as Torgama swung a spear around, knocking Kenan off Neb's back. Riphath, who had stayed behind on every other battle, now found himself face-to-face with Enosh, and he plunged wildly like an angry cat at his enemy. A slight slice cut through Enosh's arm, and he backed away stumbling, though he kept his eyes fixed on Neb. Kenan had been knocked to the ground by a blow to the head and was now lying motionless. Both Neb and Enosh saw him at the same time. Neb rushed forward to finish his work while Enosh jumped over two bodies and stood with one foot on each side of his fallen brother. Despite his cuts, he felt invigorated and strong, secure in a secret knowledge that he would survive this battle.

"You will not kill any more members of our family! The days of your conquest are over. Another man will rule the people of Hezeki…as a true leader should."

Neb let out a laugh that rang loud across the bloody field. "So you can see the future now? Tell me, as you face your last moment, who will rule the people of Neb?"

Enosh was looking directly at Neb, but then his eyes shifted just a bit to focus on something directly behind his enemy brother. Suddenly his expression changed dramatically. What he now saw claimed all his attention. It was so unexpected that he desired to rub his eyes to clarify his vision but he simply stared, as Neb began to notice the change in his reaction. His laughter died on his lips. Neb turned for an instant. There was a cloud of some sort coming upon them. Something was moving across the grasslands at a determined though frightening gate. It did not look human, and yet it moved with purpose. It was not a cloud. It was not smoke. It was not anything he had ever seen before. Neb slashed once at his brother, cutting his hand very badly and forcing Enosh to jump backward. But when Neb turned again, he saw clearly the approaching menace, and he gasped for this was nothing of his doing. Suddenly the men up and down the grassland battlefield all began to shout and bellow. Neb's men began stomping and running. They were trying frantically to get out of the way. The men of Havilah stood their ground, staring as if a vision of God had appeared. But no one would be spared. This strange cloud was upon them, and it was a fabric made entirely of locusts. They were jumping and chomping and landing by numbers uncountable. No man could stand still as the creatures landed sharply on their arms and legs and in their clothes, crawling, spitting, jumping, being crushed as yet more and more would fall every moment from the sky. Neb stood with his hands at his sides in utter stupefaction. All of his plans were undone. He had never met an opponent like this before. There was nothing to stop them. He called to his men, and they began to follow him south, away from the advancement of the cloud.

Enosh knew that he could lose his hand if he did not act quickly. He thrust the bleeding mess under his arm as he rushed to find his brother. He was terrified that Kenan would be crushed by the rampaging men, but Kenan had called out from the depth of the thick mass that he was alright and had found Kryce who needed help. The two gathered all their strength, Enosh using only one arm, and they thrust Kryce into an upward position. Suddenly Jubal appeared from the darkness of the insects thick in the air, and he thrust Kryce up over his shoulder. The nearly frantic men rushed as fast as they could away from the maddening cloud.

The battlefield was unlike anything the men had ever seen before. They could not clearly see anything, even the bodies of the dead, for the insects were still in mass for several days, and no man dared approach the mysterious undulating field of horror. The injured had been retrieved with fear and dread. Death they were accustomed to, but this was a strange impersonal form of destruction which they had never met before. Neb's men were silent, and Neb himself watched and waited without words of comfort or praise. He knew where Enosh and Kenan had gone. He knew that Kryce was injured nearly to death. He knew that his enemy was dispirited and confused. He also knew that his own men felt much the same way. He was aware that victory had been snatched from his hands like a child who had a toy taken away without comment or explanation. He also knew that he was becoming ill and that it was a sickness unlike any he had ever known before.

Torgama had seen and reacted to everything with a contradictory sense of fascinated revulsion and slavish duty. He realized that Neb had attempted to kill him, but he had spared Neb's life. He wondered at himself.

Leah sat alone in silence, hearing of the wonder and the horror of the terrible cloud and asking where her son was. No one could answer her question. Serug returned to her first, for he had stayed on the outskirts of the battle the whole time. Neb had positioned him well within the thick of the battle, but when the first screams and yells thundered in his ears, he ran with all his might for the safety of the camp, which was immediately at hand. He had not looked for his mother to warn her of the danger. He had not looked for any man to tell him his duty. He had just stood back and watched, and when the cloud came, he grew afraid beyond words and ran to his mother to tell her that they were all doomed. She said nothing in reply at first until she finally asked, "Where is my first son? Where is Madai?" Serug looked into her face and knew he would find no safety there.

For several days, Kryce lay in a dreamless sleep, sweating with a fever that would not abate. He could not lead his men to victory. Seth sat watching him, wondering what the battle had done for them. Where had the evil cloud come from? Seth reached back in his mind to various stories, and he remembered hearing of strange events in nature that changed the lives of men. Always he had been told that the great God above who made the rain fall and renewed the race of men through the honor of Noah had done all these things to assist the just and afflict the wicked. Yet the cloud had come upon them all. How could that be? It had fallen upon the just and the unjust alike. But this did not make sense for surely as there was a God, then Neb was the wicked one. He followed the ways of false gods, called upon powers of darkness, violated the innocent, killed the valiant and enslaved the defenseless. The Men of Havilah had followed the precepts of goodness and generosity. The People of Seth were followers of the one true God. Surely they were good and Neb was evil? So why had the cloud fallen on them all? Was it because Enosh and Kenan were of the blood of Neb? Had they carried the unclean spirits into their midst? Was God cleansing them all for the sins of the few? Seth propped his exhausted head upon his hands as he sat cross legged by the bed of his friend.

Kenan slipped into the room and knelt down by Seth who was staring vacantly at Kryce's still form. His shoulders were slumped, and the grief of recent days was clear in every feature. Seth let his eyes rove over his silent friend and then fall upon Kenan. Without knowing what he was going to say, he found words embarking on a search for the truth.

"Why do we all suffer for the crimes of a few?"

Kenan looked over at Seth, and he shook his head vacantly. His words broke forth like hot waves of lava on burned rock. "I would have killed him. I almost did, but then fate intervened. I wanted to kill him with all my might. Why was I denied my glory? I could have repaid much."

Seth rubbed his temple a moment. He heaved a deep sigh, for he did not know the answer. Yet he found himself speaking as if he did understand. "Perhaps this has happened because we were not ready for victory. I mean, maybe we do not see the kind of victory that God has in mind."

"What other kind of victory is there? To kill one's enemy in battle is the final and complete victory."

Seth nodded in agreement, but his words searched for another truth. "Perhaps we are becoming too much like our enemy."

Kenan raised himself up and a fiery bolt of fury nearly flew from his eyes. "You sound like Enosh! He says that God wants to spare Neb to purge us of some malady, but he was speaking like a fool. We fight to end a terror. We have that right; it is our duty. We need no purging. It is Neb and his men who need to be removed from the earth!"

Seth looked over at Kryce who was stirring now. "When he awakens, do not speak of the battle. Allow him some time to heal. Above all, do not tell him of his sister."

Kenan looked down, his expression changing from anger to grief, for it had been his fate to find Leah, killed by a knife thrust to the heart. There was no one who could tell how it had happened or why, but her body had been left near enough their village to be found on a routine boundary check. Kenan had carried her body into the village, and all the People of Havilah surrounded her fair form and mourned for they had the utter misfortune to lose her twice. They all knew that she had suffered much and that she had never deserved the fate thrust upon her. It was Dodan, the eldest son of Uzal, who buried her while Tamar watched and suffered in terrible grief. Sari watched also, and she understood that there was an end to all things—even to this world's afflictions. And for that, she was secretly glad.

A few days later, Jubal called forth a meeting of men and asked whether they would sit and wait forever in confusion or whether they would go forth and finish the job they had begun. Kryce had recovered enough to be at the meeting, though he could not sit up yet. Seth sat stoically listening, for he was not sure what to advise, and Kenan sat next to Enosh, though they had become divided in spirit of late. Enosh's hand was still aching, but with the aide of skilled healers he had been able to save it from destruction. It would never be as strong and agile as it had been in his youth, however. Enosh had felt the weight of his years more than ever in this last battle. All the men came who were able to attend, and though they had suffered much, not many had been killed as the battle had been interrupted before there was a terrible slaughter on either side. It was while they were thus assembled that a runner came up bearing the news that Accad was coming and leading a small host of men. Everyone except Kryce stood and watched their approach in silence, though there were a few muffled questions and surprise acclimations. Kryce was not yet fit to welcome his friends, so he motioned for Seth to do the honors. Seth stood waiting until Accad came within reach, and the two embraced. All the men behind him stood back. Seth noticed something strange about them, but his immediate attention was upon his friend.

"How are you Accad? Is there news from home?"

Accad looked a little puzzled. "Have you not been awaiting us?"

"Why should we? The battle was fought days ago and not to our glory, I am afraid. We are now considering what action to take now."

Accad looked at his brother who was peering over at him with an expression mixed with surprise and suspicion. He countered his brother's look with a bold smile as he made his announcement. "Why, we have brought you victory!" At this

Accad called for Adam who came and stood before them all with a strange new weapon in his hand. Before anyone could say anything, another man flung a fruit high into the air. Adam swung his bow and arrow around, letting go with a sharp twang. The fruit was pierced and fell to the earth amidst complete silence.

Seth stepped forward in awe. "This is the answer to all the questions. Here is the reason for our delay. We were not defeated. We were held back until victory could be ours completely! Do you not see? God the Almighty is with us!"

There were relieved smiles everywhere, and even Kryce attempted to sit up as he reached out for the new weapon. "I will heal quickly now - for I must practice. I must be as good as our friend here on our next day of battle."

Adam smiled as he accepted the grateful nods and words of praise for what he had brought to their fighting hands. Madai had stayed in the background. His disappointment had been keen when he realized that the battle had not yet been decisively fought. He had secretly hoped that he would find his father's grave and his uncles in leadership over the clan of Neb, but this was not to be. After a time, Enosh came over to him and tried to comfort him, speaking in a low voice. Madai asked him the question he knew he would ask, and Enosh had taken the youth to his mother's grave on the south side of their village. It was a quiet and lonely place next to the mound of her father and mother and other relations going back through time unremembered, but it was beautiful, too, for nearby a great tree grew near a gentle stream which had its tangled roots in the water. They both stood in contemplation of the life that found meaning in bringing forth life, even in the midst of slavery and oppression. Enosh looked over at his brother's son, and he spoke quietly.

"So what will you do now?"

Madai stared at the mound of silent dirt and wondered what would be the right thing to say. Finally he sighed and murmured, "I guess I will fight, though the only person I ever really cared to fight for is dead and gone."

"Surely your life has meaning even after the loss of your mother?"

Madai looked over at his uncle who could not seem to understand. "Did you not suffer when your mother died?"

Enosh looked ashen. "Has my mother died then?"

"She has been dead a good many years, but I see now that of course you would not know of it."

"How did she die?"

"Eva said Neb killed her, but the poisoned vile was emptied upon the ground and it could have been that she died by some other cause."

"Had Neb been with her the day she died?"

"Neb was the last one to see her alive."

Enosh closed his eyes. "Is there no evil that man will not do?"

"He has not killed his brother yet—or his son."

Enosh opened his eyes and turned his gaze to Madai. "How do you live knowing from whence you sprung?"

"And you?"

The two men looked once again upon the graves of the innocent, and they wondered in silence.

CHAPTER 34
MADAI

Kryce healed better than they expected, but that did not matter in the end. Neb was determined to bring victory to his men before their ardor for battle had cooled. The unexpected menace of insects moved off after a time, and the battlefield was cleared of its dead. Burials were hastily accomplished, and his men stood ready to surprise their enemy as they had been surprised. There were no more terrors that could stop them, and to be absolutely sure of that, Neb had called forth his men and decreed a night of mighty worship in order to bind all powers to them. A slaughter of animals was accomplished, and a great fire was built. They would feast and call out with all their might for the strength of the blood poured out for them. They would become mighty in the spirits of those who had died to this world but wandered yet looking for a home.

Neb supervised the care of everything, even as he pretended that he was not ill and that the loss of his wife did not bother him. He had returned from the battle expecting to find her glad that they had not won, but Serug told him that she had gone off alone after he had told her of the mysterious cloud and that she had not returned. Neb looked for her and questioned his men, but there was no clue as to where she had gone. Only Torgama returned his questions with an odd stare. Neb understood that though Torgama still acted as his faithful servant, he was not to be trusted. His feelings for Torgama were no longer a secret between the two. Neb had ordered Riphath to take Torgama's place and insisted that Torgama was to be posted on the outskirts of their camp to watch for any sudden approach. Neb would deal with Torgama in his own time. But Torgama had simply nodded as if he had no preference as to where he stood. It was just as he was leaving that Neb asked him if had seen his wife. Torgama had not smiled, but a light had gleamed in his eye that Neb regarded with grave suspicion. Torgama only shook his head while keeping his lips pursed in silence. But that night while he lay alone in his tent, Neb remembered Torgama's eyes and their proud glint of disdain, and he knew what had happened to his wife. He would have his revenge.

Neb allowed his men all manner of wildness the night he chose for their battle. This time he would not wait for the light of day. He would strike while the moon was high and all of the Men of Havilah were sleeping. With an enormous fire glowing in the distance, the site of their camp must have informed the Men of Havilah that there was a great feasting and wild celebration occurring in the camp of their enemy.

Seth was relieved, for he knew that Kryce still needed several more days of healing before he could even attempt to lead his men into battle. But during the late evening as the fire shone brighter in the great sky and reports told of a commotion of from Neb's camp, Madai came to Enosh and spoke to him in earnest.

"You have not seen my father for many years, but if you knew him at all, you must know that he serves something that rises in the dark times. Though he claims to have bound all powers to himself, I am convinced that he is more bound to them - than they to him. I know that when facing a fearful challenge he likes to send his men into a wild frenzy so that when they attack they will be unlike men anymore. I have seen them do this, and it was terrible to behold. We must get ready to strike now…before they come for us."

Enosh listened and said nothing at first, but then he stood and walked over to Seth's dwelling. When he was allowed to enter, he brought Madai forth to explain his concern. Seth listened and said little, but then he stood and the three of them went to the dwelling of Kryce. There it was decided that they would assemble all the men and take their new weapons with them, even though they had only had them for a couple of days. They would have the advantage for they could wreck havoc on Neb's men before they had recovered their wits form their wild feasting.

While everyone was assembling, Madai stood to the side, alone in his thoughts. It was thus that Accad found him. Accad turned his one good eye fixedly on the youth.

"You do not have to go into this battle, for you were the one to bring us the weapons of victory. You have done enough."

Madai looked over to where his uncles were preparing themselves. "They go into battle. Shall I do any less?"

"They do not have the bond of father and son between them and the enemy."

"Is the bond of brother and brother any less?"

Accad put his large bow to the earth as he looked at the youth who in the darkness appeared very much like a stooped old man. "You suffer a burden not of your own making. But let me tell you - I understand your grief. When I was captured, I was forced to endure humiliations I thought would kill me. I had never paid much attention to the beliefs of my father or the heritage of our people. I had lived a carefree life until Neb came. Then I saw something I had never known before. I saw chosen evil. I had always imagined that evil was thrust upon a man's spirit like a sickness, but after Neb left and when the terrors of real battle came and I lost my freedom, so I lost my foolish innocence. I saw that evil, in order to do the greatest harm, must be chosen freely. I was beaten and humiliated for the pleasure of those who were no longer men as God had created them. They had become like wild beasts—worse than beasts even—for their violence was to no purpose. And then I met my wife...and I loved her. When I beheld her suffering, it nearly crushed me for she was a kind, gentle person. I went out of my way to get to know her better, and I found an unexpected strength. In her meek manner, she accepted her situation but refused to be crushed by it. She maintained her innocence of evil by believing that she could remain honest in the sight of God. I strove to follow her example, and my spirit was calmed. I found I wished to live again. Before God we bound ourselves to each other forever. We were given children by the Almighty and then the worst horror of my life occurred. I found that my enslavers were going to sell my children away. My wife's strength began to break. She was terrified unto death for her little ones, and so I did what I had not been able to do before, I escaped. I had tried before of course many times, but I had always failed. Now this time, strange events occurred that allowed me and my wife and children to get away, and we were made free by our daring courage and by a strange gift of circumstances that blinded my master's eyes to our absence for some days. We were found by our friends who took us home, and our lives have been very happy since then. When the time came to meet Neb in battle I wanted to fight, but Seth said I was better suited to protect those at home. I knew what he meant. I was too broken a man to serve in the midst of battle. But still I wished to serve. And then you and Adam showed up at my door, and you brought me a gift I could never have imagined. I will never be a slave again, of this I am sure. But more importantly, I have accepted the most important truth of my life."

Madai stared through his grief. "What could that be?"

"I understand now that there can be no life, nor hope, without God for He cares about the fate of men. If I had not been a slave I never would have found my wife nor had my children and if I had escaped early I would not have been there to save them. God had better plans."

Madai looked out across the vast darkness into the glimmer of a great fire, which burned some distance away. "But can he save us from ourselves?"

Accad looked up to the stars above and put his hand on the young man's shoulder. "I believe so."

CHAPTER 35

SERUG

Serug arched his neck back as he watched the burning arrow fly high into the air, and then he brought his head down as that same flaming arrow landed in the midst of his men. He should have known! But it was too late now for useless second thoughts. The son of an idiot was not so stupid after all. He did have a worthy secret, and if only Serug had known, Adam would never have lived long enough to run away and give their enemies the advantage. Serug shook his head in utter vexation. But the enemy was near at hand, and Serug knew more than anyone how hopeless this battle was going to be. Neb was very ill, though he would not admit that to anyone—not even to himself. Serug saw his father's yellow pallor and had noticed the weak spells as Neb fought to stay on his feet. It was true that Neb had always overcome every challenge, but Serug had noticed lately that his father was no longer the man he had been. Too many things were going wrong. In truth, he knew that his clansmen were already defeated and that the best thing he could do now was to get himself and his father as far from this battlefield as possible. The burning arrows were setting the field on fire in some spots and the men, even in their bewildered, intoxicated fury, were becoming unnerved. Serug ran up to his father who was watching the falling arrows as if they were falling stars.

"I have a plan, Father. Come with me. The men will follow, and we will attack from another place where they do not expect."

Neb looked over at his young son, and his eyes were almost completely expressionless. He hesitated and seemed to sway a moment. "Did I ever have the blessing of Uz? My leg wound proved my vulnerability. I never really became a god…did I? For gods are not made and then unmade. If a man strikes me down, I will bleed and die like any mortal. The spirits have abandoned me to death and destruction. What difference does it make where I go now?"

Serug closed his eyes. He knew all too well that his doom was too closely connected with that of his father to allow Neb to accept his end as inevitable and imminent. Serug heard shouts all around him as the Men of Havilah encircled them ever so slowly. Kryce had ordered his men to shoot off burning arrows into the night air as they walked closer and closer, never rushing but all the while disorientating and disheartening Neb's men. They had begun shouting words of insult and curses, and Neb's men, in their stupor, returned every insult and curse though they did not have any arrows to send back into the black night. Serug opened his eyes and surveyed the madness. The men were still stupefied with the pleasures of feasting and were not yet quite in command of their fighting abilities. They had planned on doing battle, only a little later, at their own choosing, but once again they had been surprised. Chaos was breaking out as Neb's men in blind fury tried to fight an enemy who was still too far away. The arrows continued to fly, and occasionally they made an unexpected mark as one landed right at Serug's feet. That was enough for him. Serug called to Riphath and Torgama, and he directed them to gather some of the men and to begin moving away from the center of the camp. Then Serug grabbed his father's arm and called to him to come. Neb seemed to straighten up, and he focused his gaze once again. This time he saw Serug for who he was, and he recognized the danger.

Serug knew what he had to do. "We can leave now, and the men can hold them off for a time. We will gather together at a more opportune moment, and we will slaughter them all - but not right now." He pulled at his father's arm. "We must leave at once!"

Neb turned his head away and looked at his men as they tried to organize themselves. "But the men who stay will face the enemy alone."

Serug nodded. "Yes, of course. That is your plan. You will find a better vantage point, and then we will gather everyone, and we will annihilate them!"

Neb looked at his son, and then he saw Riphath standing behind him. Torgama stood to the side waiting for a decision, but he would not wait long. The situation was becoming too perilous, and he was not going to offer himself to the mysterious weapons of his enemy. Neb stood silent and alone for a long moment, and then he nodded his head and began to move in the direction that Serug indicated. They slipped into the darkness quickly, away from the fire, even as his men were calling for him and looking for direction. Serug pushed on ahead, and Neb followed though his footing was not steady. He had a hard time keeping up with his young son. Torgama, in his disgusted fury, pushed past Neb and almost knocked him to the ground. Riphath saw Neb slip, and he stopped and put out his hand. Neb panted and looked at the offered hand, but he would not take it. Suddenly Riphath heard a yell. It was the sound of a man he knew well. He stopped and listened. Serug kept going, and Torgama did not halt. Neb had begun to move on, but he stopped and looked at Riphath in his moment of indecision. Riphath looked at Neb, and they both turned back to the camp. Finally Riphath lifted one hand and swatted at the air as if to banish an annoying insect.

"Ah, I've got nothing to lose now. I will go back and defend what I once had."

Neb peered at his man with suspicion. "What did you once have?"

Riphath threw his hands up in the air again as he turned and began to march back toward the center of the battle. It was only a single word he threw back, "loyalty," but if Serug had not pulled at his arm again, Neb might have followed Riphath, for though he knew little of love and mercy, he had always imagined he was a man of courage.

Serug was in no mood for reflection. He pulled at his father's arm repeatedly, and they began to move off further into the darkness.

Several days later, Serug counted the men that had managed to find them, and he was pleased. Not everyone had been killed or captured. He thought grimly of what Kryce and his men would do with those they found, those left behind wounded or who had given up in the end. But then he put all such uncomfortable thoughts out of his mind. He needed to make plans. Neb was clearly ill and was burning up with some kind of a fever. They were not safe yet. He knew the best thing they could do was to move very far into the dark woodlands and bury themselves there for as long as it would take to be forgotten or given up for dead. He approached his father, who was lying under a particularly large spread of trees, and he spoke softly even as bright rays of light played with leafy shadows.

"Father, we cannot rest here for long, but I know that you are ill. I think it would be best if the men carry you for a time, until you are feeling better."

Neb looked at his son, but he could hardly make out his face. The fever had now nearly blinded his eyes and made his thoughts dark and confused. He simply nodded his head and let his hands fall to the side in acceptance. Serug smiled. For him, this defeat had not been a tragedy, for now he was no longer fated to be a younger son in the shadow of an elder brother and neither would he have to endure the long years of waiting for Neb to die as an old man. As things stood now, Serug was the clan leader, and this pleased him very much.

CHAPTER 36
HIS STORY CONTINUES

The sun had set and risen again many times since Ishtar had begun to tell the story of their long ago past. After the first day, Ishtar, Ammee and Gizah began sitting in a circle around the communal fire in the evenings while many others gathered to listen. Once it was known that Ishtar was telling the history of Neb the Great, many had gathered to hear the fullness of those tales, and those that had missed pieces and parts because of other duties were filled in during the work of the day. There were many who wanted to know more about their clan's past, for few knew as much as Ishtar. Ishtar had learned much from his mother, Hagia, before his exile, and Eymard had shared his knowledge with him as well.

In those remembrances, the dead came to life again, and Ammee saw with his wide-awake eyes all that had happened more than three generations ago. He could now say that he understood the forces that had formed the mind of Neb the Great, and he no longer wondered at the long reach of Neb's arm through time and history. The wonder was that his own father had broken free of the invisible chains that had held his family in bondage for so long. The sun was setting now, and Gizah had stayed home this evening to tend to necessary duties. Often she arrived late or had to leave early to manage affairs that could not be put off, but Ammee had stayed and listened and learned all he could. He retold Gizah what she had missed during the quiet of the nights when they were alone together. Now as the evening fires contrasted with the night, Ammee looked to his father who seemed more wearied than usual, and Ammee worried that perhaps the telling of this tale had been too much for Ishtar. Still, he was afraid of not hearing the rest for he felt his life's breath waited to hear what happened next. He knew there were many others, as well, who longed to know the rest of the story as if their futures depended upon it.

Out of the quiet night came the sound of Gizah as she placed a tray laden with food and drink down between Ishtar and her husband and then sat at her husband's side.

"Everyone is settling down now, but when you didn't come in to eat, I thought I would bring something out to you two." She looked at Ammee expectantly. "How far have you heard?"

Ammee smiled at his wife's enthusiasm. He was sincerely grateful for her thoughtfulness and her continued eager interest despite her many other concerns. "He told about how the Men of Havilah brought forth the terror of burning arrows against them and how Neb had abandoned his men to a hopeless defeat. I will tell you more tonight, but I fear that father is too tired tonight to tell what happened next."

There was a hushed expectancy in the air as everyone waited to hear what Ishtar would say. They knew it was ungenerous of them to demand more than he could give, but they did not want the story to be delayed even by one day.

Ishtar tried not to yawn, but he could hardly stop himself. "It is true that I am tired, but I'm not really sleepy. Perhaps I am just a little weary, as the telling of this tale drains something from me, though I can hardly explain what I mean. I feel as if the spirits of the past are with us as we review their mortal lives again."

Ammee looked around a little uneasily, as did many others, but Gizah merely motioned for them to go ahead and eat. "In that case, maybe it is time for me to speak of what I know from my father, for Aram liked to share his story with me as we worked."

Ishtar looked genuinely interested. "Do you know much about the time when Madai ruled? He and Serug never met again after Neb left the last battle with the people of Havilah. Enosh and Kenan fall out of my story, for they stayed with the people of Havilah and never met up with Neb or Serug again. They continued to live in the south, though I did hear that once during a severe drought they moved further south and entered a new land leaving only the stone with their law engraved upon it to tell the tale of who had occupied that land."

Ammee was incredulous. "So that is all we know of Neb's brothers? They passed on, and we never heard from them again?"

Ishtar shrugged his shoulders. "My grandfather never ventured south. He went north deep into the great forest, and when my father was born after Neb the Great died, Serug moved further east for a time and then north into the low hill lands. It was my father who finally moved to the Great River when I was very little, and there my adventure began."

Gizah gestured with excitement. "In that case, let me tell you what I know of Madai. He was the Grandfather of Aram, and his story is no less interesting than Serug's. Madai recovered the humbled remnant of Neb's warriors, and he kept in contact with both Enosh and Kenan, though Enosh was his favorite I was told. This way, Ishtar, you can get a rest from speaking, and some other evening you can tell the story of Serug and his son, Neb, in its own place."

Ishtar smiled in quiet relief and pleasure, for he would dearly love to hear about the current of events that brought forth into a desperate world his old friend Aram.

CHAPTER 37
MADAI RECLAIMS WHAT WAS LOST

On the morning after the terrible battle, not many men of Neb the Great had survived, and those that did were worse than defeated; they were lost and dead to the world as they had known it. Neb was gone. He had abandoned them, and such a possibility had never occurred to them before. Kryce and Jubal were all for slaughtering those that remained alive, but Seth and Enosh would not allow it. Kenan had been injured again, so he was brought home to be tended by those who knew how. Kryce had put up a fierce argument; for all their suffering the People of Havilah deserved the right to completely vanquish their enemy, and Jubal had earnestly supported him in this. Seth had held them back with the objection that something more was required since they did not know everything that had led Neb's men into their terrible deeds. Were they certain that all those men had been willing conspirators with Neb? Was it not possible that some of them been forced into a role they would rather have not taken? This thought did little to cool the fire of vengeance in the hearts of the men of Havilah for they did not care to know the minds of their enemies but rather receive the justice they had fought so hard to win. Enosh could not do much to deter the bloodshed, though he felt that when a man no longer had a weapon in his hand, it was wrong to merely slaughter him. It was at that point that Madai had stepped forward. He had stayed in the thick of the battle and acquitted himself valiantly, and no one could deny his right to speak. If he had not left his own clan in the first place and accomplished his mission, Neb's men would not be standing helpless before them completely at their mercy.

Madai was covered in blood though not seriously injured. He stood straight and tall, and no one could question his manhood at this moment. He was most certainly the son of Neb, for it showed in his features, but the man before them was not Neb. He had declared—and they believed it to be truth—that he was also the son of Leah of the people of Havilah. Yet as he looked around at the circle of men penned in by the angry warriors who wanted very much to see them die, he threw up his hands in a gesture of defiance not unlike something his father would have done.

"They are mine! I am Neb's eldest, and these men belong to me by right. I have conquered them by force of arms, and I will not see them slain."

Kryce looked astounded and turned to stare at Madai. "What gives you the right to take our prisoners?"

"I claim the right to take these men back to our clan and reclaim the inheritance of Hezeki, which was lost to us during the time of Neb." He looked around into the faces of the defeated men, and he pointed to them as they hung their heads in stoic silence while his eyes flashed in fury at Kryce and Jubal. "Do you condemn the families—the women and children—to death, too? Surely they will perish if they have no men to help them. Are you going to march to their village and dispatch them for justice's sake too?"

Jubal put up his hand and tried to speak, but he had to look away from the conquered enemy. What Madai had said caused a multitude of groans and sighs to rise from the despair of the defeated. "We are not without mercy. We will allow you to tend to the women and children. Those that wish may join with our clan."

It was then that Thubal, Hezeki's lead warrior who had joined with the people of Havilah, stepped forward. He had been a faithful clansman, and no one doubted his loyalty. He had married into the clan and had several children. He was trusted and much respected, though he rarely spoke in open assembly. He stood tall and spoke clearly now. "I think we have forgotten the memory of Hul and others like him. There were many who wished to go with Hezeki at his departure from Neb, but they were unable to leave their families. They had wives and young children, aged parents and crops to tend, and they could not do what I and my free men were able to do. We were spared the years of torment under Neb's leadership, but these men stayed true and were led into their deeds by a force that was beyond reckoning. Their leader demanded their obedience and loyalty. Would you admire them more for blind defiance?"

At this there was utter silence. Kryce took a large step backward, and Jubal threw up his hands in acceptance of the verdict. Madai swallowed hard in relief for this second victory was no less great than the first. He stepped forward and called to any who would assist him. Thubal and several of those who had followed Hezeki stepped forward. They said they would assemble their families and would return with Madai to the village of Neb. It was clear that these defeated and betrayed men would never follow Neb's will again. Arrangements were made for the feeding and care of the prisoners while preparations were begun to return to their home village. Madai took charge of all the details.

Riphath had stayed well in the background during all these proceedings, and he felt like he had swallowed an enormous stone. He saw in his mind all the years he had dedicated to Neb, and yet Neb had abandoned them all in a moment of weakness and confusion. Riphath had come back to save a friend who had a young wife and several children, but he had been too late. Now all he would have to offer his friend was a deep hole to bury him in. He thought of his own wife and daughters, and relief washed over him that he would be alive see to their needs and protection. Then he thought of all the others whose husbands had left them to follow Neb. There had been men left to die in a lost battle and women to perish for want of need and care. Neb did not care what happened to anyone…except himself…and for the first time in his life that struck Riphath as unforgivable. Riphath stood silent in the face of the mercy that allowed him to bury his friend and to assist the others left behind, and he who never liked to show any emotion wept in silence, still as stone, in his grief and overwhelming relief.

After a time, two surprises occurred that saved Madai from absolute defeat in his mission. First, Adam came forward and said that he would like to travel with him still for he had come to appreciate his honest wisdom. He smiled as he spoke, "Besides,

I want to see what happens next in this little adventure. Since meeting you, my life has taken on a whole new perspective, and I am not ready to return home…just yet."

"Won't your family be worried about you?"

"They are not a worrying sort. My father will look for me, but he will wait for many moons to fill and empty before he becomes anxious." Adam looked at his friend appraisingly. "I think it would be most interesting if, after a time when you have your people settled again, you were to come with me and meet my people."

Madai smiled widely at this suggestion. "I would like to do that."

"Then it is agreed. I will go to your home and help you settle in, and then you will come to my home and help me."

Madai had started to look away, but his eyes swiveled back to Adam's face in puzzled concern. "Help you? How?"

Adam merely grinned as he began to walk toward the prisoners who were being ushered along. He spoke over his shoulder toward Madai who was waiting for an answer. "Oh, didn't I tell you? I have five sisters."

Several days later when everything had been arranged, Madai was about to set out for his old home when a man little known to him came up and introduced himself.

"I am Dodan, Kryce's elder brother, though his servant in war. I usually stay at home to tend to the matters of the clan and guard the village when Kryce and his men are off on a hunt or in battle. I saw you when you came to us first, we met briefly, but I fear you do not remember me."

Madai looked at the diminutive form of Dodan, and though he had not remembered the name, he did remember the man. Dodan had something about him that demanded respect. "Yes, Dodan, I do remember you." He tried not to look impatient, though he needed to be off soon for there were many matters to attend to.

Dodan understood the situation, and he cleared his throat carefully. "I have come to offer you my services. I spoke with

Kryce, and he has agreed that the more successful you are with these men, the better things will go for all of us. Also, I can be a liaison between you and the people of Havilah. If ever Neb should try to come back or there is any serious trouble, then you will have the firm assurance of our clan's arms."

Madai was taken aback. This was an unexpected boon, yet in a way he thought he might not want to have a man of Havilah come back with him. He felt a certain stain of shame would be forever connected with this clan, and he wondered if it would not be best to leave the past…in the past.

Dodan appeared to read his thoughts, and he spoke softly so that no one else could hear. "I am not a warrior, as you can well see, and I have not fought in the battles between our men. I am one who heals, not one who destroys. I do not think your men will even know who I am unless you tell them. Only Thubal and his men would know, and they are men of great discretion."

Madai looked up to the bright sun above and wondered at this sudden decision he was faced with. Would this be what leadership was like, trying to read the future with uncertain knowledge of the present situation? "Word might get out. Someone would know the truth, and they would tell the whole clan."

"And what would they tell? That I am not a warrior? That I am merely a man who stays at home to protect the innocent?"

Madai saw the justice of this observation and shrugged his shoulders. He was feeling less and less like the bold leader he had proclaimed himself to be only a few short while ago. "I am willing to allow you to come with us but please…travel inconspicuously. Do you have a family that will join you?"

Dodan looked over Madai's shoulder at the empty air and shook his head. "No, I am a man set apart."

Madai was not sure what to make of this comment, but he accepted the truth of it. They quickly agreed to the time for departure.

It was a long tedious march back to the Village of Neb, and there was a mournful scene awaiting them. Word had spread that Neb had abandoned them, and several of the men who were supposed to watch over the women and children had gone off to find Neb and bring him back. Those who were left behind were in sad shape. It had been dry of late in this place up against the southern hills, and the main creek that ran down from the northern mountains was running very low. Even the fish seemed to be trying to run away, as well as most of the animals. There had been no hunting, and very many of the women and children were sick with fever and hunger. Madai's face flushed with rage when he saw the conditions in the village, and he wanted to run after his father himself and see justice done upon him. It was the hand of Thubal that stopped him and reminded him of his duty to stay and take charge. Madai reluctantly agreed and decided to form a council. With the help of Adam, Thubal, Dodan, Eva and the few ancient men of the clan, Madai was able to form hunting parties, arrange for the collection of medicinal herbs and get the women to work together to gather what harvest they could.

After several moons, things were much better arranged, though the drought had not lessened. Several clan members had died, and Madai was beginning to despair of saving his clan. One day he had gone to the river's edge and had seen a few dying fish upon the bank. Madai simply stared at them as his shoulders slumped in exhausted weariness. He had worked so hard and done so much, but he was not at all certain that he had really done any good. Suddenly, out of the corner of his eye, he saw the form of a man moving along the bank, bending and rising while throwing something back into the nearly still water and then repeating his actions almost identically. Madai watched and waited for the figure to come closer. Finally, he realized who it was. Dodan was walking along the bank picking up each of the stranded fish and throwing it back into the water. Madai shook his head. He called out in exasperation.

"What do you think you are doing? There are so many fish, and the river is long. Besides, with this drought it will probably do no good, it won't make any difference."

Dodan stood to his full diminutive height, his slight form contrasted with the greatness of the massive earthen bank behind him. He held one dying fish in his hand, and he looked at it before swinging his arm up into a great arch. The fish flew unnaturally and then fell in the middle of what was left of the stream. "It made all the difference in the world to that fish." Dodan smiled and walked closer to Madai. He bent down and retrieved yet another fish and threw it into the water. Finally, he walked up to Madai and spoke with a deep sigh. "It has never been my privilege to be the master of great events. I am a small man in stature but not in imagination. Many have been the times when I wished I could go into battle and slay the enemy and change the course of my people's fortune, but few are those who look to me for such noble deeds. No, I must be content to change the fortune of a fish or a single man or a child if the situation presents itself to me. As I have pondered my life and watched the forces that both control and are controlled by the leaders of men, I have come to the conclusion that my fate is not such a bad one. I may not arrange matters for the clan as a whole, but by my simple services I have made all the difference to certain individuals. I have to ask myself, is a single man worth less than the whole?"

Madai stood and stared down at the little man who, with the smell of fish about him, knew more about the matters of life and death than any man Madai had yet met. "You speak like a man of faith in something beyond the sight of men."

Madai shaded his eyes from the brightness of the sun, which shone down upon them both. "My people believe in the One, but I am not one of those who sees visions or can foretell the future. Like I said, I am a simple man, and content with that, for in my role I do the duty assigned to me as well as can be done."

Madai smiled and looked at Dodan in silence a moment. "I am glad you joined with us. I am not an experienced leader, and I fear I lack your wisdom. I suffer from the loss of my mother and the inheritance of my father. I fear the return of my brother, and I despair the future of my people. Perhaps you can do more than you imagine; perhaps you can council my confused mind and encourage my doubt-filled heart thus enabling our people to survive despite our present despair."

Dodan put his hand on Madai's arm. "I will be glad to be of assistance, for that is why I came."

Thus it was that the time of trial was shortened, and when the rains did come again, the men of Madai were transformed into a new clan. The prisoners were freed from their allegiance to Neb, and the families began to prosper in ways they had not known in a long time. The clans all around heard of the change, and there were a couple of attempts to attack them. Madai was strong in the face of such threats, however, and his warriors knew all too well how to fight. Several of those who had gone off to find Neb had returned to find the clan thus altered, and they were glad of it. Their bitterness against Neb was even greater upon their return. No one had found Neb or Serug, as they had buried themselves deep in the woodlands and covered their trail very well. But with Adam's ingenuity, Thubal's loyalty and Dodan's wisdom, the clan of Madai knew prosperity. Madai's only wish was that his mother had lived to see it. Many were the times he dreamed of her and imagined her with them again, but always she seemed to yearn for another place and he awoke with the certainty that though she was gone from him, still she lived on in some form he could not yet see. When he told Dodan about his dreams one hot sunny day, the son of Uzal smiled and told him the story of Ophir and how she had been taken away to a foreign clan and the tragedy that took over her life. He told him about the love his uncle bore her and how, when she died, he was certain that she lived forever in a more perfect world where all the past horrors had been wiped away. Madai listened with ardent concentration. He wanted to believe that another world existed beyond the world he knew, for it seemed to him, that for many, this life was cruelly unjust. But how could he account for such a land…so beyond his vision and experience?

"My mother is dead, and I fear it is the wishful thinking of a child to believe in an unseen world where those that suffer in this life are rewarded with joy in the next."

Dodan rubbed his jaw in thought. His hand was grimy from digging in the soil, as he was helping one of the families sew their next crop. "I too wonder about my people's belief in the unseen God. Why does He hold His hand back from a man like Neb? Yet as I work the soil I wonder if perhaps God merely allows the weeds to grow up with the fruit until the time of harvest." He put his wooden spade into the stirred-up dirt and rubbed his dirty foot upon the edge of it in thought. "I sometimes think that we believe God to be like us, and we think He should reason as a man does. But really, who is man to stand in judge of so mighty a hand? Who are we to be His counselor?" He smiled at Madai, for he saw Madai as more than a friend; he felt him to be almost a son in his endearing need and devoted trust. "We are only men after all, and we do not have the vision of God."

Madai blanched as a new thought struck him. "Do you believe we will ever see Him?"

"One day...I hope to look upon His countenance." Dodan put his spade back to the purpose for which it was intended. "But for today, I must dig the earth. The family who lives here is in need of help. The father is sick with fever, and though Eva has done everything in her power, she has not been able to cure him of his malady."

Madai looked up at this to the dwelling they stood before, and he nodded his head thoughtfully. "Yes, you are right. I have duties to tend to also." He took a few steps away and then he stopped. He stared at Dodan who was digging with the effort of a small man at a large task, and he spoke softly. "Thank you."

Dodan did not raise his head, though he did smile as he spoke. "You are welcome."

CHAPTER 38

TRAVELS

Adam watched as Madai worked to make a fire, and he grinned. Then he looked over at Dodan, and he shook his head silently. Dodan pursed his lips and let out a low whistle. Finally the eldest son of Uzal stood up and sauntered over to the blazing inferno that was supposed to cook their dinner, and standing behind Madai, he spoke very quietly.

"Are you planning on cooking the birds up in the trees?"

Madai swung around in surprise. He had been deep in thought and had not even realized how much brush he had put onto the fire. "Oh, no…not really." He looked over to his uncle and let a sheepish smile break the intensity of his concentration. Only here, in the company of these two friends, could he dare to express his uncertainty. "I was not really thinking about the fire at all."

Adam let out a laugh. "We noticed."

Dodan pulled one of the branches off to the side to keep it from catching entirely. "It is best to pay attention when you are working with fire. Though we have had some rain, this grassland will still burn. Adam's family might not like it if we send a raging fire on ahead of us."

Madai nodded thoughtfully. "Yes, of course. I wouldn't let that happen. It is just that I have a lot on my mind."

Dodan returned to his perch on a rock not far from the fire. Adam waited in silence. He did not like to be pestered, and he knew that Madai would speak more freely if allowed to speak in his own time. After a while, Dodan decided to go in search of game, and Adam joined him. Madai stayed and watched the fire, pensive and uncertain. By the time the two returned and several large rabbits were roasting nicely on a spit, Madai had formulated his thoughts well enough to speak his concerns to his friends. They were all sitting around the fire, watching the meat sizzling on spits while the light faded from the day and the cool evening air invaded the quiet grasslands. Suddenly Madai stood up and threw a small dry twig into the fire.

"I have been thinking about my role in the clan."

Adam looked at Dodan who stared straight into the flames in front of him. Neither of them said anything.

"I don't think I should lead the clan anymore." The silence continued. Madai shifted from one foot to another. "It is not that I do not want to. Actually, I would like to, and I think I could do a good job. I am nothing like my father, but I have learned much from his mistakes. I am young, but I am stronger than I look. My youth is an advantage really because I will live long enough to give the clan stability and . . ." His voice dwindled off.

Dodan cleared his throat and spoke evenly. "It sounds like you are the perfect person to lead your clan."

Madai shook his head. "But I am not—not really. The truth is that I am the son of an evil man, and I have a brother who will always hate me. It is too much like Enosh and Kenan's fate. I know enough of the past to realize that everyone who knew them fell under their shadow of their doom. It would be best if someone completely new took over the clan—someone who was raised up well and did not inherit an evil shadow."

Adam spoke very softly while he rubbed his tired eyes. "You would not have many men left if you took away all those who have to contest against evil." Madai attempted to speak, but Adam put up his hand. "No, listen a moment. I have not told you the whole truth about my own people, and it is best you hear it from me, especially considering the fact that I have hopes that you will . . . . well, never mind. I just hope you will be happy with us during your visit. You see, the truth of my clan was only half told when I shared the reputation of my grandfather. I told you that many considered him mad because he liked to do new things. And that is true. In fact, they tried to kill him because his madness. One day he left for a long stretch of time, and when he came back, he told stories about strange dreams he had had. He tried to explain how things worked in his imaginary place, but the more vivid the pictures he painted, the more alarmed my people became. One of the elders especially disliked my grandfather and looked for any opportunity to catch him in some doubtful act. My grandfather, in his foolishness, complied by insisting that someday men would fly like birds, and he imagined that if one made wings large enough and strong enough, one could in fact fly. Several of the youths thought that perhaps my grandfather was gifted with wisdom from the spirit world, and they encouraged him. One youth even went so far as to make his own set of wings. Now, as much of a dreamer as my grandfather was, he would never have consented to this youth's project, and the horror which later occurred would never have happened if the youth had come to my grandfather first. But as it was, the youth made his own imperfect wings and climbed to a high place, and he jumped a great distance. He died in the fall. The whole clan blamed my grandfather for bringing such wild notions into the clan in the first place, and my grandfather was devastated by both the death of the young man and by his own part to play. He stopped traveling, and he stopped dreaming dreams. He is an old, old man now, and though my parents nurture him, he is just a shell of his former self. This is one of the reasons I decided to travel. I wanted to see the world and think thoughts and perhaps…dream dreams. I wanted to figure out if my grandfather had been truly wrong or if evil can stem from a man even when he does not intend it."

Adam stopped speaking and sat still merely staring into the flickering flames which danced across Madai's face. "As you know from my story, I gained a great benefit from perfect strangers that was not deserved and was completely unlooked for. You were born into an evil family not of your choosing, but you used the knowledge I brought and together we saved an innocent people. I do not believe that a man's fate is set by others but only that we can give in to despair when we doubt our imperfect goodness too much."

There was silence as Madai continued to stare silently into the fire. Dodan nodded his head very slightly and then spoke only a few words. "We inherit both good and evil. Leah would not want you to give up, for she lived…so that you might live… and perhaps you would be a better man than your father."

Adam rose and started to pull the meat off the fire. "Enough talking! I am terribly hungry, and it is time to eat."

Dodan rose and looked critically at the roasted flesh. "I do not think it is ready."

Adam took out his knife and sliced off a healthy chunk. "But I am ready!"

Madai and Dodan looked at each other, and they both stepped forward to get their share.

It took many long days of travel through the southern lands across low hills to get to a rich land of ancient woods and grassy plains. The people were both calm yet expectant, and they showed great interest when Adam introduced Madai and Dodan. Adam was pleased to introduce his own father, mother and his five sisters. Madai was quiet for the most part, but after a while one of the sisters caught his eye, and he looked on her with favor. Her name was Ester, and she was quite beautiful. Her hair was long, thick, and a rich, dark brown. Her eyes were large and shy, and her figure was petite but perfect. She was the softest spoken of all the sisters, and Madai was drawn to her. Her simple attraction to his youthful manliness made him feel stronger and braver than he had ever felt in his life. Adam and Dodan noticed the budding attraction with glad hearts and kept their own council, for they knew it was a man's own business whom he choose for wife. It was near the change of the season that Madai realized it was time for him to go home and that he must speak to Adam and his father of his intentions. Adam's father merely smiled his approval, for he knew the worth of this clan leader and had heard all his son had to say about Madai's goodness and honor. He saw his daughter's heart plainly expressed through her eyes and he was glad enough that one of his girls would find a good home soon. After their visit with Ester's father, Madai thought the matter was settled, but Adam shook his head in silence and motioned for Madai to follow him to the outskirts of the village. There Adam stopped in front of a dwelling unlike anything Madai had ever seen before. It was built of timber, river stone plastered with mud and thatch. It was large with rounded corners and had a second story—something completely unheard of in that part of the world. Madai stared, and his mouth hung open for a moment. Finally he spoke in a whispered voice as if he didn't want to arouse anyone of their presence.

"Is this the home of your grandfather?"

Adam nodded. "Yes, he has been building and rebuilding it for years. It is one of the few things he allows himself to do. Despite my parents' protests, the clan exiled him to the outskirts of the village. It is not considered good form to speak with him or associate with him in any way, though my parents are allowed to bring him food every day."

Madai looked at Adam with large, angry eyes. "But I thought you said he did nothing wrong. The boy died from his own foolishness."

"That is the truth, but too often the truth does not appease angry hearts. They were angry at him for being different long before the youth died from the fall. They were glad that misfortune gave them an excuse to exile him."

"How can you live with such people?"

Adam smiled as his eyebrows rose in ironic silence. "I have not been among them much lately if you remember." He looked up when an old man came softly padding out from inside the dwelling. He looked at the two youths, and a great smile beamed over his face.

"Visitors? For me? It has been so long!" His searching gaze met that of Adam, and his eyes squinted in recognition. His lips trembled, and he held out an old, gnarled hand. "Is it you, my son?"

"It is me, Grandfather, Adam. I am your son's son."

The old man nodded understandingly, and his smile widened again as his eyes began to sparkle. "Yes, yes, of course. You have come to say goodbye for another journey, is that not so?"

Adam looked at the dirt on the ground and nodded in silence. Grandfather spoke again. "Ah well, it is best. You know what might happen if you stay too long. There would come a time when you might start dreaming dreams…and then trouble would follow."

"Yes, I know, Grandfather." Adam looked into the eyes of the old man, and they understood each other perfectly. Then Adam gestured toward Madai. "Here is a friend I brought. He is the son of Neb the Great, and he is going to marry my sister Ester."

The old man stopped startled. "The son of Neb the Great did you say? I know that name, and it is not a welcome one. Are you sure—"

Adam stopped his grandfather. "No, you do not understand. He is his father's son, but he is also the son of Leah of the people of Havilah. He left his father and has taken over those abandoned by Neb. He is the leader of a new clan—one much better than anything Neb ever imagined."

The old grandfather shook his head in distress. "Neb had imagination alright, but it was all the wrong way. He looked for glory in taking from others and not from the gifts within himself."

Madai was becoming baffled. "My father was evil and selfish—he had no imagination what so ever."

Grandfather shook his gnarled finger at the son of Neb. "Oh no, there you are wrong. Neb was brilliant, but his intelligence was directed toward things of fleeting value. He could have used what was naturally given to him to share with others, and then he would have grown in wisdom and strength. Instead he tried to take from the spirit world a power which was not his to have. That was his doom."

Madai was startled. "How do you know all this?"

"There is little that I do not know about the clans around here. I know all about the people of Havilah and the people of Seth, and I even know that there is a great land beyond the far northern mountains. But I am content to live my last days here in my own dwelling. There is not much out there that is all that different from what happens in this clan. The same passions rule everywhere." There was silence for a few moments as the old man seemed to lose himself in thought. Then he looked up and stared intensely at Madai. "No, I see it is true. You are not made of the same stuff as your father. There is an honesty in your face that was never on Neb's." He paused. "I met him once you know."

301

Madai's eyes widened in surprise. "You met my father?"

"Yes, it was during one of my travels. We bumped into each other you might say. Though he did not say much, I could discern by the quality of his men and the way he spoke that he was a man full of deception. I felt grieved for those who believed in him."

Madai looked sorrowfully at his own feet. "There were some who had no choice but to follow him."

"Yes, of course. It is always the case. Even among those who fight on the side of evil are those who would not…if only they knew another way."

Madai looked up, and he squared his shoulders a bit. "I found another way, and I do not follow Neb the Great. I am Madai, son of Leah of the people of Havilah. I have chosen another path."

The grandfather smiled and pointed to his house. "That is good to know. Now won't you come in and enjoy some of my hospitality? I realize that I am but an outcaste, and through my own foolishness I have become separated from my own kind, but before you return to your home, come and eat with me, and know that though I am considered strange, my will is only to learn about the wonders of human invention."

Madai spoke softly. "You are not strange."

The old man chuckled as he went ahead inside. "Oh, no? I hope not, but sometimes I have had to wonder. I certainly can be terribly foolish."

Adam laughed as he followed Madai and his grandfather inside his dwelling. "Well, in any case, I hope to become just like you!"

CHAPTER 39
EVA AND ESTER

When Madai brought Ester home to his people, Eva stood off to the side, watching the introductions with an interested though wary eye. The death of Leah had been devastating to her, and even though Neb was exiled to a far-away place, her heart did not recover from her utter desolation. Though she knew that Neb had not killed her friend and that he was seriously ill when he left for his last battle, still she could never forgive him for falling out of love with Leah. Of all the people that Eva had ever known in her difficult life, Leah had been the best. It was true that Leah was innocent, but she was more than that; she was strong in her innocence, a quality that tugged mightily at Eva's heart. She needed to believe that Leah had not lived in vain—that her strength had meant something. She had watched Madai grow up with apprehension and agitation because she knew that Neb would inevitably become jealous of his son's closeness to his wife. Yet Madai was formed in his mother's image, of that there was no doubt. And despite all of his father's manipulation and deception, Madai would not abandon his mother or the memory of her simple truthfulness, and for this Leah was very grateful. But even though Madai was an extraordinary young man, still he could not comfort the aching grief in Leah's heart. He was not even aware of it.

After the death of Leah, the defeat of their clan at the last battle and Neb's abdication, Eva found that she was completely exhausted. Her heart was wrung so tight that she had ceased to feel anything at all. When Madai shared his desire to travel a bit and meet Adam's clan in the far south, Eva simply assented without comment. She could not have told anyone in the world what she thought about anything at that time, for she herself did not know. She watched as Adam made himself at home in the clan, and she felt nothing. When Dodan, the eldest son of Uzal, came and asked to travel with Madai, Eva's soul stirred a bit.

Dodan was unlike any man she had ever met before, and she could see in him a reflection of her lost friend. During the men's long absence, nothing remarkable occurred in the village, and Eva moved about in silence without any trace of enthusiasm.

But when Madai returned with Adam and Dodan as well as a bride, suddenly Eva did feel something. It was like a dull ache that hurt her very intestines. Ester, she soon learned, was the most cherished daughter of Adam's parents, and besides being quite beautiful, she was also considered wonderfully skilled in weaving and decorating clothing. There was great rejoicing among everyone in the clan, for it was always a happy time when the leader choose a wife. But Eva was not glad. She watched and grew more and more sulky. In her mind, she believed that Ester was nothing more than a spoiled child who knew nothing of the hardships of life, and this burned a resentful hole in Eva's heart.

It seemed to Eva that everyone had forgotten the losses they had suffered and that the lessons of the past were being abandoned. She felt no small alarm over the fact that one day Neb could possibly return, and he would find them so lost in their simple everyday matters that they would be completely unprepared to deal with him. She wanted to speak of her concerns to Madai, but he was a man so absorbed by his new wife and his plans for building a larger home for their expected children that he did not care much for contentious discourse. Instead Madai had burned down the dwelling of his father and had decreed that no one should build on that site. He wanted to forget the past entirely. Now that he was creating his own dwelling, he wanted to start fresh, and his earnest endeavors took much of his time and attention. When Eva attempted to speak to him about the past and her fears for the future, Madai tried to turn the conversation to other things or found that he had other immediate concerns. Eva felt deeply hurt by his rejection and she retreated further into her injured soul.

After a time, Eva began to show her disdain openly. She would not speak to Ester when she was in her company, and even when Madai brought his wife to her for some small matter, Eva would speak as if the girl were not there. At first, Ester accepted the humiliation as a part of her testing in the new clan, but when even her husband grew surprised and irritated, Ester began to unleash her resentment. She had never been treated like this before. Ester was not one to think matters over for any length of time. In very much the same way that she fell in love with Madai, so she fell in hate with Eva. Soon there was a dangerous and ugly passion between the two women with each doing whatever small thing they could to anger the other. Ester was not very inventive, and her talents lay in the area of taunting Eva for not being married and by making unflattering comments about her skills as a healer. Some who had known Eva for many years but had never really felt close to her enjoyed this dispute and did what they could to encourage it. Eva, however, would not lower herself to the commonplace insults against the girl or her family, but she did manage to express her disdain for Ester's intelligence. Every time Ester made a remark in her hearing, Eva shook her head in a sorrowful manner as if to mourn the stupidity of the girl. There were also those who were jealous of Ester's sudden rise to prominence in marrying the clan leader. So the small battles were encouraged, and they increased in vehemence and duration.

    Then there came a day when a youth in the village was brought in with a serious injury. He had been traveling deep into the woodlands, and a wild cat had dropped upon him from above. If it had not been for the bravery of his friends, he would have been killed outright. As it was, he was terribly torn up, and during the long trek home, he had lost a quantity of blood. Eva was called for and she came, as did most of the clan with Ester with Madai, and they all watched the healer's every move with breathless attention. Ester was so excited by the unusual event and the sight of so serious an injury that in her curiosity she edged her way closer and began to ask questions. Eva and her skilled helpers were busy working on the youth, trying to keep him alive, and the irritation of excited whispering quickly became too much for Eva. When she looked up and saw who was interrupting her work, she flew into a rage like she had never experienced before. Everyone around her was startled, and they feared both for the young man under her care, as well as for Ester, for it was an ill omen to have the enmity of the clan healer. Madai quickly took his wife away, and he tried to persuade her to understand Eva's outburst, though he himself felt uneasy. From then on Madai had to keep the two women away from one another, and he hoped that they would forget their animosity in time. But that was not to be. The youth lived, despite his many injuries, and that put Eva in a new light, for many considered it a miracle that she had been able to save him. Suddenly Eva was praised and reverenced as having special powers, and in her renewed pride she felt more justified in her disgust of Ester.

It was about a full turn of the seasons when Ester learned that she was carrying a new life, and her pride at this wonder gave her a renewed strength to strike back at Eva's treatment of her. And so it happened that after several moons, Ester was coming close to her time to deliver, and Eva had done nothing to assist her. Other women of the clan had stepped in, however, and instructed her in the matters of becoming a mother, and Ester had never felt the loss of the attentions of the clan healer. In fact, she had experienced a very joyful pregnancy, and she had enjoyed herself as much as possible. Even when Madai asked her to be more careful and to slow down, Ester carried on, determined to show no weakness and to make it very clear that she had no need of friend or healer in the person of Eva.

It was during the change of the season when the air had suddenly cooled from blazing hot to windy and cool with a mild rain falling from dim grey clouds that Ester found she could not do whatever she wanted. She had been visiting with friends on the outskirts of the village when she slipped down a slope and injured her hip. She found herself in a great deal of pain. One of the women went to get Madai, and he returned terribly concerned. When he tried to carry her, she cried out in such anguish that Madai rushed back to the village and got Dodan to assist him. He wanted to bring Eva to help, but he knew that Ester would not want her assistance. So it was that Dodan did what Madai could not, and he found a way to lay Ester on a makeshift sled. He brought her back to the village, and then he helped to tenderly care for her in her injury. Eva watched all this, and her heart smote her more than ever. She had tried on several occasions to speak with Dodan, to share her skills with him, and thus make a friendship with him, but though he had always been friendly and had willingly learned of her skills, he had never seemed inclined to visit her by his own will. Eva had hoped that one day he would come to her, but he never did. She had watched him with her big, silent eyes, wishing that he would notice her, but he did not. When he cared for Ester, it seemed that every ounce of tender concern he could have shared with *her* was lavished upon her enemy. Eva felt crushed and desolated in a manner she had never known before. Even the loss of Leah had not injured her soul as this did. So she watched and suffered in silence.

But Dodan had quickly become almost as good a healer as Eva herself, and Ester was soon mended from the sprain and feeling much better. There seemed to be no harm to the child inside her, and they all expected Ester to have a perfectly normal, healthy delivery. But this was not to be.

It was not long after this incident that everyone noticed that Eva was keeping much more to herself and did not speak to anyone. She spent a lot of time in her dwelling, and there was an unusual amount of smoke coming from inside, as if she had more than the usual number of daily meals. But few dared to ask Eva about the matter. As a matter of fact, few even cared what the matter could be, for they were all expecting with joy-filled anticipation the arrival of Madai's first child. But when Ester went into labor, it was apparent right away that something was wrong. Dodan and every experienced mother were called in to assist, but things went from bad to worse very quickly. Soon it seemed that not only would they lose the child, but the mother as well. In the silence attending Ester's labored and distraught breathing, Madai took Dodan aside and begged him to get Eva to come and assist.

"You know her for you have spent some time with her discussing herbs and the qualities of various brews. She respects you, and she knows your intelligence, so she will listen if you tell her that this is a serious matter and that we need her assistance."

Dodan looked grave and nodded his head several times, but he had seen with growing uneasiness the change in Eva, and he feared for her sanity. He had thought several times that he should go to her, but the memory of Ophir was still clear in his mind, and he feared madness as a grief that he had little skill to heal. But when he looked at Madai's tormented face, he knew what he had to do. "I will go to see her and do what I can. But do not hope too much, for my words are mere breaths of air to a hurt and angry woman."

Madai turned his head and looked at Dodan with an intense gaze. In a flash of sudden awareness, he realized that perhaps he had neglected Eva and that it was possible that Eva had never been allowed to explain herself to him. He had brought home a new woman, making her his own, and Eva had suddenly been blotted out from his mind. Now he suddenly recalled all she had done for him and the long years of quiet torment she too had endured under the rule of Neb. While he had escaped into a position of leadership and importance and had been able to marry well, gaining an attractive companion, Eva had been left to languish alone and forgotten. Madai put his hand on Dodan's should and spoke with great haste. "It may be that I have a part to play in allowing things to come to this pass, but more than anything under the sun I do not want my wife to die. Eva may not have the cure she needs, but it would be murder not to try. Ask her, for my sake, to save my wife and child."

Dodan nodded once and turned to go while Madai sped back to his wife. When Eva heard Dodan calling for her outside her dwelling, she stopped all motion and was as still as a mouse being sought out by a cat. She did not know why she did not want to see him anymore, but she realized that she was suddenly afraid. For the past many days, she had taken to making stick and clay dolls and burning them in a fire. She made a doll to match Ester's image, and then she made one to match Madai and several other clansmen who had hurt her with their comments or their silence. Finally she had made one to match Dodan. It was this doll that had been the hardest to make. She spent long hours carving out each feature, and she had even added hair to this one so as to make it more life-like. She was just about to burn it that morning, but she had not been able to do it. When she held it over the fire, she told herself that with the burning of this image, she would be released from all suffering connected with this man, and she believed that perhaps he would suffer a bit to make up for all the suffering she had had to endure. But she could not drop it into the fire it as she meant to, so she had waited a bit. Now the figure was over in the corner of the room, staring at her as she went about doing the simple duties of her day. She heard Dodan's voice, and she instinctively looked at the little figure with bright, large eyes. Then she heard the call again, and she stood straight up, realizing that Dodan was really right out in front of her dwelling. She put down the garment she had been working on and went quickly outside.

"Dodan? I am surprised to see you. It is not often you travel out this way."

Dodan smiled despite himself. Eva had a smear from her breakfast on her chin, and it looked somewhat amusing on so serious and proud a countenance. But then he remembered his task, and all traces of his smile vanished. "I have come to beg for your help. Ester is near death, and Madai fears for both her and the child. No one can calm her or help the situation. We need you to see what can be done, or both are lost."

Eva stared at Dodan for a long, silent moment. "Why do you come to me now? Why have you waited until there is little hope? So that I can be blamed for their deaths?"

Dodan's eyes grew wide as he looked back at the woman he had once admired so much. He shook his head solemnly. "There is no such thought in anyone's head. We did not ask for you for the simple reason that everyone knows you do not like the girl."

"I do not like the girl? Is that how it stands then? I suppose I am a cruel and unjust woman who dislikes a poor girl for no reason!"

Dodan looked off into the distance and saw someone beckoning to him. He saw their agitation, and he spoke quickly and a little more loudly. "I do not have time to understand your feelings right now, though I know that that would be a very good idea, and I would very much like to... perhaps at another time. Right now a woman and her baby are dying, and if you ever considered yourself a healer, this would be the time to remember that your mission is to help and not to hate."

If lightening had reached out from the low, dark clouds and struck Eva with their full force, it would have seemed like nothing compared to the bolt of shock that went through her system now. Suddenly, as clear as day, Eva saw her father as he stood in their last moments together, and she remembered her vow. She remembered why she had made that vow, and a dark blush spread across her face in shame at the burning of the carved images of her clansmen. Without a word, Eva began to run. She sped up the incline toward Madai's new dwelling, and she pushed through all the bodies of men, women and children crowding around wanting to know what was happening. Eva yelled at everyone to go away, and when she reached Madai, she said not a word as she reached for Ester and took her hand. She saw the sweat pouring off the girl's face, and she cursed herself inside for her stubborn pride and obstinacy. She started giving orders like birds flying from the nest. Ester tried to turn her eyes to Eva, but she had barely strength to move, and her pain was too great to allow for speech. Her eyes, however, pleaded with unspoken humility.

Eva worked in a fury to do all that she could for both mother and child while Madai and Dodan were sent to care for the rest of the clan and tend to the duties of the day. There were women enough to see to carrying out of her orders and getting her all that she needed. It was a long night with rain coming down in a cold drizzle and a chill wind blowing, but Eva stayed by the new mother's side, and even though she almost despaired for them both at times, by the next day she knew that not all was lost. Ester would live, but the baby came early, and it would take everything that Eva knew to keep the baby alive. She used every skill she had—and invented a few she had never thought of before—and the babe lived.

Madai, in his gratitude and joy, did everything he could to make up to Eva for his earlier negligence, and Ester, in her complete gratitude, treated Eva as her new mother. She offered respect and the love of a daughter and sought Eva's advice in everything. Dodan stood by while all the excitement abated, and the rosy glow of gladness settled into the more ordinary peace of the usual pattern of days. But he paid attention to Eva's doings, and he was very glad for her transformation. He saw her resentment melt and her hurt heal, and he decided it was time for him to be going back to his own people. Adam had gone off to travel again, and though he said he would return at times, he was not a man who wanted to build a home right now. Dodan stood and watched as Eva took care of a small sick child, and he knew that he could go home now but that there would be little he needed to do there. Kryce was a strong leader, and Enosh and Kenan were as much his brothers as any men could be. The clan was strong and prosperous and they did not need his ministrations. He felt a little deflated. But Madai was still young, and he had relied on Dodan for an infinite number of small matters, which, though unimportant, had helped Madai make a good transition from leader's son to leader and helped the men of Neb adjust to new leadership. As important as all that was, Dodan was not sure it could justify his staying any longer. He knew Madai would welcome him forever, but he felt he must have more reason to stay. After all, perhaps he was intruding and had not the wits to realize the signs. Then his eyes traveled across the wet ground to where Eva was sitting now with a little baby in her lap. She had taken Madai's son to herself as if he were her own, and Ester and her both lavished generous amounts of attention of the infant. Madai's son had been named Keram, and he was the darling of the entire clan. Dodan watched Eva, and something began to burn in his chest. He wondered at himself. What was it he wanted? He had accepted the fact that he was not born to be a great hunter and warrior. Though he could furnish game for the clan, it was not something he would ever be renowned for. Yet he yearned inside of himself to be renowned for something. He well remembered his clan's admirations when he had faced Ophir's past of terror and brought enlightenment to his father. Even the great Uzal had looked upon him as a hero in those days. Yet his father had died and so much had changed. He had been of little use in beating back the enemy.

He was not the hero of anyone, and yet he dearly wished he could be. Even in the matter of Ester and her baby, he had been at a loss as to how to save them both. It had been Eva's grace to heal what he could not heal. He watched her, and before he knew what he was doing, he found himself standing before her. She looked up, and there was a wide smile in the place of the sullen pout that he had seen formerly. He smiled in return, though his smile was not as great. Eva spoke with a cheerful lilt.

"Good day, Dodan. What are you about today?"

Dodan shrugged his shoulders. "I am not doing much, I am afraid. It seems I have outlived my usefulness. Perhaps it is time for me to go back to my own clan."

At these words, all the sparkle went out of Eva's eyes, and she sat still and even appeared to stop breathing. "Surely that is not so. You are very useful here. Madai would not know what to do without you and—" She seemed to falter for lack of words.

Dodan looked at her with sudden attention. "And?"

"Well, there are others who need you as well. You are a healer and not just of bodies. You saved me from my rash ways with only a few words."

"Your rash ways?" Dodan smiled at this. "You were merely angry and hurt, and it took someone to remind you that you were more than just those feelings."

Eva nodded soberly, and then she looked hard at Dodan. "It seems to me that you do much the same yourself. I suppose it is ever the condition of men to define themselves by a trait or two rather than by that which makes them truly human."

"What do you mean?"

Eva shifted the baby onto her other leg and smiled into the little one's sweet face. "It just seems to me that sometimes you do not realize your value. Just because you are not a warrior, it is as if you do not think of yourself as a man."

"I am a very small man."

Eva smiled. "Not really. I think you are every bit as large as any man I have ever met. In fact, the image I made of you was several sizes—" Eva put her hand to her lips and closed her eyes tightly in her embarrassment.

Dodan looked at her, and he remembered the fires and the secretive behavior, and he guessed much. He was truly shocked, but he could see tears forming at the corner of Eva's eyes, so he slid over next to her and put his arm gently around her. She laid her head on his shoulder and tried to stifle her memory and her grief. There were so many things she still grieved over, and she could never explain them all. In this moment of shame, it seemed as if they all came at her with renewed vigor, and she felt like she would never be able to stop crying. Dodan held her, and he understood. He knew in a way he had never understood before that the real value in being intimate was not in the shared joys but in the shared sorrows, for only then, when you have nothing left to give but your grief, do two people really unite over that which binds the best of all of us—selfless love.

Dodan took one hand and stroked Eva's cheek and checked her tears. He looked down at the little sleeping baby and smiled. "I would like to have a child of my own."

Eva looked up at him and nodded. "I too."

Dodan stroked his chin a moment. "Well, we best not drown Madai's baby then. I have a favor to ask of him, and it might be a good idea to keep his first son dry and peaceful."

Eva smiled up at Dodan and then rested her head upon his shoulder once again. "It takes a man among men to father a whole clan, and you have done so. I have no fear of your fathering a child."

Dodan sighed deeply and he let his chin rest gently on his soon-to-be wife's soft head.

CHAPTER 40
THE NEXT GENERATION

Gizah looked at her husband, and though he was still listening, she could tell that he was getting very tired. It seemed that everyone in the clan had fallen into a quiet, restful peace. Eyes were open, but no one was moving, and even the homes were silent. The fire had burned very low. She looked over at Ishtar, and his head had dropped on his chest with his eyes closed. Gizah smiled and motioned for her husband to get up with her so that they could go home without making any noise, but then suddenly Ishtar looked up.

"I was just resting a moment. I heard every word you said."

Gizah smiled. "It is getting late, and perhaps we should rest and start again another time."

Ammee nodded agreeably. "Yes, Father, it has been a long day, and I do not want you to get over tired." Ammee began to get up again, but Ishtar put up his hand and stalled his son.

"Yes, I admit I am tired, but I feel a great desire to hear up to where Aram is born. Perhaps you could just tell . . ."

Gizah laughed good-naturedly. "Yes, if you want, I will continue. I will go along more briskly, for in truth, there is not much to tell of the clan of Keram. His people lived quietly enough but there is an event that occurred later and changed everything. Do you want me to tell of that?"

Ishtar took a drink from a skin bag at his side, wiped his mouth and sat up a bit straighter. "Yes, that would be very good."

Gizah looked at her husband, and he got up and threw a little more wood on the fire, bringing the flames back to life. Everyone stretched and then settled back down into comfortable positions. Gizah leaned her weary back against her husband with his arms nestled gently about her large waist. Her eyes reflected the flickering flames as she continued her story.

"Thanks to Dodan and Eva, Keram grew up strong and healthy, and it was not until much later that his little brother was born. But this babe was not as lucky as the first, and he died in his first year. There were several others who followed, but Keram was raised to be the inheritor of all that Madai had established from the clan of Neb, son of Hezeki. Rarely was Neb mentioned, and it was as if all memory of him had been blotted out of his people's memories. Eva spoke at times with Madai of her concern that their people might forget the dangers of Neb, but Madai always assured her that Neb would not return, and so he was proved right. Neb did not return, and the clan lived on in peaceful security. Eva was, herself, blessed with several children, and with her recaptured desire to fulfill her vow to be of service to others, she came to be the most capable of women in the area. Clansmen from all over sought her advice in treating serious injuries. Dodan continued in his role as mentor and father figure to Madai, and the two of them brought an established peace to the clan. Adam came now and again and brought them new ideas he had gleaned from the clans from near and far. And so it went for year after year with only births and deaths to change the pattern of their days. But then as Madai grew into old age and his son, Keram, was nearing an age to become leader, an event occurred that drastically changed the fortunes of all. A new people came traveling through the area, and though they were friendly enough, they brought something with them that could not be seen but which brought disaster to the whole clan. A terrible sickness invaded, and though both Eva and Dodan did everything they could, there was no known remedy for this silent stalker, which claimed lives with horrible speed. Several of Madai's younger children were taken, as well as Eva's infant daughter. Many old people succumbed in a matter of days, and even those who had lived through years of drought and poor crops and other hardships now failed to survive the present danger of this new illness. After nearly a third of the clan had been laid to rest in numerous mounds, Madai called together all those still able to make a clear choice, and he stated the matter in definite terms.

"Whatever is killing our people will claim us all in time if we stay here. We must move on and make a new home away from these southern hills. The strangers came from the south, and they were heading east. I think it would be best if we head west into the wilderness where few venture to hide from this formless terror that stalks us." Keram was man enough to help make the decision, and though he loved his home, for he had many happy memories there, he knew that to stay would be certain death, so he supported his father's plan. Dodan and Eva agreed, and it was soon decided and those that were able to pack up did so, and those that needed help were laid on stretchers to be carried by the stronger youth.

It was a heartbroken assembly that thrashed a trail through the dense woodlands, heading they knew not where. But even as they hacked and broke away all barriers, new terrors began to haunt them. Wild animals they had never encountered before attacked them in the black night and killed those unaware and unprepared. There was one enormous creature that had thick and hard, bumpy skin, short flat legs and feet with enormous claws and a mouth that opened wider than anyone had believed possible that came out of the great western river and devoured two men. Madai swiftly turned northeast away from the river of blood while trying desperately to hold his people together. But as time went on, it seemed as if they would be taken one by one until their ultimate and complete demise.

Keram had grown into a strong young man of medium build with thick dark brown hair like his mother and dark brown eyes, but he was not quite so shy and soft spoken as his mother. In fact, he was quick to make rash decisions and very unwilling to change his mind about anything. It was he, as eldest son, who decided that it would be best if the clan split in two and each tried to make its way so that at least some might survive. Everyone protested that this was the worst thing they could do, as each group would be less protected, but Keram would not wait for death to find him. He wanted to move further and faster than his father. So after much discussion and argument, a final decision was accepted, and Keram did move on with a few who were brave or foolish enough to follow him. One of those who went with him was Miriam, the youngest daughter of a large family who had lost every other member of her family. She believed that she had nothing to lose and everything to gain by going off with the only man in the clan she trusted. Keram had gone out of his way to comfort her in her grief, and he knew that the best thing Miriam could do would be to separate from all that reminded her of all her loss. So he conceived the idea of going off on his own, and he led her and several others forth into the deepest part of the woodlands. Keram never saw or heard from his father, mother, Eva or Dodan ever again.

All the knowledge and storage of learning that had been accumulated for the last couple of generations was lost in that departure. Keram knew the stories of his father and his grandfather, and he knew much about healing herbs from his mother, but he had not studied much of weapons or the ways of growing crops or the things of an established clan. He had to reinvent his own people, and so they were made anew as a woodland clan that wandered from place to place and lived completely off the resources of a dark, rank forest. Keram and Miriam married young, and they gave birth to a son very soon after their joining. The son born to them was great in size and very strong, and he soon showed signs of being very much like his great-grandfather, Neb, for he wanted to rule the clan before it was his time to do so. This first son's name was Elath, and he was the bane of his father, Keram. But after the loss of three sisters, there was a second son named Aram. Here was a son who loved his father like no other son had ever loved his father, and he had no desire to lead his clan. His only hope was to grow up strong, but as sometimes happens, history repeats itself. Keram found himself having to choose between his sons. But this time, the first son, Elath, had no desire to destroy his father. He liked to travel to the high places, and so when he was barely old enough to be considered a man, he claimed the right to separate. He called forth any who would follow him, and though most did not, there were some who did, and Keram was left with his wife and his son, Aram, and a little over half his clan. And thus began the personal history of Aram and his rise to become a leader of men."

Gizah looked away from the flames, and her eyes meet those of Ishtar. He was not smiling, for his pondering thoughts were very deep and serious. But then he tilted his head and spoke a few words. "You have explained much. Thank you."

Gizah nodded as she and her husband rose in the night air and stretched themselves. Ammee reached down to help his father up, but Ishtar waved his son's gentle hands away. "I can sleep here as well as anywhere." He looked at the dying embers. "There is not much more to tell, but I will share the rest of Neb's history with you tomorrow. Thank you, Gizah, for what you have kept in your memory. Now I understand that which had been a strange mystery to me. I had never understood why Aram's people were so primitive when it was clear that Aram himself came from a developed heritage. Now I see the lost years where all advancement had been buried in the suffering past. Strange to say, but much the same loss occurred in my grandfather, Serug's clan. It seems that men may move forward only to have to step back time and again." Ishtar sighed deeply and then nodded slowly. "It is a beautiful night to watch the stars go by. Get a good rest, children. Goodnight."

CHAPTER 41

AND TO DUST WE SHALL RETURN

The next afternoon after Ishtar had done a full day's work, he went to the bank of the stream that meandered near their village. His feet were resting comfortably in the cool water, and his back was bowed with tiredness though he could straighten himself up as well as any man. When he saw Ammee leading Gizah toward him, he smiled and pointed to the water.

"Rest your feet and refresh yourselves. It is a warm day, and the sun and the water feel good."

Ammee laughed and stepped into the stream and splashed water all over himself. "I remember when you did this every morning, Father. You said it helped you to think."

Ishtar nodded. "Yes, ever since being in the hot, dry lands beyond the mountains, I never cease to be grateful for the refreshing beauty of abundant clear water. Pity those who have never known it." Ishtar's eyes seemed to scan the past to the time before he returned to his own people—the time of his exile—and Ammee, seeing his father's far-away look, spoke quickly for he had no desire to return to those memories.

"Father, tonight will you tell us about Neb the Great's last days and explain how it was that Serug brought another Neb into the world?"

Ishtar glanced at his son and then looked up into the bright blue sky as if he were soaring from one memory to another well beyond the sight of the present world. He knew the grief that was awaiting him in the telling of this tale, and he knew also that his son would be grieved by the truth. But there was no way to grow beyond the past other than to go through it. One had to accept that evil existed even in one's own bloodlines and then admit that all contain the stain of evil in their hearts. However, straightening himself up again, he reminded himself that the story did not end there. Beyond the past was a future, and beyond evil lived an undying hope.

"Yes, son, we will gather once again in the evening twilight, and I will tell the final tale of Neb the Great." He looked up again and took a deep breath of fresh air, stretching out his arms and letting his feet stir the cool water. "But for the moment I will live in the present and rest and rejoice that the past is no more."

When evening came, there was the largest crowd they had yet known for it seemed that no duty or sense of exhaustion could keep any clan member away from hearing the last part of this most magnificent tale. Ammee sat straight and tall with his wife leaning against him again, and though his eyes were wide awake, it was almost as if he were already drawn into another world for he felt the presence of more than those visible clan members gathered around. For some strange reason, it was as if in the retelling of this tale they had acted as a sort of council meeting in which the spirits of the dead were accused and judged as they had never been in life. There were no secrets now, and all knew the truth that many sought in vain to conceal. He shuddered involuntarily, for he realized with a sudden shock that someday it may be his turn to hear his life recounted by those who lived to judge his actions in a light of reason and by a measure that he had never considered. He looked at his wife and knew with a certainty that he had never experienced before that his own child would consider his actions of supreme importance. He could never again think that what he did in the course of a day, secret or not, was of no importance, for there would be a record somewhere, in someone's mind, and someday it would be recounted out loud before all.

Everyone leaned in to listen as Ishtar sat up tall and continued the story once again.

"When Serug found a suitable hiding place, he laid his father's tormented body in a quiet cave and tended to him himself. Serug was not so concerned with his father dying but rather that the men might revolt and pick another leader before Neb formally left him in charge. Serug was very careful that everything was seen to, and the men began to begrudgingly believe that Serug was more than he had formerly appeared to be. They watched and waited while Serug both tended to his father's needs and also hunted in the woodlands, feeding everyone better than they had dared hope on rabbits, deer, cats, hogs, birds of various species and even a wolf or two. They made suitable shelters from various nearby caves and stone embankments, and after a time they no longer regretted having left their former homeland.

It took a long time before Neb was well enough to sit up and speak coherently. He had seen all that his youngest son had done for him and his men, and he was frankly amazed. He had not imagined that Serug was capable of such clear thinking and studied self-discipline. When he felt well enough, he called Serug and those men who were most capable to him for a council meeting. As he looked at the solemn faces around him, Neb could not help remembering Hul and how he defied him after they left the people of Seth. The picture of Hul dropping everything to stand defenseless before him rocked him a moment and brought a taste of bile to his mouth. He swallowed hard, but the taste was still there, so he turned and spat off to his side. His men merely stared back at him with unmovable concentration. Then he remembered Riphath, and rubbing his temple, he wondered what had happened to him. Had Enosh and Kenan killed him as he would have liked to kill them? He decided that he did not want to think of that matter further. Then he felt a sudden choking sensation, and he gasped for air as the vivid memory of Kittam falling in battle by his own spear appeared before his face. Neb tried to thrash the memory away by blinking furiously and shaking his head in little jerks. He was looking more and more like a mad man. He forced himself into a willful calm by chanting in his own mind that Kittam's death had really been Torgama's fault. It was Torgama who had pierced him through the thigh first and caused him incredible torment, and it was Torgama who had looked upon his wife and had seen a chance for revenge. Neb demanded himself to believe his own inner conviction; it was Torgama who killed Kittam! It was all Torgama's fault. Neb clutched at the thin skin blanket that covered him, and he was filled with unutterable disgust. Of all his good and faithful men, only Puti had died as a noble warrior should—in battle, fighting the enemy. Neb knew that his men stood before him waiting for him to speak, but the faces of the past seemed to be rotating around him as shadows in the night and he found it difficult to speak. Finally Serug looked from the men to his father, and he spoke loud and clear.

"My father wants to thank you all for your loyalty and faithfulness." There was a sneering grunt from the background, and all eyes wavered, though no one dared to turn their heads except for Neb and Serug. Neb looked up, but even before his eyes found the face, his heart knew who dared to openly sneer at him. Serug called out shrilly.

"Torgama? Was that you? What are you saying? Do you doubt your master's gratitude?"

Torgama stepped forward slowly as if he had all the time in the world. His face was scarred, and in it was etched in a permanent look of sour disdain. He threw his head back to be heard all that more clearly. "I know what Neb is grateful for, and it has little to do with us." He looked around at the other men in the small, crowded space, and he shook his head as his gravelly voice rose. "He is no longer the man he was. He cares for nothing and no one. He is weak now. You can see it in his eyes. He is lost and knows not where to look for his past glory."

Serug clenched his fat fingers into stubby fists and screamed in uncontrolled fury that Torgama should die. "You are a worthless traitor to your master! You ought to be speared through the heart. No one wants a man like—" but Torgama put up his hand and shook his head with a slightly bemused expression on his face.

"Before you say anything else, I would like a word with you alone, Serug, for I do respect your opinion." Serug stopped short. His eyes squinted at Torgama in a distrustful but inquiring manner. He stepped off to the side, and Torgama moved off to follow him. Neb watched them, knowing what was about to happen, and he felt nothing at all. In all his life, he had never known true defeat and now, when he was weak and his mind was plaguing him, he knew beyond a shadow of a doubt that his end had come, if not physically, then at least as the man he had always been. His life had always been about ascendancy. It had never occurred to him that he might live to see his own decent.

When Serug returned a few moments later with Torgama trailing after him, a faint smile quivering about his lips, Neb knew that Torgama had done him in just the same as if he had taken his spear and pierced him through the heart. Serug walked up to the men, and he nodded his head silently in understanding.

"I have been informed by Torgama of the wishes of you men, and I understand your needs." He looked back fugitively at Neb and spoke in a grieved undertone. "I agree with your assessment. You are quite right, and though I am an honorable son, I do see the importance of making a quick and firm decision." Serug tapped his fingers against his thigh for a few moments trying to decide how he was going to act out this particular betrayal so it would look honest and good. He turned suddenly like a man who has decided that the best thing to do at the moment would be to jump into a cold lake.

"Father, the men have chosen me as the new clan leader. You will always be a very important member of the clan of course, and you shall live out your last days in peace and security. However, I will the one to make all the decisions from now on. I will convene the meetings with the men, and I will form a new council when it suits my interests to do so." Serug was still quite young, and even this bit of amazing good luck was startling enough to shake him a little. He looked to his father, nodding his head several times in succession as if to convince himself what he had just said in certainty. Neb simply stared at him as pictures of his own father floated before his possessed eyes. Suddenly he broke out into a loud cackling laugh as if he had been part of an enormously funny joke. Serug stared at his father, his eyes growing wider with every fresh burst of mad merriment.

"Father, what is it that ails you? I thought this would be a relief. After all, you are a very sick man. You deserve a time of peace and rest." This just brought even more laughter from Neb. He was practically choking with uncontrolled amusement.

Finally he spat out his words well enough to be understood.

"You offer me in life what I denied my father at his death, yet you condemn me even more surely than I condemned him." His laughter rang out in a rage of broken fortune, and his men turned one by one and walked away. Only Serug maintained his position, not quite sure what to do. He was not angry but simply a little confused. He took a deep breath. He was quite glad that he was the acknowledged leader. He knew he owed a great deal to Torgama, for it was clearly through Torgama's maneuvering that the men had been united in this fortunate wish. Yet he also felt fairly certain that it had been Torgama who had killed his mother. And he knew definitely that Torgama would like very much to kill his father. Serug began to tap his fingers against his thigh again, waiting patiently for his father to settle back into calm. Neb had finally stopped laughing, but he was alone now in a world of his own mind and seemed to be speaking to the air. Serug tipped his head to the side and studied his father. He had no desire to end his father's life any time soon. He was not threatened by him. For some reason, it satisfied some little place in his mind that now Neb the Great was subject to his own son— and a second son at that. If he had been the laughing sort, he might have laughed in his own turn, but he merely stared ahead in thought. He thought little about justice and cared nothing for mercy, but a secret smile played around his lips as he walked away from his father, planning for the future of his clan.

CHAPTER 42
İNNER EXİLE

The days slowed down for Neb. It was a strange exile inside the remnant of his clan and also inside the remnant of his own mind. The days were mild now, neither hot nor terribly cold, except at night when a bitter chill would descend and he would wrap himself up in his thin skin blankets and shiver despite himself. Serug kept a distant watch over him, and slowly each day he would mend in both mind and body. He would take slow walks along the meandering stream and say nothing and think very little. He would simply observe the small changes of each day, and some part of him began to stretch toward a light he had never noticed before. Quiet had always been a useful tool to him in which to collect his thoughts and make his plans, but now he realized that he had no plans to make. There was a moment once when he considered the possibility of overthrowing his own son the way he had overthrown his father years ago, but for some reason that idea did not appeal to him. He was truly exhausted and even the slightest effort toward serious exertion would send him back to his pallet for days. No, this time he could not rule as he had in the past, yet as the days flowed into longer and longer stretches of time, he began to wonder if there were not many ways to rule. He thought about Leah and how she had ruled him more than anyone had ever suspected—more than even she had imagined. But he knew that his passion was far spent. He did not think he would ever feel that way toward anyone ever again. Still, he realized as he circled around trees and meandered along streams that as time passed, many things could change. There was more to leading men than arranging for their next battle. One particularly perfect day, he wandered through the woods to a great tree that drank directly from the stream with its enormous roots both in and out of the water. The sun was at its peak in the sky when he decided to sit down and watch it creep across the vast blue expanse. He needed rest and thought that perhaps he would nap a little. He rested his head against the broad, dark tree trunk and let his shoulders slump in utter relaxation. He was not sure how much time had passed when he awoke to the sensation of being shoved in the side. The sun was eclipsed by the shadows of the vast trees all around him, but Neb soon realized that he was not alone. He had most certainly felt something jolt him, and he felt a wet spot on his arm and still could smell the scent of a large furry animal. He sat up ever so quietly and looked all around. There to his right side stood one of the largest bears he had ever seen. It was a matriarch of the forest, and quite likely she had cubs somewhere about. Neb let his eyes scan his environment, but he made no other motion. There were no other large moving animals in the near vicinity. He turned his gaze back toward the great she-bear. He remembered his first great hunt and his ignominious defeat by the failure of his throw to reach its mark. But a slow grin crept across his face as he remembered what he did in revenge of his defeat. He became renowned throughout the clan for his daring accomplishment of skill when he brought home his dead enemy. It did not matter that it was not the same bear. What mattered to him and everyone who heard the tale was how he had conquered himself and had accomplished what few would have attempted at his age. Neb knew that he was not in fit shape to kill this bear, and she had not been particularly threatening to him. In fact, she was ignoring him as if he did not exist. He was not in any danger, but Neb remembered his thin blankets and knew for the first time since his sickness and exile that he wanted something. He wanted her skin. He felt his knife in his belt, and he knew he would need more than his one blade. But knowing that she was near was all that mattered. He could accomplish this task in his own time. When he was ready, he would get for himself a beautiful fur blanket. Her fur was a tawny dark brown that changed sheen as the broken lights filtered through the branches and leaves. He imagined himself wrapped up in the thick fur, and he could almost feel its soft fullness against his skin. He smiled and began to slip slowly away, edging out of sight, smell and imagination of the great animal.

A cold night when the moon was full, Neb awoke to the sound of howling, and he sat up in a state of near panic. The great fur he had won for himself had fallen down near his knees, and he clutched at it wildly but could not escape the sudden chill that had enveloped his body. He had seen the face of Uzal in his dream and felt his grip upon his shoulder. Neb wrapped the blanket around himself tighter and shook his head in disbelief. Why now? Who was Uzal now that he should come to haunt him? Uzal was dust in the ground by now. Leah was dead and gone. All the battles that ever mattered were over. Neb was only a man who lived in the wilderness in quiet obscurity. What did Neb's guilt or peace of mind matter now? Neb sat down and heard the screaming wail of the wind as it tore through his small dwelling. What had Uzal promised? To haunt him in life and death? Neb laughed grimly, for surely he was living that very contradiction; he was neither fully alive nor definitely dead. The warm fur rubbed against his bare shoulders, and Neb smiled even in his uncertainty. No, he thought as he sat on his haunches, he would not succumb to terror and madness. He would not. He had something left to accomplish, if not in this life than in the next. The future still existed, and he could still affect the outcome of another's fate. Suddenly he understood for a moment how his own mother must have felt when she tried so desperately to control him. But Neb was not Meshullemeth. One thought led to the next, and Neb nodded his head as he imagined the son that Serug would one day have. He knew without a doubt that his life was not quite over. He still had one great victory to accomplish. Uzal would have to wait through eternity to accomplish his reign of terror. Neb was not afraid of anything, be it from man, beast or the spirits of hell.

Serug watched his men with a jealous eye. He was the leader, but he was never secure in his own mind that he would stay the leader. There was one man who had come with them during the final battle who most certainly did not belong to them. He was of the family of Torgama, but there were never two so different mortals to walk the earth. His name was Eymard, and he was as silent and thoughtful as his kinsman, but his eyes betrayed a very different mind behind them. Eymard had followed the wishes of his father and served Neb faithfully, but he had seen very little in the way of battle, as early on it had been decided that he was a better healer and provider than he would ever be a warrior. So it had been in this capacity that he had worked in silence among the men of Neb. Neb himself had never taken the slightest notice of Eymard, and when illness came, he simply called upon Eva as was his habit. But now that Eva was no longer a part of their small exiled group, he found himself forced to notice this medium-built, brown-eyed, nondescript individual. Eymard never spoke unless he had to, and when he needed something, he spoke in the softest voice imaginable. It was not the same conspiratal whisper as some of Neb's men used, but rather the whisper of a man who speaks seldom and wishes to be heard only by those he is attending. Eymard never once called attention to himself, so it was no wonder that no one ever seemed to notice him and that Neb barely even realized his existence. But Serug was a different sort of leader. He was not afraid of warriors who might try to challenge his might. He knew that he was not the strongest in the clan in terms of physical strength but that rather his power was based on his ability to see danger ahead of the turn and face it with a well-executed plan. As he watched his men work and his father rest, Serug became more and more obsessed with Eymard's quiet ability. Something about his nature disturbed Serug greatly. It was during the big hunt of the fall when the men banded together and went out to bring in much game for the dark days that Serug noticed Eymard doing things differently than the rest. He was building a structure to live in that was more permanent, and he had instructed several of the men to bring any very young animals they came across to him to raise, especially pigs and goats. Apparently Eymard had ideas of his own making in his head. Perhaps he remembered the ways of Hezeki and the stories of the settled clans and he wanted to try something of his own invention. This was very threatening to Serug who saw, like his father, the necessity of keeping his men tied to him through fear. Settlements were too closely allied to security, and security bred a kind of free thinking that left little room for leaders like

Neb and Serug. So Serug went to his father, and they spoke of Eymard and his ways.

Neb listened to his son's complaints and nodded his head in understanding. He knew what his son feared, and he had the perfect solution for him.

"We need to move on from here. Keep the clan moving, and do not let them rest too long. They will look to you for direction, and Eymard will find his plans come to nothing. You need not approach him directly. Just say you have knowledge they do not have and that you know that now is the time to move on. Make it urgent. Make it imperative that they do just what you say, and they will follow you."

Serug knew his father was right, but he was a little confused as to why it was true. In absent thought, he spoke under his breath, "But why will they believe me?"

Neb smiled a secretive smile and leaned in toward his son. "You see, men want to be led. They do not want to think everything out for themselves. Of course there are a few who think they would like to lead and could do it better than the one in charge, but the truth is that few really want the role." Neb looked around and saw that they were completely alone, and he resumed speaking a little louder and with more confidence. "Men want to do whatever they like, but nothing ever turns out as planned. Even in the dullest man, there is some realization of this. So even more than directing, men like to complain about others and blame everyone else for the evils that we all must endure." Neb nodded slowly. "You will see the truth of my words. No matter what decision you make in any matter, there will be many who will complain bitterly. Just give them time to wear themselves out. Leaders are always despised while they are in charge. It is the fate of a leader. Never care for the opinions of others. It is the only way to rule."

Serug looked blankly ahead. He knew what his father said was true, but he could not help lusting after the position of leadership. He did not care who he had to conquer or kill; as long as he could give all the directions and be obeyed, he was most content. He looked over at his own father, and his eyes narrowed just the least little bit. "Do you not want to lead even yet, Father?"

Neb looked off into the distance. "I am leading, Son."

Serug pursed his lips together and thought about those four simple words for several long moments, and then he decided that he could accept them. For the time being, as long as he appeared to be the one in complete charge, it did not matter that he sought advice from his father. He was the one who made the final decision. His father had accepted his own position with apparent indifference, and it suited them both very well for the time being. As for Eymard, Serug would find a way to rid his clan of this dangerous influence of a man who was not content to follow in blind obedience. Men who thought for themselves were a danger to everyone, and this he could ill afford. He needed men as his father described—men who did not want to lead but only complained in their sterile effort to relieve themselves of all responsibility. Serug stood up and looked down upon his father.

"I will give the order today, and it will become a matter of life and death to my men to obey me."

Neb nodded absently. Then he stroked his chin in a thoughtful manner. "You might be interested in heading north toward the great mountains. I have heard stories about many small clans in the valleys, and I suspect you might find yourself a young wife who has never been tainted with the blood of the Men of Havilah."

Serug nodded in agreement, but then he spoke in uncertainty. "But what about the Men of Seth? Do they not come from the north?"

"Not this far west. They are higher up in the hills. We will stay in the low lands."

Serug nodded in acceptance. He did not even notice that his father had planned his future for the next many years. He simply tilted his head to the side as if pondering a question for the first time. "A wife for me?"

Neb let his eyes close as he pictured their future. "Yes, a wife and a son. You will have a son who will be just like me."

Serug felt like a mighty weapon had just been put into his hand. A son who would do his every bidding. A son to bring power and glory to his name. A son who— Serug paused a moment. What if he had a daughter first? He had been told such things happened. Neb seemed to read his mind.

"Do not worry. Girls are fragile things. If one is born first, she would not live to matter. Eva taught me many things even when she did not mean to. I know how to dispose of a mistake easily enough. Besides, I am a first son of a first son going back for generations."

Serug squared his shoulders and looked perplexed. "But I am a second son."

For the first time Neb seemed pulled out of his reverie. "I have no other son, so therefore you must be my first son."

Serug nodded decisively. He would lead his clan toward the mountains, he would find himself a wife and he would have a son, all as his father directed, and he would be the recognized leader. He was pleased. His future was growing bright.

CHAPTER 43

TORGAMA AND EYMARD

The weather had turned cold, and the nights were bitter. Neb was immensely grateful for his thick fur blanket as they huddled against the bare rock of an overhanging cliff. Nothing had gone according to plan. Their journey had been much longer and more difficult than they had imagined. Several of the men were expressing their discontent, not the least of them being Torgama. Torgama began to openly question the purpose of their migration and the direction they were taking. When Serug asked him where he wanted to go, Torgama had merely responded that he would go somewhere warm, and there was amused grunted approval at this. Serug merely rolled his eyes and said that weak men complained the most. Nothing was said in response to this charge. Still Serug was tired and hungry, and though he had followed Neb's direction into the north, he had now run into a barrio he could not get around. They were up against a cliff that went straight up into the sky as far as the eye could see. The hills to the west were dark forbidding things with great trees growing straight out from the ledges of massive rocks. To the east there was easier travel, but much of it was swampy. Serug doubted his men could navigate their way through it safely at this time of the year. He was not sure what to do when Torgama came up to him and with his arms folded across his chest spoke in a biting tone, saying that they were men captured by the very stones and that if an enemy approached they would have no escape. Serug was irritated and exhausted, for he had led the men every step of the way and had set the pace faster and faster so as to halt any questions or unbidden remarks. He looked Torgama up and down, and though he knew that Torgama had once done him a great service, all that was forgotten in his sudden rage.

"I need no escape from an enemy! The enemy fears me. I fear no one."

Torgama smiled belligerently. "It did not seem like that on the night of our last battle when the fire fell from the sky. You were quick enough to flee then."

Serug's face turned almost purple with suffused rage. "You will see who flees when we attack next."

"Who will we attack? These rocks?"

Serug looked back to his father who was resting calmly against a rock face. Neb had a long stick in his hand, and he merely pointed to the east in a general sort of fashion. Serug forced himself into calmness as he took a deep breath and faced his other men. "We will head east, and we will conquer the first clan we come across."

Torgama shook his head in wonder. "I suppose you will lead us through the marsh lands?"

Serug smiled as a sudden light came into his eye. "No, you and Eymard will lead the way. You are so very brave, and he is so very smart. I want you two to head out tonight and come back tomorrow and show us the best route to take." Serug smiled at Torgama's blank look as his mouth hung open in an unspoken retort. Serug shrugged and put up his palms in unbidden acceptance of an unpleasant truth. "Unless, of course, you are afraid."

Torgama shook his head and looked slowly over to Neb. Neb never raised his head. He simply twirled his stick between his fingers looking vacantly ahead into the fading light.

Eymard was thoughtful as he gathered his small bag for the journey that was to decide his fate. He knew that Neb was possessed by an evil that he could not control, and he knew that Serug was possessed by his father. Yet he had stayed with the men for reasons he could not explain. He had felt called to live as a man set apart in the midst of these beasts, for he considered Neb and his men as little more than beasts of the field. He had decided that though he could not fathom his own purpose in his loyalty to an evil man, he had accomplished all that could be accomplished in such circumstances. He had survived, and he had helped a few others to think with minds not wholly absorbed in the will of Neb or his son, Serug. It had not been much of an accomplishment for all the horror and trial of this life these past

333

years, but he trusted that something more would come of his life. This mission to go into a swampland was nothing more than an order to commit certain suicide, and both he and Torgama knew this. Neb and Serug no longer had need for them.

Eymard studied his companion in silence as they made their way into the dark wetlands beyond the light of the campfire that Serug had ordered to be built. There had been no farewell. There had been no slight expression of regret or grief. They had been told to go, and none of the men would look at them as they picked up their bags and headed out into the night. Even when Torgama came and stood in front of Neb on his way into the darkness, Neb had refused to even look up. Torgama waited a moment, thinking of all the parting words he could thrust at Neb, but he knew that nothing he did or said would affect Neb now. A chill went down Torgama's spine, and for the first time he really wondered if Neb was human at all. He still stood before his leader and then dropped his words like pebbles in a pond.

"Leah was not surprised when I followed her. She seemed to know I was coming."

Neb did not move at all. He was as still as the rock he leaned against. Torgama continued. "She died quickly. I don't think she felt much at all. Once her son was gone, she had left this earth. I was acting out of mercy, in a way." Neb still said and did nothing. Torgama became a little agitated. "It wasn't about her at all, you know! I just wanted—" Eymard strode up to Torgama and put his hand on his shoulder.

"We have a job to do. Let us go."

Torgama shook his head in sudden fury. He bent down swiftly and grabbed Neb by the shoulder. "I hate you. I have always hated you. Everyone who has ever known you hates you!" Torgama tried to shake Neb, but Eymard pulled him roughly away as Serug came running up to see what was the matter. Torgama began to walk away into the darkness, muttering to himself in loud, querulous tone, "Is that what he really wanted?"

There was no answer to his question. As the two men entered the muck of the dank reed-infested swamp, they instinctively held out their hands and grasped each other to keep their balance. Eymard knew that he would never go back to Neb, and he knew that Torgama was a dead man if he ever returned. Their fates were set in the direction of a dark, wet swamp, and for the moment that was all they knew. They traveled pulling up each foot sucking out from the muddy water for many long hours. They wanted rest. They needed rest. But they had no place to rest. There was no solid surface in which to stop and sit down. Even standing still was not an option, as their feet seemed to sink further and further into the wet ground if they stood still even for a moment. A horror of the place seemed to grow on them, but they could not stop to contemplate their situation clearly. Finally as exhaustion and despair seemed to gain the upper hand in both their spirits, they began to grunt and groan almost in unison, and Eymard broke the silence with a whispered comment.

"If I slip and fall in, do not try to save me. Use the rest of your strength to get out of this place." Torgama was so shocked at these words that he stopped moving for a moment.

"What did you say?"

Eymard kept moving ever so slowly and waved his hand impatiently. "Keep moving or you will be sucked in that much sooner."

Torgama picked up his foot with great effort and realized for the first time in his life that he really was about to die. He began to laugh. It was almost a giggle at first, very much unlike his normal, deep threatening intonation. "Would you care if I lived a few more moments?"

Eymard slapped at a mosquito that had settled on his face. The insects had been tormenting him the whole long night, but as the sun was just beginning to crest over the horizon, he could see better. The sight of those miniature monsters urged him to retaliate by killing as many as he could before he met his own end. He heard what Torgama said, and with a heavy sigh, he pulled his own foot out of the sucking mess and nodded slowly.

"Yes, I would do everything I could to help you survive this nightmare."

Torgama shook his head in wonder as he tried to speed his steps to get a little nearer to this man he had never paid attention to before. "Why?"

Eymard shook his head as if he did not know the full reason himself and the mystery had baffled him for a time, but then he slowed his movements a bit and looked back at Torgama. "I am related to Hul. I found out from Riphath how it was that Hul died, and I have remembered what kind of man Hul was. There are stories in the memory of our people that speak of a God who lives, and I sometimes wonder what kind of greeting we will receive when we leave this world and enter into His unseen land."

Torgama rubbed his muddy hand under his nose and then slapped at one of the mosquitoes on his arm. "I have never heard about a living God. I only know of the gods of the dead. I know that Neb works their will upon others. He is theirs, and they are his. I have never loved them or him." Torgama felt a pain in his head as if his mind were being pressed by the light of the new sun. "But what has that to do with me? I still do not see why you would want me to go on and leave you behind."

Eymard stopped a moment and shook his fist at Torgama in frustration. "Then I would not be like you. I would not be like Neb. I would not live and die like a beast."

Torgama came up beside Eymard and grasped his shoulder. "I have been a beast all my life, and it was all I have ever known or wanted to know. But now, as we sink into this morass of hell, I wish I had known something else."

Eymard looked at Torgama with bright, brim-filled eyes. "Then do not stand still. Let us keep moving. Perhaps there is more to this life than swamps and dark pits."

Torgama shook his head. "I do not believe it is possible—at least not for me. I killed the only good person I have ever really known, and I did it not because she deserved to die or because I hated her, but because I hated *him*." He jerked his hand backward and seemed to contemplate walking back through the labyrinth to Neb's camp. "I do not deserve to know any fate other than that which I have embraced all my life. I am as evil as Neb, though I like to blame my evil on him."

Eymard sniffed and stopped moving a moment. He held up his hand in sudden alert attention. He held his head high and sniffed again. "Do you smell that? It is a fire burning. There is a camp somewhere out here."

Torgama looked askance at Eymard. "You are dreaming in the light of day. There is nothing to burn. We will walk until we sink. There is no hope; you only imagine it so."

Eymard looked all around him and then pointed excitedly. "You see, there is smoke rising into the air. We are not far away. We will touch land again. Our fate is not sealed."

Torgama looked and saw, and he hung his head in silence. "I do not deserve to live again."

Eymard began to walk as swiftly as he could, pulling his feet out of the muck and making great but horrible sucking sounds. "I do not deserve good fortune either, as I have assisted an evil man for many long years, but if the God that lives gives me a chance to try again, then I will not hesitate to try again."

Torgama watched as Eymard began to outdistance him, and he suddenly began to hurry to follow as fast as he was able. "If you are willing, then I am too." And the two were like swimmers at high tide moving in slow motion against a force that would have overwhelmed lesser men, for despite all appearances, they were not alone.

The old men who were drying fish on the shore of the stream near to their home watched in complete amazement as two figures came forth out of the misty murk that was called the forbidden lands. They never went to the south in that area because all knew it was a death trap, while just paces away was sound land that supported the life of numerous animals and a healthy, clear stream flowing next to it. They never wondered at the contradiction of good land and life-giving water so near to a terror that swallowed whole men and animals without mercy. They had lived near this reality for all of their lives, and never in all their born days had they ever seen anyone return from the lands of sinking sand. Most certainly they had never seen anyone walk forth coming from this land and nowhere else. When Eymard and then Torgama alighted in their midst exhausted and covered with the muck of the swamp, they were speechless with a wonder that mixed with horror. Were these men alive, or were they spirits of the dead come back for some unknown reason? The old men sat upon the soft earth and with gapping mouths wondered but did not speak. Finally Eymard panted out his first words, and they were received with comprehension.

"We have come from across the swamp and barely lived to see this new day."

Torgama just kneeled on the solid ground and patted it over and over as if making sure that it was solid indeed. Then he bent down and spread his arms wide as if to embrace the whole of the solid world, speaking in a hoarse whisper. "Oh, God! Oh God! I still live. I am still alive."

At this one of the old men stood up and walked over to the two men. "Surely it was God who saved you, for no man has ever entered the swamp and lived to come through to the other side. You are blessed indeed."

Torgama groaned loudly at this and threw himself upon the ground. "I could have died gladly in battle or while killing Neb, but I could not have born the horror of dying in that swamp. My spirit had already made ready to leave me behind."

The old man smiled at this. "My name is Aaron, and I think you had better come and rest a bit, or your spirit may still decide to depart for another land." He reached out his strong arms, and he grasped both Eymard and Torgama by the hand, leading them toward a simple village and a sense of peace they had never known in all their lives.

Several moons later, Eymard and Torgama were sitting together in quiet peace watching the sun set on another day. They had learned about these simple people and their quiet existence as if coming to know a new kind of human being. For Torgama it was not unlike the first time he had entered the clan of the People of Seth, but then he had been a different man and had seen those people with different eyes. Now he had survived something that had taken him apart, and only these people had the strength and wisdom to put him back together again. He was not healed from his exhaustion yet, for he had become quite sick from utter weariness the first days he had been among them, but with gentle care he had found himself growing strong enough to sit and then stand again. Today he had taken a slow rambling walk with Eymard. Though they had spoken little, they knew the moment of their parting was near.

Eymard spoke first. "I must move on from here. These people have been very good to me, and I have learned much, but I want to find our people—the ones we left behind at the last battle. I want to help them."

Torgama nodded. "I would have liked to go back too, but for a different reason. I would have liked to find Neb and kill him as I always planned to do. But now . . ." He took a long breath. "It doesn't seem so important anymore. Neb will die. Serug will see to that. And those who follow Serug will follow his son, whoever that might be. But I will be free of them all. I will stay here. I will make myself a small hut down by the shore of the stream, and I will watch and wait for any weary travelers who cross through the swamp. I will be there ready to help them."

Eymard smiled as he turned and looked at Torgama. "You may wait a very long time. Aaron has told us that we are the first and only ones to make such a journey."

Torgama set his jaw in stubborn decision. "Still, I will be there. I will watch out for anyone who embarks on such a journey and makes it to the other side."

Eymard stood up and put his hand upon Torgama's shoulder. "I do not expect we will meet again, but know that I am very glad we traveled together. And I am very glad indeed that we both survived."

Torgama nodded with his head down a moment. His shoulders hunched, and then he raised his head to speak. "What you said to me that night when we were utterly lost was unlike anything I had ever heard before in my life. As much as anything that ever happened to enlighten me, you were the one who first broke through my darkness."

Eymard swallowed hard and patted Torgama on the shoulder in a friendly fashion. "I will remember you wherever I go. Keep your vigil, Torgama, for who knows, there may be others." Then he turned and walked away.

CHAPTER 44
THE CONSECRATION

Serug stood with his bloody hands at his hips, heaving deep breaths. He felt exhalant, for he knew the victory was his. His men had surprised the small clan and overwhelmed them quickly. Every man, woman and child was now cowering before him. He had no desire to kill them all. He just wanted some provisions and a few slaves. He had gone to his father before the battle, and Neb had given him explicit directions. All had gone according to plan. Now he looked for his father, but he could not see him. Disappointment cascaded down his face. Certainly Neb knew the outcome. He would undoubtedly be quite gratified at their success. Serug walked along the line of forlorn folks and stared hard at each of them in turn. He knew what he was looking for, and he set his eyes upon every young girl in an appraising manner. Neb had said she would be among these captives, so it was only a matter of searching through the small throng to find his mate. But as he walked along and came to the end of the assembly, he saw no one who even began to spark his interest. There was no beauty, no intelligence to be seen in the whole crowd. Surely his father did not mean for him to align himself with a dog? Serug took a deep breath and then choked, wrinkling his nose in the sudden unpleasant scent that gripped his nose.

"What is that?" Serug demanded.

A shrunken old man quavered over a step nearer and whispered almost imperceptibly. "It is the rendering of fat for preserving and cooking our food."

Serug spat on the ground to rid himself of the smell and taste in his mouth and looked again at the old man out of the corner of his eye while swiftly gesturing with his hand. "Are these all the members of your clan?"

The old man shrugged. "There may be a few wandering here or there that you have not seen, but we are all the same to you. So what does one more or less matter?"

Serug could not contradict this reasoning though he wanted to. He merely spat again and looked around. It was then that he saw a small cluster of young girls off to the side near some bushes. One was brave and devoted enough to be tending to a large fire over which hung an enormous pot. Serug allowed a small gleam of light to enter his eye, and he sauntered over to the timid gathering. He appeared not to notice the girls when he looked into the pot, examining its contents with disgust. He then put his hands near the fire as if to warm them, though he was not in the least bit cold. The young girl stirring the pot was stiff and kept her eyes away from Serug even when he finally turned and looked at her intently.

"Why didn't you come with the others when I called for the village to gather? You are a defeated clan, don't you know?"

The girl, Athaliah, by name, would not turn her eyes toward Serug even after so pointed a question. She merely shrugged and waved her hand vaguely toward the pot and the bushes. "My father told me to keep stirring no matter what, and my mother told me to watch over the younger children."

Serug shook his head in disbelief. "You listen to your parents above me?" He grabbed the arm of the girl and pulled her so that she stood before him. "I am your master now. Your parents have no authority here anymore. You do as I say from now on. Do you understand me?"

Slowly Athaliah's eyes rose from the ground, and she looked Serug in the face but said not one word. There was something in her eye that arrested Serug's attention. He grew impatient. "What is wrong with you, girl? Can you not hear?"

Athaliah nodded her head and spoke in a whispered voice. "I hear and will obey you, but it will be hard to have both parents and a master."

Serug was startled by this. "Why? You just do whatever I say, and everything will be easy."

"My parents will want me to work for them. I have always done so."

"You will work for me from now on." Serug looked around impatiently. "Where are your parents? Show them to me."

Athaliah looked around, and seeing them a little distance off, she pointed in their direction. Serug followed her gaze and took her by the arm, leading her toward them. Athaliah moved reluctantly. "If I do not stir this, it may burn. Then we will lose a whole season's work."

Serug stopped in mid-motion and turned Athaliah's face up to look up at him. "Look at me! Don't you see the blood on me? I have just killed men from your village who opposed me. I have taken over the lives of all of your people, and I am telling you that my will is all that matters. And yet you stand there worrying about a pot of rendering? I will think you are mad soon. Now come with me!" Serug pulled Athaliah's unwilling form across the village until they stood directly in front of a middle-aged couple. They were dirty and disheveled. Their eyes glared at Serug with undisguised hatred. There was no uncertain opposition here. Serug was unnaturally pleased for now he knew that he had conquered someone indeed.

"Is this your daughter?"

The man looked and nodded his head with a quick jerking motion. He let his hand fly up into the air as he let out an oath. "You have conquered to be sure, but you can't take that one. You can take one of the others. There are plenty to choose from if you look around."

Serug looked from the father to the girl, and he swore an oath back. "By the gods, I have never seen so stupid a people! Who are you to give me orders? I choose whom I take and whom I leave. I have decided to take this one, and so I shall."

The woman put up her hands in a warning gesture. "It will be to your peril if you do."

Serug laughed as if the woman's words had tickled him. "My peril? Why, I could put you two to death in a moment if I wanted to." He looked down at his hands, rubbed them across his chest and spat to the side again. "It just so happens that I have had enough blood for the day." He took a step nearer the couple and whispered for their hearing alone. "You are nothing but animals, and I could slaughter you for our next meal." Serug looked back toward the girl and shrugged his shoulders. "Besides, why should she be so important? She is nothing to look at, and she is as stupid as a post. Why do you want to keep her and offer me another child?"

The mother looked at her daughter with down turned lips and a little grunt escaped under her breath. "She knows the gods, and they know her." She looked back at Serug and shrugged. "Besides, she is very obedient." Then she sneered ruefully. "Yes, you will find that out. She is very obedient." The man sniffed sarcastically at this nodding in apparent agreement, and then they turned their eyes away. Serug turned abruptly and took Athaliah by the arm.

"That is exactly what I want. Come girl. I want you to meet someone before we go."

Neb appraised the young woman in front of him with slow moving eyes. He tilted his head to the side and stared while she kept her face downcast and her eyes on the ground, sweeping side to side almost as if she were looking out at the world from a tiny opening. Finally Neb looked over to his son and shrugged.

"Are you sure you want this one?"

Serug pursed his lips in annoyance. It had been Neb who had suggested he attack this small clan in the first place. He was the one who hinted that there was a wife to be found among them. Now that he had brought a girl forth, he felt he had stated his choice and did not want Neb think he did not know his own mind. "Yes, I am certain of it. Her parents vow that she is very obedient."

Neb took a deep breath and looked her over one last time. "I wonder who it is she obeys."

Serug could not understand this. Here he had done everything his father had wanted and had even obtained the prize of the village, and Neb still did not seem satisfied. "She will obey me, and we will have many sons."

There was a rustling sound in the background, and several men came running up toward Serug. "We have been followed. There are men coming upon us. Scouts say that there are enough men to overwhelm us. We must flee." The lead runner was out of breath from his exertions, and he barely panted out his words before another runner came up calling for them to flee.

"The enemy is upon us. We must gather what we can and leave immediately."

Neb stood and walked over to his son and gripped his shoulder. "I thought you won your last battle."

Serug looked at his father with a deep red color flushing through his features. "I did. It is not they who come but another clan from the hills. Others have heard of us and want revenge or to take prizes from us." Serug sighed deeply. "I will gather my men, and we will put them to flight."

"Are you sure that is wise?"

The runners came a little closer, crowding around. "Beg your forgiveness, Serug, for being so bold, but you have not seen this great throng. They are too many. We would do well to flee."

Serug looked from his men to his father and began to shrug his shoulders as if to accept the inevitable decision, but then Athaliah took a step nearer. She leaned over and spoke quietly into Serug's ear. Serug took a step back and looked at the slight, frail young girl again with wide open and appraising eyes. "Yes, I meant what I said. You will be my wife and the mother of my sons." The young girl nodded and looked over to the horizon, which was dull in the afternoon light and overcast by a blanket of grey clouds.

"Then you do not need to run away. The land has been dry of late, and we are on the crest of a hill. Set fire to the bushes and trees to the north, and in a little time no one will be able to pass through to bother you. When the wind rises, it will carry the fire far. When the rain comes to put it out, there will be no enemy left."

Serug glanced over toward his father, and Neb's eyes gleamed in sudden appreciation as the barest suggestion of a smile played upon his lips. Serug nodded once and gave the order, and the men ran away to fulfill the command. And so it was to be. The enemy fled from the flames, and Serug took Athaliah for his wife. Neb accepted Athaliah as his daughter, and as he had never known a daughter, the sensation was new to him. In this mysterious child, however, he found a kindred spirit. It was true what her parents had said. She knew the gods, and the gods knew her. But she was not like the sorceress of old or even like his franticly driven mother. She was a woman who worked in silence and mystery. No one knew her thoughts, and though she appeared to be completely subservient, her obedience could have a very high price. If someone attempted to force her to do something she saw no reason for, she would get a certain look in her eye, and before long the petitioner knew to take back the request before it was too late. She had an uncanny ability to know everyone's weakness and fears, and though she spoke softly, those quiet words she murmured under her breath were like spells that fell like molten rocks on the listener for she knew how to threaten without ever appearing to do so.

Once there was a woman named Zipporah who liked to advise the other women as to how best to decorate their clothing. Decorating clothing was now becoming something of a competitive pastime, and those who could display the most ornamented clothing and blankets were considered superior to the rest. Zipporah had a truly magnificent touch when it came to decorating everything she owned. She sewed designs into her and her husband's clothes, and she etched designs into her clay pots and carved pictures on her husband's tools. She was skilled with painting designs too, and there were few who were not impressed with her skill and ability.

Even though Serug took her as his wife, Athaliah and some others who joined the clan with her were seen as nothing more than slaves. She made no protest but rather did her work silently and made no attempts to correct anyone until the day that Zipporah came and saw how Athaliah was working Serug's clothes. Athaliah liked to make her own designs, but hers were unlike anything the clan of Serug had ever seen before. She made circles that wove into themselves and four and five sided figures that fit together in colorful repetitious patterns and caused the eyes to stare as if in a trance. When Zipporah saw the shapes and patterns, she felt a momentary jealousy. However, she could not refrain from correcting Athaliah, telling her that no one would like such eye-blazing decorations. Athaliah stared at the woman expert and said nothing but looked back down to her work and continued without change. Thus every time Zipporah saw Athaliah, she commented on her overwhelming designs. Then one night Zipporah did not sleep peacefully as usual. She had had strange dreams the whole night through, and when she awoke she discovered that she had a strange rash on her skin. It seemed as if each mark was a strange shape not unlike the shapes of Athaliah's designs. For days Zipporah stayed in bed and grew sicker. Even in her weakened state, however, Zipporah dared to complain against Athaliah. Her wounded skin grew worse and worse until she eventually died. No one else from the clan became sick with skin eruptions, but no one else expected to either for there was too certain a look of quiet satisfaction on Athaliah's face every time Zipporah's fate was mentioned. No one ever said what they thought about the contest between the two, but everyone knew how it ended. That was enough for them.

Serug was pleased with Athaliah for she did his every bidding, but he, too, learned that there were times when she wanted to be left alone, and he learned to respect those times for her potent anger was more than he wanted to bear. He could not say he loved her or that he even respected her, but he knew that she held some sway over Neb and the rest of the clan. She understood people even better than he did, and she was more skillful in her manipulation of others. But when she presented him with the news that she was carrying his child, Serug did feel something. He was proud beyond words and went to tell Neb that he would have a grandson. Neb looked his second son over with a bitter grin. "How do you know it will be a boy? Or more to the point, that it will be the boy that you want?"

Serug looked positively bewildered. "I know the mother."

At this Neb let out a loud and terrifying laugh. "Yes, yes, that is true. You do know the mother. And that does make a difference. May the gods save you!"

Serug avoided his father for a time after this, and he did everything that he could to see to the comfort of his wife. Athaliah found that she could no longer do common labor, and it was accepted without comment. It was determined too that she could no longer be expected to make the meals, and other women were brought in to see to all the menial tasks of their daily care.

When the time for the birth came, Athaliah called for only two old women whom she had made friends with, and they alone cared for Athaliah in the time of her delivery. Every time Serug came to see what was happening—and whether he had had a healthy son—he was told he could not cross the threshold. It took several days, and then even Neb had become impatient for news. He went to see Athaliah, but as he approached, the three women, cleaned and well-dressed, stepped from Serug's dwelling. Athaliah held a small bundle, and she strode purposefully to the center of the village and stood directly in front of the communal fire pit. There was no fire but only some smoldering embers. She spoke quickly to one of the women, and the old crone moved off and called to some other women and children. Soon there was a great haste and bustling of activity. Serug noticed the sudden change in the village and came out of his father's dwelling to stand before his wife. He saw the bundle and all the preparations being made, so he stretched out his arms.

Athaliah stood tall and spoke with a slow, deliberate speech. "You shall not touch this child until he has been consecrated to the gods."

Serug looked slightly bewildered. He had heard of such ceremonies before, but he had never known of an instance where the father was not allowed to look upon his own child before the whole clan. "I will see my child first!" Serug stepped up toward Athaliah, but there was no glad smile upon his face now.

Athaliah slowly shook her head and stared at Serug very intently. "If you come one step nearer, you will die before the sun sets!" Serug stopped in mid-motion. He looked at his wife, and then his eyes roamed the village to see who was witnessing this conflict. Every eye was upon the two of them. Serug let his other foot slide into position under him and he put his hands on his hips in a petulant manner not unlike the stance he had taken with his father many long years ago when he had been a child. "Why? Is it wrong for the father to look upon his own child? Unless there is some doubt about the child?" He allowed his speech to echo across the village to Athaliah where she stood with her well-wrapped bundle.

"There is no doubt as to who this child belong to. I will make very sure of that."

The young men and girls who had been put into action by the urgings of the other women were now successfully building an enormous fire. The mere embers had been fanned into flame, and so much dry wood was added that the fire was building into an inferno. The young girls became timid at the sight and backed away while the boys continued to feed the flames for a little while longer. Everyone was silent as this procedure was allowed to continue. Then finally one of the warriors shouted out that it was enough. They did not need to set the sky one fire. But Athaliah lifted her hand in the air and called out in a strange voice, and there was a rumbling sound from somewhere in the distance. There were many who began to look sideways at one other and there was much repeated swallowing. Athaliah gestured for more wood, and several of the warriors began to throw on the largest pieces of wood that they could find. Finally the fire was so high and bright that it lit up the evening as if the sun had never set. Neb stepped forward and walked over to Athaliah and put his hand upon her shoulder. Serug looked on with consternation, but he found that he could not move a step. Neb put up his hand and spoke but a single word. "Enough."

Athaliah stepped several paces away from Neb and began to walk around the flames first in one direction then in another. Neb watched her in silence. Serug's mouth hung open, but he said nothing. The whole clan moved in a circle around the fire, but there were no whispered commentaries or questions. It was all done in silence for a long time. Then finally Athaliah took her little bundle and very carefully unwrapped the child, letting the ornamented blanket drop to the ground. She took a hold of the infant and held him high for all to see and called out in a dry, deep voice, "He belongs to the gods, and he will bring many to serve."

Serug quickly took several steps nearer, reaching out for his son, but his father was closer and reached over and took the babe in his own arms. Though the words were never said, Serug knew that his father was taking his son for his own. Serug's arms fell to his sides. He was frozen in thought and stock still in his loss. What could he do against such a man and such a woman committed to a cause?

Later that night there was a feast to honor the consecration of the new child, and though Serug knew more than he wanted to, he now wondered in the silence of his own mind if he would ever have another child. He had not realized until this night how much he had been looking forward to having a son of his own to raise, but now that those hopes had been crushed by the usurpation of his own father, he found that he was hoping that Athaliah would be quick to have another child. But that was not to be. In due time, the child was given tasks to prove his strength and ability. It was Serug who decided that his son should be named Neb to honor his father, for it was only too obvious whom the child resembled.

Neb the younger lived with his mother up until the time of weaning, and then he moved into the dwelling of his grandfather. Serug watched the child grow with mixed pride, for though he knew that the child neither looked nor acted like him, he could not find fault with the babe or the boy. Whenever he attempted to challenge his son as his father had challenged him, little Neb would astonish him with his quick wit and curious agility. The boy was thin to the extreme though Serug went out of his way to make sure that he ate well. But the boy favored only a few foods and would have nothing to do with any others even if he had to go for a long time without eating. Serug marveled at the boy's discipline and tenacity at so young an age. Then came the day when Neb's grandfather felt a shadow cross over him, and he knew that his time upon the earth was dwindling. He spoke to Serug one afternoon and told him that he wanted to make plans for the future. Serug was too pliant to his father's will to make any objections or even suggestions. He merely asked how he wanted to make his will known. The boy was now nearly nine summers old, and Neb said that he wanted a feast similar to the one they had had when the boy was born. He had a gift to bestow on his grandson, and he wanted to state his last wishes before he departed for the spirit world.

So Serug made all the preparations, and a hog was duly caught and roasted, the meal preparations were piled high on platters in the center of the village and the fire was fed to the point of becoming a tower of massive flames. Serug walked with his young son around the village, saying very little but nodding to those who showed their competent service. The child bowed his head slightly as he came to favored members of the clan as if to show them some small token of his appreciation and acknowledgement. Athaliah had secured for herself a quiet dwelling near the inner edge of the village, and she did nothing but what pleased her to do. She worked at making figures and decorating them, often with paints she brewed from plants of the meadows and berries from the woods. Occasionally she took the husks of nuts and boiled those down to make a very dark stain, which she would use very sparingly. Her figures had become more recognizable over the years, and she seemed to have a theme she was building on as if she were making a portrait of a person she had never met but had only heard about. She would change this or that aspect, but always the main features would remain so that you knew you were looking at Athaliah's god, for her god it most certainly it was though she would not say so in words. It was only by her looks and gestures of respect and the reverent care she took of her images that told a person what the figure meant to her. But dread born of experience taught every member of the clan to say nothing unkind about her figures and to complement them as strong or worthy of some unnamed greatness.

When the time for Neb's great feat came, Athaliah became even more secretive than normal though she had several of the clan's warrior's working for her. There was a great deal of activity in the woodlands behind the last dwelling in the midst of a ring of enormously old trees. Anyone who was curious and dared to ask ill-advised questions was told that they would know all the night of the feast and that those who came looking about might find their eyes would not work so well in the morning. So none came to see, and everything was done in secret.

Serug walked his son around the village, and they both nodded and spoke little. When the night's blanket was well wrapped around them, Neb the elder came forth and directed everyone to follow him. They left the comfort of the blazing fire and stepped into the dark woods, but soon they saw a circle inside a circle of fired torches stuck into the ground. There in the midst of the circles of flames was an enormous rock that had been dug out from the earth and rolled into position. There were several audible gasps as thoughts flickered from mind to mind and parted lips bit off astonished questions. But most surprising of all was the figure that was standing on the top of the massive rock. There was a figure of a creature with a massive bullhead with horns coming out of its head and a body of a man but with the feet of a bird. Every member of the clan stood still, amazed at the apparition in front of him. Finally Athaliah spoke in her curious voice, which was so deep and controlled. "Here is the god you serve. Bow down and worship."

Every man woman and child knelt on the leaf-strewn ground and bowed his or her head except for the two Nebs. Serug had his head hanging down in silent, cold thought, wondering how long this ceremony would take before they could get to the feasting. His eyes now strayed over to his father and his son, and he saw that they were standing in front of the figure not bowed down at all but merely looking at it with cold understanding. Even Athaliah was bowed down, and as she began to stir to a standing position, she looked and saw that neither her son nor her husband's father had bowed down, and a curious furrow grew between her eyes. The elder Neb led his grandson back to the village, and there everyone stood around the food ready to eat. Neb held up his hand for attention.

He looked over to a particular attendant, and the man slipped forward toward the firelight holding something massive and heavy in his arms. Neb, though he grown weaker with age, was still strong enough to grasp his bear skin in both his arms and carry it over to his grandson. He put the enormous fur about the boy's shoulders and then took a step back to survey the effect. The boy was dwarfed in the great fur, but he grasped the edges with his two small arms and pulled it around him as if in a tight embrace. The night air was warm and the fire hot, but the child acted as if he could not get enough of the great blanket's warmth. His fingers slid up and down over the soft fur in a caress that they would grow very accustomed to over the long years ahead.

Neb looked at his grandson and then surveyed the clansmen before him, and he spoke loud and clear for all to hear. "Listen to me my people. I am Neb, your leader of long years and the father of Serug, your present leader, and the grandfather of Neb, son of Serug, your future leader. I declare that all gifts bestowed on me shall be given to my grandson and that when it is his time to serve, you will follow him faithfully. I have seen a new land for you in a vision, and you will depart from these vast woodlands to live on the edge of a mighty river. Your greatness will not be measured. Your hands reach out, and you will take for yourselves the power to rule over all others. I bestow the mighty spirit of the bear onto my grandson. You will worship the gods, especially the god of horns, which Athaliah has made known to you. If you obey, you shall prosper. If you do not, a curse will be upon you and future generations down to—" Suddenly there was a sound that broke through the cavernous tones of Neb, and there was a cracking sound and a great tree limb broke free and began its weighty decent from the upper regions of the sky and fell through lower boughs crashing and tumbling as it came. It fell like a message from the black sky and landed in front of them all. It was so big that in its decent several people had to scamper quickly out of the way lest they be crushed by the fall. Neb stood silenced and Serug merely stared in surprise for nothing of this nature had ever happened to them before. Always it seemed that every act of nature was to assist them. Though he had to admit the flying locusts of old had amazed and dismayed him also, but he did not think of them now. He just stood with his mouth open unable to decide what to do next. But his son had no such qualms or confusion. He strode up to the massive limb and began to tug at it while everyone watched and wondered. Then suddenly as the smaller Neb got the wood to the fire, everyone at once understood, and they all reached out and began to pull at it forcing it onto the fire. The ancient limb caught quickly and made the fire that much greater. Neb smiled in satisfaction. He had forgotten what it was he was going to say, but it did not matter now. His point had been carried, and the incident had only made his point that much clearer.

In a gesture not unlike the one he had used to the People of Seth on the night of their big feast, he motioned for his people to commence the meal. There were no more ceremonies or words, for everything worth saying had been said. The future was set. Neb could leave the earth, and his spirit would live on in his grandson so that he would never really die.

Serug watched everyone begin to feast for a few moments and knew that his father had undoubtedly prophesied correctly and he would lead his people to a Great River, but he also wondered how long he would rule before his son felt the need to take over. He knew the whispered stories of how his own grandfather had been relieved of his rule, and as he stood staring into the flames of the great fire, he pondered just how much like his grandfather his son would be.

CHAPTER 45
THE FINAL JOURNEY

Neb labored to breathe. He did not want to die like this. He knew that he could live on getting worse and worse for many more miserable days, and he looked wildly about for anything that might end his torment. He wished that Torgama had not buried himself in the dank marsh but had instead lived for this time when he could finally be of real service. He tried to call out, but no one could hear his slight whispered voice. It was late at night, and Serug was undoubtedly fast asleep in his own dwelling. Athaliah lived in another dwelling even further away near her god. Neb had almost laughed when she told him of her desire to keep her god company, but he had seen the flash in her eyes and had quickly suppressed all inclination toward even a slight smile. He had ordered several men to build her the finest dwelling in the village, and he told her to choose several maidens to build their own dwellings close to hers so that they might assist her in any need. She had quickly seen the advantage of this and had done what was proposed. Now she lived in order to meet the needs of her god and of no one else. Serug did not argue or oppose this action, for he knew it would be useless to do so and might incur the ire of the god whom he did not really understand. Though he saw Athaliah's devotion, he himself could see nothing special about the clay and wooden figure. He merely shrugged at his wife's decision and allowed her to do as she pleased. But now that he was feeling so poorly, Neb wished that she or someone might be closer to him and care for him in his final days. He had attendants of course, but they did not watch over him like a sick child, which was very much how he felt of late. He wanted a mother's care, and there was no one to give him that kind of devotion. He looked wildly around for his grandson knowing that he would see to his needs, but perceiving neither the sight of his slumbering form or his slight soft breathing, Neb remembered that the youth had gone off on a long hunt several days ago. He had ordered the young man to kill the largest animal he could and to bring home its skin. The young Neb had dutifully sharpened his blade and set off. He had not been seen since.

Young Neb was exhausted and sweating from his prolonged exertions. He had been on this hunt longer than any other hunt in his short but full life. Last night he had heard the yowling of a cat on the prowl, and by the resonance of her voice, he knew that she was in the area and was very great. When he finally tracked her down, her paw prints sent a shiver down his spine. He wanted so much to find her and return home with this prize that he forced himself to move on well past his natural endurance. But she was reluctant to show herself. Finally after falling down on his knees in the midst of layers of decaying leaves, he lay down and slipped into a deep slumber. He awoke in the dead of night with the voice of the cat in his ears. He raised himself just enough to place his blade and his spear into a good position for the expected fight. He did not have long to wait. As she circled nearer and nearer, he watched until she came just close enough to get proper aim. When she was near enough, he threw his spear with all his might into her side and then pounced upon her wounded form and stabbed her repeatedly in the neck. Even wounded she was a fierce and formidable opponent. She whirled around and scratched and bit, but Neb was almost as quick as a cat, and though he was wounded in the fierce encounter, nothing injured him unto death. He knew he would have scars to remember this adventure for the rest of his life, but when the cat finally fell over on her side, he knew he had conquered. He watched the light from her angry, tormented eyes slowly fade away, and for the first time in his young life, Neb fell on his face and cried.

Neb the elder tried to sit up, but the effort was painful. His chest burned with the pain of trying to breathe. Finally in desperation he began to yell as loud as he could, but all that came out of him was a sort of choking, croaking sound. Neb leaned back and tried to calm himself. He knew that panic would only make the situation worse. He slowed down his beating heart and took long breaths to settle his confused brain. As he lay there in the dark, images of his past life came before him as if he could see himself as a young man once again. He watched his own mother as she carefully covered him with blankets on a cold night and kissed his forehead. He saw her determined, proud stare as she told him she wanted to rule when he went away for a short time and the look of injured fury that took her when she saw that Neb no longer needed her. Then he saw her face as she lay on her pallet the night she died. He heard her mumbled conversation and then he saw her throw the poisoned skin away, and with eyes large and surprised, Neb realized for the first time that he had not killed his mother. But then he knew he had, though perhaps not directly. She grabbed her chest in her fall and stared ahead until all the light of understanding faded unto a blank glaze. Neb blinked his eyes to shut out the vision, and it worked for a few moments. But then as he tried to shift his weight, his action was arrested for he could see his father clear as day before him as he stood when he first taught him how to throw a spear. But then he saw his brothers receiving the same guided care from his father, and he felt the burning resentment knowing full well that he should be first in all things including in all hearts, but he was not. He could see his father's contemptuous expression when he cornered him in the weaver's dwelling in the village of the People of Seth. He could feel the knife go in and the blood seep over his hands as he pulled his blade away. He looked and saw to his utter amazement a look of grief that he had not seen before, and he closed his eyes to shut the image out though it was before him still.

    Neb jerked himself up higher so as to breathe better, and now he heard the mocking contemptuous voice of Uzal as he cursed him. Neb almost choked as he laughed bitterly at this image. "You can do me no harm now, you forsaken ghost! I have accomplished my ends. I have a son's son who is exactly like me, and I will live on into eternity."

But the boast was cut short by the sudden image of Uzal's face and form perfect and content with Leah at his side. They were together in a gentle embrace, with Leah's head resting on her father's shoulder. For a moment Neb stared, and without his knowledge or consent, his hand reached out to touch her face once again. She was of another world, however, and touch her he could not. She seemed to see his motion though, and even as her father nodded in acceptance, she raised her head and spoke a single word. "Repent." She gestured with her hand for him to come to her, and though Neb saw, he could not understand. Repent? Repent what? He was Neb the Great, and he was going to live forever. He saw his own hand reaching out to her, and he quickly drew it back. The vision melted into the black night air. He lay back and heaved a deep sigh. He had lived as he wished, and soon he would die as he wished.

Serug came in as the sun was cresting over the horizon though it was still hidden by the vast trees. He saw his father with beaded sweat on his forehead, panting for each labored breath. He crouched down beside him and reached out for his father's hands. They were thin and very cold. Serug could see his father's agony, so he whispered in his ear.

"What can I do for you, Father?"

Neb looked up and rested his eyes on his son. For a moment he thought he saw Madai, but he realized Madai had been gone from him for a very long time. He croaked out his words. "Get me the black vial from my shelf." He reached up as well as he could to point to the only shelf in the dismal dwelling. There upon it rested a water skin and braided basket with a few dried viands. But to one side, alone by itself, was a small black vial. Serug stood, and in the dim light he reached out for the thing his father wanted. He pulled out the wooden stopper and gave a faint sniff and quickly coughed and sneezed in furious procession. Suddenly he knew what the vial contained. He looked down upon his father's contorted face, and he shook his head. No, he would not ease his passage. His father had let others suffer, and it was now his turn to know what helplessness felt like. Serug put the vial back and knelt down by his father and took hold of his two hands. "I cannot see any vial father." Neb tried to squeeze his son's hands, but the effort was too much. Serug grew queasy at the sight of his father's struggle, so he moved back a bit and grabbed at the water skin. "But I can get you some fresh water. I will be right back."

Neb wanted very much to keep his son with him, for the panic of not being able to breathe was very hard to keep at bay, but his son would not see his feeble gesture or the unaccustomed look of pleading in his father's eyes. Serug was glad to get out of the dwelling of the dead. He knew it was only a matter of a few moments more. He felt frozen with fear, and he did not know what to do. He would not call for help nor would he get the water. He simply walked away from his father's dwelling as fast as he could.

But Neb the younger had made it back to the village early that morning with the skin of the great cat upon his shoulders. Though he rarely showed the least sign of excitement, he could not help rushing forward to his grandfather's dwelling to show him his prize. He entered the room and heard the labored breathing and knew at once that the end of life as he had always known it was at hand. He crouched down beside his grandfather's form and spoke gently.

"Grandfather, it is I, Neb. I have brought you the greatest cat skin ever seen by man."

Suddenly, Neb the Great felt a calmness come over him. Here was his posterity. Here was his hope. Here, indeed, was his future. He tried to sit up, and though he could only manage a slight motion, the boy knew what was wanted. He eased his grandfather into a sitting position, and the elder Neb took an easier breath. He wondered at himself. Was he getting better? Was the very presence of this youth a curative? He looked over at the boy, but his face was hidden by shadows. "Come closer to me, Boy, and let me feel the skin." The youth pulled the still damp skin off his shoulders and placed it near his grandfather's shaking hands. The old man caressed the fur softly, stroking it across toward him.

The old man gestured for his grandson to move closer so he could whisper in his ear. "Bury me in this."

Suddenly a frown crossed over the boy's face. Bury an old dead body in this? Something he had risked his life to earn? He wrinkled his brow in distaste. He looked down at the sweating, shriveled old man and realized that there was no strength or merit left. He pursed his lips together. Then he thought of the right question to ask so as to settle this question completely.

"How did you bury your father, grandfather?" He paused as he looked around the room. He knew very well how his great-grandfather had died, for his own father had told him. "I will do just as you did."

Neb's eyes grew wide in sudden horror. He must die quickly. No more suffering. He must be buried with great honor so that everyone would know his greatness in the next world. He reached out to his second self, and he grabbed the boy's tunic. "You must save me!"

The youth reached down and took his grandfather's old claws off of him, prying each finger loose at a time and speaking in that clear, precise manner of his that was a full imitation of his dying forerunner. "Save you? Save you from what? From yourself? It is too late for that, I think."

The helpless old man raised his head and spoke a single gurgled word. "Vial." Neb looked up to where the old man's eyes searched, and he stood and took the small black vial down from the shelf. He looked it over curiously and then crouched down near the dying man.

"You don't want to die like a poisoned dog or an unwanted baby, do you?" He shook his head in disbelief and apparent grief. "No, that is not right. You should die like your father did or like a man in battle at least." Slowly he reached inside his tunic and withdrew his blade. He flashed it before the old man's terrified eyes. Neb had never been at anyone's mercy before, and now he felt the horrid sensation of complete powerlessness in the hands of one who loves no one. Surely he had done his work too well. He squirmed to move away from the blade, and he grunted in a last feeble attempt at fury but could hardly manage it. But then he thought of Madai and his sister Eva, and he knew that despite all his ways, they would have treated him differently in the end. They would have been merciful. But mercy was not something he had valued up until this moment. He looked into his grandson's eyes, and a shaft of sudden light entered the room. He could see for a brief moment his own eyes reflected in those of his grandson, and he knew he was lost, though he need not have been.

With the last of his strength, he grasped his grandson's hands in his and whispered as he plunged the knife deep into his heart, "So we will be together forever, cursed throughout eternity!"

Neb felt the blood seep over his fingers, and he realized a strange sickness. He was not actually intending to kill the old man. He was his own grandfather after all, but somehow it seemed to make some kind of strange sense. He laid his head down, and for the second and last time in his life, he wept.

CHAPTER 46
HAGIA

Serug trailed after his son, watching him move swiftly and confidently through the tall grasses. Apparently Neb knew exactly where he was going. He was heading directly east. They had reached the edge of the woodlands several days ago. Now they were pushing their way through a forest of tall grasses, and because it was such an open land, Serug felt exposed. He wanted to move back closer to the edge of the woodlands, but Neb saw no reason for this. The sky was becoming overcast, and a misty rain was falling in the distance. It appeared to him that they were moving toward the center of a cloud. Serug continued to plod along silently for some time, his heart heavy and his mind almost numb with suppressed irritation, but suddenly he stopped. Athaliah, who has been moving behind his left elbow, ran into him and nearly tripped. She gave a high-pitched "Chaaa" sound, which meant nothing at all except that she was irritated. Serug looked at her, and his brows wrinkled in reflection of his own deep thoughts. Why? Why were they making this trip? Why was his son leading the way? Why did he allow everyone to direct his life? Was he not the leader of this clan? Had he given over control of the clan to his son? No, No, No! He had done no such thing, and yet it seemed to have been assumed that Neb had some special right to set their direction after his grandfather had died. Serug waved his wife away and told her to step back from him. He had not spoken so sharply to her since the first day he had met her. She had taught him to respect her, but at this moment he cared for no one's respect. He felt a reckless anger surging through his veins. He would not allow his son to usurp his role as leader. He would not go to an open land where they knew nothing of the people or the creatures that occupied it. The vision of a great lake was just one more of his father's devious maneuvers to get others to do his will. Why his father had wanted them to move to the east was beyond his imagination at the moment, but what was definitely clear was the fact that he would no longer follow the will of his son. He had been forced to obey the manipulations of the elder Neb, but he would not allow history to repeat itself. Neb was dead. He was dead and buried deep in the ground. Serug had made a big ceremony of the final burial so that all could see the cold, still body being swallowed by the cold, still earth. There could be no doubt in anyone's mind that Neb the Great was dead and gone. He would never rule the living again. Still he had to give some recognition to the passing of so great a man, so he had allowed Athaliah to pronounce that Neb had become one with her gods. This seemed to please everyone very much. But all of that was not enough for his son. Now, Neb was marching along at a quick pace, trying to grasp—no he had simply assumed—leadership as if there were no question who should rule now. Serug's face was red with rage. He would not move from this spot until he had a clear understanding with his son as to who ruled the clan. He stomped over toward the head of the line of waiting men. He saw his son standing impatiently and looking back irritably for the cause of their delay.

Serug stalked up to his son and stood as close to him as he could get without actually standing on his toes. His tone was clear and commanding. "I will not settle in the open lands. I will lead my people into the low hills." He pointed northward. "There are caves and shelters, trees and plenty of animals. We do not know what we will find out here other than snakes, tall grass and strong winds."

Neb looked at his father a moment. He was not quite full grown, but he would probably never be quite as tall as his father. He was strikingly more lithe and agile, but his lack of height and weight was a definite disadvantage when the two stood side-by-side. He titled his head to the side, which was a peculiar trait he had when considering a new idea. His eyes were a light shade of green that had surprised everyone at his birth, and since he had become a man, his eyes seemed to have even taken on a cat-like shine. Those gleaming orbs searched his father's face for several moments as if discerning the seriousness of his father's attitude.

His lips parted a slight bit, and his tongue circled around as if he could taste his decision. Suddenly his eyebrows went up, and he put his hand up as if ordering everyone to stop though they had all been standing around for some moments in anticipation of the climax of this contest of wills.

"We will head toward the hills in the north. It is my father's wish, therefore it is my wish."

Serug grunted. He was pleased, but yet somehow he still felt that things were not quite right. He spoke to his son in a quieter tone, putting his hand on his arm to lead him off to the side. "You see, I am the clan leader, and it is best that all commands come from me so that the people will not get confused. I know your grandfather led you to expect to be leader in his lifetime, but his earthly existence was cut short, and I am not in need of someone to replace me just yet." He tried to laugh, but it sounded forced. He put up his two arms to demonstrate his point that much clearer. "You see? The strength has not yet left my arms. I have wit and will enough to lead for many long years." He attempted to pat his son on the shoulder. "Do not worry. I will not burden you with the concerns of leadership until I think you are ready, and that may not be for quite a while yet." Serug stared at his son, willing him to understand and not to oppose him. Neb simply stared back and said nothing for a long time. He just turned and walked back toward the head of the line and made a forward motion with his hand. The entire clan looked between the two men and stayed in place for a moment. Neb was moving forward, and Serug was not sure what to do so he simply started to walk toward the front of the line also. He called out. "Come, we head to the hills." When he came alongside his son, he looked at him from out of the corner of his eye. Neb did not turn or look his way, but after they had marched some distance he spoke a few soft words. "We will see."

Serug had been right—they found shelters aplenty among the rocky cliffs and hills in the north. But the weather was different there. It was cooler now, and in the winter they even had snow a few times. As they had never experienced such a thing before, it had bewildered everyone, but while Serug was pleased with the novelty, Neb was distinctly displeased. That was only one of the many differences between the father and son. Neb was not content to choose a wife from among the women of the clan, and he did not want to accept a woman chosen by his father, so one day he asked to go on a long hunting expedition where he might hunt for more than meat. His father had grown tired of his son's eccentric attitudes, so he was actually relieved when Neb told him of his plans. Enough time had passed, and Serug was secure enough now in his role that he felt more able to tease Neb about his manhood.

"Go on son. Take some men, and have a good hunt. I will be here waiting for you. If you find yourself a wife in addition to meat, all the better. I took your mother from a clan that I raided, and I have never been sorry." He winked at his son at their shared joke. "Of course she may not feel the same, but then women are never happy." He patted his son on the back as the young man went on his way. "Come back with more men than you take with you, and I will be impressed!"

Neb said not one word though his ears did turn a bright shade of red. He walked soberly up the incline toward a rocky ledge, and a plan almost complete came to him in startling detail. He looked up past the incline into the vast blue sky, and he could almost see his grandfather's face looking down on him. He was sure the spirit of his grandfather understood, and he knew he would be pleased.

Neb had taken ten men with him. His father had been surprised at first by the required number of companions, but then Serug remembered his first experience with the bear and how disastrously it had turned out. He supposed that Neb had a little better sense than he had had at that age. Serug was pleased that he was going well prepared. Actually, even though Neb well knew the story of the ill-fated bear hunt, he had no qualms about his ability to hunt a bear or any other creature of the wild. He did know, however, that it would take a few well-armed, ruthless and battle-tried men to take over a defenseless clan. Ten was a very small number of warriors to attempt such a feat, but he knew the men of his clan, and he knew what he was promising them so he was not overly concerned about their ability or their desire to accomplish this task.

He found a small cave-dwelling clan high in the western hills, and he circled around them for a day until he could spy out the perfect attacking vantage. His men were skilled in this sort of thing, and his Grandfather had told him stories in graphic detail. He looked forward to his first kill. It was not long in coming. One of his men inadvertently alerted the clan to their presence, so the battle was commenced earlier than he expected. The outcome was also accomplished quickly. Neb was very pleased when it was over. He looked his slaves over and decided what his next move would be.

For weeks Neb moved from one small clan or single family to another. He killed at random and took what slaves he wished. More often than not, he simply told the people that he was son of Serug and that they controlled the land from the grass to the mountains. Everyone who heard reports of him feared him, and he was quite pleased.

Finally after they had taken their rest for several days up in a forested area at the foot of a great mountain, Neb realized it was time for him to claim a wife. He had heard stories from various sources that there was an ancient community far to the west and that they had woman who men only dreamed of for wives. They were said to be the most beautiful women in the world and were thought to be more intelligent than average. Neb wanted to claim one of these special women for his own, but he knew he would not be able to fight a large, well-protected community for her. He wondered if he could barter for one. So he traveled further west than he had ever done before, leaving most of his men to make their way back to Serug's small village with all of the slaves. Just he and two men traveled to a far region, and there they met clans like none other they had ever met before. The verdant land was near an enormous river, and everywhere there were farms and villages. It was very green and fruitful, but Neb was not interested in their agriculture.

He went to the center of the greatest village and found a market place unlike anything he had ever heard of before. He and his men trailed around looking idly at various foreign foodstuffs and weapons. His eyes were hooded, and he kept his thoughts to himself even while his men looked with wide eyes and spoke in whispered tones. Neb felt a burning sensation in his stomach as he considered how primitive his own people were compared to these people, but then as he watched the various buyers and sellers, he realized that none were really any better than he. He thought to himself, *"How many of them can subdue a clan as quickly as I can? How many of them can rule as I can? These people are simply bees in a hive, workers and laborers and nothing more."* He walked continuously around the village until he came to a lane he had not seen before. It led forward to the center of the village, and he could see there was a great crowd gathered around. He walked along, and as the crowd grew thicker, he had to push and elbow his way to go onward. Finally he saw what it was that everyone was looking at. There was a tall structure built of stone with steps leading steeply up the side. It was taller than the greatest tree he had ever seen, and he wondered why he hadn't noticed it before. Now as he looked upon it, he marveled for it was beautifully wrought. There were stone carvings of men and beasts guarding the walls and the doorways. There were paintings etched into the walls with illuminated figures telling amazing stories for those who had time to stay and decipher them. But what caught Neb's eye the most was a procession of young girls walking with baskets of food from the market into the structure. They were the most beautiful women that Neb had ever seen. Their clothes were various colors and looked so terribly soft that he wanted to reach out and touch just a piece of one of the garments. The girls were covered from shoulders to ankles, but the material swayed and billowed with their every movement. They eyes were outlined by some magic color, which made them larger than natural and so entreating that even as they all looked downward, they appeared both glorious and modest all that the same remarkable moment. Neb stood transfixed when the last girl in line accidentally stepped on the garment of the girl in front of her, and she tripped. She fell forward with her tray, and the precious burden slid from her grasp. Neb's mouth opened to order someone to assist her, but another man, large and burly, saw the mishap and rushed over to the girl as the food splattered to the ground. He struck the beautiful child across the cheek, and she cried out, putting her hand over her face for protection. Neb leapt forward and put out his own hand and blocked the man from striking her again. The guard looked at Neb in amazement for it was forbidden to interfere with the maidens dedicated to the temple gods. Neb knew nothing of their traditions nor would he have cared if he had known.

"You will not strike her again. If you do not want her, I will take her."

The guard stood back amazed, for Neb's calm but absolute assurance of authority caused him to hesitate. He looked Neb up and down and shook his head in doubtful assessment. This could not be a royal son or even a distant relative of the most high, for he wore strange and rough clothes, and his barbarous speech told more than words could say.

"Who are you to give orders to a man of the royal house?"

Neb stepped forward while necks craned to watch this interesting exchange.

"I am Son of Serug of the mountains and Grandson of Neb the Great, high spirit of the neither world. I would advise you to obey me, or you will suffer the fate of those cursed who walk in utter darkness even on the brightest day!"

Being of the royal household, this servant well understood the threat, and he stepped back in dismay. "Do not lay your wrath on my shoulders. I do what I am ordered. I will bring you to the master of the temple maidens, and you may speak to him about this worthless one." He shook the young woman's arm in rage for bringing this unwonted attention and duty. She winced in pain, but she would not cry out. She threw back her head and spoke clearly though softly.

"You will meet an ugly fate yourself, for it is forbidden to strike a maiden of the gods. Let me go now, and you will be saved from more harm than any of us. Now the procession is late, and if you leave the gods to wait any longer, another sacrifice will be demanded before the usual time. Only the gods know who they will strike next, for their vengeance is terrible and complete."

The servant's eyes were over large at these words, and he quickly thrust the girl in Neb's direction. "Take her and go away from this land quickly, or I will pronounce this ill-fated delay as all the doing of your foreign god!"

The servant shouted out a series of commands, and everyone began to move at the same time in various directions much like a river that suddenly broke free from the winter's frozen grip. Neb looked from his own warriors to the girl and quickly retreated out of the city, across the mountain pass and back toward his own people. He kept the girl moving in front of him while a secret smiled played around his lips. He had accomplished his goal and more.

It was not until late the third day of their travels that he bothered to ask his newest acquisition what her name was, and she looked up at Neb with a mixture of hope and disdain.

"My name is Hagia."

Neb merely nodded silently, accepting this as a fact that could not be changed. He stared at the girl for a long moment and then asked another question.

"You did not seem to struggle against your fate. I have watched you travel with us these three days, and you never looked back or appeared to pine for your lost home."

Hagia merely nodded in silent acceptance of the truth of his statements. Neb blinked like a cat appearing impervious to her lack of revelations, but inside he was beginning to feel a buildup of sincere curiosity. "So do you hope for a new future or just hate your past?"

Hagia wrapped her soft mantle a little tighter about her shoulders, and her response came out with a sigh. "Both."

Neb stood and threw some more wood on the fire and then walked next to where she stood. He let his hand rest on her head as he stood by her. "Tell me about your people and your home. I would like to know."

Hagia did not move her head at all, but she shifted her weight just a bit. "I can tell you little about my people, for I was given to the gods as a child. First I lived with the other children and was taught to cook and make the special meals for the servants of the temple. I did whatever service was required, and I rarely went out into the world at all. Most of my life was spent in the compound around the temple, which has a high gate, and no one but those with special permission are allowed in. Only recently was I moved into the house of the maidens, and I was taught to serve as well as cook." At this Hagia looked down at her hands, and a frown puckered between her eyebrows. "I am not a very graceful person, but I tried to do my best." She shrugged in resignation, "I did not please those who oversaw my work, however. My cooking was good, but I did not move quickly or gracefully and I . . ." She faltered a moment. "I was told that if I was not equal to the tasks assigned, I could offer myself to the gods in another way—a way that would not fail." She looked up at Neb for the first time. "After my last mistake, I am sure I would have been moved to another house, and though it is not difficult to live there, no one stays for long."

Neb offered one of his silent nods of the head again. He let his hand rest on Hagia's head a moment more, and then he walked toward the fire. He was quiet for some time, and then with his back to her, he spoke softly but clearly. "I will never offer you to the gods. You are mine now, and I keep what is mine."

Hagia stifled a sniff and ran her hand across her face. She shook her head and let her eyes rove up toward her only hope. "I will do whatever I can to serve you well. Perhaps I will give you many sons."

At this Neb turned suddenly and shook his head in determination. "Of all the things you do upon this earth, the one thing you must never do is give me a son!"

CHAPTER 47

A NEW DAY

The sun was just beginning to send out rays of pinks and yellows from the eastern horizon to herald the beginning of a new day. Ishtar's shoulders were slumped as he let a deep breath escape from between his lips. He looked over at Ammee and Gizah and put up his hands in a gesture of surrender. "And so that is my background—the fertile soil from which I sprang."

Ammee sat up and looked intently at his father. He could see that he was worn thin with his great effort, and though he had many questions he wanted to ask, he knew that there were other days and that it would be better to wait awhile. Though he knew the story now, he did not quite understand how it was possible to escape the destiny of evil that he had been born into. "Father, you have a remarkable memory. I feel as if I have lived through all those years and seen the youth of my ancestors before they became aged and the stuff of burial mounds. When you speak thus, I realize how relentless is the passing of time."

Gizah nodded her head in somber understanding. She took a deep breath and stretched. "Speaking of that, the sun is about ready to shine upon a new day, and none of us has slept. It would be best to rest now and speak again another day."

Ishtar nodded his acceptance. "I know the story is not really finished and that you must have some questions, but remember that you are in this story too, and it will never really end until the last human heart stops beating. Your child and future generations will live on into a future we have yet to dream of."

Gizah let out a little gentle laugh as she attempted to stand up. "And dreams are what I need most right now. She put out her hand to her husband who stood up quickly without any aching restraint. He bent down and helped her to a standing position, and the two looked down at Ishtar. Ammee then reached down to help his father up. Ishtar accepted the offer and stood up to his full height. He smiled in return.

"I, too, am in need of dreams, for in reviewing the evils of the past my heart is heavy." He started to step toward his dwelling. "I am not the man my father feared, nor am I the man my grandfather hoped for." As he moved forward, he held up a depreciating laugh. "I suppose I have surprised every generation going back through time unremembered."

Ammee put his arm about his father as they moved in unison. He looked over to his father and nodded. "And knowing what I know now, I will be forever grateful." The three walked on, and Ammee saw his father safely into his own dwelling.

CHAPTER 48
AND IT BEGINS AGAIN

Eoban was almost as old as Obed, and Obed had to admit that time had not exactly left him untouched. Still, Eoban knew he could wrestle the young jackals who vied for his attention to the ground if need be though he would have to stifle back threatening groans for days after. He put up his hand to block the bright sun as it glimmered down upon him. Even though it was a clear day, it felt cold—colder than he had ever known it to be. It actually was rather refreshing in a way. He looked at Obed one more time. It was odd that Obed had ended up being the infirm one. With his brilliant mind and his ability to think out problems, and sometimes get into problems, he was the last one Eoban would have thought would end up helpless in bed. Yet there he was, acting like an old man unable to rise from his pallet. Eoban rubbed his chin in his usual thoughtful manner. Still, as Jonas was as attentive to her husband as ever, life could not be too hard for his friend. He shook his head. Obed was no Onias, but he had managed to be a good husband and a good father despite his personal failings. He had raised Tobia and Onia well into manhood, and they were both strapping, strong men well able to care for the needs of the clan. Onia had become the traveler while Tobia took care of all their domestic concerns. It was an arrangement that had worked out well. Eoban looked at Obed once again. Obed's hair was now quite white, and his frame, though never robust, was shrunken and quite a bit thinner than ever before. Strange that time would not stop, even for a moment, to let a man catch his breath.

Eoban attempted to saunter over to Obed's pallet, which was lying out in the sun, but his gate could not have deceived even the youngest member of the clan. He would never saunter again—it was simply too hard on the hips. Still, as Eoban looked down upon his infirm friend, his old familiar, teasing glint showed through his eyes.

"You have enough blankets to make a bear jealous."

Obed twisted his head up as far as it would go and proceeded to work his jaw muscles in an exaggerated fashion as if he were preparing them for a truly devastating response. Then he beckoned Eoban to step closer. When Eoban did step near and bent down on his haunches to look Obed in the face, Obed reached over and tapped the large man on the arm. His voice was a little husky, but his words were distinct and clear.

"No creature alive could be jealous of an old man like me. But you now . . . that is another story!" He smiled the rest of his thought.

Eoban blinked, trying to discern just exactly what Obed meant, not sure if he was being complimented or teased, but then he dismissed his confusion with a gesture of his hand. "Speaking of stories, have you heard about Ishtar's great tale? I heard so many reports of it that I had to go myself and hear what was happening. I learned things I had never known, and I thought I knew everything."

Obed nodded his head encouragingly. "Yes, Tobia went too, and he gave me many reports. Even Jonas was eager to hear all. We sat around the fire, and those who had been there told us bits and pieces as they remembered them."

Eoban had a thought and was instantly eager to communicate his idea. "We haven't all been together for a long time. I would like to see Ishtar and everyone gathered together again and talk about times past. Perhaps we should invite him here. We don't have to discuss Neb the Great, but we could just talk about how things were, and how they are now, and what the future might hold."

A faraway look came into Obed's eyes. "Yes, I would like that too. Ask Barak to come and Lud also, for though he has experienced much, still he will live long enough to face the great unknown." He looked up toward the moving clouds and pointed with one long finger. "See up there—those great billowing clouds sweeping across the sky? They remind me of something Aram once said."

Eoban looked up with a blank uncertain expression. "Clouds? What about them? They are but illusive things, like the mist I think."

Obed smiled. "Yes, that is what Aram said too. But he made a point at the time that seemed unimportant to my mind—back when I was a stubborn and brash young man. He said that he always wished he could stop and enjoy the sky, the clouds, the sunrises and sunsets and the wild life and his family a bit more, but he never had enough time. Time on earth seems like an enemy, but it is really a friend, for it is a good and honest teacher. In time's demanding limits, one has to choose how to spend every moment for it can never be rolled backward. Somehow, he thought, time taught man a valuable lesson that nothing else could. We have to know our limits, or we will go crazy for we would never be forced to decide anything." Obed looked at Eoban. "I guess I would add we would never know the regret of not using our time well." He took a deep breath. "It is when faced with the end of time that a man really thinks about what he has done with his life, and he rejoices—or regrets—much." Obed tried to smile, but his eyes were much too serious. "I wish I had taken better care."

Eoban stretched out his hands expansively. "I suppose we all do as we near our ends. It is so hard to realize . . ." He looked up and paused in silence a moment. Then a smile over spread his face, and he nudged Obed's shoulder. "Sit up my friend and grow young again, for great minds think alike. Here comes our past to visit with us a while." It was Ishtar with Barak walking toward them. They were talking together in quiet tones. When they got a little nearer, Ishtar looked up and saw his friends and put up his hand up in salute.

"I thought I would find you two together. Word has it that Obed has decided to travel again, and he is putting Eoban in charge while he is gone."

Eoban laughed out loud. "By the great sky above, I will not let him go anywhere without me for fear of that very thing. If he wants to wander far afield, he will find me at his heels."

Obed had managed to get to a sitting position, though the effort had cost him much. His breathing was no longer as regular as it had been, and he seemed to be struggling though he did everything possible to keep his appearance normal. "Do not say such things, my friend, for where I go next you must not follow too soon. Ishtar spoke more truly than he knew. I am leaving the clan in your hands, though my sons will see to the daily cares of the people. All I ask is that you stay behind to guide them with your wisdom."

A stricken look crossed Eoban's face as he shook his head in disbelief. Ishtar too looked downcast and grieved that he had made light of so serious a situation. It was not until he had surveyed Obed's appearance more carefully that he realized the tragic change in his friend.

"I am sorry for my rash words. I was only attempting to make light fun, but I see the situation more clearly now and only wish that I could still the movement of the sun so that we could enjoy each other's company for many long years to come."

Obed waved Ishtar's words away. "We were just speaking of you both actually. Word has reached us of your epic story, Ishtar, and we wish to celebrate once again with all our friends. Let all three clans gather, and let there be a feast the like of which we have never had before. Let us eat and drink and be joyful, for we will not live forever."

Eoban clapped his hands in approval and reached over and slapped Barak on the back. "Just like old times, eh? We can sing even! Remember how we sang on our journey together, Barak? You can retell your tale about the great cat hunt and how your clan migrated to the Great Lake for all the young who have not heard the stories of Aram's courage and your . . . adventure." He offered a mischievous wink. "Well, at least we can teach the younger generation something, can't we, about the wise and the foolish?"

Not seeing Eoban's quick jab to Barak, Ishtar nodded his head in eager agreement. "Yes, we have many stories of goodness and strength to tell that the young people have not yet heard. Jonas could explain about Onias and Jael and how they lived and died for their people. Lud could tell the story of Pele and her long journey and describe the Sky Warrior that she saw. There would be many interesting tales to share, and the young would know not just the horror of Neb but also the glory of those who have gone before, leaving us legacies of honesty and courage."

Tobia had come up behind the men as they were speaking, and now he stepped forward and bent down to put his hand on the shoulder of his father. "It is a good idea. For in truth, we all need to believe that there is more to our past than the overcoming of horror and grief. We need to do more than refuse the void of darkness—we must choose a lighted path and only those who have done good upon the earth," he looked up to the men around him, "overcoming whatever obstacles they had to, can show us the way."

And so it was decided that a great festival would be arranged on the night of the next full moon. Excitement ran high throughout all three villages, for everyone wanted to partake in the festivities. There was a great hunt arranged days in advance, and women planned and competed against each other as to what special food they would bring. Jonas had Tobia and Onia working for her from morning till night. The great event was to be held in their village, and she wanted everything perfect. Mari was busy with her own household, but she managed to assist in preparing for the event. Barak assisted Milkan with an assortment of viands, while each of their children either helped in the shaping of the great banquet site or prepared more food for the event. Bethal and her husband and Suraram were going to bring their own families, and they discussed various stories to share with everyone about their father. Gizah wanted very much to come, but her time was drawing near. As the days passed, she felt more and more weary and uncertain about whether she should appear in public. She was afraid to hinder her husband's and friend's enjoyment with her pale and exhausted appearance. Lud and Hawin and their children all planned to come, though they did not expect to say much. For them, the pleasure would be in listening and learning the stories of their adopted clan's triumphant past.

For Obed, the event was something he longed to see like a green plant longs for the last rays of the evening sun. He felt that he could hardly wait for the event, for he felt he did not have much time left upon this earth and wanted to be with those people who had helped to shape the texture of his life. He wanted to see everyone one last time, and most of all he wanted to see everyone happy.

Eoban looked forward to the day of the party with mixed joy, for though he had agreed to the idea at first, he also realized that no memory could be brought up in isolation. They were a people who had known much sadness, and though they were joining together to celebrate, his old distrust of perfect joy held his heart in check.

Ishtar worked alongside everyone else with a strong, good will though he, like Eoban, knew that there were many sad memories that would inevitably be revived along with the good ones. He knew that he, himself, had been the source of much grief and that even if he could outlive every one of his friends, he could never outlive the bad choices he had once made. They were with him forever. Each clan member may have forgiven him, and he may have put the past in the past, but he was still marked by the reality of where he came from and how he had lived his life at one time. He sighed even as he worked in the bright day, for he longed for a perfect world in which all evil would pass away and there would be no bad left in him to mar the good.

The night came, and everyone assembled. Though Obed could walk short distances, Jonas had her sons bring him out a large and comfortable pallet on which he could recline and receive his friends in comfort. Eoban looked at him residing in splendor and sniffed rather loudly. When Obed looked his way, he was about to speak, but Jonas put up her hand to stop him. She turned upon Eoban, squaring her shoulders just a bit, and asked very politely if he had caught a cold. Eoban shook his head disdainfully and waved his hand imperiously. "Not me! I don't go around catching things I don't want, and I keep too busy for colds to catch me." There was a general murmur of approval and some stifled laughter. Just as Tobia was about to step forward, he mumbled under his breath, "A practice I could recommend to some others." Tobia's eyebrows rose slightly, but then he continued to move forward and spread his hands wide, gratefully welcoming everyone to their festivity. There were cheers of approval and shouts of rambunctious play from the younger members. Tobia acknowledged Ishtar's presence, and that of his son Ammee who was now the leader of their clan. He recognized Barak and his large and growing family. There were very loud cheers and acclamations at this. Aram's children, Bethal and Suraram and their families were recognized amid blushes of the young and old alike. Then finally Eoban and Lud and his well-respected though shy family were brought forward, and there were smiles as Eoban tried very hard to look modest while ushering Lud out in front of himself. Once the formal salutations were made, there were acknowledgements of the various helpers who had brought this feast to pass, and everyone was duly thanked for their great contributions. Tobia finally began to run out of words when Eoban yelled across the compound, "So when do we eat?" There was a general burst of merriment at this, and Tobia bowed low and graciously as he invited everyone to partake of the feast and playfully ordered everyone to tell as many stories as the night could hold. Continued cheers and acclamations greeted their formal release, and everyone surged forward to the heavily laden boards with cries of surprise and delight. Though everyone had helped, no one had expected such a sumptuous banquet. It was an event without parallel in their whole experience. Great was the exuberance and joy as the night wore on.

  The moon sailed on its appointed trip across the sky, and everyone felt invigorated for there was a great deal of very good wine and meat, and in their secure joy, they partook abundantly. By the early morning, everyone had laughed and cried to their hearts' content. Jonas had remembered episodes of Onias' life, and tears spilled down even the maiden's cheeks who had never known her heroic husband personally. Young men found renewed strength and fortitude as Barak told about Aram and his long journey leading his people from a dark, dangerous forest into the new and wholesome world of light and beauty. Milkan told about Eymard and how a man ancient in years had still much to offer the world, for he brought hope to the dying, life to the forlorn and faith to those who had lived in a void of understanding. Tobia shared stories about his older brother, Jael, and his great heart that would echo forever in the young and the valiant. Ammee told about his little brother and the gentle love of a child who would not forget his father or abandon his brother and who had lived his innocent nature to the fullest. Lud described Pele and the Warrior Spirit so clearly that there were many who looked up and around wondering if they were not with them even yet. Eoban spoke of the friends he had met on his many adventures, those who had saved him and taught him to love and respect the greater world outside his small village. Finally as the sun was just cresting into a new day, Obed spoke about his journey from doubt to faith. He told how he had doubted everything that he could not prove with his own senses until he learned the horror of real evil. It had been a long journey from the knowledge of horror to acceptance of a living God, but now he believed, and he understood his friends better. Eoban sniffed loudly again. Obed looked over to him quickly, but he did not say anything. Eoban just shook his head slightly. Finally when everyone had moved into little groups and some were heading back to their beds for rest, Obed called Eoban over to him. Eoban shuffled rather slowly, rubbing his eyes as he moved.

Obed put up his hands and stretched and then looked at Eoban out of the corner of his eye. "So, was the night what you hoped for?"

Eoban nodded. "Sure enough! I am so tired that I won't be telling another story for a very long time!"

Obed snorted softly. "I find that hard to believe!"

Eoban turned and looked down at his friend, and something snapped like red fire inside of him. "What do you mean by that? That I talk too much? That I never quit? That I—"

"Oh stop acting persecuted would you! I didn't mean anything except that you always tell stories. You can't help yourself. You are a born storyteller—a man who sees a great story in every event!"

Eoban bent down and spoke with distinct clearness. "And

what is so wrong with that? At least I don't go around giving up!"

Obed stirred under his comfortable blankets. "What do you mean by that?"

"Oh, please, everyone heard you giving your farewell speech. 'I am a changed man, and everyone can admire me before I die and remember my wonderful life'."

Obed tried to stand up, but he was so cramped from sitting so long in the cold that he could hardly move. His face had contorted into an expression of real anger. "I did not give any speech. I just told the truth as I see it! I *have* changed; I *am* a better man than I was . . ."

"You don't need to tell everyone about it then! It's not like you are going to die this minute!"

"I might! I might die today, and it is better that I say what I want before I go. I don't want to be like those who left without saying goodbye."

Eoban reached down and motioned for Obed to get to his feet. As Obed tried to comply, Eoban took his arms and grabbed him to help him to a standing position. The sun was just cresting the horizon, and there were various shades of pink and blue vying to take control of the sky. Eoban helped to steady Obed and then nudged him as he pointed toward the rising sun. "Remember what you said the other day about how Aram wished he had more time? Well you have today, and it is a good day to live. No one gave you permission to give up or give in or die off!"

Obed looked toward the slanting rays of the new sun, and he smiled a little as he shook his head at Eoban's dictatorial tone. "Do I need permission?"

"You just need to live each day and not worry about goodbye speeches." Suddenly he saw Ishtar coming toward them, and he grinned with all his good humor restored. "Look who is coming this way. Now behave yourself!"

Obed finally got settled on his feet, and they all stood around talking for a little while, watching as the sun's white glow took over the sky and began to make its upward accent. After a few minutes, Ishtar began to look all around, first in one direction then in the next, and a concerned expression crossed over his features.

Eoban looked at him. "What is the matter? You look worried."

Ishtar shook his head only slightly. "Oh, it is nothing, I suppose. I just haven't seen Ammee for some time. I hope he is alright. It may have been hard for him to remember Amil."

Eoban scanned the environment, sweeping his eyes every which way. "Half the clan has gone home to bed, and practically everyone else is seeing to their duties." He shook his head at Ishtar. "You can be such a worrier sometimes!"

Ishtar smiled at this and then stretched and yawned. "Well, I guess it is time for me to get some rest as well. All the food has been eaten, and all the stories have been told. Every youth in the village must be full to the brim with the history of our people."

Eoban smiled and nudged Obed. "You should have seen Rula's face when I was telling about Gimesh. Oh, she liked that one very much!"

Suddenly there was a loud yell, and a figure came running across the compound. It was Ammee, and his hands were up in the air as if in the ecstasy of triumph in battle. He ran up to Ishtar and grabbed his arm, shaking it violently.

"Father! Father, I have a son!"

Ishtar blinked in sudden surprise. Tears rose to his eyes, and he tried to speak. "Gizah has . . .?"

Ammee shouted with his joy. "Yes, father, she has born this day a son to me and a grandson to you."

Eoban clapped Ishtar on the shoulder. "Congratulations, Old Man! This is good news indeed. Another warrior for the good of our people!"

Ishtar blinked and looked over to his son, and he put up his hand in the style of an oath. "No, this boy will not be a warrior, though he will know well how to defend his people in time of need. He will be a man of—" But there was a sudden commotion which arrested all their attention, and Eoban ran forward as Barak came jogging toward them with a look of urgency on his face. Eoban and Barak met some distance away, and then without explanation they both turned and ran out of sight. Ishtar looked at his son in surprise, but they were both so elated with their private news that nothing could worry them over much.

They began to walk back toward their dwelling when Milkan came running toward them.

"Jonas says that Gizah needs rest right now and that the baby is sleeping but you can come and see them when the sun is a little higher." She smiled as she patted Ammee on the back. "You will have many long years to enjoy your son, so just give them both a little time now, and you will see how wonderful they will look after a rest."

Ammee nodded his head in acceptance and looked back toward where Obed was still standing, watching as the new day made itself clear. He called over to his friend. "Come on, Obed, I am sure we can find a place to rest out of the way until the duties of the day call us." Ishtar turned and beckoned also.

"Your wife will be busy for hours fussing over the new baby, and I am sure we could all use a little rest."

Obed smiled as he began to shuffle up toward them. "Yes, a rest sounds good to me, though Eoban and Barak don't seem to need any sleep. They are running all over creation like little boys!"

Ammee smiled sheepishly. "If I know Jonas, she will have jobs enough for all of us before long. Don't worry about Eoban—he knows how to stay out of her way. There is nothing like a new baby to get the women busy—and get me busy too!" He put his fingers through his hair wearily. "They'll probably want me to clean up the house, the yard and the entire village if I know them!" He looked over at his father. "Do you think there is a chance under the great sky that just maybe she'll just be so dreamy about the baby she'll—" but he didn't get to finish his sentence as he saw Eoban and Barak bustling back toward them. There were huge smiles spread wide across their faces.

Ishtar turned at the sound of their approach and smiled in return. "What is this? More memories to review?" But it was clear that Eoban was in an unusually excited state. He practically ran up to them, moving as fast as he could, quite out of breath for his excitement.

"You'll never guess what we just saw."

Obed, Ishtar and Ammee turned their heads from side to side

almost in unison, but Obed spoke first. "No, probably not, and please do not try to get me to guess. I am no good at games."

Eoban made a sour face. "Oh, you! As if I would want to play games at a time like this! Ishtar, you and Ammee need to call forth your best men, and we need to get Tobia and Onia here. We need to hold a council meeting."

Ishtar's face had suddenly gone white with aggravated concern. "Why? What has happened?" His eyes darted toward the dwelling in which Gizah lay resting with her infant son.

Before Eoban could speak, Jonas appeared. Her steps were a little slower than in times past, but she was as determined as ever. She saw the gathered men, and at first a smile spread wide across her face, but then she noticed their expressions and the smile faded quickly away. She began to walk a little faster toward them.

"I am hoping you all are here to welcome Ammee's first son, but you better wait a little while. I sent Milkan to tell you. But what happened? Your expressions are too serious."

Ammee spoke up quickly. "Eoban says there is important news. He and Barak have seen something." He turned back toward the two men and gestured impatiently. "Hurry up and tell us what has happened!"

Jonas turned to Eoban with questions darting from her eyes. "What has happened, Eoban? Why haven't you told me anything?"

Eoban looked like he was going to burst. "How could I tell anyone anything? Everyone keeps asking me questions, but no one listens!"

Ishtar put up his hand. "We are listening now. Tell us what has happened."

Eoban hesitated the smallest moment, and before he could usher out his announcement, Barak straightened his shoulders, threw back his head and clapped his hands in joy. "A new clan has arrived!" He looked around to see their shocked expressions. "It is true! I was just at the lake talking with some people, and we decided to go across the lake for fun. We were going to go up into the grasslands a bit near the woodlands, and we saw a large clan that had just left the great forest. We signaled to them, and they sent runners up to us and we talked a bit. They are difficult to understand because they use a different dialect, so I came and got Eoban, for he understands just about everyone, and they told him about how they are being pursued by warriors. They need our help." He looked around. "So, what are we going to do?"

There was a dumbfounded silence by everyone, but finally an exasperated Eoban spoke up. "We will assist those in need of course! Come on, Barak. We will get Lud, Onia and Tobia and meet with Suraram and the new clan. We will learn all about what has happened and how best to help. Ishtar, are you coming?"

Ishtar nodded his head while holding up his hand. "Yes, Ammee and I will follow close behind. Just give us time to tell Gizah and see the baby."

Barak nodded and turned while Eoban threw up his massive hands in the air. "Just like old times, isn't it? I guess our journey isn't over till it's over, eh?"

Obed nodded and whispered rather stoically. "Just don't start singing, whatever you do!"

Eoban only laughed and spoke with exuberance. "We will go and gather everyone and bring the leaders to meet with us. They seem like nice enough people. I wonder who they belong to?" But without waiting for an answer, Eoban gestured for Barak to follow him, and the two hurried away.

Ishtar turned toward Jonas and put out his hands into hers. "Can we leave Gizah and the babe in your capable care for a little while?"

Jonas smiled, though her eyes followed Barak and Eoban for a little ways before they traveled back to Ishtar's face. "Yes, of course. My little ones are grown, and it is always a pleasure to hold a baby once again." She looked over to the opening of their dwelling and spoke softly. "I best go in and let her know the news. Perhaps I can calm any fears before they start." She smiled and turned and walked through the entrance into the dwelling.

Ishtar looked at his son. "Let us go and take our leave before we begin this next adventure. By the way, what have you decided to name the child?" Ammee smiled. "Gizah and I discussed that for a long time. She wanted something from her family, and I wanted something from my family, but we could not agree so we decided on a new name altogether. He shall be called Thare for he shall remember his history and yet he shall be his own man with his own future."

Ishtar rubbed his chin, and his smile grew wide. "Yes, we have been most blessed by that man who came out from the great forest and forged a home in our midst. You and your line are destined to make the world a better place. Let us meet the next generation before we face this next challenge."

Ammee turned and went into the quiet dwelling to see his wife and child first while Ishtar stood silently a moment, alone in his thoughts. He looked up into the great sky above. His eyes peered at the bright blueness, and he knew with a certainty that he would never be able to describe to anyone that he had never once in his life ever really been alone at all. He saw Obed standing still and silent, and he walked up to him and put his arm over his shoulder in a gesture of comfort and friendship.

"And so it begins again."

Obed turned and let his gaze sweep across the village and toward the great lake. His voice was husky with strong emotion. "Thank God!"

Ammee was off with the men now, helping Barak, Obed, Tobia, Eoban, Ishtar, Lud and all the rest to assist the new clan and to plan a strategy of proper defense should they need to face open battle once again. Gizah shook her head. She knew she should be worried, but for some reason she was not. She smiled at herself. Her confidence in the men of her clan was strong, and she suspected that any plundering clan would think twice when they saw what they were up against. She could hear the natural sounds of the deepening day, and the smells of a good warm dinner were wafting in her direction. Oh, but she was hungry! She looked around, but she realized that Jonas had gone outside to do one of the many various duties that made her an invaluable friend. Gizah brushed her long black hair back from her face and looked down at her newborn son. She smiled again for she could see the serious furrowed brow of her father and the determined stare of her husband reflected in this baby's first expressions. He was quite tired, for in coming into the full glare of life on earth he had joined the multitudes that had come before him and stood alongside the many that would form his present world. In due time he would stand at the head of the line of those who would come after him. Gizah felt a single tear slip down her cheek in an odd mix of protective love and joyful triumph, for just as she had suffered in bringing him into this world, so she knew she would suffer caring for him as he traveled the steep and treacherous path to manhood. But she knew that no matter what powers of evil might assail him, there was also a path of goodness and strength forged by those who had come before. Aram and Ishtar were proof that men could overcome their own worst selves and become greater than their forbearers. Gizah hugged her little one tight, for she knew that it had just as truly been the woman—the daughters, the sisters, the wives and the mothers—who had cared for their men with undying love who had made the impossible possible. She stood up ever so carefully and walked to the open doorway to watch the last rays of this day's bright sun linger on the horizon in a melody of colors, and she knew that though she stood in silence with a sleeping son in her arms, she was surrounded forever by those who knew and loved her best.

Suddenly Aram was there beside her, and she once again felt his protective strength. Acting out some deep sense of rightness, she lifted her newborn son up high into the last bright rays of the pure light, and she silently offered him, and all who came after, to the same God who had protected her father, Aram, led Ishtar back to sanity and loved her into being. She knew without a doubt that this same God would be with her people until the end of time.

FAMILY TREE

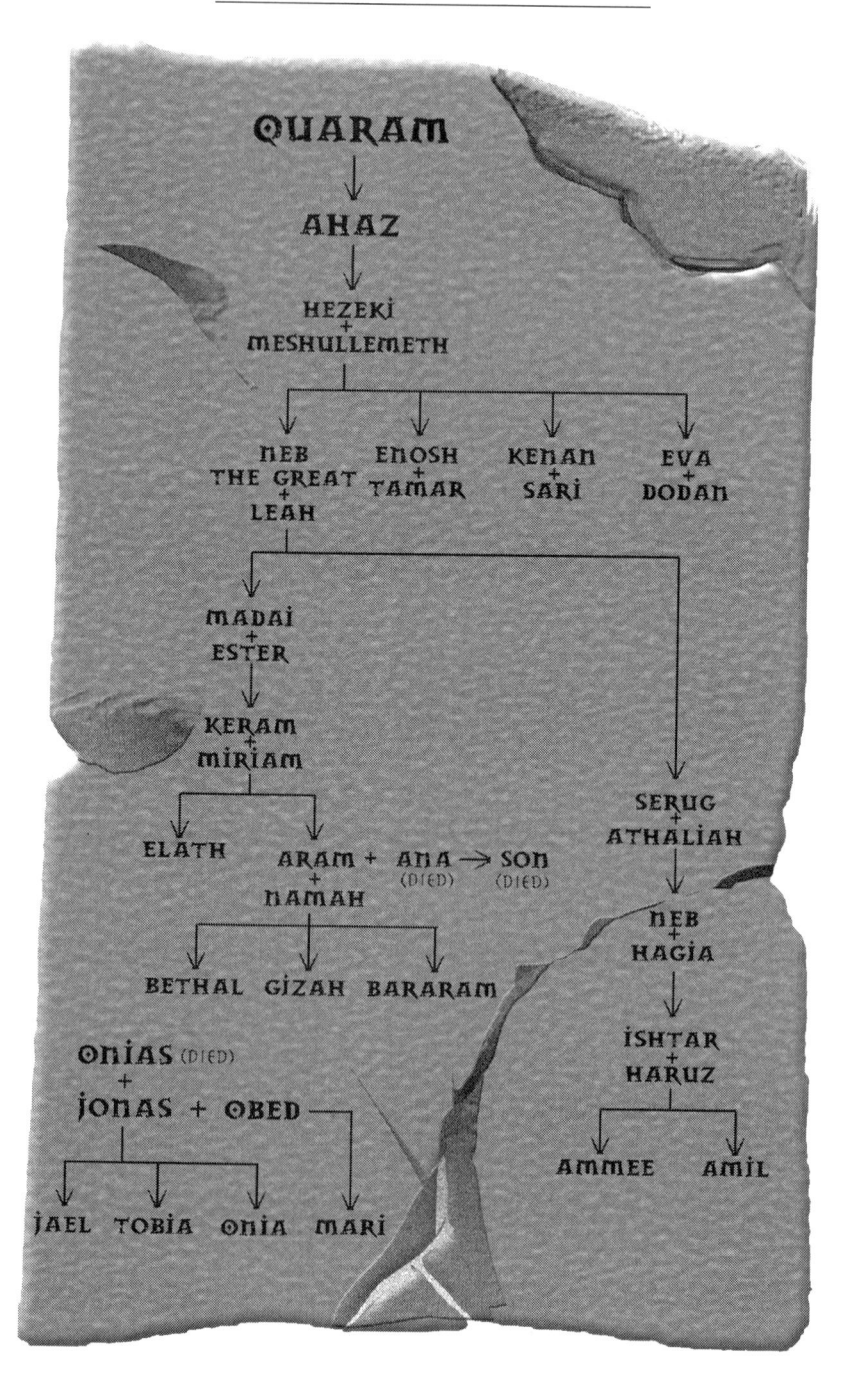

- **QUARAM**
  - **AHAZ**
    - **HEZEKI + MESHULLEMETH**
      - **NEB THE GREAT + LEAH**
        - **MADAI + ESTER**
          - **KERAM + MIRIAM**
            - **ELATH**
            - **ARAM + ANA → SON**
              (DIED) (DIED)
              + **NAMAH**
              - **BETHAL** **GIZAH** **BARARAM**
                - **ONIAS** (DIED) + **JONAS + OBED**
                  - **JAEL** **TOBIA** **ONIA** **MARI**
      - **ENOSH + TAMAR**
      - **KENAN + SARI**
      - **EVA + DODAN**
        - **SERUG + ATHALIAH**
          - **NEB + HAGIA**
            - **ISHTAR + HARUZ**
              - **AMMEE** **AMIL**

388

ALSO BY A. K. FRAILEY

A Christian Journey Through The Lord of the Rings is a reflection on the characteristics of the heroes and villains in the Tolkien classic and what influence virtue and vice have in our own modern world.

For more information and updates
on new books by A.K. Frailey
check out: www.akfrailey.com

Made in the USA
Charleston, SC
15 April 2014